THE SWARM

BLACK CARBON #4

A.J. SCUDIERE

GRIFFYN INK

PRAISE FOR A.J. SCUDIERE

"There are really just 2 types of readers—those who are fans of AJ Scudiere, and those who will be."
  -Bill Salina, Reviewer, Amazon

For *The Shadow Constant*:

"The Shadow Constant by A.J. Scudiere was one of those novels I got wrapped up in quickly and had a hard time putting down."
  -Thomas Duff, Reviewer, Amazon

For *Phoenix*:

"It's not a book you read and forget; this is a book you read and think about, again and again . . . everything that has happened in this book could be true. That's why it sticks in your mind and keeps coming back for rethought."
  -Jo Ann Hakola, The Book Faerie

1

      ————

Cage felt his muscles clench as he almost tipped over into the clear, blue water.

The water itself terrified him. He'd told himself—and Joule—that it was okay. This was clear. They could see anything coming and it would only be fishes and dolphins. The good marine mammals. They'd certainly had enough of bad fish in the past.

But his lungs froze as the shape lifted out of the water beside him, the hump large and gray. Pasty and rough, it's skin broke the surface, swelling upward, and his brain went haywire.

Surely it was the Loch Ness Monster.

It was huge. In case he thought it was just his imagination running toward real and imagined terrors, the thing bumped at his pole. His toes clenched against the board. He hadn't been the most upright paddle-boarder from the start, and he was going in. He'd go under. He'd die.

His eyes darted quickly to his sister, and he saw Joule, too, was frozen with fear.

"Breathe!" he wanted to yell at her. To tell her it would be okay. But he couldn't even tell himself that. His own lungs hadn't expanded. His eyes were trying to squeeze shut even as he forced them open to the warm, sunny Florida day. If he closed them, he'd see the murky swirls and rising floods they'd faced before.

This.

Wasn't.

That.

Through sheer force, he sucked in air. He tightened his core muscles and managed to stay upright, despite the bump he felt from the monster from the deep.

Around him, squeals and screams cut the air.

"Oh, my God!"

"Look!"

He didn't want to, but with a second forced inhale, he did. Eyes downward, he watched as the hump slowly went back under the water, the dark beast receding beneath the surface.

"It's a manatee!"

This time, the words broke through his racheted-down thoughts. *A manatee.*

Safe. Not dangerous.

Cool, even.

It had taken Joule and him two years to use the tickets for this trip. Job opportunities had interfered. Grampa's health had worried them. But finally, they were here, and he was going to enjoy it.

"They aren't supposed to be here this time of year!" another voice called out.

"Actually, manatee haven't had 'normal' migratory patterns for the last twenty years," the guide informed them. Jeff slowed his own paddling to let his group stop and watch as five of the giant beasts slowly checked out their poles and shadows. The crystal clear water here was a natural aquifer fed by underwater springs. Something both the people and the manatees appreciated. It was why Cage and Joule had been willing to spend a half-day of their vacation on the surface of the water.

They'd been to the beach, but only stood on the shore. The waves, though blue and bright, were not clear. Cage knew with more certainty than most—with far more conviction than he'd ever wanted—what waited beneath the breakers. The salt air, at least, hadn't smelled like the flood. And here in the clear backwaters, he'd felt... not comfortable, but safe enough.

A manatee. *He could handle that.*

But his eyes went immediately to his sister. Joule's face, though pale, was now looking downward. Her cheeks were pink and rounded, and she was smiling at what she saw. He then found his own courage to look at the water.

Pink fishes, almost a foot in length, darted between the sea cows. Black fishes, smaller and often striped, zipped between them with a vivaciousness that neither the big fish nor the manatees felt compelled to mimic. Even smaller, gray, minnow-type fish moved in tight schools between the others, and he thought he saw one of the pinkish fish open its mouth and inhale a swath of smaller ones. The little guys had been there one second and gone the next.

The big fish hadn't changed expression at all. But that was life. Big fish ate the small fish. Sharks ate the students when they fell overboard. But manatees ate only grasses and ... he didn't know. He hadn't finished that marine biology degree he'd started. He'd moved to the biology of more land-based creatures after the waters had risen. So the manatee habits were beyond his knowledge.

He stayed still as he looked down. Tracking the gentle beasts, with only one ear listening to the guide explain their habits. What they ate. That the scars on their backs—Jeff had pointed to one in particular—were from boat rotors and careless tourists. "When they say *no wake*, they mean *no wake*. When the sign says under ten, this is why."

The scars tugged at Cage's heart... which was now almost back to a normal rhythm again. Not that it had been low and relaxed since he'd climbed on the board and learned he was *not* a natural at this. Not since his toes had begun gripping the board's rough surface and his pole digging into the bed of the shallow waterway every handful of seconds, just to stay upright. Jeff had been good, though. He'd been calm and soothing, full of information to distract them.

Cage looked up just in time to see the guide slap at his neck. "If no one has anywhere they have to be," he said, "we'll stop and let the manatees roll on past us, and then we'll continue our tour."

No one protested. Not even Joule. Not even Cage. *He could do this.*

Wasn't this part of why they'd come? He and his sister had never openly discussed it, but they each had something to prove here.

"Ugh!" Jeff slapped at his arm and this time—though he didn't seem to notice—Cage was close enough to see a slight smear of blood. *At least he'd gotten the sucker.*

Cage looked to his sister. Joule shook her head and shrugged her shoulders. She probably would have raised her hands, but her death grip on the pole didn't allow it. It wasn't her, anyway, who was allergic to bites. It was him. She was just sweet. The biteys liked her. He, on the other hand, already sported one quarter-sized reaction to a simple mosquito bite after a morning at the botanical gardens. The tree crabs had distracted him. He'd not even realized something was buzzing around until he'd felt the almost imperceptible pinch.

Now, Joule shook her head again, and he could read it. She'd sprayed herself with bug repellent. Something she'd concocted from internet instructions using essential oils. She'd also used commercial stuff that he was pretty sure had DEET in it. Her look told him, "Not me. Not getting bit."

He'd done the same. So when Jeff reached down and slapped at his leg, and almost tipped. Cage didn't feel much sympathy. The man was supposed to be a professional. He did this every day, probably twice. He should have known he'd get bit.

"Okay, the big guys are moving on, it seems." Jeff pointed toward the lead manatee, though if that was the actual leader, Cage didn't know. Jeff hadn't said, or Cage had just been paralyzed with fear over some gentle sea cows and he'd missed it. But the manatees were swimming the opposite direction of the paddle-board tour.

Despite knowing what they were and that they wouldn't hurt him, Cage found himself relieved to see them go. He didn't need them bumping his board. At least this was cool and he'd tell people he had been out with the manatees. But he was grateful they were moving on.

"If you look up and to the right, on the shoreline you can see a nutria. It looks like—" Jeff coughed. A harsh throat-clearing, then continued. "It looks like a big rat. But they aren't rats, they're—"

He coughed again, as though to move something lodged. "One second," he told them. But even that sounded raspy.

As the guide reached down by his side and pulled up his water bottle, he coughed again.

That couldn't be good. He tipped his head back to take a sip and Cage heard his sister's gasp just as he saw it.

Jeff had a rash blooming in real time across his neck. Pink welts moved down his arm like an army of marching ants.

"Umm, Jeff?" one of the other tourists, a mom with several teenage kids in tow, asked with her most mom voice. "Jeff, I think you have—"

But Jeff didn't answer. He was clawing at his throat, opening his mouth like one of the big pink fish, only he was terrified. Sucking sounds came from his lungs as he tried for air and failed. His eyes grew wide, and he looked at Cage as his face began to turn purple and his frantic motions toppled him into the water.

2

Startled by both his tour guide's sudden spasm and splash into the water below, Cage lost his tenuous grip on his own stability. He tipped and flailed, his lack of attention dooming him.

So he did the only thing he could do: he went into the water. Pushing his hands in front of his head, he shoved with his foot off the board and tried to dive as cleanly as possible. The water wasn't deep, but it was deep enough for manatee and clear enough that he could see where to aim.

The water, cool and soft, closed in around him, a sensation that almost paralyzed him. The sound of voices, frantic above him, didn't help.

His head popped up in time to see the manatee darting away, not liking the sudden commotion that humans had caused. He spun quickly, his feet not touching the bottom and his arms paddling frantically, to shouts of, "Right behind you!" and "Find Jeff!"

The twins had been given swimming lessons when they were small. They'd even been on a swim team and raced competitively during the summers. Though they'd won their handfuls of ribbons, they'd been nothing special. Still, a couple quick crawl strokes brought Cage to Jeff.

The guide was now face-down in the water, twitching and thrashing. Flipping the man over, Cage saw the now-swollen face and the rash. Maybe the cool water had made them easier to see. Above him, he heard Joule taking command. She had seen that Jeff wasn't able to breathe. Cage's own lungs stopped working as his adrenaline kicked up another notch and Jeff's flailing arms nearly hit him.

It was supposed to be a vacation! he thought as he looped an arm under Jeff's chin. This was certainly not the best way to haul someone, but if he tucked his arm under the man's shoulders, Jeff would surely swing back and clock him. Also, it wasn't like he was what was cutting off Jeff's air, and he needed speed.

"To the shore!" Joule was yelling to everyone, aiming the paddle-boarders in the same direction Cage was moving. Luckily, the waterway was narrow. The crystal clarity of the water was the only thing keeping Cage from panicking.

Quickly, his feet found purchase in the sandy bottom. Several places sported dark patches and though he assumed they were mossy rocks; Cage avoided them. The place seemed far too beautiful and far too serene for an emergency like this.

Jeff, who had been rocking back and forth when Cage first grabbed him, now started to diminish his fight. It seemed his airway had been completely closed, or very close to it, when Cage flipped him over. Jeff had had enough oxygen in his system to fight for air, but even that was gone now. The sucking sounds that insisted he was trying still to breathe through a narrow pipe had all vanished as his forehead broke out in a fevered sweat.

With quick, muscle-aching steps, Cage dragged what was now a lifeless body onto the shore. He thought about CPR but couldn't make sense of it in this case. *ABCs.* He'd learned that somewhere and he was pretty sure they were failing at *A—*

Airway. No airway, no breathing. No breathing, and pretty soon there would be no circulation.

His own breath sucked in frantically, his body taking over when his brain didn't want him to breathe at all. For a moment, he thought through all the things he wished. He should have taken CPR or first-aid classes. He'd had a bit of it, and the twins had gotten some on-the-fly medical training from Dr. Brett Christian a small handful of years ago. But this hadn't been included.

Cage tipped his head up and looked into the crowd. The roaring that blocked his ears suddenly disappeared and he heard a cacophony of voices. "Is he dead?"

"If he's not, he will be soon."

"What's the rash? Is it contagious?"

"He can't breathe."

And then Cage heard Joule. "It looks like an anaphylactic reaction. Does anyone have epinephrine?"

The tourists all looked to each other, eyes wide, motions short and stunted. Each expression clearly said, *Not me.* But then one of the teenagers tapped his mother's arm.

"Mom, do you still have mine? Do you have it?"

The woman's eyes flew wide and she began to paw through the small bag strapped to her waist. Cage looked back down at Jeff. His head had lolled to the side, his neck and face obviously swollen now, red blotches covering every inch of him.

"Holy shit! Holy shit!" It was the woman.

Cage snapped his head up to see her. Though his hope was running thin, she held out an oddly rounded plastic device. It was covered in orange and yellow direction labels.

"The EpiPen! It's out of date," she warned even as she pushed it toward him. "We haven't had any trouble with Sterling in years."

The excuse didn't matter as she thrust the small thing at

him. But instead of taking the device, Cage moved back. "Can you do it?"

He'd never worked an EpiPen. All he'd seen was the movies where someone jammed a large-bore needle directly through the sternum into someone's heart and pushed the plunger until someone gasped themselves alive again.

Before he could finish asking, the woman was on her knees next to him, tugging at the hem of Jeff shorts to expose his thigh. With her teeth, she yanked what Cage now saw was a cap and she stabbed the pen deep into the spotted quads. A small click told Cage the needle also had a mechanical action.

He was fascinated by the tiny machine, but the mom already had her head turned, counting to herself as she looked toward Jeff's face. Cage couldn't quite bring himself to look elsewhere until he heard the sharp intake of breath and watched as the body twitched. Only then did the mom pull her fist away, revealing the small, exposed needle of the EpiPen.

"Holy shit! Holy shit!" she said again. Probably not the phrasing she'd taught her kids, but Cage wasn't going to call anyone on their language even on a non-emergent day.

Jeff was still wheezing and sucking air, still sweating and feverish. It wasn't quite the instantaneous revival that movies and TV shows would have led Cage to believe. But the man was alive.

This time, Cage rocked back on his heels, his own breath whooshing from his lungs as he took his first deep breath. He'd been on heightened emergency mode. And God if he didn't know what that felt like from too many times in the past. But this time, it was going to be okay.

It wasn't always okay. Today it would be.

However, he didn't have a clue where they were. Their tour guide was still incapacitated. But they were all upright. Joule was still on her feet, not even wet like he was now, and she was marshaling the crowd.

"Who has cell signal?" she asked, but her tone brooked no argument. "We need to call a medevac for Jeff and someone to get us the hell out of here."

Still sitting on the ground, knees folded under him, not quite ready to stand up, and not quite certain if his legs would hold him if he did, Cage let her run the show. He needed a few more deep breaths. So he watched as his fellow tour groupers flexed their phones, held them high, and began the odd human ritual of searching for a signal.

His brain was still coming down off the rush, and it took a moment to register that one husband and wife were standing slightly aside. They waved their hands in front of their faces and scowled as they looked at the screens on their phones.

The man waved to his wife in question as he shook his own head *no*, then resumed holding his phone up high. Though he was burly and wide, he was also tall. And the couple wasn't that far away. Cage could hear him as he said, "Hey, babe. I think I've got a sig—"

But his words cut off as he reached up and slapped at his neck and offered a grunt. As he moved his hand away, Cage saw the small smear of blood.

3

Joule carefully scanned each member of the tour group even as she held her own phone out, trying to catch a spare signal. She'd seen the slightly older gentleman slap his neck. Her eyes darted immediately to her brother's only to find that Cage was looking at her with a worried expression on his own face.

The tour guide had clearly had an anaphylactic reaction to something, and he'd been bitten several times. Joule and Cage both kept wary eyes on the older man. She watched as he slapped again at something.

Did it take several bites to take someone down? Or was Jeff just suffering an odd reaction? She didn't know, and when Joule didn't know the answer, she tended to turn to the things she could do. She raised her voice. "Does anyone have signal?"

"One bar!" one of the kids called as he moved farther away from the water, back into the dense trees. His bare feet walked on ground she didn't trust. They weren't supposed to get out of the water. Then again, they also weren't supposed to have their tour guide stop breathing and splash face-first into the manatees.

"Me too," the older man called back, appearing absolutely none the worse for wear.

Joule told herself what happened to Jeff was just something freak. Anaphylaxis was basically an allergic reaction as far as she knew, which meant Jeff had been allergic to whatever had hit him—maybe the bug bite, maybe a plant he brushed by, or even a food from lunch. She didn't know. But surely, it was just a quirk of Jeff's.

The older man seemed to be fine.

"If you've got signal, call 911."

"But just one of us needs to call," the mom pointed out.

"I got two bars!" her kid called from even further back into the trees now.

Joule felt her brows pull together and her gaze narrowed. She didn't like it, but his mom did seem to have an eye on him and he wasn't her kid. She put her effort where it could make a difference. "*Everybody* with signal should call 9-1-1. If the calls drop or doesn't connect, then hopefully at least one of us will have gotten through."

Some of her fellow tourists were already dialing. Joule held her phone aloft, swaying it back and forth and cursing her phone plan and cell towers alike. Her eyes still darted everywhere.

She'd long ago lost the faith that she was safe. That she could stand with her eyes in one direction and nothing would sneak up behind her. She was pushing buttons and watching her phone attempt to connect, even as she checked all corners. She didn't trust what might be lurking in the trees and marsh.

"Hello?" the older man was asking, and Joule's heart soared. *He had a connection!*

She was looking at her own phone, still trying to connect and holding it higher. It was probably a futile gesture, but she couldn't not try.

"I'm Gary Mitchell. We were on a tour—"

She'd taken a deep breath of relief only to hear him cut himself off mid-sentence.

"Honey. What's that?" Gary sounded worried and Joule felt her head swivel at the sound.

She wasn't the only one alarmed by Gary's tone. Cage had bolted to his feet and was rushing to where the couple stood. Still a little separate from everyone else, the man was turning to his wife, no longer paying attention to the emergency operator.

The group had been out paddle-boarding. They were in swim suits, a few in wetsuits of the tank variety. Some wore shorts. It was a hot day and Joule herself was in a two-piece with a pair of shorts pulled on over the bottoms.

They were all just exposed skin... waiting.

She could see—they all could—the small red welts that started at the woman's feet and crawled up her body in a pattern somewhere between a leopard and a giraffe, but 100 percent petrifying.

For a split second, Joule froze, and then she, too, bolted into action. She almost asked, *Is anyone here a doctor or a nurse or an EMT?* Maybe someone had been a lifeguard previously. But the fact that Cage had still been on his knees, monitoring Jeff the tour guide, and that the mom with the expired EpiPen had been the one to deliver it, told Joule that *no*—no one here was any of those things.

The wife reached up as though to scratch at her throat, the pink welts now popping up on her forearms. A frown appeared on her face and Joule wondered what she felt. Early signs of her throat closing, most likely.

She wasn't sure if the woman's face was beginning to swell. It was hard to tell as she didn't know anyone else here personally, except for her brother. She couldn't say she'd gotten a good enough look at everyone to recognize early signs.

The mom, who was now desperately calling her three boys back, gathered them into her arms, despite the fact that two of them were much taller than she was. Looking frantically around the group, she blurted, "I'm out of EpiPens!"

Of course she was. It had been lucky that anybody even had one—expired as it was. Still, it had worked well enough to save Jeff. That there might be another one in this small crowd would be unheard of.

They were out of luck.

Joule scanned the crowd as though she might find something in their eyes this time. That someone might know or remember something they hadn't when Tour Guide Jeff had toppled into the water. Instead, what she saw was a tall, teenage boy smacking at his forearm.

Shit.

She had only her tiny backpack with her, but it held the one thing she thought she might need now. There was nothing she could do for Clara. She knew the woman's name now because her husband was frantically repeating it.

"Clara, can you breathe? *Clara!*"

Cage was there, telling her, "Tip your head back!"

Smart, Joule thought. It would open the airway as much as possible. But she couldn't deal with Clara. There had been ten other people on this tour. Though she couldn't see any bugs flying around, she'd certainly seen enough of her fellow tourists slapping at their skin.

With her bag now hanging from one hand in front of her, she pawed through with the other, looking a lot like the frantic EpiPen Mom. She knew it was here.

She was too panicked to search methodically. She knew that, but she couldn't make her heart rate slow down, couldn't control the jerky movements. She was not going to die here, in the stand of trees, next to the beautiful water, her throat closing from something she couldn't see.

The backpack wasn't that big. It should have been easy to find.

Her head snapped up as she heard it again—the horrible sucking noise that Jeff had made right before he went into the water. Clara still stood, making the scary sound, her feet planted wide apart. Her small hands clawed at her throat, ringing her neck, almost as though she were trying to strangle herself. But Joule understood. The woman couldn't reach what was harming her. She couldn't stop it, but her hands were still trying anyway.

Clara's head tipped back, her face aiming to the clear blue sky and puffy white clouds overhead. Joule looked up, too. It was easier watching the sky that peeked over her head where the water cut through the trees, but it didn't change that all she could hear was Clara gasping for air.

4

Cage's thoughts went two different directions simultaneously as his heart tightened into a small, lead weight in the center of his chest. There was nothing he hated more than being helpless.

There were no more EpiPens, he had no CPR training, and there were no doctors in the group. They all watch helplessly as Clara pawed at her own throat, her husband frantically trying to help.

Did they even have the supplies to perform an emergency tracheotomy? Lord knew they'd all seen it done on TV often enough, but could anyone here even find the trachea if they had the necessary items? He turned next to that list. Did they have a knife and a pen or a tube of some kind?

Cage didn't think so.

They were stripped down to the minimum—only what they could carry on their paddleboards. He wouldn't have listened, but the noises were inescapable. Birds chirped and called in the trees, there was a soft rush and burble from the water, and there was Clara, desperately trying to suck in any air she could get.

This time, the sound was harsher, the wheeze of the constricted airway louder. But Cage turned his face away and watched Joule. His sister busied herself digging through her bag until she pulled up a white can triumphantly.

Though the two of them generally worked hard to use sustainable products, right now, he'd never been happier that they'd found only an aerosol can on the shelves. With one continuous motion, Joule pushed the top and sprayed herself down again.

Then she shook the can and moved to the next person. She didn't ask permission, just assaulted them with high-end bug spray.

His parents had always referred to Joule as *bait* when she was little. His mom, too, had been of the "sweet" variety, she'd always said: one of those that the bugs particularly enjoyed snacking on. But with Joule around, even Kaya Mazur hadn't been bitten as much as her daughter. Cage, on the other hand, was actually allergic to bites. Mosquito marks swelled up the size of quarters or even silver dollars. Sometimes, he could find a faint bruise where he had been bitten a good week or two later.

So the twins had started the day doused in the serious stuff. Now, he turned his head to the side and held his breath as Joule enveloped him in a cloud of chemical spray. She was hitting everyone, but she'd beelined for him. He wouldn't say thank you now, but he knew she understood and that it would go the other way when it needed to.

Even as he thought that, he realized some of the spray was liquid now, running down his arm. Ah! She wasn't wasting it into the air, she was holding it close, putting streams of it directly onto people and telling them to rub it in.

On a normal day, he would have done no such thing. Today was different. Today was punctuated with the sound of Clara, suffocating in open air.

Joule turned to aim for Gary. Gary waved her away, his attention entirely on his wife as he issued orders that made no sense. When Joule finished with him, Cage offered what little comfort he could as the woman began flailing in her attempt to get oxygen.

Joule still fought for her task and managed to hit Gary in the back of each leg, before turning away. With bold and almost frantic motions, she lined up the mom and her three sons. Joule sprayed up one person and down the next. She motioned for them to turn around after she'd hit them, and then quickly she moved to the next tourists.

Cage heard this behind him. His eyes were now solely trained on Clara, her lips turning a pale blue. She wasn't transitioning quite as fast as Jeff had. With her head tipped back, she was still able to suck a wheezing breath.

Without looking away, Cage called back, "Did anyone get through to 9-1-1?"

"Gary did!" one of the boys said.

"Get his phone," Cage instructed, hoping the operator was still on the line. He watched as Gary absentmindedly pulled it out of his pocket and handed it back to a kid he couldn't see. His gaze was changing from confused and panicked to accepting and petrified.

Gary kept issuing instructions. "Look left. Look right! Tip your head back, Honey. Take a deep breath." None of it seemed useful, and all of it sounded frantic.

Joule stepped back. Her work was done. The group was small, and she'd hit everyone with the repellent. Cage watched as she shook the can near her head, feeling and listening for the weight of the liquid left. *Would they need another hit? How long would they be out here?*

He listened to the boy who'd grabbed Gary's phone talking to someone.

"We have someone with a closing airway—anaphylaxis!" Jeff called from behind him.

Cage's head snapped back. Though the tour guide was still on the ground, his hand pressed to his chest as if to assure himself his heart was beating or he was breathing, Jeff's eyes were wide, perhaps over-alert. But he *was* alive, and he was breathing.

His rash even seemed to be fading. The man would probably need treatment for being hit with an expired EpiPen, and he might need it right away. It was possible Jeff wasn't out of the woods yet, but no one had the bandwidth to worry about the tour guide when Clara was still clawing at her throat.

Cage then had an idea and turned to Jeff. "Did *you* have first-aid or CPR training?"

Now towering over the tour guide, Cage pointed back toward Clara, sending the second worst-shape person to take care of the first. Then he began pushing through the small crowd. Everyone now reeked of chemical bug spray but was hopefully safer. "Do you have a knife? Do you have a pen? Do you have anything like a small tube? Is it clean?"

Though people dug quickly through their pockets or the small bags they carried, no one really had what he needed. Cage had no idea—if they even had any rag-tag supplies— whether any of them could do the kind of emergency tracheotomy Clara would need. Hopefully, Jeff could.

But Clara was blinking frantically, tears squeezing from her eyes and sweat breaking out on her forehead as the fear took hold. Cage didn't hear noises from her anymore and she was starting to sway on her feet. It was Jeff who jumped up and motioned to Gary to grab his wife. The two of them laid her down into the dirt and rocks and leaves, Jeff tipping her head back and attempting to breathe into her lungs.

Cage didn't want to get into that. Exhaled air still held plenty of oxygen, he knew, but less than the external air did.

But her problem wasn't her breathing so much as the airway that led to her lungs, which was swollen shut now. Still, Cage hoped Jeff knew what he was doing. He hoped maybe the force of attempted rescue breathing would get some air in where Clara struggled.

Cage couldn't figure it out, so he continued to search the group for supplies. There was no knife. EpiPen Mom managed to find a ballpoint pen. The little sack she carried had apparently been on numerous trips and held leftovers from previous expeditions, because there was no need for a pen here.

Jesus, it was a ballpoint. Worst-case scenario, they could jam the point into her neck to create the hole and then break the pen case and use it as a tube. But that was stunningly un-sterile, and the pen was so tiny. How would she get enough air? Still, it was better than nothing.

Gripping the pen in his fist, Cage turned around in time to see Clara's eyes roll back.

5

"This is all I could find." Cage stood over Jeff, holding out the ballpoint pen.

Jeff didn't seem to see. He and Gary were frantically moving Clara about, one way or another. They tipped her head back. They lifted her shoulders. They lifted her feet, as per Jeff's instruction. But she thrashed only once, then immediately passed out again.

When she didn't respond to several gestures in a row, Jeff finally looked up. Seeing the blue ballpoint didn't do much for his expression. It didn't even have a cap.

Cage shrugged. "Emergency tracheotomy?"

"Can you do it?" Jeff was quick to turn it away, as Gary looked up and asked the same thing. The older man, however, had hope shining in his eyes.

Cage had none to offer. "I've seen it done on TV. I'm no better than anyone else."

Cage thrust the pen toward the tour guide again, waiting for Jeff to take it from him. This time he added, "You, at least, have CPR and first-aid training. I don't even have that."

Jeff nodded and finally reached for the pen. He clutched it tight but didn't do anything.

"What are you waiting for?" Joule asked, having come to stand beside Cage. Somehow, he hadn't even noticed.

He understood that she was asking a real question. When Jeff looked up at her, brows together in a frown, she raised her hands. "Just curious. I don't have anything to add, I'm sorry."

The last part, she directed at Gary, who looked back down at his wife, the slump of his shoulders showing that he was losing faith fast.

Though Jeff didn't answer Joule, it was clear that he was taking her thought into consideration.

What *were* they waiting for? "Do you think her airway will open any other way?" Cage asked.

Jeff only replied, "You shouldn't have used the EpiPen on me."

"We had no idea there would be more." It was the only reply Cage could think of that didn't argue the logistics of someone not wanting their life saved.

Jeff had the decency to look to Gary for decisions. "Here's what we're proposing..." He described the grim details of an emergency, in-the-woods tracheotomy with a ballpoint pen.

Gary did not look pleased, but Clara was turning more and more blue. The older man looked to both of them as though they would have answers. "What's the alternative?"

"Prayer." Jeff was decisive about that much. "We can hope that her airway opens up on its own enough and that she can breathe. We can do chest compressions to help push her heart and her lungs. But if the airway isn't open, we won't move any air by doing that." He waited a beat, then looked into the small crowd of his tourists. "How long has she been out for?"

It was one of the boys, fancy watch on his wrist, who flicked it up and rattled off, "It's been five minutes since she started showing signs of welts and forty-five seconds since she passed out."

Damn, that was sharp! Good kid. Also, that was a way-too-fast timeline. There wasn't any wiggle room. He looked back to Gary. "She was already oxygen-deprived before she passed out."

Jeff reached out and put a hand on Gary's shoulder, as if to comfort him in a situation where no comfort could actually be offered. "She probably has another minute or two."

"How long will it take you to do the trachee— the trasty— the—" Gary couldn't even say it. "How long can we wait before this is our only option?"

Once he'd rephrased it, the words were solid, his tone forceful. The man was in the process of watching his wife die, and he didn't have the vocabulary, but he knew what he meant. Cage respected that.

Jeff looked up to Cage and Joule who, merely by standing there, had somehow been granted a level of expert status. Cage did his best. "Most people have three minutes of oxygen before brain death. She has fewer because she was airway-compromised before she passed out. She was low oxygen for several minutes before this."

Gary nodded along, but it clearly wasn't the answer he wanted. Cage was grateful when Jeff said the words.

"I don't know how long it will take to do this. I don't know if we can do this right, but I don't think we have any more time to decide."

"Do it." Gary's tone was full of conviction.

"Does anybody have any alcohol? Even hand sanitizer or hand wipes?" Jeff asked into the crowd.

Shit. Cage hadn't even thought to look for something like that. But infection could be dealt with later. And hopefully the medevac was on the way. He turned to look behind him and found the mom still on the phone with 9-1-1, shaking her head no at the request for sanitizer.

The woman multitasked like a pro, but Cage found her catching his gaze. Through his confusion, he saw her mouth something she clearly didn't want to say out loud. Cage thought it was *thirty minutes*.

No, they didn't have thirty minutes. If he'd read that right— and the expression on the mom's face said he had—there was no way in hell Clara was holding on for the medevac.

Reaching out, Cage motioned for the phone. The mom handed it over immediately and Cage began speaking harshly to the operator, not even introducing himself. "We're considering an emergency tracheotomy with a ballpoint pen."

"Is the airway closed?" the operator asked calmly, not seeming flustered by his radical announcement.

"I'm confident that it is. It has been for over a full minute, and we think she was low on oxygen before that because her airway was already closing. Hold on." Having reached the point where he was standing at Clara's feet, Cage handed the phone over to Jeff.

With the phone pressed to his ear, the tour guide nodded several times before saying, "Yes, I'm confident her airway is completely closed. She's passed out and not breathing at all that I can tell."

With shaky fingers, he put the phone onto speaker, as Cage looked down to check the battery. Only five percent. *Jesus, they were screwed.*

"I see it."

He listened to Jeff get talked through what they could do, though mostly Jeff was saying no, they didn't have anything better—just the pen.

Cage turned around. "We need to get someone else on the line with 9-1-1. This phone is almost dead."

He waited as everyone else behind him began scrambling to

pull their phones back out and dial. Then he turned back to see Jeff gently pushing at the base of Clara's throat, testing for something the woman on the phone was instructing him to find. Then he pulled his arm up, pen poised, ready to stab, and he plunged it into her neck.

6

Joule went to stand at the edge of the water. The clear view to the pale, silty bottom was mesmerizing and relaxing. She took a deep breath and tried to tune out everything behind her.

But the second she let her shoulders sink, the sound of rotors pulled her attention upward.

Hovering above her was the medevac helicopter. Her hands raised high of their own accord, waving over her head as if one tiny person could draw their attention. She was the only one though—the others were a short distance back, hidden under the canopy of trees.

A moment later, she heard a voice behind her. Jeff called out, "They see you."

She stopped waving. The chopper wasn't going to send a basket down. They were here, hovering and waiting in case anyone else went into anaphylaxis before the rescue team came in. But there was no one to save right now. Nothing worth risking the basket being dropped and crew coming to the ground.

"How far away are the crew?" Joule asked.

"They think five minutes," Jeff replied. He'd come up to stand close behind her. *Maybe the water soothed him, too.*

Most of the group stood around, somber. No one had spoken until one of the boys said he thought he'd heard the helicopter a short while ago. It had taken five more minutes before they began to catch which direction the sound was coming from.

Gary sat silently on the ground, holding Clara's hand. Clara hadn't made it.

The emergency tracheostomy had not been good enough. Or it hadn't been the right thing. Or it had been too late. They wouldn't know until an autopsy was done. Even then, Joule thought, she and Cage likely wouldn't get the results. Who was going to tell them about the autopsy of a woman they'd met for a few brief hours and barely spoken to on a paddle-boarding tour in Florida?

Joule stayed where she was, her gaze glazed over, the water barely touching the soles of her feet through the aqua shoes she'd carried in her bag. She'd slipped them on after Clara had died. Only then had she remembered that she'd brought them. She had rinsed her feet in the water, shaking them one at a time to remove the soft, silty sand that covered the bottom of the crystal clear waterway.

No more manatees had come by. Maybe the people had been too noisy. There were still fish, though—they didn't seem to scare quite as easily.

Joule felt much calmer, standing and facing the open water and the light that reflected from the slash of open sky above rather than facing what was behind her. The tour would not go on. Jeff, though able to walk, was going straight to the hospital. The rescue team apparently would be moving Clara—actually Clara's *body*, Joule corrected herself.

Though she heard the rustling of the approaching rescue crew in the distance, Joule stayed where she was. Having applied another layer of bug spray to herself and to Cage, she felt reasonably safe. Still, she knew "safe" was relative and it was just an illusion.

The mom and the three boys had readily accepted when Joule offered them another chemical dousing. Everyone else had declined, saying they could still smell it. Joule couldn't give two fucks about what she smelled. She wasn't going to get bitten, even though she wasn't positive that it was the bug bites that had caused all of this.

She'd watched as Gary slapped his neck and his arm, but nothing had happened to him. She couldn't even say with certainty that what had happened to Clara was the same thing that had happened to Jeff, but it sure looked like it

The noise behind her became louder as the other tour members began moving to meet the rescue team. The odd noises threatened to pull her attention, but Joule thought that if something was going wrong, she didn't want to know.

"Hello?"

The voice was in the distance, and she didn't respond.

"Can anyone hear us?"

Other members of the group called back, a few sounding almost excited, the rest dejected as the crew arrived.

Joule took one last look up and down the beautiful waterway. This vacation had made her happy until about an hour ago. She and Cage had gone out on a boat in the bay and watched dolphins. They'd visited the botanical gardens and another sculpture garden. The weather had been beautiful.

It wasn't full-on summer, just far enough into spring for Florida to be the right temperature. It wasn't even likely anyone's spring break, so the tour spots had been easy to book, the little bungalow available for the week. She hadn't asked if the three boys on the trip were homeschooled or what?

She and her brother had rented a little house and enjoyed having their own four walls. There was a patio set where she'd eaten breakfast most mornings. The backyard was fenced. They tried restaurants that they passed that grabbed their attention or just seemed like a good idea. She'd eaten some of the best shakes and burgers in a long time.

Neither of the twins was much for the ocean. So aside from standing on the beach and watching the waves roll in, just so they could say they had seen the Gulf, they hadn't done much more. The boat tour was about as much water as she could stomach. Each time she'd watched a dolphin surface—as excited as she'd been—Joule had also wondered if something would grab it and pull it under.

She didn't like water that she couldn't see through. Now, she didn't even like water that she could. She knew in her head the water wasn't the problem, but her feelings didn't agree.

Turning around, she answered the question she heard, but only vaguely processed. "Joule Mazur." She gave her age and hometown to the young woman quickly tapping away on a tablet.

Did she have an internet connection? Did it matter? A team of seven had arrived to take their guide and the eight still-standing tourists and one body out of the woods. Several of the team hovered over Clara. It was clear from their complete lack of urgency that they, too, understood there was nothing that could be done for her now.

The one with the tablet was apparently done once she got Joule's information. So Joule turned softly back toward the group and watched as her brother slowly walked over to stand beside her. The tourists were starting to cluster in family units. Only a young man, probably close to her and her brother's age, stood alone.

Joule was about to say something to him, when Maria introduced herself, explained that she was a paramedic, and motioned to him—Ethan, apparently—to join Joule and Cage.

The twins nodded and welcomed the stranger the best they could.

"It's a two-mile walk out of here. Mostly flat." Maria was looking at each of them as she said it, gauging reactions. No one flinched. A two-mile hike was nothing after the last hour they'd had.

Then Maria looked at their feet. "No one has shoes?"

Most shook their heads. Joule lifted one foot to show off what could hardly be called "shoes." The mom said, "They told us to leave them when we got in the water. So, we did."

Maria only nodded. No one had expected to have to hike out of the woods. "We'll go slow. Please step carefully. If you step on anything, let us know. We have first-aid."

She seemed to finally notice Joule's aqua socks. "You three will be in the front."

Joule nodded along. Aqua socks made her a leader? That was sad.

Maria lined them up, subtly checking each of them for physical condition, probably wondering who might fall behind, who she and her team might have to pick up and carry.

The walk out was solemn. It began with everyone stepping past Clara's body. Though the team had her strapped to a backboard, they all knew. Her head had lolled to the side before the sheet was pulled over her. The four rescuers carrying her would bring up the rear.

It was almost an hour before Joule could see the trees begin to thin and hear civilization in the distance. The walk was slow and agonizing, having paced to one of the kids—the slowest among their group, who was always complaining about stepping on rocks he didn't seem to be looking out for.

Joule wasn't a fan of kids, and this didn't help, but she couldn't fault him. She knew what a shock to your system it was the first time you watched someone die. She knew what it was to have that happen at sixteen. But she kept her gaze ahead, searching for the end. Quickly, they cleared the edge of the trees and picked their way across a small, open field with a brightly colored playground.

In the far parking lot, several ambulances waited, and it was another hour before they were each checked out, though none of the living needed much beyond care for their feet. They were loaded in and driven back to the small building where they'd first put into the water for what was supposed to be a two-hour tour. Their shoes and purses waited in lockers. The woman behind the desk—who'd been so exuberant when they left—now merely directed them to their belongings with soft hand motions.

Cage and Joule had given over all of their information to the rescue team, fully expecting some kind of inquiry in the future. After all, it was Cage who had found the pen and asked Jeff about the tracheostomy. At least that wasn't what had killed Clara.

Maria was checking them out one last time. Her team had returned to the transport truck, the ambulance having headed a different direction with Clara's body and Gary beside her for the last time. Maria finished taking information from the young woman behind the desk and was saying goodbye as she headed out the door.

Just then, her phone rang.

The sound was soft; few of the tour group even heard it over the bustle of grabbing their things and putting the water tour behind them. But Joule and Cage had picked a locker close to the front door.

So they heard most of the paramedic's side of the conversation.

"What?" Maria asked as she pulled up short. "Another one? That's our second one today and our fourth this week."

7

"Look, it's a three-pack!" Joule held up the box to her brother, her eyes widening at the price tag.

"It's the last one I've got. I don't have singles for you," the pharmacist warned.

Joule didn't care. She was trying to get Cage's attention.

"What allergies do you have?" the pharmacist asked.

"He's extremely allergic to bug bites," Joule fudged it a little bit. "A singular ant bite put him on crutches the first time." *Almost true.* "It made his ankle swell, and everyone thought he'd stepped in an entire nest of ants. But it had just been one. And the last time he got an ant bite, he had a systemic rash and his throat started closing on him." *Well, he complained that his throat was itchy.*

That was all Joule needed, though. The pharmacist was sold, even if she didn't have to be. They had called Cage's doctor as soon as they got back to the little bungalow and reactivated the prescription that scratchy-throat episode had afforded them. They'd been on campus at the time and had just never filled it. Joule was grateful now.

The pharmacist seemed to be just doing her due diligence

and making sure she was getting her customers what they needed. What Joule didn't say was that they'd seen two serious anaphylactic reactions the day before and that she wasn't quite sure what caused them. The man who'd gotten the epinephrine had survived and the woman who didn't, hadn't.

Cage only offered a small nod at Joule's exclamation; mostly, he just perused the shelves. He picked up a few big bottles of antihistamines and small ones of generic painkillers, adding them to the counter as the pharmacist began ringing everything up for them.

They left with the bag tucked securely under Joule's arm. She already felt better just holding it. She was probably also trailing a cloud of bug spray behind her. She absolutely did not care.

What had happened on the tour was definitely an allergic reaction to something. She'd heard Maria talking to someone in dispatch as she'd headed out the door. Joule had quietly followed as far as she could without being detected. It was enough. She'd heard most everything Maria said, right up until the woman had closed her car door.

Clara had been Maria's second case of severe anaphylaxis, unknown cause, today. The fourth in the past several days. It sounded like hers wasn't the only team fielding these cases, either. And they were definitely out of the ordinary—or at least, the numbers were.

Joule was happy to be in the car, though she was certainly looking around for any bugs they might have let in. She'd traveled to places that had bugs that bit. She hadn't been surprised at all the first time someone had slapped at an arm or a neck. Today, though, she was grateful for all the times she'd been bitten in the past. All the times she'd said it wasn't fair that the other kids didn't get as many welts as she did. Because she was always certain now to cover herself in bug repellent.

It might have saved her life and Cage's yesterday.

They'd walked out of the woods, the equipment all left behind. Joule wondered if part of the team was out today or if they'd closed up shop and canceled today's tours. A death would certainly warrant that. Had someone gone back to the site to collect the boards and poles?

Cage had suggested the twins cancel their own plans today. One of the guided tours hadn't been able to offer a refund, but Joule hadn't cared. The other event they'd planned was one they paid for when they showed up—which they didn't do—and they'd talked about playing mini-golf later that night, if they had the energy. Their father had always taken them to mini golf. They sometimes played now as a way to reach back and remember.

She wondered sometimes about him. If Nate Mazur were somehow still alive.

It couldn't be, though. He wouldn't have gone over seven years without contacting his kids. He would have shown up at the house. The twins hadn't sold it. Though with no one living in it, it was slowly falling into disrepair. The shingles still tore off in high winds, but no one was there to put them back or even to notice. The toilets had struggled to flush when they'd gone back, and the sinks had sputtered for almost twenty-four hours as the water had figured out the system again.

Dad hadn't been there.

So instead of tours and mini-golf, they'd gone to the pharmacy and followed it with drive-thru tacos and "homemade" lemonade.

"Was that our only outing of the day?" Joule asked as she sat at the high dining room table, watching her brother unwrapping his taco.

As Joule opened the box of EpiPens, the food beckoned her. But so did the comfort and the weight of the needle system in her hand. It was like a small machine, plastic and ready. She slipped one into her ever-present, tiny backpack and handed another to Cage.

She held up the third. "Where does this one go?"

"On one of us," he said easily around bites that decimated the small, street-style taco. Then he wadded up the waxed paper and sighed. "Where are we going? There are four more days of vacation. Do we cut our losses and leave?"

He unwrapped his third taco, took another hearty bite, and waited on his sister.

Joule sipped at her lemonade, knowing she needed to eat but not quite ready to do it. "If we leave, where do we even go?"

She didn't have to say all of it. They'd wedged the vacation between jobs with Helio Systems Tech. Though they were both full-time employees, they logged long days and overtime on jobs and then logged days off between. The pay was lower than the market rate for the work, but HST paid for their housing during jobs.

They'd developed a system: Put what few possessions they had into a trailer and haul it to a self-storage at the next location. Then either check out the city or go somewhere else for a short vacation. Right now, they were essentially homeless and all their things were in a mini-garage unit just outside of Charleston.

Their apartment at the new job wouldn't let them move in for another week, and the weight of that filled the air between them. It hadn't been a problem when they were planning to check out the manatees and the mini-golf on the west coast of Florida for a week. But now? Joule didn't feel bad about running from death. She'd seen too much of it to stay close.

"We can get a hotel room. Closer to Charleston. Scope out the area," Cage suggested. They'd done it before. The little vacation house was paid for already, but Joule didn't care.

"Basically, just not be *here,*" Joule murmured, finally taking a bite of a taco that was less tasty than it looked. It had to be her.

Cage just shrugged. His tacos were gone, the EpiPens dispersed, the decisions were not made.

This vacation had been a challenge to both of them. Could they be near the ocean? They had wanted to try, to see the waters and actually enjoy the dolphin tours. That was the part Joule had anticipated would be difficult.

Though, statistically, she'd known it was stunningly unlikely for the boat to tip, she'd still been petrified they would all go into the water. She told herself friendly dolphins would save her. In the end, she'd done all right. Her heart had pounded out of her chest for the first thirty or so minutes, but then they'd sailed right into a pod of dolphins and it had taken her breath away.

This, though, was not where she'd been expecting to be tested.

It was only later, while she was sitting on the couch watching a movie and thinking about maybe just having a slush for dinner, that she put together the pharmacist's words: *This is the last one I have.*

Joule paused the screen and thought for a moment. Then she ran a small experiment. Finding the number for a nearby pharmacy, she dialed. "Hello.... Yes, I'm looking for injectable epinephrine... Yes, I have a prescription."

"I'm sorry. We are all out of them, too."

Joule had planned to call several places, but this one had been enough.

The pharmacist had said they were out of them, *too*. She not only was out, but she knew other places were as well. She sounded like she'd heard this same call before.

There had been a run on EpiPens. People were replacing them because people had *suddenly been using them.*

8

"What about the car?" Cage asked, not sure how everything would work.

He felt as if he were being swept along in a raging current. Once the idea had taken hold, Joule had not been able to let go of it.

Cage would have packed their vacation suitcases and headed toward Charleston. They could have spent a few days exploring the city. The area was full of wonderful, touristy things. In fact, it had been difficult to choose not to do that this time. But there had only been so many free days, and this vacation had been a long time coming.

Then Joule had suggested that they go back home to Rowena Heights. And when Joule clamped her jaws around something, she didn't let go. She was a master at arguing her side. While it hadn't been Cage's idea, and he wasn't as enthusiastic as she was, he had no real objection.

Still, before the idea had truly had time to simmer, Joule had called the power and water companies and had the house utilities turned on. She'd called Kayla Reeves-Lopez, the neighbor down the street, and left a message for her and her wife, Ivy. The twins would be home by tomorrow morning.

"We can fly back here," Joule offered, having already worked all of it out without him. "Then we drive up to Charleston. It's not that far."

He'd only tipped his head. Joule may have run her brain at a mile a minute, but she'd missed this one thing. "Let's drive up first and get flights out of Charleston."

She frowned at him until he said out loud what he'd realized. "Do you really want to fly back here? Spend more time *here?*"

He didn't even have to finish the full thought. They were done with this area. They probably wouldn't come back until some kind of report said whatever this was, it was over.

First, local public health authorities would have to admit that something was happening. Cage hadn't seen it yet and he was not a fan of watching danger come at him head on, when no one else recognized it yet.

He wished he could hold to the conviction of just never returning to this part of the country. Unfortunately, Florida was sunny. The company they worked for? Well, it provided a variety of environmental services to business and governments. They were known for installing eco-friendly solar panels and systems. He would have to pray they didn't get an assignment here in the future. That might be the point where he and Joule drew the line.

Though they hadn't heard of another case of anaphylaxis, what they'd seen and what Joule had heard from the rescue guide later had been enough. Something was happening and Cage was tired of being in places where things were happening. So, he found himself first in the car for long hours, then immediately on a flight, desperately trying to sleep in an uncomfortable position. They touched down before he'd really accomplished it.

He couldn't say Joule was excited, but she was certainly on edge. They were both anxious to see the old house.

Though they'd come back to Rowena Heights several times since moving away for college, it had been a year since they'd last opened the door themselves. It would take far too long to rent a car and deal with all the paperwork and extra fees to get it. Then there was the drive from the airport. Conversely, the distance seemed much shorter now than when he was a kid.

Before he was ready, they were pulling down the dead-end street and up to their house. It faced directly onto the end of the cul-de-sac, so it was easy to see the grass was a little long. The yard people were coming only often enough to keep it reasonable.

Joule didn't need the moment that he did to stop and settle and take a breath. She was out of the car and putting her key in the lock before he was even close by. His sister struggled with the mechanism for a moment, though whether it was because the lock was actually resisting a little now or if it was just something psychological in his sister, he didn't know.

A moment later, the door swung wide onto... nothing. And everything.

The room was empty and still. The space smelled just a little stale and old. He stepped in, knowing it wouldn't get better until they'd moved the air around themselves. For a moment, his brain flashed, and he was unable to ignore the far-too-vivid image of his mother's body on the floor with the Night Hunters she had killed lying dead around her.

Cage blinked again, and the vision vanished, leaving only the tile and his gasp of surprise hanging in the air.

His mother had saved their lives that night. While it no longer haunted him every waking moment of the day, and some of the sleeping ones, her death still offered an internal drive to do his best. He would do everything he could because someone had loved him enough to sacrifice everything for him and his sister.

Pushing past the memories and the feeling that his parents should have been here, he went through the kitchen into the dining room, where a pile of mail waited on the table. A box taunted him. Kayla and Ivy brought everything in twice a week, but he and Joule hadn't ordered anything sent to this address in ages.

In the middle of the room, a small contraption sat with a light and a reflector on one side. Startling him, it whirred, clicked on brightly, and changed directions. He hadn't seen the little motor in the bottom until just then.

Joule came to stand on the other side of it looking down, her hand on her hips. "That has to be Kayla's little invention."

The neighbor had rigged them a light that ran on battery power. It turned itself off and on at random intervals and aimed itself in different directions, all in an effort to make the house appear more occupied than it was.

Cage looked around the mostly empty room. The dining table and chairs remained, but the twins had hauled much of the furniture off over the years. Some had been donated to charities, other pieces sold when they had the time. There remained only a couch, a small, old TV, and a bed in each room upstairs.

The darkness had settled in on the street beyond the wide front window. Cage was both apprehensive and exhausted.

Luckily, the weather was just shy of cool. The fact that the AC hadn't really regulated the house yet wasn't going to be too bad. Turning to Joule, he asked, "Can you call Kayla and Ivy and tell them that we arrived?"

Even as he said it, he could see the words sinking in. His sister finally lost her exuberance for the journey. Her shoulders slumped as if she was only just now realizing she was exhausted.

"It's weird being home," she said.

It was obvious in the stilted words and dry air that he agreed. But there was nothing to do about it, so he tamped down the dread that threatened at the corners of his memory and headed upstairs. Pulling sheets out of the closet, he quickly made the bed and crawled in.

As he fell asleep, he couldn't help but worry about what lurked beyond the windows in the darkness.

9

"Morning." Joule said it without much inflection as she reached across the table, picked up the sandwich in waxed paper, and held it out toward her brother.

There was something satisfying in not only being the first one up, but having been up for long enough to get dressed, go out, buy breakfast and get a gallon of milk for the fridge. It felt even better to be sitting at the table, eating her own sandwich before Cage even came downstairs.

He didn't ask what the sandwich was. They were twins. They'd always been together. They'd graduated high school together on their own after their parents had died. Suffering tragedies like that so close together, they'd been reluctant to split up as so many siblings did. So they'd gone to the same college, graduated at the same time, and then taken jobs at the same company.

They were roomed together on job locations and took many of their vacations together—a small, tight knot that was the only thing left of their original family unit. So she knew the sandwich in her hand was built exactly the way he usually liked it.

Sitting down, he grabbed the lemonade she'd gotten him and began slowly unwrapping the sandwich. Her brother was not yet moving at full speed. She waited as long as she could. "You want to open the box?'

"Why is there even a box?" he asked. They'd both noticed that the night before. Anyone sending something to the house was most likely mistaken.

"It's from grandma and grandpa," Joule told him, having already inspected what she could this morning. She was curious. They'd had a conversation about checking in with the grands. Were they getting a little senile in their older age?

The twins had visited at least once a year, and though there weren't true signs of dementia, sometimes their grandparents seemed to think they were still the small kids who visited with their parents, so long ago. Joule had dug through the junk drawer to find what she needed—that was not one of the things they'd cleared out. Now the scissors were ready and her curiosity piqued. Who knew what it might be? The box had been sent several months ago, according to the postmark.

Now that her brother was here, she unceremoniously began swiping at the tape. When she opened it, she saw two sweatshirts, one red and one golden yellow. The red would be for Cage. Then she corrected herself: *If they'd gotten it right.* It was possible the shirts said *Stanford* across them. The grandparents had been more than proud about the twins' acceptance and subsequent graduation. Though they weren't in college anymore, that would at least be acceptable. She was more afraid one might say *I break for penguins,* or something similar. But as she shook it out, she saw that the golden yellow one was indeed for her.

Two beakers sat on the front, both wearing frowning cartoon faces as one claimed the other was overreacting. Cage's hand was already in the box, more interested now that he'd seen hers. He held up the shirt, unable to help the expression that crossed his face. The corners of his lips turned down and his eyebrows rose.

He, too, was impressed.

"Show me."

He held it up for her to see a Venn diagram of a cow, a mermaid, and a potato that resulted in a manatee. It was funny, but a little too close to home. Still, her grandparents had sent the shirt long before their tour guide had plunged into the water and scared the manatees away.

"It's a good thing to come home to," she said. "Not exactly work- appropriate, but..."

Not only did the grandparents remember that they were no longer thirteen, but they'd managed to catch their respective professions and senses of humor. "We should go visit again."

Cage nodded. "After this job."

With the mystery box open, she resumed her earlier task, sorting the mail into multiple piles. Her pile, Cage's pile, their pile, definitely junk, probably junk, and so on. Without a word, Cage took a bite of the sandwich that he held in one hand and reached out with the other, helping her sort. It was only a moment later that he stopped suddenly and held out a full manila envelope.

He swallowed as though his food had suddenly become a lump and Joule froze as she saw the front of the letter. Apparently, he wasn't going to open it. Even as she took it from his hand, he said, "I think this is it. It's been just over seven years."

Her heart almost stopped. She told herself there were positives to things being finalized. They'd been so young when they filled out the paperwork. But they'd been eighteen, legal adults, unable to be placed in foster care because their father was missing. Dr. Brett had helped them fill it out. Joule remembered it vividly, a hard day—but still, they'd told themselves their father could come back.

This notice would change the world for them again. It would open old bank accounts and drop another gush of life insurance money onto their laps. Their parents had each planned, in the event of their death, for the other to be able to stay home with the twins, cover childcare, and not have to work and still send both kids to a high-end college.

The money had allowed the kids to pay off the house and let it sit here and slowly rot for their own nostalgia. The life insurance their mother left had already covered Stanford for each of them and left a good enough-sized chunk in savings. They had both taken the jobs with Helio Systems Tech, but they didn't have to. Mostly, the money had saved them early on, when their father disappeared and they had to pay the bills themselves.

Joule now took a deep, fortifying breath and slipped her finger under the edge of the envelope. They'd known this was coming, but she'd chosen to ignore it. She couldn't ignore it anymore.

With reverence, she lifted the flap and reached in. Her lungs didn't want air. She didn't want to admit what they'd both likely known all along. When Cage had insisted Nate might still be alive, it had been Joule who said, "You know he isn't." If their father was alive, he wouldn't have abandoned them. But now, she wanted to be wrong.

The paper inside was slightly thick and felt like linen under her fingertips. That's how she knew this was it. Sure enough, she pulled out her father's official death certificate.

Cage looked down at the paper and then up at her. "Now what?"

10

Joule was not prepared as the arms came around her in the fiercest of hugs. Ivy held the hug tight for a few moments longer than Joule would have, if it had been up to her.

Before Ivy even released Joule, she'd looped an arm around Cage and pulled him in close, even though he was noticeably taller and bigger than her. Ivy wasn't quite taking no for an answer. Her inky bob swung as she breathed her way through the deep welcome. Her smile reached up to the kind, violet eyes.

Luckily, Joule didn't feel like saying no, and neither did Cage.

"I think you've grown again," Kayla said as she hung back. She was not quite one for hugs, certainly not the way that Ivy offered them.

"How are you doing?" Cage asked, looking between them.

"Same." Ivy shrugged.

"My job has a new project," Kayla told them, her ponytail bouncing softly with her almost staccato words. "The light in your living room uses a motor that I designed for a much larger machine that we're building."

"What are you building?" Joule asked, curious. She'd noticed that morning that the little bot strolled around the room and changed positions, too. It worked even better than she had originally thought.

"I can't tell you." Kayla merely smiled.

Ivy smiled with her, though whether that meant Ivy knew or not, Joule wasn't going to push to find out. But with the hugs and warm greetings out of the way, she said the thing she hadn't really wanted to. "I saw the signs on the way in last night."

Kayla tucked her hands behind her back, her gaze going to her sneaker clad toe as it dug at the gravel of her driveway.

Joule had been prepared to knock on the door, but Kayla and Ivy had run out of the little blue house to welcome them as soon as they'd seen the twins walking down the street.

Luckily, it was the weekend, and many were home. This was merely the first stop.

"Hey, you two!"

Joule turned at the sound of Steve's voice. His wide face was blooming into a wider smile, brown skin beaming, glad to see them as he came up the driveway behind them. His booming voice had managed to alert her just in time to another hug. Not the way neighbors usually treated each other, Joule knew. But they had been through something unique. She wrapped her arms around his girth and hugged him back. It was good to see him. Good to see that he was well. Susan would not be hugging them, despite the fact that she ultimately turned out to be quite the badass.

Steve's had been their next stop anyway. He grinned while he hugged them, then stepped back and nodded. He'd heard Joule's question.

"We're seeing more of them," Kayla spoke from behind her,

and Joule stepped back, making them into a small triangle of sorts. Kayla and Ivy at one apex, Joule and Cage, and then Steve holding the others. "People didn't put up signs for a while."

"Because they knew it wouldn't do any good?" Cage asked.

"Maybe? Maybe because there weren't any pets left for a while to go missing." Kayla shrugged again, her words driving the point home.

"But now there are more signs..." Joule let the prompt trail off. "Did they slowly just creep back up in number?" She looked at all the other eyes.

Steve and Kayla and Ivy all lived here. It was she and Cage who had been away for so long.

Kayla shook her head. She could always count on Kayla for the details. Kayla would sometimes speak without the tact of holding back—the kind Ivy was so good at. Sometimes it hit a little hard, but Joule appreciated the truth.

"It's been recent." Ivy picked up the thread. "Only one or two, about six months ago. And then the signs came down, as though somebody had found their missing cat. Then there were more..."

Joule had seen several *missing dog* signs—and not for small dogs, either. The dates on some indicated the dogs had been gone for a month or more.

The small team stood silent for a moment. They all knew where this could go. They'd fought a gritty battle with only each other and their wits. And they'd all survived. Joule could see the look on her brother's face. She could see him thinking the same thing she was: the signs not coming down meant the owners hadn't yet found their animal or a body.

When no one said anything again, it was Steve who shifted the conversation. "Are you two moving back?"

The twins just shook their heads in tandem as Cage added, "Just here for a visit. Barely an overnight."

Joule had wanted to see the old place. To look over the house, maybe clean the gutters, check for leaks in the roof. *Oh, my dear God. She was such a freaking grown up.*

She'd thought all she wanted was a chance to come home. But home wasn't here without her parents. The death certificate had tightened the noose on the last of her hope for her father.

"You clearly don't want to sell your house," Kayla jumped in again. "But you might rent it. Ivy and I can keep an eye on it."

That made Joule's eyes go wide. It would be quite the effort. She looked to Ivy and saw the woman nod and offer a reassuring smile. This wasn't Kayla offering something that hadn't yet been discussed.

Joule could only turn to Cage. It was something they hadn't considered. They'd said one day they would sell the house, but that day simply had never arrived. Here they were, years later.

Dr. Brett Christian had convinced them to file the paperwork declaring their father officially missing. This was a definitive time marker to have him declared officially dead. There was a job to go to; they couldn't stay. But there were new considerations, new worries.

They talked to Kayla and Ivy and Steve about much more mundane things, easier topics that made them smile and laugh. Ivy was traveling and doing restoration of historic homes. Steve had officially retired the year before. He loved it. The twins told about their next job.

"It's for a company that works on jet engines. Just outside of Charleston. They're expanding the industrial park and building a new garage, and they want everything outfitted with solar to run their entire campus."

Kayla jumped in and asked specific questions about the build and the panels. An engineer herself, she managed to turn the conversation in a way that only she and Joule could understand. That managed to get some eye rolls from the others. But then it was time.

The twins had only a short window here. They turned away, with Cage wishing everyone well and letting them know they'd stay in touch.

"We'll consider renting the house. It's a good idea," Joule said, surprising herself. She offered hugs before she stepped away. Then she turned her brother. "You know who we have to see next."

11

Cage headed up the front steps, reaching for the brass door knocker.

When the veterinarian had volunteered to meet them, Cage had quickly replied, "We can come to you."

They didn't mind getting out of the house with its sad memories and magnetic pull. There were good memories there, too, but Cage wasn't quite ready to dig through the others to get to them. He'd seen flashes of his mother's death more times than he could count. He could feel himself, huddled in the central upstairs hallway, reading a textbook all night so he could hide his light, listen for anything breaking in, and learn how to kill it.

But the vet's quick smile and obvious delight at seeing the twins again banished the rough memories for now. The three went through a few minutes of greetings and quick hugs with claps on the back. Dr. Brett, as they often called him, had followed them through the years. He'd texted them occasionally at school, checking up and asking about their grades, making sure they were okay. At no point had he ever made an effort to replace their father, but he'd definitely filled in a few of the gaps for their missing parents. Cage and Joule had welcomed the oversight and caring.

He led them through a home more modern on the inside than out and motioned them to join him at the art deco table. The twins pulled out matching chairs and joined him. Cage was glad to be sitting and having what he wished could be a fairly normal conversation.

"So what's the new project?" Dr. Brett always seemed genuinely interested. Cage didn't have to catch him up to their current status; the vet had stayed up-to-date on all the other changes.

This, Cage thought, *was good.* It had felt good to see Kayla and Ivy, but they'd all been standing in the street, the very street where they'd lost people. The intersection—where they'd fought for their lives in the dark with just the weapons they could design themselves—had been in his line of sight.

Dr. Brett's house was new to them, almost neutral territory.

"We're outside of Charleston," Cage told him, explaining about the jet design company campus.

"That sounds like a cool project." Dr. Brett leaned forward. "Are you excited?"

An interesting question, Cage thought. "I guess so."

He looked to his sister to see she seemed to have the same response. Though she managed to put it into words a little bit better.

"It's a good job. The company is good. They take good care of us. We get to see a bunch of different places."

"But?" Dr. Brett prompted them.

"But it's the same thing again," Cage filled in now. "Technically, each job is new..."

"—but they're getting repetitive." Joule picked up the back half of the sentence.

Dr. Brett shrugged. "It's common for smart people to get bored. Are there promotions in your futures?"

That offered a little jolt—something Cage hadn't really thought of. He'd gotten his degree, initially intending to be a marine biologist, but that had changed when the waters had risen and the sharks had come. Instead, he'd switched over to a more general biology degree, focusing on land animals, mammals, lizards, bugs, and the like. When the twins graduated, they'd applied for jobs and gotten this one together. It felt appropriate.

"We probably won't get promoted much without an advanced degree," he told Dr. Brett.

Joule nodded along, pointing out, "All our team leaders have a master's at least. All the bigwigs have PhDs."

The doctor didn't reply, but there was something in his nod that told them, *maybe it's something to consider.*

"So how are you doing?" Cage changed the conversation. "How's the veterinarian business in the area these days?"

"I can't complain." Dr. Brett offered half a smile. It was clear that something big was happening, though he always loved the topic of veterinary medicine.

But Joule jumped in. "We saw more missing pet signs on the way in. The neighbors are concerned."

Luckily, Dr. Brett shook his head quickly and decisively. "I haven't seen it here, and I don't think the numbers are high enough to draw any conclusions yet. These things do normally go in waves."

That was good to know. Cage felt the breath softly escape from his lungs. It was probably just old fear sneaking in around the corner. He'd had a rough night. His room at home was now mostly empty except for the bed. The windows and doors still had the bolts, despite the fact that the need for them had long since passed, and even so, he tossed and turned.

He'd slept numerous different places over the past seven years. Each time, he'd moved to a new climate, a new area, a new level of rural or urban cityscape. The noises always bothered him less than they had the time before. He was beginning to think he could sleep just about anywhere.

But then he came back home. It was specifically these noises that were keeping him awake. The sounds of the tree of his childhood clicking against the window that had turned into the rustle of the Night Hunters just beyond the grass. He'd sat up, stock still, listening into the night, hearing the thrum of his own pulse in his ears, but nothing beyond the walls. He'd finally convinced himself to lie back down and go to sleep. Until he did it all over again, just a few hours later.

Charleston would be a welcome change.

"How long are you here for?" Dr. Brett asked, though he deflated a little at their answer.

"Just today."

"We leave tomorrow morning."

"I wasn't expecting you to be home anytime soon," he added as though it were a consolation. He looked a little older. He was married, but they didn't have any kids of their own. And Cage and Joule didn't have parents. Cage was just about to suggest that they could spend the holidays together when Joule jumped in again.

"The opportunity to come back just happened at the last minute," Joule said, her eyes darting to Cage's.

He offered a small nod to indicate she should go ahead.

She told Dr. Brett about their tour and the manatee, and Cage watched as the man's face lit up.

"You got to see manatees?"

"Five of them!" Cage smiled, but Dr. Brett's expression quickly fell. He knew the kinds of things that were happening. He probably expected them to say one of the manatees had leapt out to bite someone. But no.

Cage explained how the tour guide had fallen into the water and scared the manatees away. How first Jeff and then Clara had sudden anaphylactic reactions.

"And you only had one EpiPen?" Dr. Brett burst in.

"Expired!" Joule said. "But it worked. We were lucky we even had that. There were fewer than ten of us on the tour."

"No wonder you came back home." Dr. Brett's eyes flipped to the side, his expression one of careful thought. Though Cage didn't know why that meant *no wonder they had come home,* there wasn't time to ask. The vet asked the next obvious question. "Was it something they ate?"

"We think it was mosquito bites."

"That would be weird."

"Actually, what's really weird is that we filled my old epinephrine prescription, just to have it on us. We got a three-pack, and apparently it was the last one in the whole area."

"So, the two you saw weren't the only two." Dr. Brett paused, his hand flat on the surface of the dining room table, pressing downward a little until slowly he stood. He added, "If the pharmacies are out of EpiPens, then there were a lot more people reacting who managed *not* to die.... Mosquito bites, you said?"

Shit, Cage thought. Dr. Brett knew something

12

Cage ran his fingers through his hair in frustration. "Really?"

He looked at the other three members of his team, as they stood together in the Charleston heat. He hoped he didn't come across as blaming anyone.

"We should do it again," Sarah said.

"We should get one of the engineers," David threw out at the same time.

"We've run it twice already," Cage said in frustration. "And we got the same results both times."

Sarah nodded. She and Cage had been through this together on several other projects, though they'd worked on other ones separately in between. They'd been in Alabama together. Cage and Joule had started with Helio Sys on that job, and Sarah had been their roommate as well as a disaster-mate. That formed a bond that was hard to shake.

"Dr. Murasawa is going to have us run it again. So let's just run it again," Sarah sighed. "But like David said, let's reach out to one of the engineers, too."

Ground soil samples and percolating tests were handled

mostly by the biological team. Until, like this one, they went awry. Too much red clay had packed to dirt. Not enough water drainage. Given what the company had given them to read in the week before, he'd not expected this.

None of them had.

He dialed up Melinda Gonzalez and asked if she could get them one of the engineers. Not surprising him, it was his sister who showed up less than fifteen minutes later.

"What's going on?" Joule asked the group at large.

Three hours later, they were explaining it to their bosses.

The whole build would have to be moved. That wasn't unusual, Cage knew. Often, they'd gone out to build something and—being at the leading edge of technology the way they were—it rarely went the way it was expected. Certainly not from the initial plans.

But they'd been here for three weeks already. Each week, they'd picked a place to build the garage and, each week, it had failed the soil samples and the environmental testing and had to be moved.

"I thought testing was completed before the first build site was selected." Joule was frowning at them, watching as Gonzalez leaned over the paper map she'd spread on the table. Several large, red X's mocked them from places they'd already tested and rejected.

"They did." The environmental team leader had proved herself a bit of a badass in Alabama, but now she just looked as frustrated as the rest of them.

"So why are we getting different results?" Cage asked.

"They did preliminary work. We're doing much more thorough testing."

As the manager walked them through each rejection process, it sounded more and more to Cage like they were about to be out of a job. But at least Melinda Gonzalez didn't think so.

"The first site had better ground clearance. We could go back with a remodel. You—" she pointed to the members of the biological team, "—I want you to go back and do a wider net survey. Do all the basics again at the first site, so we can confirm the initial findings. It looks like what was wrong with it was an endangered species problem."

Cage watched as the other bio team members raised eyebrows at the term "endangered species problem," but Gonzalez was still going.

"Figure out how we can move them. You—" she pointed to Joule, "You're coming with me to engineering. We may have to go down to a single- or dual-story scenario. I don't think we can support what they originally wanted."

"That means a much larger footprint." Joule pointed out the obvious.

Gonzalez only nodded. "Yes. We've got to go back to Dr. Murasawa with this and see if we can get it approved. And that's why they are redoing their initial survey."

At least it made sense, Cage thought as he nodded at her and, with his whole team, turned to leave. He'd see Joule again at dinner. Or maybe not.

There wasn't much of the day left and they'd barely gotten started with the second round of site surveys before they called everything off for the night. No one said it, but it was understood they'd be back early to continue the testing the next day.

Though they hadn't been at it long, the team size had already grown. This problem could hold everything back, so it wasn't surprising that Dr. Murasawa was throwing everyone at it. Some teams had found other suitable ground, but not as near to the main buildings as the company wanted for a parking lot.

The situation would have been more upsetting if it wasn't par for the course for Helio Systems Tech jobs. So, Cage wasn't sweating it yet. He and his sister were no longer project-based employees now. As full-timers, the failure of this site would mean the end of *this* job but not *their* jobs.

He headed home. This time, home was an apartment with two bedrooms, but still small. Unlike Alabama, where they'd been forced to room four to a place for simple lack of housing. They hadn't known at the time that the dorm-like conditions were unusual. Now, he and Joule had their own apartment. He set about flipping on all the lights and starting something for dinner.

She came in about an hour after him, having texted that she'd be there soon. The weather had turned gray. He'd been hoping for nice spring weather, but summer was coming—the hot and muggy phase hitting them hard and fast.

"Wow!" Joule said, following her nose to the small kitchen. "You did pretty good for an electric stovetop."

He preferred a gas top by a wide margin, not only for the ability to control the heat, but for the option to turn the gas on and blow the place sky-high. Not a protocol he'd ever needed to enact, but history had taught him to take note of when it was and wasn't an option.

He'd made burgers, with mac and cheese and broccoli. The broccoli had been a bit last-minute. He'd heard his mother's voice telling him he really needed a vegetable.

"I could say the same to you." He waved the spatula at her. "You managed to come in right as I got everything ready."

She shrugged as if to say, *It's a talent,* before she offered to clean up after they ate. Cage easily agreed to that one.

The living room and dining room space was small; the table that had come with the unit was now tucked deep into the corner. The twins pulled out TV trays and turned on the news as they sat down with their furnished-apartment-plates and glasses.

They'd come in at the middle of the main report, catching only the tail end of what the commentator was saying.

"Though the new infection hasn't been identified, it's clear it's not Zika. It appears to be triggering severe and sudden anaphylaxis—the closing of the throat and airways. There are currently just over two hundred people who've been successfully treated for this. They're the lucky ones. They are expected to survive because they received proper treatment early enough in the process. Currently, thirty-two people have died from this sudden and severe reaction."

Cage looked to his sister. His hand almost unconsciously patting down the side of his cargo pants, feeling the EpiPen next to his wallet. He kept it there all the time now.

Joule turned as if to ask if he was putting it all together. But she didn't have to say the words.

Cage shook his head, but his words were the exact opposite. "It has to be the same thing. It's been less than a month since..."

She didn't ask *since what?* She didn't have to.

"And this is local news," he added it too softly, not liking his own conclusions. "That means it's *here*."

13

—————

"I call it *Fuck Off*," Joule told the others on her team and Cage's. They were out in the field again today, but this time she was being a drug pusher as she stood there with her small spray bottle in her hand.

Her heart thudded a little bit too hard, though. She shouldn't be so invested in dousing her coworkers with her essential oil bug repellent.

"You don't use the regular stuff?" David asked.

"I did. I do sometimes," she admitted. "But it smells so bad. And the commercial stuff that works best has DEET in it."

She'd been torn between solid protection from bites of all kinds and the known negative ramifications of the harsh chemicals. Some of the other brands that didn't have the harsh smells—sometimes just a "clean fresh scent that bugs don't like"—didn't work so well. She'd tried them and she had more than one little red welt on her calf or her arm to show for it.

She and Cage had come out of Florida scared of bug bites. Though they still weren't entirely sure that that was the cause of the paddle-board tour incidents. So each time she found a new little red mark, she reminded herself it was all conjecture;

it could be something entirely different. She also breathed a sigh of relief that Jeff was alive.

Then again, Clara wasn't.

"You're very adamant about this." Sarah was looking at her askance.

Joule shrugged. She didn't want to tell them that she and Cage had watched someone die. Again. She was grateful when Cage stepped in.

"When Joule was little, we called her *bait*. We still do."

She grinned at his words, though internally she cringed at the use of *we*. It had been him and her parents who called her that. Now, it was just him.

"No matter where we are," he went on, "if you don't want to get bitten, you just hang out with Joule. Of course, now that she's covered in bug spray, that won't work anymore."

She jumped in, just to make herself sound less extremist. "On one family beach vacation, when we were little, I got so many bites. I didn't think my mom and dad were going to believe me, so I got a permanent marker and numbered all of them."

"Oh!" Sarah's mouth fell open. "I'm sure your mother loved that."

"Actually, she laughed hysterically. It was my father who was a little embarrassed to be seen in public with me. Especially after the bug bites faded, and the numbers remained.... I had ninety-six."

"Wow!" David was impressed.

It was an impressive number. Still, thinking of her parents made her heart tug. Something about the trip to Florida had twisted her up a little bit, and she hadn't quite unloaded it all yet.

Cage went on. "I, on the other hand, am occasionally allergic. I've had a bite on my arm—" He held his forearm up across the front of his chest. "—that swelled up enough to make my arm look curved. Sometimes I react normally. We don't really know. So the two of us? We just don't get bit."

"Eh, I'll take your home-brew spray." Sarah shrugged at them as she held out her arms for Joule to douse. "They don't bite me that much anyway."

Maybe having been their roommate before made her trust the twins' judgment, or maybe she just gave them a pass for being a little crazy. Joule didn't know.

"Look." Joule planted her hands on her hips when she finished over-spraying Sarah. "There's something coming up from Florida. Did you see the news last night?"

They all shook their heads, except for David. "Yeah, something about people dying from anaphylaxis."

Joule almost laughed. Leave it to a team of engineers and bio-researchers. For the biologically educated half of them, that word just rolled off the tongue in casual conversation.

"We saw one of the people die in Florida." *Fucking monkey balls,* she thought. She was not letting her friends get bit. "According to the news last night, whatever it is, it's *here*. And we think it's caused by bug bites."

"Bug bites don't send you into anaphylaxis," David said. He shook his head at her as though she were a little nuts.

She might be, but she wasn't wrong about the possibility.

"They do if you're allergic to their venom or saliva," Cage responded as quickly as David had opened his mouth. "I took an ant bite to the leg one time, and I got a full body rash and a scratchy throat. The doctor gave me an epinephrine prescription for it."

Joule saw what Cage didn't say. He almost absentmindedly reached down and patted the pocket on his ever-present khaki cargo pants again, as if reassuring himself the EpiPen was still there.

Hers and the spare still lingered in her small backpack.

"What's in the spray?" David asked Joule. But she didn't breathe a sigh of relief yet.

She quickly rattled off several essential oils before adding, "mixed with deionized water and vodka."

"What's the vodka for?"

But it was Sarah, her fellow engineer and Chem major, who explained. "The water and oils won't mix without it." Then Sarah sniffed at her shirt and shrugged. At least it wasn't too bad. "Do it, David. Make your friends happy."

"Nerd peer pressure is the worst!" he lamented, but he didn't let them spray him.

One mission mostly accomplished, Joule thought, as the other five team members came forward. This time, she handed over the bottle and let them spray themselves. She wasn't their mom. Dousing Sarah like she was a toddler had probably been a bit much.

Some of them asked Cage questions as they took turns, more curious about his previous reactions than concerned about dying. Maybe that was good. Joule wasn't a fan of spreading her paranoia.

"That smells pretty good!" Aliyah handed the bottle back to Joule with one hand as she lifted her shirt to sniff with the other. "And it works?"

"I haven't gotten bitten in the last few days."

Aliyah raised one thick, dark, expressive brow. "If you're as bait-y as you say, then that's good data. Though—" She held up one dark-skinned arm, "rumor has it we just don't get bit as much. My mama will tell you that's a lie, but not me."

Joule grinned at her friend and held the bottle out toward David, the last one.

David wrinkled his nose. "I'm good. Lord knows I'm going to be close enough to this one. The fumes from him will keep me safe." He motioned with his chin toward Cage, who definitely smelled like a bottle of essential oils himself.

"We got to get going, guys." Sarah turned away, motioning for the team to get back out into the field. She wasn't a team leader yet, but she definitely had seniority, so her people trailed along.

Cage and the other bio-team members followed her right into the high grass. Joule and Aliyah turned the other way. Their grid was closer to here, where they started, but Joule couldn't help herself; she surveyed everything she could see, as though she were arriving for the first time. Last night's news had tilted her world a bit.

A stand of trees and wet ground from the rains yesterday made her concerned. Though Cage had told her a single twenty-four hour span wasn't enough for the puddles to host and hatch a new batch of mosquitoes, she didn't like it. *What about tomorrow? Was two days enough?*

"Come on," Aliyah said, turning away. "Murasawa wants us to pick up something before we start."

Probably some preliminary sketches for a lower, flatter parking structure. Designated points they would have to check for stability and more. The bigger footprint would cause as many problems as it solved.

But as she followed Aliyah back to the team trailer, Joule turned one more time and looked back over her shoulder. Though he was too far in the distance to be positive, she thought she saw David reach up and slap at the back of his neck.

14

"I don't know if I can handle another day of this," Joule told her brother, her exasperation flowing even if there was no real reason for it. She paced the small living room, hating the feeling that something bad was coming. She wasn't always right, but she wasn't often wrong.

Cage didn't reply. He just handed her a granola bar.

Her stomach had the tendency to refuse breakfast, so he often didn't cook it for her.

"Eat something. It'll work itself out." He held the wrapped food out until she took it. "It always does."

"And if it doesn't?" She watched him work his way through several pieces of bacon and a scrambled egg he'd slapped between toast.

Holding onto the granola bar, she didn't open it yet. The idea of putting food in her mouth hadn't quite formed as a need yet. She gave her brother a cold, hard stare until he answered.

"I didn't mean the job. And nothing has happened since Florida." Cage shrugged.

"We've been doused in bug spray. That's why nothing happened."

"David wasn't. I've been watching him. I'm pretty sure he got bit, and nothing happened to him," her brother repeated. "Also, we didn't douse the entire Helio Systems team in your bug juice."

Still clutching the granola bar in one hand and pulling her small spray bottle out of her backpack with the other, she started to relax. He was right. "A lot of them were working outside."

Still, she shook the bottle to mix the oil, vodka, and water before dousing herself in it before she even left the apartment.

"Maybe it's not about bugs," Cage said. "No one in Florida seemed to think it was the bugs. In the news here, they didn't seem to think it was the bugs."

Joule nodded. "I know they said they thought it was some food that they figured people were allergic to, but... that doesn't make sense with what we saw."

Last night, when they'd arrived home, she'd watched every single news report she could find. So far, whoever was contact-tracing the victims hadn't found a thread linking them all. Or even most of them.

Though Joule wanted to believe her brother was right, she didn't. "It's not random."

At least he agreed with that. She didn't think she could go on if it was truly random. Too many things had been pulled away from her too many times. She didn't handle things well if they didn't at least offer some measure of control. So, she squirted more of her bug repellent on her ankles because— necessary or not—it was something she could *do*.

"But whatever it is, it's *here*." She stood up and looked her brother directly in the eyes.

He tipped his head for a moment. He was her best friend. She had other friends, but if she ever had to choose one person, it would be him. He understood. And even when he didn't agree, he *listened*.

"Well," he offered, after a quick thought. "The local news is for Charleston. We're definitely inland. Not even in the Charleston city limits."

The jet lab that Helio Sys was constructing the parking and solar system for had bought the land on the cheap originally. Now the city had grown and was slowly spreading outward, closer to the site where they were working. But it still wasn't coastal.

"Maybe it's not *here* here," Cage said. "The local news reported it in Charleston, but maybe not in the surrounding areas yet."

"Is there a map of mosquito migratory patterns?"

Cage shook his head at her. "I'm sure there must be somewhere, but I don't know about it."

Her anxiety was rising, and she wasn't quite able to push it back down. He was thinking the problem through, but it didn't make her feel better. If the mosquitos were the culprit and they just weren't here yet, that didn't make her any safer.

Her brother stood up and put his dishes into the sink. "We need to get to work."

Joule picked up her backpack and pulled out her keys as she headed for the door. But Cage shook his head and dangled his own keys in front of her. He pointed to her granola bar, still clutched in her other hand. "I'm driving. You eat."

The snarky words *Yes, Mom* almost fell out of her mouth, but she didn't let them. It might have been funny if they'd still had a mother to tell her to eat her granola bars and take her vitamins. So she sat in the car silently thinking and fuming up the air with a mix of bug-repellent essential oils.

Slowly, she fed herself the granola bar. She didn't taste it, but she managed to finish it as they pulled up. The drive to the job site was short, only a few miles. Honestly, it might have been walkable, if not for the humidity and the fact that they were supposed to look vaguely professional upon arrival.

"I don't like this," she repeated as Cage pulled into the grass lot the team was using for parking. Of course, there was nowhere to park. It was their job to build the structure.

"I don't like it either." He twisted the key, but he only looked straight forward.

The good news was, the number of deaths was down. Though it had gone upward, the rate had slowed before doubling. For some reason, that was the number at which Joule had decided to panic. So she wasn't there yet.

With a deep breath, she exited the car out of force of will and managed to lose herself in some of the work for most of the morning. But at lunch break, Aliyah had headed off one direction and Leslie another. Joule had gone alone into the main building and eaten her sandwich with her thoughts.

She liked the downtime. Several workers approached, but she huddled over her phone and tried to look busy. When she finished her food and tossed her plate and fork into the wash station, she still had time before her fellow teammates returned.

With another deep breath—she needed too many lately— she looked around the cafeteria and large lobby. Though there were corners away from everyone, she didn't want to do this here. It was ridiculous, she told herself.

Still, she headed out to the car and turned on the air conditioning, even though she might not need it. She dialed the first number she found and waited on hold before pressing the prompted series of buttons.

As she asked her questions, her heart sank.

She found another number and dialed. Again, she waited and heard an answer that she disliked just as much. By the third one, her tone had clearly changed. She was starting to sound desperate.

"I'm so sorry," the pharmacist apologized, even though it wasn't his fault. "We've had a run on them just this week. Everybody's getting their refills right now. We weren't stocked up quite enough for it."

The center of her chest hardened into a tiny little knot that rose slowly, threatening to clog her throat. She'd called to settle her nerves. The answers had done anything but that.

"We'll have some more in a few days," the pharmacist said, an upbeat tone in his voice this time. "We've ordered a shipment of epinephrine pens. But, unfortunately, right now, we're all out."

15

David turned toward Cage, an angry glare in his eyes. "You and your sister are my least favorite people right now."

He reached one hand up to his other elbow, scratching lightly at new, small pink welts that raised on his skin as Cage watched.

They were nothing like what Cage suffered when he'd had gotten bitten. So, he merely raised one dark eyebrow and pointed to the perfectly spaced marks. "Vampire?"

David sighed in response. "Yes. The dumbest little vampire ever. No one gets blood from an elbow."

Cage grinned back. "I'm not sure how you getting bitten is mine and my sister's fault."

"You're the ones who bug sprayed everybody," David snapped back.

"Yes?"

"And now I'm the only thing available for these fuckers to eat."

"Oh," Cage said as he reached the obvious conclusion. "So

we should have offered ourselves up as food so you didn't have to use bug spray? Yeah, *no*."

He almost laughed. It had been five days. He'd spent them surreptitiously looking at the arms and occasionally exposed lower legs of his coworkers. He knew he had seen bites, but no one had died and, in fact, no one seemed really bothered by it.

Except David.

"Give me some of the stuff," David demanded. He held out his hand, rolling his eyes as he motioned for the bottle. "I'm tired of being the only feast out here. But let me tell you, I'm not looking forward to smelling like gingernuts or fuck thorn or whatever the hell is in there."

Cage did laugh this time. He didn't quite know the recipe, but he was confident those weren't real plants. "I don't have it. Joule does. She's with the teams on the other side of the campus today."

Besides, Cage told himself, it probably wasn't the bug bites. Joule had told him a few nights ago that there'd been a local run on epinephrine. People were refilling their scrips, and that had to mean something.

Their medications couldn't have all expired at once. A rash of refills must mean there had been a rash of sudden uses, but the news wasn't touting strange, new deaths. A few more people had died. They said the CDC was watching the food supply. They'd followed that with calm reminders that most everything had to be safe.

Since Joule didn't seem to be able to sleep unless she'd watched every report out there, Cage figured they were pretty up-to-date on what was going on.

These weren't the first two bites David had gotten. Cage watched as, absentmindedly, his fellow scientist reached over and scratched at his elbow again, even as he leaned down to check a trap.

David's head popped up as he caught himself scratching

and forcibly stopped himself. "Well, the next time we see your sister, I will take her magical anti-bug spray."

"We might catch up to her at lunch," Cage offered, trying to be hopeful. He hated bites and itching, and he felt bad for David, though it was his own doing. He could try to run into Joule, but the groups tended to break whenever they could. And honestly, they didn't work at having lunch together, most days.

They worked together. They lived together. They'd rarely been apart from the time they'd been born. Hell, she'd even stabbed him in the leg once. Granted, it had been dark, and she absolutely hadn't meant to, but they'd glued his leg back together.

It had been a wild ride, even if it hadn't all been good. Cage wasn't making any major life moves without his sister, but he didn't need to have lunch with her every day, either.

"I'll see what I can do," he told David, even though he was becoming more and more convinced it wasn't the bugs.

The two continued working, sending notes to Kelsey and Sarah, who were checking similar data on the other side of the open field. Eventually, he figured, he should just ask David if he knew anything.

David had joined the team about two jobs ago and Cage had worked with him before. Now, they were mostly tracking small mammals and lizards, but David had been hired as their resident insect guy. "So, what do you think bit you?"

"Garden variety mosquito. Probably *Anopheles*." David rattled it off as though everybody knew the genus names of common insects. "There are a handful of species here, though."

"Is it bad here?" Cage waved his hand to indicate the whole field. "It's rained for several days. Is that enough standing water?"

Though he initially reminded Joule that mosquitoes didn't

reproduce overnight, he wasn't quite positive about how long it did take.

David stood up, coughing briefly, then stretching his back while answering the question. "With standing water like this? Absolutely. While it's raining? No, but the rain leaves behind puddles—" they'd stepped in more than one hidden among the tall grasses each day, "—and though the puddles shrink, and that helps kill them, any standing water with a surface will do."

"How long until they hatch? Like three days?" Cage wanted confirmation. Mosquitoes were one of the big concerns about global warming. They were the base of many a food chain. "Can we wipe them out?"

"Yes, three days, and no. Disrupting them disrupts everything. So, we can't completely kill them off." David walked several yards away to check a different trap.

Cage wasn't surprised, he just didn't like the answer. Mosquitoes screwed things up going the other direction, too. "Well, it's why we're here."

David gestured to the open field then added, "We have to alter the warming of the earth or deal with the consequences."

Cage already knew plenty about consequences, but he figured those weren't the same ones that David was talking about. But his friend was still going on. "The one-degree climate increase everyone talks about, is so dangerous—in part —because it gives us three more days above seventy each year. Every day above seventy is another day for mosquitoes to breed."

Cage filled in the obvious conclusion. "One more life cycle—"

David interrupted, "Yes, but one more cycle doubles the population."

Cage felt his head yank back at that. The math made sense, but he hadn't thought it all the way through before.

David wasn't giving him time to process. "*And* double the

population at the *end* of the summer means double the population of mosquitoes making it through to the following spring."

"So, it isn't just double each year. The following spring starts with more mosquitoes each year after?"

David nodded, letting him know he was right. "Not all of them make it through, not even close, but three more days above freezing means you have double the population at the end of the summer than you would have, and double the population starting the next summer than you would have. It doesn't take very long for that to get wildly out of control."

Cage sighed. That was shitty news, especially right at a time when he and Joule were most concerned about mosquitoes. But he'd learned because he'd asked. "At least we install solar panels and work for a company that's reducing its carbon footprint."

David coughed again.

Cage asked snarkily, "Do you need me to hit you on the back?"

He always offered the treatment his mother had foisted on the twins when they were small.

"I'm fine!" David choked out between raspy sounding coughs. No one wanted to get whacked on the back.

Cage looked over again to see if his friend really did need help, but he said only his friend's name and he could hear the fear in his own voice as the tone rose. "*David?*"

Cage struggled with what he saw. David coughed again and held his arms out in front of him.

The red rash climbed quickly to his elbows...

16

Cage stood frozen, only able to watch as the welts appeared and climbed his friend like an army of little ants marching toward his torso.

It took a moment before he snapped out of it. Though Cage wasn't certain how long he stood there staring, he grabbed David's hands and flipped them over. He pulled on his friend's arms, extending them and looking to see how far it had spread.

The sharp urge to yank his hands away surged through him. He wasn't consciously afraid to touch David... but should he be? Cage didn't give into that fear, and he hoped his hesitation didn't show.

Instead, he put his hands on David's shoulders and turned his friend around. It was already too late. There was no way to distinguish if there were bites now, or even how many there might be under the rash. But looking for bites wasn't even the right thing to do! Cage spun David back toward him.

He realized then that something they'd done or said had drawn attention from Sarah and Leslie, who were working on the other side of the field. The women were already racing toward them as David stood stock still and tried not to panic.

Sarah called out to them. "You guys need help?"

"Yes," Cage yelled back.

David looked as though he were going to open his mouth but, instead, he closed it and swallowed awkwardly. It was obvious, even from the outside, that swallowing was getting difficult.

For a moment, Cage felt his own throat restrict. Was something happening to him, too? Or was he just having sympathy reactions?

He looked down at his own hands and saw that they were free of bites and rash, so he forced his mind back to the problem at hand.

"Are you allergic?" he blurted.

"To what?" David's voice scratched out. Cage took that as a no.

He considered asking his friend if he had any medication on him for anything like this, but quickly tossed that idea aside. David was obviously confused. This wasn't something that happened regularly.

His friend shook his head, swallowing again, then tilting his head up—a move Cage now realized involved trying to lengthen and open his windpipe.

Sarah pulled up, drawing herself to a quick halt. "What's going—oh, my god! David!"

Her assessment and conclusion that this was scary was immediate.

David nodded to her, one hand pulling away, though Cage was still holding on to him. It was stupid, but Cage gripped his friend's fingers tightly, as though if he held him upright and held his hands out, the rash would stop moving.

But it didn't.

It was now starting to show on his neck. It wasn't instantaneous but followed a clear path from the tips of his limbs to his core, then to his head. When it hit David's face, Cage would worry.

He glanced at his own bare arms again, just to be sure he didn't have it, too.

With his now free hand, David wrapped his fingers around his own throat as if there were anything he could do from the outside.

"Do you have an EpiPen?" Cage blurted out to Sarah and Leslie, who'd now come up alongside them. He had his own, but he was starting to be afraid of using it up.

"Does he need one?" Sarah asked.

Cage leaned in close, looking at David's face now with small, giraffe-like pink welts all over it. "Are you having trouble breathing?"

David shook his head *no*, but then his mouth opened, and they all watched as his lungs tried to expand but didn't do so very well. The air was not getting in this time, not in the way it needed to.

David changed his answer and nodded Yes.

"Do you want an epi pen?" Cage asked, his fingers already working the flap of the pocket, tearing at the Velcro and digging around. He was trying to distinguish the plastic device from the wallet it sat beside. He suffered more selfish thoughts about rationing the lifesaving medication.

Maybe David didn't need it.

What if he or Sarah did?

The other two pens were with Joule. Three total had meant there was no even division. Could Joule get here quick enough to get them a second EpiPen if they needed it? He didn't think so.

David still hadn't answered. He was eyeing Cage oddly. The problem was, Cage wanted to jab the pen into his friend's leg right now, but he wanted a clear answer about whether he should.

In Florida, when they'd used the expired pen, it was obvious was nothing more to do for Jeff. The medication had been the last resort. But now? David was still upright and answering questions. Cage couldn't just jab him with such a strong medication.

"I don't think so," David managed to wheeze out the words, his throat obviously tight. But he looked at all three of them as though they were a little crazy. As though this were a coughing fit where he'd swallowed something wrong, and it would simply pass.

It wasn't.

Cage wasn't sure how much he could believe his friend. But he didn't quite know how to change his mind. As Cage was opening his mouth, Leslie tried a different tack.

"I think your throat is closing up. I think this is anaphylactic shock. David, you're having a reaction to something. But what?"

This time, David mostly mouthed the words as his hands rose and his head shook back and forth frantically. Cage saw that his lips were starting to turn blue. Sweat was beading on his forehead. Leslie stepped away from the small group, but Cage was too busy watching David to pay much attention.

Cage couldn't tell if the color meant David was getting worse, but that had to be it. Didn't it?

Sarah stayed in close and asked another question. "If your airway closes up and you pass out, do you want us to use the EpiPen?"

This time she was more forceful, putting her face up close to David's, her concern showing. She, too, now thought this was the only likely path they had.

But David didn't give a solid *Yes*. He swung his gaze from side to side, his fingers clutching and twitching at his own throat. The red welts were now everywhere. Cage couldn't see any open patch of skin.

He was tempted to lift his friend's shirt up and check and

see if they'd moved to his torso. But that seemed the least of their worries.

Cage had seen Jeff react, and he had seen Clara. And if this wasn't the same, well, he'd eat his own socks. And that would still be a million years better than what was happening to David.

Behind him now, he could hear Leslie talking on the phone. "Yes.... No...." She turned to Cage and Sarah. "Do we have an EpiPen?"

David turned and looked at her. She was a few feet away, where they had stepped back to make the phone call easier to hear.

"I've got one." Cage pulled the device he'd been fingering out of his pocket.

Leslie turned back to the call, as though everybody should carry EpiPens and Cage's answer had been expected. But Cage simply pushed his attention back to David as he heard Leslie behind him say, "yes . . . yes . . . yes."

Then she stepped closer, her eyes darting frantically. "The online operator says to use the epi pen on him, *now* . . . Lay him down. Push it right through the pants if you have to . . . It's designed for that."

Leslie was speaking in short bursts of sentence fragments, clearly relaying what she was hearing. Cage and Sarah were trying to get the instructions correct before they stabbed their friend with a drug that would require a hospital visit.

Each of them now had a hand on David, who was looking less and less solid. Cage felt the tug at his hands as his friend's weight shifted.

They hadn't laid David down, but his grip slackened. Cage, still holding tightly, was being pulled awkwardly as David sank to the ground.

"Sarah!" he yelled. "Catch him!"

17

hy me? Why me? Why me? The phrase was going through Cage's brain as he pulled the epi-pen from his pocket and yanked the thick cap off, exposing the short, sharp needle. Why did he have to be the one to jab his friend?

But why not him? He was the one who had the pen. He'd seen it done, just over a month ago.

David was out cold now and clearly not breathing. Every second counted as Cage struggled with his decision.

Leslie was standing over them, the phone still at her ear. "Jab it right into his thigh. Now! Go! Go!"

Cage felt her words pierce his gut. Not quite knowing how much force he would need, he pulled his hand back, needle gripped in his fist as if to strike. He imagined it was a heart problem and he would thump David's chest and demand his friend to come back to life. Instead, he plunged the needle down through the thick khakis and into the thigh muscle.

"In." Leslie breathed through the phone line to the operator. "It's in."

Cage held his breath waiting.

Was the area too noisy? Too many birds and crickets? They seemed so loud right now.

Was this pen different? Maybe they'd used an older version on Jeff and this one was different. He didn't hear it. It was supposed to click... *wasn't it?* Did the plunger go down, or was it also encapsulated so that he wouldn't see anything?

David didn't twitch at all. His eyes didn't open. He didn't inhale.

"It didn't work." Leslie barely whispered the words into the phone.

She'd clearly been given instructions that she should have seen some change by now.

Cage couldn't tell. He didn't know if it had been one second, or fifteen, or a minute. But David still gave no reaction.

"Instantly?" Leslie asked none of them there. Cage listened with half an ear as she began describing the needle. Helping out, he bent down and read off the brand name to her.

"Really?" She sounded desperate, then she looked at the group. "Sometimes they don't work."

"*What?*" Cage fought to stay down on the ground, rather than bursting up in anger. These pens had been expensive, and they didn't work? He tried to direct his anger to the hot sun beating down. To the fact that they were only out here because the geology tests hadn't passed the second round like expected. He felt the water soaking into his pants and wondered if mosquitoes had laid eggs in it.

David had said if there was water and there were mosquitoes, the answer was yes.

"Why?" Cage asked. "They're *supposed* to auto dispense." His own breath came in angry huffs, the words falling out haphazardly. He struggled to string his thoughts together.

Could he take the needle out? Could he check to see if it had dispensed? He looked down and could only think that it hadn't. He was moving to check as Leslie yelled, "Don't touch it!"

She almost as quickly relayed the next thing. "Did the needle deploy?"

Well, he'd have to touch if to find that out, wouldn't he?

But he didn't actually have to. It was clearly stuck in his friend's leg. "Yes."

Leslie frantically told the operator while they all waited for any sign from David. None came.

"Don't pull it out!" Sarah repeated Leslie's command and Cage wanted to turn and snap, "Then *you* get in here and do it." But he managed to hold back.

Leslie was still relaying information from the 9-1-1 operator, and Cage could barely hear, but he tried to follow along. The small snippets of voice sounded far too calm for the situation as she used Leslie to talk him through pulling the needle out—the irony—and taking the back of the pen apart.

"It's been a minute and ten seconds," Leslie reported.

Cage's head snapped up at that. Someone was counting. *Good.*

Three minutes was the mark. So, he had almost two minutes to fix things, he told himself as he worked frantically to get the plastic to come apart and reveal the inner workings.

The emergency operator obviously had everything at her fingertips—she was googling it or flipping through a book or whatever. But she managed to describe what he was seeing with only a few bits of information about the brand and the date.

When it was ready, Sarah looked at her watch and said, "Two minutes."

Leslie, now crouched down next to David on the other side, told him, "Do it again. But this time, push the plunger down manually."

There was no time to hesitate. The time it had taken him to get the pen apart had cost David precious seconds.

For whatever reason, a clear thought told him to get the other thigh. *Don't bruise the same one twice.* It was stupid, with David's life on the line, but Cage was no longer thinking entirely rationally.

Raising his hand up again, Cage plunged the device down through the khakis and prayed the already-used needle made a clean cut through the fabric, not pushing any fibers into the hole. He wasn't even sure that was a possibility with such a small, sharp needle. With the needle embedded and his right hand wrapped hard around the barrel, he reached in with his left hand and shoved at the plunger.

They all watched as, almost instantaneously David jolted. His eyes and mouth simultaneously flew open. It looked as if the world around him expanded his ribs and reflected in his now-open eyes.

Did it work? Cage panicked again. He wanted to hear breath. He wanted to hear David say something and know that his friend's airway was open again.

Was the EpiPen broken in more ways than one?

But David's hands were pushing to the ground behind him. He was trying to sit up. All of which Leslie was narrating into the small cell phone.

"Sit him up! Sit him up," she instructed Cage and Sarah, who immediately went to work doing so.

They reached for David's shoulders, each grabbing one and holding on to him. This time, when his rib cage expanded, they could all hear the air sucking into David's lungs.

He did it twice before looking frantically at his friends and saying, "Holy shit. What happened?"

Cage felt his own consciousness twinkle at the edges as the relief flooded him, the way the epinephrine had surely flooded David. But he didn't pass out. He'd been through too many emergencies—and he'd only survived because he'd stayed alert and on his A-game.

Looking around, he saw they were now surrounded by people. More were rushing across the field.

Cage heard the sirens even as he heard Leslie say the words, "I think I hear the ambulance." She leaned down and whispered, "We need to keep him here. Now that he's breathing well, he can sit up or lie down. We have to keep watching, but someone should be here in just a few moments."

David shook his head at her. "I'm fine."

Cage shook his head back at his friend. "You are anything but fine."

In fact, the needle still protruded from his leg. Quickly, Cage grabbed it and yanked it out, thinking that way it wouldn't get knocked around. But then he realized he should have asked first. David didn't seem to notice and no one commented.

They all stayed there, waiting an interminable amount of time before another rescue team walked up, not unlike Maria and the crew in Florida. At least this time they were relatively easily accessible and not miles deep in the trees.

He'd also seen the ambulance as it drove most of the way out on the grass, which was handy. But as they strapped David to a back board, and loaded him into the vehicle, Cage gave a cursory glance to everyone else.

David was their patient, but Dr. Murasawa was striding across the field like an avenging angel. She motioned to Leslie. "You were on the phone with 9-1-1?"

She nodded quickly.

"Then can you go in the ambulance with him?" Dr. Murasawa seemed to check her own take-charge tone, though Cage appreciated it. He'd seen her take-no-prisoners attitude in action. "We need someone to stay with him and make sure everything goes okay. Answer any questions that he can't and so on."

Leslie quickly agreed to this and was off, running the short distance before climbing up into the back of the ambulance.

Cage stood with his feet apart, thinking that if he moved them any closer together, he might sway and pass out himself. Adrenaline was the only thing keeping him upright as the group turned in unison—almost like a drill team—and watched the ambulance driver maneuver deftly over the uneven field.

Reaching up, he brushed his hand along the back of his neck, feeling the cold sweat that had formed. He was now heating up again as the sun beat down. If this was the beginning of the summer, he couldn't imagine what the rest of it would be like.

Either he didn't sway, or no one noticed. Maybe they were all just fighting their own shock, but they stayed still, solemn for a moment. Then, as they began to move, he could tell almost everyone was getting ready to say something, ask something. Maybe they should just sit down, put their heads between their knees and take a few deep breaths.

But it was Dr. Murasawa who spoke. "Oh, damn, this is annoying," she muttered as she slapped at her forearm.

18

———

"What?" Joule asked, unable to keep the panic out of her voice.

She was running before she'd even made the conscious decision to do so. The few words Cage had gotten out told her more than she needed to know.

He'd said David was already in the ambulance and leaving, and that he'd used his EpiPen to save their friend... leaving her two pens as the last ones. "And, just so you know, Dr. Murasawa —" whom Joule adored "—just got bit."

She tried to keep it together.

His voice came over the line, pretty much reiterating her thoughts. "I don't have the bug spray on me, you have it. And now I'm out of EpiPens."

His words were sharp and clipped, an underlying panic driving them at a rapid rate. She looked out the window as she passed by but didn't see them.

"I'm on my way. Where are you?" She had a general idea to head to the field behind the main campus. She was bolting through the cafeteria, wishing she'd run track in high school instead of taking volleyball for one short season.

Her speed was drawing stares from the people she passed, both those with Helio Systems T-shirts that looked much like her own and those who were clearly jet lab employees. Her people were distinguishable from the business-casual people who worked here permanently, not just by their shirts, but by their questioning looks that asked, "Is everything okay?"

She couldn't answer them.

Not yet.

"Joule, is everything okay?"

Kelsey stood in front of her clutching a tray full of food. But Joule shook her head. She could only say what she knew. "David's headed to the hospital. He had a reaction."

She pushed past, but Kelsey simply abandoned her tray on the nearest table and turned to follow.

"Cage used his EpiPen," Joule added, but that only made Kelsey look oddly at her. There wasn't time to explain.

She turned her attention back to the phone as Cage gave her directions and then disconnected. Joule kept running, her lungs already feeling the effort. She'd have a stitch in her side any moment. And if these past seven years had taught her anything, it's that she needed to be able to run, to jump, to swim, and probably even to fly.

She couldn't do all of it, but she did her best. Kelsey paced her relatively easily. It wasn't long before they pushed through the doors to the back and spotted the small cluster off in the distance, slowly making their way toward the building.

Why didn't they run? Was something wrong?

Joule's eyes scanned everyone but didn't find anything concerning. Still, she pushed forward, her backpack bouncing against her side with each step. Right now, instead of annoying, it felt reassuring.

She had two life-saving doses in there and they brought some peace of mind.

Calculating the distance between herself and the group

proved difficult against the open landscape. She wished she'd been there when it happened, rather than getting news after the fact, but she'd been working inside today. Her healthy fear of bug bites, and knowing she could wind up out in the fields at any time, had left her dousing herself in her ridiculous oil spray again.

As she pushed forward, she lifted her arm to see if she could still smell it. She couldn't. But was that because she was frantically running across an open field, or had her protection faded? Was she about to get bit?

There were no answers as she and Kelsey intersected with the group. Bending over, hands on knees, huffing heavily, she was grateful that Kelsey looked just as worn out as she was. Her friend wasn't making her look as though she'd completely faked all levels of high school PE.

Falling into step beside her brother, and trying to slow her breathing, she watched as Dr. Murasawa looked sideways at Cage.

"I don't think she needed to come out here. I'm fine." Their boss lifted her arm, the brown skin already showing a red welt.

But Joule's eyes scanned up and down the woman. She didn't see a rash forming. As she looked at her boss's face, she felt her smile forming.

Dr. Murasawa must feel okay. Her throat wasn't closing up on her, or if it was, she was hiding it incredibly well. Either way, it was the only thing that kept Joule from swinging her backpack around front, digging through it, and coming up with an EpiPen in each hand, like a gunslinger from a particularly disturbing version of the Old West.

She did see though, that her arrival—despite her heavy breathing and obviously having run too far—had calmed her brother immensely. Joule understood.

She fell into step and listen as Kelsey asked questions and

tried to sort out why she and Joule had come blasting out here like the field was on fire.

Cage explained, in a low voice, what had happened.

Joule shook her head. "I told him to wear the bug spray."

"Do you think it was the bug bite, though?" Kelsey asked. "Dr. Murasawa got bit, and she's fine."

Sarah leaned over, explaining more of what had happened, but it only confused Kelsey, who pointed out, "Anaphylaxis is usually brought on by something people eat."

She sounded confident of that diagnosis, and Joule wanted to sink into it. Sarah would know, wouldn't she? She was on the bio team. She definitely out-ranked Joule in that arena. Joule replied, "That would be great. But what was David eating?"

"We all had lunch at the cafeteria. But that was a while ago," Sarah commented as Cage agreed.

That made sense, Joule thought. She and Kelsey had gotten sidetracked this morning and they had only made it to the cafeteria when Cage had called. She still hadn't eaten.

The thought was enough to make her hungry, but the information tended to quell that. If David had eaten something here, then had a full reaction, she didn't want to follow suit.

Still, she didn't have to decide right now, did she? She walked along, letting the cadence and the group soothe her jangled nerves. The fear had drained her. The slight tremor that wanted to start in her fingers told her that she needed to eat.

Then again, Cage had eaten in the cafeteria today, and so had Leslie and Sarah, and they were fine. As they approached the building, Joule was thinking seriously about getting herself through the line and getting some food in her.

Even as she thought about it, Cage motioned for her to step out of the group. "Before we split up—" He held his hand out and she fully understood without him finishing the request.

Joule pulled one of the pens from her bag and pressed it

into his palm. Once again, she could see his form relax just a little bit at the touch of it. Then she tucked the last one back down into her backpack. It was good there.

"I think I'm going to go buy lunch again," Kelsey announced, though she didn't seem bitter about needing to buy it twice. "That was enough excitement for one day."

She and Joule had just turned away from the group, aiming themselves back to the cafeteria, when she heard Dr. Murasawa behind them.

"Oh my god. Look at this!"

They quickly turned back to where the doctor held her forearm up, her wrist braced in the other hand as if she needed help displaying it.

But displaying the arm wasn't necessary. It was obvious even from this distance that the bug bite that she had told them before was of no worry was now the size of a silver dollar.

19

"Oh no, that can't be good."

Joule watched as Dr. Murasawa reached to scratch at her arm and stopped herself, a little too late. "What is even happening with this?"

This was her boss. This was the woman running the whole build site, and that bite looked bad. Scary bad.

Joule told herself the reactions weren't caused by the bites. It was some random food that was doing it. But she couldn't ignore this as the doctor looked around the group of her employees.

For a moment they stopped walking, but then Joule decided to pick up the pace a little. She wanted to keep them moving, to get them back closer to solid ground and paved roads. If Dr. Murasawa was also going to need an ambulance, Joule wanted her where one could race in and whisk her away.

Her own breathing shallowed out as Joule's throat started to feel scratchy. But she hadn't been bit. Surely it was just psychological sympathy or fear.

That had to be it.

Not only did Joule simply like her supervisor, but Dr. Murasawa had taken over after they lost Dr. Radnor on the Alabama job. Then Dr. Murasawa had helped save Joule's life.

If Joule could ever repay that kind of favor, she would. But she didn't want it to be now.

"It looks like an allergic reaction," Cage said to his boss as she moved her feet to keep up with the group but kept her focus on the weird welt on her arm.

Joule's eyes snapped to the side, catching Cage's expression. His voice sounded far too casual for the situation, but she saw the tic just under the jaw line he'd developed in recent years. He was not as calm as he appeared.

"And?" the doctor asked.

"That's what a lot of my bites do," Cage said, it as though it was reassuring rather than alarming.

"Is this what happened to David?"

"No." Cage shook his head with confidence, but then rolled back his words. "I mean, I can't promise that. But David just started getting the rash."

"Do you know what he ate? They think it's something in the food." So Dr. Murasawa had been following the news.

Joule had been wondering if anyone else was keeping tabs on the story, or if she and her brother were lunatics.

Helio Systems Tech was full of people who got rearranged and regrouped as projects came up or changed. So while she knew half the people on this project from other places, half she hadn't worked with before. Still, she could count a good number of them who'd been in Alabama, who'd survived a disaster.

She and Cage weren't the only ones who would encounter these threats. Radnor wasn't the only one who'd passed during their short tenure. Micah and Peter, and the other Alabama employees who'd been killed by the twisters weren't the only ones who'd been lost on the job or at home. She and Cage weren't the only ones who'd seen the epic floods.

She wasn't sure if anyone else had seen the same things that were in the floods they'd had in California. But she still wasn't quite ready to talk about it or ask everyone else about carrying their own traumas. She liked to keep her baggage zipped.

Instead, she turned to Dr. Murasawa, "Does your throat feel tight?"

The woman shook her head no. "My arm feels itchy. Does anyone have any Benadryl or something?" Immediately on the heels of that she added, "Not the pills. I need the topical. The pills will knock me out."

Some of the other workers shrugged and held their hands up. Sarah had a small fanny pack that she wore completely unironically. She was already holding out a pill bottle, but she pulled it back.

"I have one or two of everything," Sarah said, even as she tucked it away. "But I have the pills if you decide you need one."

Cage probably didn't have Benadryl on him either, though he should, Joule thought. Even though he tended to get very itchy bites that reacted, he was more the "ounce of prevention" kind of guy these days.

"Don't scratch it," Cage told their boss, reaching out as if to slap at her hand. Joule could see the moment he realized that smacking Dr. Murasawa was not the best idea.

They walked relatively slowly, Cage holding the pace back when others might have gotten a little faster. Her brother looked sideways at her and quietly shook his head.

Joule frowned, wondering why he was holding back.

He leaned in and whispered, "You get upset, you get adrenaline, and your blood pumps faster. So, it spreads poisons, toxins, even allergens, faster. The slower and calmer you stay, the slower it spreads and the slower you react."

"Is that true?"

"As far as I know."

She wasn't sure if anyone else had heard them. But Joule

slowed her pace and even moved back closer to Dr. Murasawa and motioned to ask if she could take a look at the bite one more time. It was really a ploy to help stall them. As if she knew anything about diagnosing anything other than structural problems.

Was it wrong that, in part, she did not want the doctor to have a reaction because she would have to use her EpiPen on Dr. Murasawa? She didn't know right now if she could replace it, which would leave only one between her and her brother. She was already feeling naked with just the two.

She would absolutely use her drugs on Dr. Murasawa if she needed to. She just didn't want to. In fact, Joule would use it on anyone who needed it, because holding it back for something that *might* happen was unconscionable.

Joule had lost too many people to think about letting someone slide away just to save herself. But she'd still had the thought, she'd still counted her EpiPens and considered holding them close. She'd still made a mental note of where it was sitting in her backpack.

Joule tried to look sideways to Cage while keeping an eye on the doctor's arm.

Her boss had darker skin. Would they recognize the welts as fast if they formed?

"Can you guys not walk a little faster?" Dr. Murasawa tried to push them along. "I've got to get something on this bite to stop it from itching."

"I think there's a first aid station," Cage said.

"But—" the doctor swallowed, hard. "I'm also thirsty. I need something for my throat. I think I'm coming down from the adrenaline of watching them haul David away."

Then the doctor reached one hand up to touch the base of her throat as she swallowed visibly and twisted her head.

20

"Can I do that?" Cage asked his sister. It sounded like a good idea.

"I don't see why not. It's the truth."

Joule had told him to call his doctor and get his epinephrine refilled, even though they had two pens left. She was feeling squirrelly at the thought of not having spares anymore.

Cage understood her math.

"Tell them you used it on someone else," she went on. Joule was often good at building a case. "The doctor gave you that prescription because they want you to have an EpiPen on you. They don't know we used it for a three-pack. But when we get the refill, we get another set of them."

"Do you think they check on it? That they know we got three last time?"

"I wouldn't think so." But she shrugged before further convincing him, or maybe herself. "I mean, why would they even care? Who's running around selling epinephrine on the black market? Or overdosing on it?"

"Fair." He figured he'd call the next morning. They'd barely gotten into the car after a very tiring day at work. He backed out of his spot in the grass and turned around, aiming to climb the small berm onto the pavement. Not his favorite parking situation, but today his brain was racing as they left the campus.

Dr. Murasawa had never developed a rash. Though she'd complained about a scratchy throat, she'd gotten a soda and said she was fine—to the point where she'd shooed them all back to work. Still, she'd put them into larger groups, making sure that each group had people who'd eaten different things for lunch... just in case.

Cage still didn't quite buy that it was something in the food causing the reactions. If it was, a whole swath of people should have fallen ill. It had just been David. Still, that had been more than enough. Leslie had stayed with David at the hospital until he was discharged, at which point they'd both been sent home for the day.

Joule's stomach growled and interrupted his dreary thoughts. "What do you want for dinner?"

He did not have it in him to make anything. They debated getting takeout. But Joule had questions.

"If it is from the food, then what if it's *this* food?"

"By the same issue," Cage countered, "what if it's grocery store food?"

She'd only replied with a sharp, "Shit, that's just as likely," and motioned him toward the nearest drive-thru. Twenty minutes later, they were opening plastic bags and pulling out toasted sub sandwiches and fresh cut fries. He was going to be okay with that.

His mother would have wanted them to have a vegetable, but his mother hadn't lived past the Night Hunters. She hadn't seen the floods or the tornadoes. If she had, though, he was confident she'd be proud that her kids were still standing. And so, he was going to count the grilled onions and peppers in his Philly cheese steak as vegetables, just for today.

He was about to set up in front of the TV—he had to turn off his brain and let all the tension drain out of him—but Joule motioned him over to the table.

"Here," she countered, motioning with her still-wrapped sub.

He didn't want to eat at the table. He didn't want to think. He already had too much to process. But he knew he wouldn't be able to really rest until he had it sorted.

Joule wasn't wrong. She even motioned to him to get out his phone. "Just call the doctor for the refill now."

He conceded that, too. It would likely happen faster, and he could relax a little, knowing he'd already taken care of it. His sister obviously needed some reassurance.

He quickly pulled up the doctor's number, hit the requisite series of buttons to get him through to the after-hours messaging, and found it was easier to leave his odd, mostly-true tale on the voicemail. Cage rattled off his birthdate and spelled his last name again, hoping everything could be taken care of by the next day.

With that one task done, he picked up his sandwich, fries, and drink and abandoned the TV tray he'd started to set up. Joule was already pulling out her laptop, setting herself up with the computer in one space and the sandwich in another. They were too close together for his comfort, but he couldn't say he hadn't done it before.

She just looked up at him as though he shouldn't argue, as though spending dinner on research was the only way this could go. "We've got work to do."

So Cage settled in beside her and pulled out his own laptop.

The sandwiches didn't disappear as quick as he'd expected. Though he was very hungry, twenty minutes later, they were only half- eaten. But he was slurping the bottom of his lemonade.

He had a document open on his screen that he was toggling

back and forth. Joule, on the other hand, was taking notes on a small legal pad, and she already had several pages scribbled over.

She looked up at him. "I started by looking at food. Anyone can be allergic to any food. And anyone can *become* allergic to any food at any time, apparently."

He already knew that, but motioned to her to share more of what she'd found.

"There were several common culprits—peanuts and shell-fish among the top ones." Joule had shaken her head at him. "Peanuts and peanut butter are everywhere." She paused a moment. "Do you think David had shellfish? And if so, when and how?"

Cage tried to remember. "He didn't have it at lunch yesterday, and I'd be surprised if he had shellfish for breakfast."

"He hasn't mentioned a peanut allergy. You'd think he would have told the people he was working with..."

They were always carrying around granola bars and snacks. It wouldn't have been the kind of thing that everyone who'd been there this afternoon could have missed.

"The news thinks it's a food allergy, and there's probably ample evidence for it. But food allergies usually occur within an hour or so after eating."

Cage agreed. "I don't think it was a shellfish contamination. I'm fine."

Joule shrugged. "So, let's say he didn't mean to eat shellfish. Does it matter if the shellfish contaminated his food, and he's allergic but you're not? Would that explain the discrepancy?"

He thought about it for a moment.

"Well, I really don't think it's peanuts. In Florida, we were all snacking right before our trip."

Joule nodded. "I remember Maria asking about that. But if somebody had a peanut allergy, wouldn't they know they had it? You would think it would have shown up before then. At least for Jeff or Clara. Wouldn't they have asked me to put my little peanut butter crackers away?"

But Joule was already pondering the answer to her own question, shaking her head at him again. "Seriously, that would mean two people suddenly became allergic to peanuts within twenty minutes of each other. I don't buy that."

Cage had to agree. "Maybe it's a different food. In fact, maybe it's something that's not supposed to be there—something everybody is allergic to—that's contaminating foods."

But even as he proposed that option, he found the flaw in it. "But if that was right, then whole families would go down. Or at least a couple people in the same restaurant."

There were a few moments of silence between them. Cage took advantage and had another bite of his sandwich. But it wasn't as hot as it had been when they first sat down, and he didn't think he was going to get the whole thing eaten.

Joule took a deep breath—maybe to assure herself she could—and said softly, "I really don't think it's food. But if it's bugs, why hasn't anyone else figured it out?"

That set his sister into silence for a while longer.

It didn't make sense. He wasn't one to believe that they were the special little flowers who'd figured it all out when no one else had. But she was right: the rest wasn't adding up.

Eventually, Joule responded, "Because they weren't there."

"What?" That didn't make sense.

"I'm just saying that all the CDC people and such working on this, *they weren't there*." Joule stared hard at him, as if to help her point penetrate. "They come to it after the fact. In fact, the anaphylaxis happens so fast that the ambulance usually doesn't get there in time to administer epinephrine. At least, that's my guess. That's why we carry it."

He had to concede that. While the first incidence they'd seen had been out on the back clear rivers just north of Tampa Bay, it put them in an odd situation where they really weren't accessible to help. Here, the situation with David had been quickly treated. Still, if Cage had not had the epinephrine on him, he didn't know if David would have been unconscious and not breathing for long enough that he would have died.

The second half of Joule's sandwich was clearly forgotten as her eyes sparked with a new thought. She clicked a few buttons on her computer and turned it around, showing him an image she'd pulled up.

It showed someone with an anaphylactic rash. And it looked exactly like what they'd seen—like Jeff and Clara and like David today. Cage wanted to ask her why she was showing him the picture, but Joule was already leaning forward, her arms crossed, her weight resting on her elbows. He was beginning to get concerned about the cheap little table tipping under his sister's slight weight. But she was already talking.

"I think it's the bug bites," she said. "And here's why..."

21

I t was clear to Cage that Joule thought she was onto something. All he could do was wait.

She'd agreed with his assessment that they weren't the chosen ones who'd solved the mystery when no one else could. But from the look on her face, maybe they had.

"The researchers are coming at it from after the fact, but we were *there* and we saw it before it happened and as it happened. We actually *saw* the bug bites."

"But other people would have seen bug bites, too. Wouldn't they?" Cage asked.

Joule shook her head and waved her hand at the screen. She enlarged the image, showing a patch of skin covered in small red welts. Staring at him, she challenged, "Find the bug bite."

Of course, he couldn't. "There's probably not one on there."

"Not in this particular picture. But if someone did have a bug bite, who would notice?"

He shrugged. "The medical examiner?"

That at least gave her pause. "Would they?"

Maybe he had her. He wasn't trying to ruin her argument, but they really couldn't afford to be wrong. They'd only saved David today because of what had happened in Florida. Because they'd watched Clara die and it had become very clear they needed to carry epinephrine.

"Would they?" Joule repeated to the room at large. "And even if the medical examiner did, let's say they are that thorough that they examine everything and they find the bite or bites..."

Cage knew nothing about the job, and he didn't think Joule did, either. She erred on the side of caution.

"So, they find bug bites on all the bodies." There was a soft pause before she added, "On Clara . . . But what would they think? Clara was out paddle-boarding. In a stream, in Florida, surrounded by the Everglades. Practically everybody had bug bites. Hell, I had two before I remembered to put my bug spray on."

Now Cage was nodding along. She was making sense. He picked up the thread. "And most of the people survived. Bug bites are really common in Florida. So it wouldn't necessarily be something you'd tell anyone asking what you had a reaction to."

"Right!" Joule said. "I only just learned a few minutes ago that you can develop an allergy to anything at any time. So, if it had been me, and they asked, I would have been very clear that I wasn't allergic to bites!" She took in a deep lungful of air as her eyes darted up toward the ceiling. "I'm guessing that allergies to bug bites are relatively rare."

"Why?" Cage asked. He thought about taking another bite of his sandwich, but it had been too cold with the last bite he'd taken, so he wasn't feeling like he should repeat it. He could see Joule's food was just as forgotten as his. She took a sip of her coke again, her face making it clear she'd hit the raw water at the bottom.

But her attention was on where the ideas were going. "I'm

guessing that because, over the course of *your* life, I've heard you tell a handful of people that you're allergic to insect bites. When you do, everybody looks at you like you're weird. I don't think I've ever heard one person say, *Oh, yeah, me too*, or *my cousin has that.*"

He thought that through. He was the one with the bug-bite reaction. He'd told far more people about it than she'd been there for. He had to. He had to explain why bugs weren't just a nuisance for him to put up with, the way others did. Joule was right. When he thought back, he could only remember hearing one person say that they knew what that was like.

"So, no one suspects the bug bites," he said, clarifying her point for himself. "And even if the different medical examiners in different places did find them, why would they connect it?"

"Look." She turned the computer back, tapped a few more keys and slid the screen around to face him again. "This says anaphylactic reactions often come on in a matter of minutes. Sometimes just a few moments from the trigger, sometimes an hour or so. What we saw definitely falls into that window."

She was right again. The buzz of a new idea caught hold in him. It didn't matter that the news was reporting something different. It mattered that they felt like they were solving it.

"Also," Cage pointed out, "it seems like most of the people that are surviving are in populated areas. That would mean they are getting treatment fast enough to save them."

"Maybe." Then Joule asked, "Is everybody running around with an EpiPen?"

"Well, we had one in Florida. And you and I are carrying them now. With all the runs at the drugstores, we have to assume people are using them. We've really only heard on the news about how many people are *dying* from it."

Joule sat back for a moment, needing to calculate something before replying. "That's a lot, but I can't imagine that would run all the local stores out of their EpiPens. So, we have to assume that more people are surviving than dying—a good number more."

They paused again, but this time neither of them even attempted to eat. He thought about wrapping up what was left of dinner and putting it in the fridge. But just as he was about to stand up, Joule started talking again.

"Everybody eats. Everybody gets bit."

He nodded along. Either option could be the culprit, so he shrugged again. Then he realized where his sister was going and he said the words out loud. "So, if it's the food, there's already a whole team of experts trying to figure it out. But if it's the bugs, no one's looking."

She nodded along, her concern evident on her face. "More than that, you and I are working out in an open field in the middle of the wetlands. If it is the bugs, we're in real danger."

"*It is the bites*!" Cage suddenly understood why. "This area ....Oh, it's got to be the bugs."

"What?" Joule asked. "Why are you suddenly so certain?"

This time, it was Cage who leaned forward to explain.

22

"Check the other news," Cage told her, moving his hand in a forward-rolling motion.

Joule jolted at the motion as he'd almost knocked over his lemonade, but then he set the drink out of the way. She did need to check, but his near-miss reminded her she also needed to move her sandwich.

She needed fuel. So she forced herself to take a huge bite, though the sandwich was as cold as she had been afraid it would be. She chewed the unsatisfying food anyway but wrapped the waxed paper around the remainder as she did and moved to grab Cage's sandwich, too. It had been that kind of day.

Her brother tapped away on his laptop as she returned to her seat and began pulling up articles and looking through them quickly. Some she parked to do a full read of later, but then she found one...

"Cage, we need to find out where the deaths are."

He nodded, understanding what she was looking for and hopefully why. She searched for news stories, autopsies, anything. There wouldn't be studies about it... not yet. *Unless ...* she paused, thinking, *unless it wasn't new.*

Checking the research didn't yield anything that really matched what they were seeing. Local news reports turned up videos and transcripts from a variety of locations. She played one stream, listening through the overlapping audio of another story her brother was checking out.

Then she looked up. "There are Jeff and Clara from above the Tampa Bay area. But I also got three dead from seemingly the same thing in Orlando. And another in Deltona..."

Joule had to look up where that was—more central, but definitely near water.

"Did you just search in Florida?" her brother asked her. She hadn't, but it was where she'd found cases. He didn't seem to care though. "I found several at Jekyll Island. And one near Myrtle Beach."

"Where is that?"

"Off the coast of Georgia," he answered, then added, "Also Daytona. And the several we saw in Charleston. That definitely means it's the bugs."

Joule frowned at him, wondering why he was concluding that from the locations.

But Cage asked, "What did you search for?"

She told him she'd been looking up *anaphylactic reactions.* Deaths. She rolled off a few other keywords she'd tried.

"Right, you didn't put in the locations."

She hadn't.

He was excited now. "And we only got hits in a string from southern Florida, up the coast, to here—"

"Up to North Carolina," she inserted, still not quite sure where he was going with it.

"Right. If this was happening in Colorado, or further inland, we should have gotten hits." Cage was grinning at her now. "It's the bugs. *Food doesn't migrate.*"

Joule felt her eyes go wide. It felt good to know that she'd been right all along. "It has to be the mosquitos."

The rush flooded her system and she popped up out of her chair. She danced away from the table, probably poorly, but she didn't care. For all of twenty seconds or so, the world seemed right. Then she stopped.

Cage had been watching. "What?"

That was exactly the problem. "What do we do?"

He shrugged.

She tried untangling her thoughts out loud. "The bugs are in this area. We left Florida because of them. We thought it was the bugs, so we just left. Now we know it's the bugs... but can we leave here?"

"We'd have to leave the job," Cage pointed out, now on his own feet. But he wasn't dancing. He was pacing and thinking.

"We can afford it," Joule pointed out. They had savings, the money from their parents' life insurance. If there was ever a time to use it, this would be it.

Cage's words told her he was thinking along the same lines. "We wouldn't just be leaving Charleston."

Joule nodded along. "We'd be walking away from Helio Systems Tech entirely. I don't think they'll grant us leave because we think we found something the CDC and all the local health departments didn't."

"How will we get the next job?" Cage moved to the logical step.

That one was beyond Joule. "I don't know."

If they left Helio Sys under bad circumstances, who would hire them? Would anyone hire them together? So far, HST had graciously put them onto the same projects. It was never guaranteed, but it was part of the reason they'd stayed with the company for as long as they had. The money they had saved was a lot, but it likely didn't mean they could retire in their early twenties.

"We know something," Joule lamented, "but there's nothing we can do about it."

She'd let the words trail off, almost making a question but she knew he didn't have an answer, any more than she did.

"What if we stay?" he asked.

"Then we practically drink that bug spray I made. And I'll be using the professional grade stuff on my clothes all the time." It would be a lot of exposure to chemicals, but it was better than having her throat close up and needing epinephrine.

Cage started pacing again, clearly trying to organize his thoughts.

Joule wanted to grab the can of spray. She had a nearly pathological need to put her hands on it and know exactly where it was. Because she wasn't going out to the job site without it, she started searching.

"What are you looking for?" Cage frowned at her, still on his feet, still standing in the middle of the room, as though he'd stopped there and didn't know where else to go.

"I want the real bug spray."

Nodding along, Cage began looking for it, too. They'd set it aside, believing that Joule's essential oil mix worked, and that the bugs weren't to blame for the people dying. But where was it now?

"I don't know what we're deciding, but I'm not going back out on the job site until I have chemicals in hand."

Cage looked around as though the walls were hiding it, and it took her a minute to figure out what the problem was. Then she caught on that he wasn't staring at the walls. He was thinking beyond them.

"We really shouldn't go outside *at all* without it."

By the time she'd said the words, he'd wandered into the back room. Her brother came back out with a smile on his face and a plastic spray bottle in his hand.

She wasn't really prepared to smile, and it came out a little bleak around the edges. "So, we just bug spray up and convince everyone else to do it, too?"

Cage shook his head at her as if to say no, but his words seemed to agree. "We have to convince them to do it, too. Which means we have to figure out how to make them understand we found something."

"—and that the CDC is wrong, but we are right."

"Or maybe we just have to convince them that there's enough of a danger that wearing bug spray is worth it."

"I think we can do that much." She was breathing a little easier now that the bottle had been found. She watched as Cage shook it to test for fullness and put the bottle next to his wallet, as if he were happy with the answer. But her thoughts had put that worry aside and moved to the next one. "So why David? You're the one who's allergic. Is it just that you didn't get bitten?"

He lifted the edge of his pants and rotated his ankle, showing off a small welt that he had on the lower part of his leg. "I've been bit, too."

"That one doesn't look like it reacted. It looks normal." She was frowning down at her brother's hairy ankle. Not her favorite thing. But it did look normal, even though for him "normal" meant "not silver-dollar-sized," like the welt Dr. Murasawa had sported earlier today.

Joule added that together. "Dr. Murasawa looked like she was going to have a reaction."

"I don't know what was up with that." Cage shook his head. "The bite itself definitely reacted. I agreed, I expected her to have the full anaphylactic thing. She was reaching for her throat, stretching her neck, and she said her throat felt scratchy. Everyone I've seen who's done that wound up covered in welts."

"Do you think it was just timing? Then maybe she did have a reaction and it was just slow-moving?" Joule asked. She and her brother had long ago learned to toss their ideas into the center of the room and sort them out later. The analysis wasn't as solid without her parents playing along, but it was still a good method.

Joule kept going. "Maybe she had a full reaction later, after she was out of our sight."

Cage sat back down at his laptop, though she wasn't sure why. Was he going to look something up? "I don't think it could happen. Wouldn't we have heard about it if Dr. Murasawa had been rushed off to the hospital?"

Joule had to concede that point. The conversation died down. They would go to work tomorrow, but do so doused in bug spray. They would try to convince everyone else to do it, too. They hadn't convinced David, and look what had happened. Joule wouldn't let anyone off the hook the next day.

Eventually, they went their separate ways, heading into the bedrooms to try to sleep though Joule didn't think she was going to have a very good night. She always liked solving something. Her parents had instilled in her a love of puzzles, but this one didn't yield anything satisfying in the solution—not other than a checkbox that she'd done it. That didn't seem worth it. So, she lay down, pulled the covers up, and snuggled between cool sheets, waiting for sleep to overtake her.

But at three in the morning, she jerked awake, dreaming of tornadoes chasing her through the woods for the third time. She figured she might as well get up and start the day.

Heading back to the computer still sitting ready on the table, she began looking for more evidence. It wasn't long before she found it.

23

C age stood over David, wanting to reassure himself that his friend was safe to be back at work. Just yesterday he'd had an EpiPen jabbed in his leg, twice, and nearly died.

"Back off." David didn't look up from the samples he was prepping.

"Sorry, man. You nearly died on me, yesterday." For the first time, Cage realized he had almost as much right to be traumatized as David did. Hell, maybe even more. After all, David hadn't done anything but be scared and then get a lot of medical care. Cage had been the one whose actions would save or kill his friend. *No pressure there, man.*

"I just have bruises on each of my legs, that's all."

That, and a directive that he work inside today. Dr. Murasawa said she'd evaluate each day and see what she thought about putting him back out. The fact was that David appeared far less affected by his near-death experience than everyone else. The main difference had been that he was loaded up with sports drinks, granola bars, and a packed lunch. He was not going back to the cafeteria anytime soon.

The twins, on the other hand, had just headed separate ways after eating together. They'd each picked out different foods as they went down the cafeteria line, as though daring their lunch to give one of them a reaction. They hadn't planned it, but Cage had been watching her choices and Joule had been watching his. Without a word, they'd run a small experiment... then they'd sat at the table until their time ran out.

They'd barely spoken until Joule said, "I have to get back."

"Anything?" he'd asked.

"Nothing."

"Me, either."

So now he was hovering over David as though his friend was going to just keel over on him again. But while Cage was going back and forth from the lab to the field, David was sequestered inside. Between the cafeteria food and the exposure to the mosquitoes, Cage was far more likely to have a problem. He wished knowing that was reassuring.

"Tomorrow, can we test mosquitoes?"

His comment wasn't as clever or subtle or whatever as he thought it was. Because David immediately looked up. "You really think it was the bug bite?"

Cage spent the next fifteen minutes not doing his job. Instead, he was showing David information about time for reaction given a bug bite allergy. "But I don't have an allergy to bug bites! That's you."

"I know, but maybe it's some special mosquito and you are allergic to that one." That, at least, made David pause.

Then Cage threw out the other evidence that he and Joule had found, and he was surprised when David only paused and turned to his own computer before pulling up a map and pointing at it. "This is where Zika went when it came to the US."

Cage peered in close at the animated image. Dots appeared and climbed their way through Florida and then up to the

Carolinas. "They also hit Texas," he told his friend, pointing at the screen as though David needed to be told where Texas was.

"So, we might look there, too," was all David said in return. "It doesn't have to follow the same pattern, but it might be indicative."

Cage was glad that David was willing to give his theory the attention it deserved. Then again, he worked for Helio Sys, and that was the kind of people they specifically looked for. Also, David had a personal stake in it now.

"Hold on." David typed at the keyboard and pulled another map up. "Zika came up through Central America."

Cage leaned in again. This time the map wasn't just the US, but global. "So, we might see if they're having problems like this, too."

"Or if they had them first."

That was a good point. The US news wasn't the best at considering what was brewing beyond their own borders. It could have been happening for a while in other places, and Americans would still be hit unaware. Cage made a mental note.

Then he told David what Joule had found in the early hours before he woke up this morning. "We found that almost two million Americans are allergic to stinging insects specifically, but almost twenty million have some kind of bug bite allergic reaction."

The number had surprised him, but it didn't seem to faze David.

"I don't have that."

"Maybe you do now."

That made his friend look up. Cage added quickly, "You can become allergic to anything at any time."

"Well, that sucks." David turned back to the samples he was prepping.

"If I bring you local mosquitoes, can you tell me about

them?" Cage asked. He wasn't fully sure what that would do, but they did analyze local insects as part of their environmental studies.

"We already looked at the ones that are local. The first team did it, way back before the project got decided."

"What?" Cage didn't realize an analysis had already been run. "Do you have that?"

Within a few minutes, they'd tapped into the original files for the project. They moved past the scrapped three-story design for the parking structure with solar panels on top. They moved past the land survey and the plot with each corner of the planned garage labeled in latitude and longitude. There were percolation studies and soil sample breakdowns. Then there were the flora and fauna results.

Three sub-species of flower grew only in the plot of land behind the laboratory campus. Two kinds of *trombiculidaes* were heavily dependent on the area, though the final analysis was that it didn't matter if they built in their territory.

Cage had kept up until then. "What's a *trombiculidae*?"

"Chigger." David didn't even look away from the screen to answer.

"Oh, those can die." Cage wanted to have a less biased conclusion, but he couldn't manage it.

David kept scrolling through the results.

There were a few varieties of lizards indigenous to the area, but nothing that would be lost if they built on this particular spot of land. They'd just be pushed back a little further. There was information on birds, and larger creatures like beavers, skunk, and even deer and bear.

"No mosquitoes," Cage murmured. They'd started with the dirt and rocks, passed through plants and trees, then insects, reptiles and mammals.

"They're filed separately." David said this as though that

made sense. "Mosquitoes are at the bottom of a lot of food chains."

"They're definitely food for a lot of things..." Cage knew that. Bats, amphibians, birds, and more had diets that consisted heavily of mosquitoes. "But couldn't they just shift their diets a bit?"

He hadn't expected a good answer, but David's was worse.

"Sure, if you want to lose a decent number that are mosquito-dependent enough to die out rather than shift. That, of course, alters every animal and ecosystem above it." Then he added, "Mosquitoes are also pollinators."

Cage felt his head jerk back a little at that one. He'd not known that. "Well, fuck."

"Here you go. This is from a year ago." David pointed to the screen again. This time, Cage was ready, reading over his friend's shoulder and hoping he didn't really mind.

There were paragraphs of information followed by tables and charts. They found a list—in order of percentages—of mosquito species caught locally.

"*Aedes Aegypti.*" Cage pointed to the screen. "Isn't that the one that carries Zika?"

David nodded, then flipped to the second document. "This one is from a month ago."

It looked much the same, but a few numbers were different. Cage felt his stomach roll.

"What am I looking at?" Joule asked. Her brother had called her in to look at the information he and David had pulled up.

It was clear David still wasn't a believer, despite his hospital visit just the day before, but he'd grown interested in the mosquitoes.

"I still don't see why it's not a food," was how he greeted her as she opened the door and walked into the lab, where he and her brother had been working.

"I'd have called you earlier," Cage said, "but Kelsey and Melinda have been in and out of here for most of the day."

"So were you," David tossed into the conversation.

That tracked. Cage had told her that they put David in the lab. It seemed they were keeping him inside today, though why that would matter if it were the food, she didn't know. Maybe they were just trying to keep his activity low. Knowing what little she did of David she was willing to bet it made him less calm.

Cage, on the other hand, had the new job of running samples back and forth to the lab for David to analyze.

"What do you do with all of these?" Joule waved her hand at a stack of clear creature carriers. They looked almost like the ones she and her brother had used when they had pet frogs or newts they'd gotten at the pet store when they were little.

"We set most of them free," Cage told her. "If not before, then at the end of the day, they all go back."

Several small lizards, roaches, and even a bird and a mouse looked up at her as she walked by. But Joule didn't ask what this was about, and she hadn't pushed about them not calling her earlier.

It wasn't as if everything was hush hush, but this—whatever her brother and David had been doing—definitely wasn't the job they were being paid to do.

"Show her." The little tinge in her brother's voice told her he was anxious to get this show on the road.

Joule had the same thought. They didn't want to get caught doing this. They wanted to get everything in order and present it before anyone else figured out they were spending time on their own research.

"Here." David pointed to a screen he'd clicked over to. "These are the relative percentages of mosquito species here. When we did our first sampling a year ago, it looked like this."

That was well before Helio systems moved their whole crew into the area. It was likely before they'd even offered their initial bid on the job.

"And here's what we have now..." David said, clicking to a second pie chart.

"What am I looking at?" Joule leaned further over his shoulder, frowning, as though the data would make more sense if she got closer to it.

"That's the problem. We don't really know what it means. Mosquito species can come and go in one area, but it's unusual for them to change quite this much in this time frame," her brother explained.

"Okay." David was clearly irritated as he brushed away the hand Cage was pointing at the screen. Not that Joule knew what either of them were going on about yet, but then David added, "What's interesting is this mosquito..."

He pointed to a very tiny sliver of the pie graph the system had generated.

"But that one doesn't exist on the first chart. Does it?" She was still leaning too far into his personal space, but the graph change was slight enough that she wanted to be close. She'd move if he told her to.

"Exactly!" David grinned. "That's *Aedes Karnatakan*."

"So, basically, we got a new mosquito here within the last few months."

"But it's such a small percent." Joule read the key at the side of the graph. Just around two percent, so that shouldn't be their problem... or was it?

"Well, four months ago, it was under half a percent. So, while this is still small, it's a huge increase for that time frame."

"Cage has been trapping us some local 'squitoes." David grinned. "And then, in a couple of days, we'll know what it is *now*."

"Is that our corporate job?" Joule asked.

At least Cage looked as if he might fudge it. David shrugged. "The family this one belongs to—*Aedes*—are the ones most likely to carry disease. Like Zika, West Nile, dengue fever."

"So, these are disease-carrying?" she asked, not quite sure she was following along.

It was Cage who filled her in. "There are three main genus of mosquito—*Culex, Anopheles,* and *Aedes.* The *Aedes* ones are most likely to be disease-carrying. *But...*" He emphasized the last word and Joule could almost sense what was coming. "That doesn't mean that every *Aedes* mosquito is carrying something. They're here, and you don't get sick every time you get bit."

"But isn't that your immune system, though?" she asked the

bio guys. This was not her forte. She just came in and helped set pylons and made sure the structures were stable.

It was David who chimed in. "If you get bit, you can often fight it off. But if you get enough of a dose of something, then you can't fight it and you'll get sick."

"So what does this tell us, then?" Joule asked.

"It tells us we have a new kind of mosquito in the area." David said it as though it were only mildly interesting. She had to agree.

It wasn't quite the answer she was looking for. "So, we have evidence of a new mosquito but nothing more.... If you trap them, can you find out if they are disease carrying?"

David waved his hand. "Probably. *Aedes Aegypti* is blamed for a lot of disease, but I don't know that one specific species is really more likely in this case... Truly, this one's just interesting because it doesn't belong here."

"Wait, what?" The conversation was roller-coastering on her. Interesting news followed by the statement that the news was of no importance whatsoever, and then her attention would be grabbed again.

"It's native to a particular region in India. It's not usually found in the US."

"So how did it get here?" Joule said.

"That's just it..." The tone in David's voice told her this ride had already taken a turn and was plummeting back down into nowhere. "Different mosquitoes get here all the time. They come on planes and in people's luggage. They come on ships, and sometimes on people's pets. Sometimes on people themselves."

"Ew!" Joule replied, and David shrugged, as if to say, *It is what it is*. She had to admit that it was appropriate that the insect guy wasn't bothered by things like mosquitos.

"So, there's any number of ways they could have gotten here. That's not interesting," he informed her. "What's interesting is that we captured them, which means they found work-able conditions and an ecological niche here in South Carolina."

Joule was beginning to think *she* didn't have workable conditions or an ecological niche in South Carolina. She suddenly wanted desperately to go home. Even more, she wanted to know where home was.

"Can we take this up the pipeline?" she asked. No one needed to know the sudden ache she'd developed—not even her brother.

David looked at Cage and Cage shrugged. But it was David who answered again.

"We found a non-indigenous species of mosquito in the area. So maybe."

"I'd hoped it would be a little more dramatic. That it would demand testing." Cage shrugged at her. He was taking it well. Then again, he'd known all of this before they called her in to see.

"If we capture some, can we test to see if they're carrying diseases? Maybe something that would drop a person in five minutes from anaphylactic shock?" That was the whole point here, not mosquito foraging.

David looked at her like she was a little bonkers. "But that's not a disease. It's an allergic reaction."

Fucking Fuck. So, mosquitoes carried diseases, and they had a new mosquito, but... they didn't have a disease problem. She was so glad she'd come all the way over here and dropped her own work to see this. *Oh, joy.*

"Good point. Can we test them to see if they're causing an allergic reaction?"

Again, it was David who asked, "How? Just let them bite someone and see if it sends them to the hospital?"

But Cage picked that up. "We'd actually have to let them

bite a lot of people, because right now they're out there and they're biting people, but only some people are reacting."

David's face narrowed and he stared at Cage. "Actually, they're only biting a few of us because *some of you* took yourself out of the bait circle."

It was Joule who hopped in this time. "Hey! Given what happened to you, you should have done it, too."

"Points," David conceded as he turned back to the computer and back to his regular work. He tapped a button on the screen and the graphs he'd shown her disappeared. He was done with the conversation and was already back on track with what Helio Systems Tech was expecting from him.

That left Joule and Cage standing behind him, still staring at each other as if to say, *but what do we do now?* Neither of them had an answer. It was interesting information, but it didn't solve anything. It didn't even give them enough material to convince anyone that David's reaction likely hadn't been foodborne.

Joule sighed. If they found out it really was something in the food, she wasn't going to be surprised anymore. But the data about people having reactions that followed a migration-like pattern still convinced her she and Cage were on the right track. The fact that they weren't finding reactions like this is Texas or Arizona or California was pretty damning. But so far, that was all they had.

Even the growing presence of a new, non-indigenous species gaining ground in the area wasn't enough. It was, however, more than they'd had last night. So she shrugged at her brother and was turning to leave when the door flew open. Dr. Murasawa stood in the open space as they all spun around, surprised.

Their boss's eyes darted among the three of them, looking them each over as though something were amiss. She demanded, "What is this?"

25

Cage's eyes flew wide as the woman in charge of the entire operation stalked her way into the lab. He was not good at playing it cool.

"Um, well..." he said, stumbling over the words. He could hear his mother telling him about how she'd always known he was lying as a kid, that she simply had to ask him the same question two or three times and he would crack like an acorn.

He was about to do it again. Though he was fully adult now, he'd gotten no better at the skill.

Dr. Murasawa pushed her arm up in front of her, holding her forearm sideways. "What is this?"

The fluorescent lights of the lab told him he'd been way off base. She wasn't angry. She didn't even seem concerned that Joule Mazur, one of her engineers, was for whatever reason in a bio lab with her brother.

"Oh shit," Cage said as he saw her arm. The swear rolled out before he managed to clamp his mouth shut. Swearing in front of his boss was maybe not his best recourse. Surely, he'd done it multiple times before. Dr. Murasawa had been there in

Alabama and—thinking he was maybe going to die, or that Joule was—he'd not monitored his language then. Cage also knew Joule could swear like a sailor, just more fluently and creatively. Joule had done it in front of Dr. Murasawa, too. His boss had not been offended by it then; he hoped she wasn't now.

The three of them moved in closer, visually examining the arm she held up.

"Is that the same bite from two days ago?" he asked. Her entire forearm had swollen on one side, glaring an angry, reddish-pink in the middle. He couldn't distinguish where her skin ended in the bite began.

"My arm looks curved!" She was clearly distressed, and he would imagine anyone would be. He'd been, too, the first time he had it happen.

"I've had that. It's an allergic reaction to a bite." She still hadn't answered his question, so he asked it again. "Is this the same bite from two days ago?"

She shook her head. "It's from yesterday, just before we left."

Now that he thought about it, he did remember her bite being on the other arm. Aside from her neck and face, her arms were her only regularly exposed skin at the worksite. But she was talking, and he needed to pay attention.

"I took an antihistamine last night before bed and it knocked me out, but I woke up and it was worse."

"Check your legs and your arms?" Joule asked, the words rushed and a little frantic.

Their boss frowned at her, and Cage was glad it wasn't at him. He did not deal well with authority being angry with him, and he liked their leader.

Joule had no such compunction and just explained herself with newfound authority. "It's an allergic reaction. Any allergic reaction can turn anaphylactic."

But Dr. Murasawa was already responding with, "I don't think I have anything like that."

Still, she held her arms out and then flipped them over so she could be inspected. They didn't find the telltale pink welts, but the movement showed just how swollen her right forearm was.

"Legs," Joule commanded, seeming to not realize she was demanding this of their boss's boss.

The doctor looked as though she didn't quite want to lift her khaki pants and show off her ankles to her underlings. But that was where it had started on Jeff, Cage thought, and he was getting ready to say so when Murasawa reluctantly pulled over a chair and propped one foot on it. Lifting her pants leg, she showed off a white sock and the skin of her calf.

Cage looked closely. Her skin was darker than his own, and he was afraid it might obscure any reaction. They couldn't afford to miss something. But he didn't see anything that scared him. His hand reached into his pocket and fidgeted with the EpiPen there. He and Joule had gotten the refill and picked up another three-pack just as the pharmacy had restocked, bringing their total to five. He had two in his pockets and another in his bag.

"Other leg?" Joule asked, her tone calming as they became more reassured that Dr. Murasawa was right that she didn't have a full reaction.

Though Cage recalled seeing the rash develop in a relatively uniform pattern when he'd seen it, he knew three cases were absolutely not enough to go by.

With a small sigh, the doctor switched feet and lifted her pants hem again. She stuck her leg out straight onto the chair and tipped her foot one way then another, as though showing off her clear skin.

Joule let out an audible sigh of relief. "Your reaction definitely looks local. You can get a doctor to look at it, but Cage has this happen sometimes. It probably doesn't need anything unless it's still there in another day."

"You can use topical Benadryl," Cage added. "But if you use too much of it, it can knock you out. It's like taking a pill."

"From the topical?" Chithra Murasawa frowned at the twins. She had a doctorate in sciences, not medicine. They definitely had the information on this topic.

"Joule once had so many bug bites that she rubbed it all over herself and knocked herself out."

"Good to know..." Dr. Murasawa murmured. "But that's it? I just wait for it to pass? I came here because I thought I remembered you saying you'd had allergic reactions to these things."

"I've had one that looks almost exactly like that," Cage replied, letting her know her memory was correct.

"How long did it last?"

Joule tipped her head, clearly trying to think back to their childhood just like him. "A day or two."

"Just enough to be really embarrassing," he remembered out loud.

"Fine." The doc sighed. At least she no longer seemed worried. "Thank you for the information."

"What made you come in here now? Why not earlier?" Cage asked, suddenly thinking that it was going on the end of the day. Wouldn't she have noticed it before? She'd stormed in like she was suddenly concerned.

"Because it was little and it kept getting bigger and bigger. I was at my desk all day, so I didn't notice until I got up. It was Angelica Stanhope that pointed out that it looked this bad." She held the arm up and looked at it again as though it might have changed in the past few minutes.

Cage nodded. At least it wasn't bothering her too much and she wasn't complaining about the work they were doing. His worry about her was now the same as the one he had about himself: if he was allergic to bites, was he more susceptible to whatever the reaction was that was killing people? Was she?

He had no answers.

However, David wasn't busy thinking about those things. He spoke up. "While you're here, Dr. Murasawa, there's something we'd like to show you."

Cage's head snapped to the left. David hadn't even gotten out of the chair or moved away from his computer. Was he going to ask her to check out their new mosquitoes?

That was exactly what he did.

He showed their boss the graphs, pointing out the change in the tiny, tiny little wedge that was *Aedes Karnatakan*. Was he also going to tell her that Cage and Joule were quite convinced that it was the mosquitoes causing the reactions—even though it clearly hadn't caused the full problem for Dr. Murasawa?

That wasn't going to go over well.

But David just rolled on. "It's not native here." He went through his same description that he'd given Joule, about how they might have arrived in a probably innocuous fashion. "But they've got a foothold. And they've changed their percent population dramatically in a short period of time. That's something we should look at further."

Cage hadn't thought of it quite that way. It was under two percent and still seemed small. But if he was thinking in terms of invasion, and the time span of the change in percentage, this could be massive.

"We might have an invasive species on this property. And I think we should check it out more," Joule added.

But Dr. Murasawa took over the computer from him, clicking through all kinds of graphs and information. She stood there for far too long. David was growing visibly uncomfortable as she checked every tab he had open and then added a few searches of her own.

Was Cage ready to go out specifically hunting for the thing

he thought was responsible for killing people in Florida and nearly killing his friend? It was one thing to be where the bugs were, another to search out their breeding grounds and stand in it.

He didn't like the idea of himself being out there and he sure as hell didn't like the idea of David being out there. His friend had basically proven he had a massive allergic reaction to... something.

Cage wanted to believe it was the cafeteria food, but he couldn't quite bring himself to buy into that. Neither could Joule, and she was the one who was most likely to sway him.

"Are you ready to go back out there?" Dr. Murasawa asked.

Cage looked up and found Joule snapping to attention as well. But their boss was only really asking David.

"I was ready this morning," he responded quickly.

"And you think this is worth investigating because it might be invasive?"

"That's a bigger concern than people give it credit for." David rattled it off when Cage couldn't figure out anything that would work.

"Why is she here?" Chithra Murasawa tipped her head toward Joule. She'd probably cataloged Joule's presence as odd from the moment she opened the door. She just hadn't said anything yet. Cage reminded himself not to put anything past the doctor.

"She's double-checking numbers for us." David's answer was swift and untrue. But thank God, because Cage was a crappy liar.

The doc still looked skeptical. And Cage held his breath as he waited for her answer.

26

J oule hunched over the black lab table, her calculator pulled up on her phone next to her. She should have been double checking the last set of numbers David had handed her. But she couldn't focus.

"Should we be worried about Dr. Murasawa?" She asked it without lifting her head. Though she was letting her laptop run most of the numbers, she was still crunching some of the smaller pieces with her own calculations, just to be sure she hadn't missed a step.

"Maybe," Cage replied. The doctor had approved their little project to follow up on the mosquitoes, even though she hadn't been told the whole truth of why they were so invested.

But it was now Tuesday. They'd had two days on the project, and Joule was frowning at the notepad in front of her where she'd kept track of a few things. She did not think this was going to turn out well. *Aedes Karnatakan* had an even bigger foothold in the area now.

"What?" David asked, swiveling his seat away from his computer screen for a moment. Maybe information about Dr. Murasawa at least interested him.

"She had a reasonably bad reaction to the first bite we saw." Cage reiterated what he and Joule had discussed over the weekend. "And then she was in here Friday with a second bite that reacted even worse."

"So, if she gets bitten again..." David let it trail off.

Joule was opening her mouth when Cage's phone went off.

"Hello?" he answered casually but almost immediately it became clear this wasn't a casual call. "Yes, I have one."

He was getting to his feet, motioning to Joule and David, even as he reached into his pocket.

The epinephrine?

"Someone got bit?" Joule asked, but Cage was already out the door.

"Already reacting!" he yelled back, but David was already on his heels. Joule grabbed her backpack and slammed out of the doorway right behind them.

Whatever it was, it wasn't good.

The medication was already in Cage's hand as the three raced down the long hallway.

Before she made it to the end, Joule's lungs were heaving, trying to get more air. Again, she thought she should have run track.

Her backpack bounced against her side and only then, as she was already too far down the hallway, did she realize that the lab had been left wide open. Laptops, computers, samples, all completely unattended. She didn't truly worry about that here, but it was something for her mind to hold onto, since she couldn't process what she was running toward.

"Who?" Cage yelled the word into the phone, still in the lead.

Joule darted her way behind them, taking sharp turns and slamming doors as the three barreled their way into the concrete staircase. They would not be waiting for the elevator, though Joule had not expected that they would.

"Kelsey!" Cage yelled back, and Joule's heart kicked again.

Cage and Kelsey had worked together a good bit. Joule wasn't surprised that her brother missed a step and almost tripped as he said her name.

But even as he stumbled on the step, she caught up and grabbed his arm as he slapped his hand on the gray metal railing. Cage righted himself, barely missed a beat, and kept going.

The whole thing shouldn't be worse because she knew Kelsey. It shouldn't be worse because this person was her brother's friend. But it was. She wished it could be one of the jet lab people. She wished it was someone in Helio Systems Tech that she didn't really know. But that wasn't going to be the case.

They slammed out of the building one at a time, with Cage still at the front. The change from air conditioning to dense humidity made Joule realize how hard her lungs were already working. The drag and pull was too much now that she was outside, but there was nothing she could do about it. She couldn't just stop running. She couldn't bend over and catch her breath when someone was waiting who couldn't catch their breath at all.

David put a little distance between them, and Joule cursed her already aching legs, but she kept pushing, backpack flapping into her side, arms pumping. She was glad she had at least worn sneakers.

They cut a path straight through the grass, no longer thwarted by buildings and hallways, staircases and fire doors. But which direction should they go? Where was the problem.

In the distance, she spotted Leslie darting toward them.

"This way!" Though she was at the back, she managed to get them all aimed in the right direction and they bolted forward.

Cage shoved his phone down into his pocket and Joule watched as his level abruptly changed. He dropped down but didn't fall, then popped back up with a swear. It took a fraction of a second to figure out that his foot had gone into a standing puddle, and Joule only realized what had happened as her own foot splashed into the water they couldn't see because of the tall grasses.

Joule's brain immediately leapt to the thought of incubating larva. But with one sneaker now squishing audibly, she kept running. When Cage veered in front of her, she was ready. This time Joule marked the spot and she leaped, managing to miss the puddle even as she watched David's foot smack into it.

But none of them slowed down. Leslie was barreling toward them and she'd seen the problem. So even though the three from the lab didn't quite know what they were aiming toward, they all kept going. Soon enough, Leslie caught up and turned around, joining them just as Joule spotted the cluster of people in the distance. Three or four of them hovered over something on the ground.

It had to be Kelsey.

The sight of them gave Joule another burst of speed. They were still off in the distance, but her lungs expanded and she sucked in an extra-large breath as though that might help. What it did was magnify the small stitch in her side to something big enough to feel like a knife. Still, her feet pounded.

David was getting further ahead and if she'd been smart—if she'd known he could run like that—she would have slapped an EpiPen into his hand before they left the lab. Cage still clutched at his.

"We're coming!" Leslie yelled, and heads popped up to watch. One of the people in the small cluster began to run toward them.

"We have epinephrine!" Leslie yelled again, though how she had the breath, Joule didn't know. Maybe it was just pure terror, because Leslie had met them halfway and covered the same distance they had.

Only then did it occur to Joule that the group had known

they needed an EpiPen before they started running. That
meant that whoever it was had been down and possibly not
breathing for more than three minutes. If they were smart,
they'd called as soon as the symptoms had begun. Though
Joule knew her coworkers were brilliant, she wasn't sure they'd
done that.

Ahead of her, David pulled up short and the group all
looked up at him expectantly. Feet still pounding as she closed
the last of the distance, Joule watched as he flipped his palms
out. He'd arrived first, but he'd arrived empty handed.

The group turned almost in unison, watching Cage and
Joule as they almost ran into people as they tried to skid to a
stop after reaching such a high speed. Leslie lagged behind
now, as if yelling out they were almost there was the last she'd
had in her.

Joule watched as her brother managed to pull the cap off of
the EpiPen even as he stepped into place.

Kelsey was laid out on the ground. Her eyes were open, her
mouth gaping like a fish. Her body jerked slightly, and she
passed out right in front of Joule's eyes.

But that was good! Joule thought. They might have made it
with the EpiPen in time.

But Kelsey's limp body now didn't react to anything. Sarah
hovered over her and prodded her. The complete non-response
sent a fresh spike of terror through Joule's heart. She could only
watch as Cage crashed to his knees next to her and jabbed the
needle into Kelsey's thigh.

27

J oule hated that she was used to this, to watching a limp body almost jolt to life. Eyes opening, hands jerking at the ends of their arms, lungs expanding as their airway opened.

She also loved it.

They were down to four epinephrine doses, and the fact that she was counting that twisted at her insides. But she herself was beginning to breathe a little easier, now that Kelsey was looking up at the people hovering around her and trying to ask questions.

Both David and Kelsey would not be alive had Joule and Cage not had their EpiPens. Or if they had not made a concerted effort to fill that prescription. They hadn't ever filled it before; Cage simply hadn't needed it, and the idea that they would carry this device everywhere for something that wasn't happening had never entered their thoughts... until Florida.

None of this would have been possible if the twins hadn't been in Florida, and hadn't watched Jeff get saved and Clara pass away. It wouldn't have happened had Cage not been close to David when he went down. Not unless someone else had been nearby and also knew what medication was needed *and* happened to have it on hand to dispense it.

That incident was the only reason this group had known to send for Joule and Cage.

It was too much, Joule thought, *too many random happenings had to link together to make this happen.* But in the end, she was happy as she watched Kelsey lifted a hand to her chest and try to push herself upright.

"I think you can sit her up for a minute," she volunteered. Joule crossed her arms for something to do with her hands and hovered at the edge of the group.

Cage added in, "You're supposed to be able to breathe better sitting up straight."

Everyone wanted Kelsey to breathe better. Kelsey had been the twins' friend for a number of years now, going back to their very first job with Helio Systems Tech in Alabama, where things had gone so wrong. So, Joule felt a deep relief as Kelsey sat upright and inhaled easier. She kept her hand pressed to her chest.

Joule took another step back, not wanting to be in the way, and watched as Cage leaned over and explained. "Your heart is probably racing. That's the epinephrine, but it also opened up your trachea so you can breathe."

Kelsey nodded along. She was a biologist, too, and might know more about it than Cage did. She hunched her shoulders in and then rolled them back, as though trying to adjust for something happening inside her rib cage. *Certainly, she couldn't feel anything in there other than her heart racing,* Joule thought. There would be no changing that until the medication wore off.

A faint noise grabbed her attention and Joule twirled to the side, quickly finding the flashing lights to go with the siren she thought she'd heard. The ambulance was almost here. Better than in Florida, these EMTs might have made it in time.

Melinda crouched next Kelsey. Had Melinda come running

as soon as she'd heard one of her people was down? Or maybe she'd been out here with the team today since Cage and David had been pulled from the standard testing they'd been working on?

Maybe Kelsey wouldn't have been out if Joule and Cage had not requested a chance to count the mosquitoes. Again, there were too many chains of actions that had come together to maybe make this happen. Suddenly, Joule didn't like it.

What had their strings of action—or maybe inaction—caused them to miss?

Would she ever know?

Kelsey tipped her head from side to side and pressed her hand against her chest again, grabbing Joule's attention. Melinda looked back over her shoulder, checking again for the ambulance. It had disappeared down the road behind the large building that housed the main portions of the jet lab. It would come around the side any moment now, Joule knew.

They'd seen this before. And that was the worst of it—that they *kept* seeing it.

They should be able to prevent it by now, and yet they were here again, needing epinephrine and waiting as the sirens grew louder. They had nothing but suspicions.

Joule turned her head again, watching as the bright, boxy truck plowed through the parking lot, finding a space between curbs, and bumping its way along the grass. The driver maneuvered clunkily along and managed to get close to the little group.

Joule frowned and worried as the driver turned around to leave, but in a moment it became clear he was backing up to bring the bay doors close to where Kelsey lay in the grass. The EMTs had already hopped out, one with a backboard in his hands, the other with a huge medical kit.

Within moments, Joule, Cage, Melinda and the others were all being pushed away. Still, they crowded as close as they were allowed. One of emergency workers had his face down directly into Kelsey's, asking her questions and making assessments. Though Joule couldn't hear all of it, it didn't matter. The other EMT looked up and asked what they knew, prompting them to all speak at once.

They explained that Cage had come with the EpiPen. That the group here had tipped her head back and massaged her hands. They'd tried mouth-to-mouth, but she still had a pulse. That they'd jabbed the medication into her thigh, and then pulled it out so that it didn't wiggle or cause damage.

"Good job," the EMT said, as though praising children. But just then, his buddy's head snapped up and the other tapped him on the leg, demanding his attention.

Kelsey was shaking her head back and forth. Her eyes were squeezed shut. For the first time, Joule realized something else was wrong. Something beyond the bite or the anaphylaxis, something they couldn't see and hadn't yet looked for.

Was there even a bite on Kelsey's skin?

Though she believed it had to be there, she hadn't seen it. And—as she and Cage had discussed—once the rash took over, would they even be able to find a lone welt from an insect bite? But now there was something beyond the reaction to the EpiPen.

David hadn't done anything like this. He'd been fine.

Jeff, back in Florida, hadn't done this.

Kelsey looked like it was getting difficult to breathe again, and her skin was turning ashy. Joule watched as her mouth opened and Kelsey began to pant, almost as if she were in pain.

Maybe she was.

"Do something!" Melinda yelled at the EMTs, even as the two men worked frantically. "Give her more epinephrine!"

"It's not anaphylaxis!" one of them spoke calmly but loudly, though whether he was telling his coworker or trying to get Melinda to back off was unclear.

Their blue polo uniform shirts moved almost in tandem as if the work of trying to save Kelsey's life one more time was almost a coordinated dance. Maybe it was.

They ran an IV line into her arm, though they still didn't have her on the backboard. The blond one slapped a bag of fluid into Melinda's hands and told her to stand up or hold it high. Now with a clear job to do, their supervisor nodded frantically and held the bag up as Kelsey became paler and paler, right before their eyes.

28

I t felt odd, sitting in a conference room. The jet lab had let the Helio Systems Tech team borrow the space, and Cage really wished they hadn't had to.

The stupid trailers they were used to would have been much better. The sound of portable AC units jammed into opened windows would have been comforting right now. He thought of small space heaters set around the corners of the room not really doing their job.

Here, a huge conference table took up most of the space in the middle of the room. The key players had snagged the front seats. Mitch, Melinda and the other team leads had table seats. The rest of the team members—like Joule and himself—crowded around the edges. They'd brought in big, comfy office chairs, but that made it more crowded.

"As many of you know," Dr. Murasawa started. "Kelsey didn't make it."

A small, collective gasp went through the room, indicating a few people hadn't known already. Cage had gotten a call last night from Sarah. He'd told Joule and then called David. Word had spread relatively quickly.

It didn't look like Dr. Murasawa was delivering the news to more than just a few people.

"Kelsey Fairfield was our second team member to suffer from this kind of a reaction." Dr. Murasawa's eyes scanned the room and landed near Cage. "David Dean survived his reaction with no ill effects. Because of that, we thought it was an odd, one-off situation. Clearly, it wasn't. And we regret we didn't plan well enough."

No shit, Cage thought. He watched as his sister's head subtly turned toward his. Gripping the arms of the oversized office chair, he hoped that no one else saw any untoward facial expressions. Joule clearly did, and she was having a few of her own.

"Your team leads and I spent far too long last night—" their boss gasped in, clipping off her own words. Her expression said that she'd only just realized what she said.

Could they possibly spend *far too long* when one of their team members had died on site?

But Dr. Murasawa was saying the same thing. "I'm so sorry. I didn't mean it that way." She shook her head and looked down and said exactly what Cage had been thinking. "There is no 'far too long' in a case like this. We did stay up very late, looking over the latest data." Having apologized and gathered herself, she plowed on.

"It appears this kind of thing has happened previously. Starting in Florida and working its way up the coast. By all accounts, it's something in the food."

Several hands shot up, even though Dr. Murasawa wasn't finished. She didn't seem bothered by this, though, and she started pointing.

"She was out in the field. Why would that be the food?" That person turned around and found David, adding, "You were out in the field, too."

Dr. Chithra Murasawa only said, "Yes. Which makes sense,

because they think it's striking within an hour after eating."

Whoever had asked the question nodded along. Cage couldn't see who it was, but he felt his own head wanting to shake *No*. But another hand went up.

"What happened to Kelsey? I thought she was treated in the field and that she was okay."

"That's what we thought, too." Dr. Murasawa was obviously very distraught by the loss of her employee. It was awful, and the whole thing felt like shit, but Cage was grateful that his boss seemed to actually care what happened to them. So many didn't. But he snapped to attention. She'd said his name.

"I want to thank Cage and Joule Mazur. They have EpiPens on them because of Cage's allergy. And it saved David's life."

That wasn't exactly true. But their project lead was still talking. "It's what we initially thought had saved Kelsey."

"So, what did happen?" the voice pushed again.

Cage wanted to believe he wouldn't be that pushy towards his boss, not one he liked, anyway. But he understood the team was now one shy, and that was hard to take.

Dr. Murasawa didn't seem to take offense from the tone, though, and she continued, this time addressing the whole room. "Upon arriving at the hospital, Kelsey Fairfield had a massive heart attack."

Murmurs fluttered about, rippling between people. Faces turned and they looked at each other, as though the person sitting next to them might have been withholding this news from them.

"But she was only.... What? Late twenties?" another voice asked.

Cage didn't even get his head around in time to identify it. But he was thinking the same thing.

"She had heart damage from an infection she'd sustained a

while ago," the doctor explained. She seemed to have a good number of answers. And while Cage didn't know where she'd gotten them, he didn't want to. He imagined she'd had to call Kelsey's family and let them know what had happened sometime last night. That couldn't have been pleasant or easy. "So, the epinephrine overworked her system."

Cage felt the air settle like lead in his lungs. *They'd killed her with the epinephrine.*

But Dr. Murasawa was scanning the crowd, checking faces until she found Cage and Joule standing right beside each other. Both their eyes must have been wide. His own breathing had ground to halt.

"As always, the epinephrine *was* the right thing to do." She was staring at him as she said it, trying to reassure him that he was wrong in his belief that he'd killed his friend. "Kelsey's reaction was apparently very rare, and had you not given her the medication, she *definitely* would have died from the reaction." She shifted her gaze to scan the whole room. "So, if this happens again, and someone's airway closes, epinephrine is absolutely the right course of action. The good news was that she was at the hospital by the time the heart attack occurred— also an advantage of the epi dose you gave her." The doctor was looking at him again.

Though he heard her, though he *understood,* he didn't yet *feel* that it was all okay.

"Being in the ER was her best chance. It just didn't work..." The words trailed off.

Cage imagined everyone in the room was filling in the gap. It just didn't work *this time.*

Nothing always worked. Life was random and cruel sometimes.

Cage and Joule knew that. It was driven home by his sister's fingers sliding quickly into his own to squeeze his hand. The touch disappeared as fast as it had come. His delightfully cynical sister was hit hard.

There were more questions, more back-and-forth. Then talk inevitably turned to *but what do we do now?*

"We just don't eat?" one of the voices asked.

Dr. Murasawa took a deep, steadying breath and held both hands up, though the question had been clear. There were still murmurs going around, and it took a moment for them to quiet. "Obviously, we have to eat. We're recommending that everyone bring in their own food until this is cleared, and that no one go out in the field until at least an hour after they've eaten. So that if anything should happen, you'll be here... close to help."

She didn't say that there were defibrillators hanging in the staircases, or that there were just more people, and that the ambulance could get to them faster if they didn't have to bump their way out through the field. What she did say was, "Every team leader will be carrying EpiPens now."

It was disturbing how much of a relief that was to Cage. They needed the EpiPens. He and Joule had been counting theirs as though they were a sacred stash. And weren't they?

Two people had reacted here but, for him and his sister, Kelsey made the fourth case.

It had been months since Florida, and it still hadn't been long enough.

"That's it?" the same voice pushed, and Cage turned. Checking from his vantage toward the back of the room near the wall, he was struggling to see who had spoken. Mostly he had views of the backs of people's heads.

"We just eat our food and hope it doesn't get us?"

Dr. Murasawa was starting to shrug.

But another voice was coming into the fray. They were all worried, scared, unsure what to do. "If it's an anaphylactic reaction to a food and no one knows what the food is, then we don't know what not to eat!"

"All we can do is try to minimize risk and maximize response." But even as the doctor was finishing the sentence, David was raising his hand. He spoke before Cage even knew what he was going to say.

"The Mazur twins have other ideas."

29

C age almost felt the wind move. Joule's head snapped to look at him so fast.

Why was David outing them?

Was this good or bad?

He didn't know.

But if Dr. Murasawa didn't agree, that meant their entire mosquito research would be shut down. It wasn't like they had the materials to do this at home on their own time. *Shit.*

The entire room had turned, necks craning, eyes wide, searching out the twins.

"I don't understand," the doctor said. Her body language was tuned to the twins, though her eyes were watching David. "You have another theory?"

Crap, Cage thought.

But David wasn't letting up. For whatever reason, he'd put his foot on the gas pedal. "They don't think it's food that's causing the reactions. They think it's mosquitoes. They're pretty convinced the reaction is from a bite."

"The CDC doesn't agree," Dr. Murasawa told the room, though she didn't say it as a harsh rebuke. She only uttered it as a statement of fact. The curiosity that lingered at the end of the sentence, though, prompted Cage to open his mouth.

"Kelsey's was the fourth reaction that Joule and I have seen."

Gasps came from around the room. "Who else?" "Someone we know?" "When?" "Where?"

Again, Dr. Murasawa made braking motions with her hands. But since most everybody was turned around, looking at the twins, no one saw her. Next to him, Joule had gone stiff, much like the proverbial deer in headlights. Cage, however, was looking forward. There was only really one person here that he needed to convince.

Luckily, the statement had piqued her interest, and she pointed to each of them in turn and motioned the twins forward.

The front of the room had a whiteboard that doubled as a projection screen. But he hadn't prepped a presentation. Joule was looking at him sideways and taking a deep breath. While she was an excellent presenter when she put her mind to it, she was not fond of being the center of attention.

Still, when they reached the front, Cage nodded to her. Without being ready at all, they had to sell this. Lives depended on it.

He'd have to pick up the biological side as they went along, but he wanted her to start the story.

"Before this job started, Cage and I were on vacation in Florida." His sister explained about Jeff and how one of the moms had had an expired EpiPen on her.

"You didn't have yours?" Sarah asked.

Cage almost frowned. He hadn't expected Sarah to heckle them.

"No," Joule said cleanly. "Though Cage is allergic, he doesn't tend to have full systemic reactions. Nothing happens to him that comes on quick enough that we can't get him to an emergency room. And I don't think he's ever had his airway close up."

She turned her head to ask, and he shook his head, muttering, "I got a scratchy throat once. That's it."

This time, it was Joule who motioned for the crowd to calm down. Because then she explained about Clara. "There were no more EpiPens. Her throat closed up, and we couldn't stop it. She couldn't breathe and she died right in front of us."

The same questions came again. And some new ones.

"Doesn't that just mean she had a reaction? None of that says it's not the food."

Joule took a breath and held up a finger for them to fucking wait. Cage could see the "fucking wait" part behind the calm expression she was trying to cultivate. Then she counted back the weeks before rattling it off.

"So why wasn't that the food?" At least this time it was polite. Questioning, not accusatory.

"I can't promise you that it's not." She shrugged at Aliyah, who'd asked this one. "But there is a lot of evidence that supports our theory. Also, people were getting bitten on our Florida trip, just like here. They each sustained some kind of mosquito bite right before they went down."

"Did you get bitten?" David asked now.

Despite how much they'd talked to him, they had not told anyone in this room the story.

Cage turned to his sister, wondering if she—like him—had found it easier to just not talk about it. Unfortunately, the lid had been pried off of that bottle and the ugly little genie was making its way out into the room.

"Cage is allergic to bug bites," Joule said. "I'm prone to them. I get two or three times as many bites as everyone else. So we were covered in bug spray, like always."

Cage stepped in and stared pointedly at David. "You got bitten not long before your reaction."

David tipped his head. Another statement of fact that he had to admit was true.

"Did Kelsey?"

Cage didn't know that one. He hadn't been there. He shrugged his answer to the to the room full of his coworkers. "Who was there? Do you know?"

Murmurs went through the room again. It was Leslie who'd come to fetch the twins and their EpiPen. Cage looked to her now, but she shook her head. Maybe she'd not been there before Kelsey reacted.

Leslie looked to Sarah, who only said, "Maybe?" Then she thought for a moment and added, "I mean, we were out in the field. Everyone knows there are bugs out there. And we were likely to get bitten. The two of you have been dousing everybody in bug spray like maniacs...."

Even as she said it, Sarah obviously only then caught on to why they had done that. "You thought it was the mosquitoes before now?"

Cage said, "Yes. From the start."

Joule solemnly nodded her head and the room finally fell silent.

There were enough people in here who had been victims of Joule and Cage's almost forcible bug spraying. They all looked at each other now, contemplating this possibility.

It was Dr. Murasawa who stepped in. "People getting bitten in a field isn't surprising, though. I don't think it's strong enough to be a link."

Cage nodded. "We agree."

But their project leader was still going, talking as she'd thought it through. "And, in Florida, you were out on water?"

"An aquifer," he told her. "We agree: It's absolutely no surprise that people got bit. It's not enough to draw real conclusions. But—"

Cage turned, looking for a marker in the tray. He grabbed

one and uncapped it before thinking better of it and handing it to Joule. "Draw the US please."

Joule caught on and quickly jotted a stunningly accurate outline of the forty-eight contiguous states. His drawing would have looked like a blob, but hers was clear, so he grabbed another marker. Her outline was in red. This one was purple. Good. It would be obvious.

He drew two little X's just above where Tampa Bay would be and then he turned and found approximately where Charleston was and added two more X's for David and Kelsey. "These are the ones that we saw."

Joule, already in tune, had picked up another marker and was handing it to him. Green this time. Cage continued. "About a week ago, we searched the internet to see if anyone else had had these reactions, and this is what we found."

He started marking the drawing again. "This is from memory, so I might get it a little wrong. But this is the basic order and locations in which the reactions happened."

He looked at the map and tried to remember all of them. He made three marks down near Miami. One near Orlando. Then he circled the two that represented Jeff and Clara. Cage kept going.

That was the problem right there, he thought. There were so many details to remember. One was in Alabama along the coast, just above the panhandle. He marked another on Jekyll Island, then Deltona, then a few in Orlando. Lastly, he made a handful of dots in Charleston. "These have been on the local news."

He and his sister held everyone's attention while the whole room leaned forward, elbows on the table, chairs creaking with the shifts in their weight.

"What about elsewhere?"

"Oh!" Joule grabbed another marker and added a few small marks in North Carolina.

But Cage said, "We looked. It's pretty localized to this section of the country."

"So, it moved from the southern tip of Florida up to where we are now?"

"Past us," Joule added, pointing to the North Carolina dots she'd just added.

Eyebrows raised around the room, but Cage kept pushing ahead. How well they convinced Dr. Murasawa would determine whether the mosquito sub-project continued or was shut down. Whether they could find out if that was really the issue or not. Whether he and Joule could stay in a job they really liked.

"It's not anywhere else," he told the room, marker still in his hand. He clutched it too hard, as if he were holding onto it for some kind of stability.

"If it's food, this seems like an odd distribution pattern." Someone breathed out the words near him. A concession.

They were getting through. Many of the faces looking at him agreed. He wanted to turn and see if Dr. Murasawa did, too. But he wasn't quite willing to give away his uncertainty.

"So, let's assume it's the mosquitoes," the team leader said, looking out at the room, taking the idea seriously now. "Does anyone have any additional evidence that would help us out here?"

Surprising Cage, David raised his hand.

30

Joule open the door of the apartment and stepped out onto the ledge—right into a swarm of small flying creatures.

Her mouth opened to scream but her brain fought the instinct, trying to glue her lips together. The last thing she needed was to eat one of these bugs. What could happen if she were bitten somewhere on her tongue or cheek?

She didn't know.

Adrenaline tripped her system and she wondered if that was what it felt like to get that EpiPen shot, or if it was much worse than this petrified startle that washed her whole body in fear.

The doorknob was still in her hand. Joule was trying to step backwards, but she felt small, tiny movements of the hairs on her arm. Looking down, she saw one of bugs had landed.

Two of them.

Now three.

All of them on her arm, heads down, in a short row.

Again, she fought the innate desire to scream.

Behind her, Cage came toward the doorway, confused as to why she was just standing there. "Joule, what are you—? Oh!"

She was stepping backwards, pushing against him. No words came. There was no way she was going to open her mouth or explain.

Finally, she managed to move. Smacking at her arm, she left a small smear of blood. But then her arm was just her arm. No more mosquitoes... or had they been something else?

Had she scared the others away? Was the blood her own or just a squashed bug that had recently fed on someone else?

Her heart was racing, her brain going just as fast, not wanting to consider the possibilities that she believed. *Maybe it's the food*, she told herself, but it didn't stop her heart from pounding or the cold sweat from forming on her palms. Her muscles were stiff except for the small tremors that tried to escape from the tips of her fingers.

She tried again to make her body move, even as she felt Cage's hand grab the back of her clothing and yank. Her brother's words from last week came back to her. If she moved slowly, and kept her heart rate low, the poison wouldn't spread as fast.

But slowing her pulse would require sucking in a deep breath. And she *couldn't*.

She couldn't do anything but react as she was hauled backwards off her feet and into the front hall of the small apartment.

The door slammed shut in front of her, whacking her ankle as it went by. She tripped and fell backwards, stumbling onto her ass and her hands. Her wrists should have hurt, but she could tell she was too scared to feel it.

Joule looked down at her legs, a new terror blooming in her chest. The weather was getting warmer. She'd worn shorts, and she saw now how much exposed skin she had. Frantically, she checked her arm where the mosquitoes had landed, but nothing appeared yet.

Maybe they hadn't bitten her. Maybe she'd killed that one little fucker before he had a chance. She clung tight to that hope. She held onto David's words that even if they were the right kind—the right species—of mosquito, they still didn't all carry whatever the trigger was.

"Jesus, Joule!" Cage turned around, looking down at her. She blinked and saw his hand was held out to pull her up. As she put weight on it, her right ankle shot through with sharp pain. The door had given her a good hard whack to the bone. But it hurt from movement itself, not from bearing weight.

"I'm okay." She hoped she wasn't lying.

They'd taken to spraying themselves down with bug repellent when they arrived at work. Sometimes they got industrious and did it in the car if the parking lot looked buggy, and sometimes they did it here, before they even got into the car.

Joule hadn't been prepared to step out her apartment door and into a swarm of possibly lethal bites. *Always be prepared—* a lesson she had learned too many times in too many deadly ways in her young history. When she'd been little, and something had surprised her or hurt her or caused trouble, her father would tell her the only thing she could do was be better prepared next time. He told her that she had to forgive herself.

But would she live long enough to forgive herself this error?

She stood there in the pre-furnished living room with her mouth gaping like a fish, trying to figure out if there was anything she could do besides simply wait. Her heart pounded, despite her every effort to keep her pulse low and slow. So whatever poison she might have been exposed to was already in her, circulating.

In her mind, she told her dad how she would be better prepared next time. How she would put the bug spray on before she even left the apartment, even though that had seemed ridiculous... before right now.

"Are you okay?" Cage was leaning in and looking at her face. Did he know she'd been bitten? Had she?

"Yes." But it was still a lie, still a question she couldn't answer. Joule shook her head, still unable to form the right words. Finally, she breathed out, "I don't know."

She held her right forearm out, watching for the welts to rise, for the itch to come. And then she felt it: The overwhelming urge to scratch her arms, her legs, every bit of her skin.

She scratched at the unmarred space, which should make the bite react faster—wouldn't it?

Her brother grabbed her hand and pushed it out of the way. "You can't."

"I can't just stand here and wait."

"Let's sit at the table." He motioned her over before grabbing her bag from where it had fallen when he'd yanked her back into the unit.

It was a mundane command, but better than thinking she could die. Grabbing for the small backpack, she tugged open the zipper and plowed her hand through everything she carried. Two EpiPens passed beneath her fingertips and she grasped one, pulling it free.

If she reacted, they would shoot her up. Then she would go to the hospital, but she should be okay. Unless, of course, she had a heart condition like Kelsey, in which case she could either die from the bite or she could die from the EpiPen. She didn't think she had a heart condition, but she didn't know.

Her brain was running too many tracks, trying to calm herself while also trying to run every possible scenario and figure out how to live through each. "We'll be late for work."

Even as the words tumbled out of her mouth, the frantic tone told her she was doing an incredibly shitty job of calming down. Giving in to the urge, she shifted her arm to look at it again.

"We'll call in," Cage told her.

"Don't tell them!" She reached out to tug at his arm as he stood to find his phone.

"We have to."

There had been no more incidents at work. Though everyone was probably developing several forms of cancer from inhaling essential oils and petrochemical, industrial-grade bug repellent, no one had even been bitten. The repellent worked, but the data sucked.

In the meantime, the whole triumvirate had not only convinced Dr. Murasawa that the mosquitoes were possibly the source of the reactions, but that it was probably specifically *Aedes Karnatakan* that they had been looking at. The bug had not only claimed a higher percentage of the local mosquito population, but the overall mosquito population was already increasing.

What David had been struggling to figure out was whether it was a normal increase for summer months or from something more. Neither Joule nor Cage knew what the normal Charleston mosquito populations were supposed to look like. But they'd reached out and tried to find someone who would know. Dr. Murasawa had even turned their data over to the CDC in several small batches.

Joule didn't know if there were new responses from the government research center. But the first times their project leader had talked to someone, she'd been told, "Yes, we know about this mosquito. And no, we don't think it's responsible."

Whatever they'd said the last time they talked, it had Dr. Murasawa thinking about pulling the plug on their little mosquito adventure. That would shift the three of them back to the building project—the one they'd been hired for.

Joule had pushed back. "We have almost zero bites and we have zero reactions. Doesn't that support a correlation between the two?" It wasn't perfect, but she didn't want to get shut down.

She didn't want to go back to thinking it was something in the food.

She'd tried again. "Just because there are fewer deaths, it doesn't mean the problem isn't the bugs."

"Or it could mean they've located whatever was in your food supply. And they fixed it."

But Joule shook her head. "No." Too harsh. She shouldn't just tell her boss *No*. "Everybody's wearing bug spray like crazy. Have you tried to find it in the stores in Charleston? It's not just us. And everybody's running around with an EpiPen. We can't get a refill."

That was the explanation, wasn't it?

"But I'm not hearing anything about that." Dr. Murasawa was trying to be kind, but it hadn't gone the way Joule wanted. "I've been looking and listening for anything that supports this. I don't want to lose anyone else." Her gaze had been serious, and Joule didn't doubt the doctor meant it. She'd put her own life on the line before. "But I have to justify the funding."

Shit.

Still, Joule persisted. "But the news usually only reports when someone dies from it. Someone like David—who was successfully treated and survived—didn't make the news."

Dr. Murasawa still seemed unconvinced.

Ha, Joule thought now. She was about to unwittingly become her own best data. Was she going to die to make her point?

Sitting on the floral couch that had been supplied with the apartment unit, she held her arm out in front of her as she watched for the skin to change.

She waited for bite marks to appear... or for the welts to start crawling up her legs or arms. Which would she see first?

But what she saw was her brother dousing himself with spray and even spraying her. "It's too late, Cage, I already got bit."

"Did you?" he asked frantically.

She answered honestly. "I don't know. I thought I did, but I don't see anything yet."

How long had it been? Mere moments? Not even a minute. She couldn't tell. Everything was moving at hyper-speed, both too fast and too slow, both warped and too linear, all at the same time. Her breathing was too heavy, or was she just thinking too fast? It was hard to tell.

Cage headed for the front door and the terror leached through her. *"Where are you going?"*

"I'm going to catch one." She saw that he had a cup and a piece of cardboard. Would that even work?

"Then you're going to *bring them inside*?" She'd finally gotten her heart rate down just a little, but it shot back up now.

"It's okay. No matter what happens, we have epinephrine. We'll be fine." He was stepping toward the front door and turning the knob as he looked back over his shoulder at his sister.

He stepped out the door before she could even launch herself from the couch. Joule dropped back down and tried to breathe, but as she did, she felt the itch on her arm. Looking down she saw two small, pink welts.

31

"Cage!" Joule yelled at her brother.

Frantic with worry for him, she looked down at her arm as if that was something to do. Something to accomplish. But it only made her blood pressure and her heart rate kick up. Logically, though she knew she was supposed to stay calm, there was no calm in this scenario.

She ran the few steps to the short front hallway, where her backpack still lay. It listed sideways on the carpet, where it had fallen when Cage had yanked her inside. Digging through, her fingers sliced through all the things that she carried that she thought were important, but right now were nothing but junk. Until, at last, she brushed the smooth plastic and papery stickers of the last dose of epinephrine that had sunk to the bottom of the cavity. She set the bag out of the way so he wouldn't trip on it if he burst back inside.

Still holding onto the first EpiPen, she went back and sat on the couch, holding it between her hands, and waiting. She knew she shouldn't jab herself until and unless she actually had a reaction. For that she would need to see welts, a rash, on all her limbs. And she would need her throat to start to close up before she did anything.

But she itched everywhere now. *Was that the rash?* No one had said if it itched or not.

David didn't remember. Kelsey had died. They weren't in contact with Jeff.

There was no one left to ask.

Jesus. Of the small batch of cases she'd seen, she counted a fifty percent kill rate. Her throat began closing up. Swallowing was getting harder, it felt like trying to push a knot down her throat.

Was it a reaction? Or just panic?

She couldn't tell.

And where was her brother? Why the hell had he thought going outside was a good idea? Was he getting bitten?

They had enough epinephrine for both of them. But they needed to retain enough brains to call 9-1-1 if they both went down.

Her breath soughed through her lungs. Again, she asked herself: panic or reaction?

This was too complex.

Joule glanced at the front door again, wondering if her sense of time was skewed or if her brother really had been outside for an eternity. He was getting mosquitoes, but what were they possibly going to do with them?

The doorknob twisted, and she saw his triumphant expression as he came back inside. "Here!"

But she didn't care what was in his tightly held grip.

Cage must have read her worried expression, because he immediately told her what she needed to hear. "I didn't feel any bites. And you saw me use the homemade spray and the commercial one." Then he shifted gears again. His face lighting up. "I got it. In fact, I got several of them."

Somewhat placated by his recitation, she was able to look at his hands. He was holding the cup he'd grabbed before leaving, firmly pressed to the cardboard. He'd scooped one or more of the bugs and trapped them.

But those little fuckers were small.

"What if one of them escapes?" she asked.

"I'll tape it down." He quickly flipped the little setup/mosquito prison over so the cardboard was on the bottom and set it onto the table. He seemed to assume that her fear was because he'd brought mosquitoes inside the house. Not wanting to startle him and let those little suckers loose, Joule let him believe that.

Standing slowly, she walked over and instructed, "Keep pressure on that cup."

He'd managed to get the cardboard flat on the table and still hold the cup firmly against it. Joule rummaged through an old suitcase until she found clear packing tape. It took several long pieces to seal every edge of the cup and do it in such a way that it didn't leave gaps an industrious little fucker could wiggle his way out of.

She continued to push down on the cup, even as Cage assured her, "They'll get stuck on the tape before they get out. It'll be fine."

But it wasn't going to be fine.

In that moment, Joule found herself paying attention to something else: A welcome sense of relief.

But everything snapped back into place as he sounded startled. "Your arm!"

"I know."

Grabbing her wrist, he tipped it one way than another. Joule let him, and this time she saw a third bite blooming. The three marks were lined up all in a little row. Just like she'd seen the bugs when they'd landed on her.

Every single one of them had gotten her.

"How do you feel right now?" Worry leached through his

tone, but he should have thought of that before he'd raced outside like an idiot.

"I'm okay."

"You need to inspect yourself.... Go." He shoved her toward the short hallway, presumable toward her bedroom. They knew, or at least they thought they did, that the pattern was first a bite, then some semblance of time before the reaction hit. Maybe even an hour.

"I'm calling work, but you keep talking to me. If you stop talking, I'm coming in." He followed her down the hallway leading to the two stumpy little rooms at the end, his phone in his hand.

Joule closed the door behind her in her generic blue and white bedroom. The matching comforter stared up at her.

"Joule.... I'm sorry." His voice came through the closed door, and she felt her anger dissipate. He hadn't known. He was trying to get evidence.

She shook her head. They could only hope he hadn't been bitten, too. Looking down, she saw she still clutched the EpiPen in her hand.

"Joule?"

She must have taken too long and not responded. Now she called back, "I'm good. I'm upright."

In fact, she was standing in front of the long mirror hung on the wall by the door. She removed every stitch of clothing, twisting her arms this way and that, then her ankles. She tried to see her back, but she couldn't.

"Joule?" his voice came again.

"Sorry, trying to find something. I'm good." So this time she kept up a steady stream of chatter like he'd asked her to. "I'm finding a small, mirror to see my back."

But she'd found one on her dresser amid the stash of makeup she rarely used. Holding it up, she turned around and looked.

Nothing.

Her breath let out. She saw the small brown mole she'd had on her shoulder since seventh grade. Joule twisted. There was another mole down close to her hip. And a scar from a kidney removal when she'd been an infant.

"I'm good. It's just these..."

"Shit."

She'd rotated her ankles each one way then another and found a small, pink mark on her calf. At the last moment.

"What?"

"Another one." She was up to four bites for stepping out her front door on the second floor unprotected.

Did they pop up this quickly? Did she need to keep looking? Or had she passed some magic threshold? Was four enough to guarantee that she would react if she was allergic to whatever it was?

"Where?"

"On my leg this time."

She thought about what they'd said, what David had talked about—that certain species of mosquito tended to carry certain diseases. But getting bit by a mosquito of that species didn't necessarily mean that this particular bug carried the disease, only that it could. With four bites, from probably four separate mosquitoes ...

Wouldn't that quadruple her chance that one of them was infected?

"Joule?"

Shit. She'd been quiet too long again. And though it was obnoxious as fuck, it was a good measure. If her throat closed up, she wouldn't be able to answer. "Hold on."

She pulled her clothing back on. Every place she'd been bitten had been exposed skin. So they hadn't crawled up her shorts or under her shirt. Joule fought a sick shudder at the thought.

Cage's voice came through the doorway, though he wasn't talking to her. He was telling someone they would be late or maybe not in today at all. She was opening the door as a tune came from across the living room.

Cage hung up as both of their heads swiveled, recognizing her ringtone.

Crossing the room, she looked down at the face. "Unknown number."

She twisted her head and swallowed, her throat feeling scratchy again.

It had a 770 area code. She held the phone up. "Do you recognize this?"

Cage shook his head.

Normally, she would let it go to voicemail, but she wasn't making her best decisions right now. She was damn curious, and she needed the distraction. "Hello?"

"I'm looking for Joule Mah-sar." The woman had pronounced the last name wrong.

Joule almost laughed and said, "I'm sorry. My family's been in America for too long to use that pronunciation." But her heart was still racing at the four bug bites on her body and the tightness that was growing at the base of her throat.

She was growing more and more concerned. But she couldn't distinguish disease from panic.

Joule said, "This is she."

"Hello. It's nice to talk to you. "I'm Dr. Noemi Achebe from the CDC."

32

"Who?" Cage felt his face pull together. Confusion was setting in, though it was a welcome distraction from waiting for Joule's bites to become something worse.

He'd barely heard the intro from Joule's phone, and he still hadn't processed it, when the voice said, "I'm actually standing at your door."

His sister's head snapped back in surprise, but Cage ran to the door and stupidly threw it open.

The woman stood tall and almost regal. She wore basic business casual khakis and a pale blue button-down shirt, making her look more like a superstore manager than a CDC researcher. Her dark skin practically glowed in the morning light and her gentle smile revealed wide, evenly spaced white teeth. Her brown eyes were soft and her words strangely discordant. "I am Dr. Achebe."

She spoke the words with an almost complete lack of accent, until she got to her own name. Then a hint of a foreign country he couldn't identify crept in.

"I am with the CDC." Her expression looked as though she

were trying to appear non-threatening, or comforting, as she reached into her pocket and pulled out a badge.

It looked official.

Cage took it as she offered it and flipped it over. He checked the wording on the back, though he didn't know what he was looking for. Maybe a misspelling or something obviously faked. But he found none. The card was made of plastic sandwiching some kind of silvery layer in the middle. It was likely some kind of magnetic strip or chip, allowing her entry to the buildings.

As he handed it back, he took another quick glance at his sister. But Joule reached out for the badge, wanting to see it for herself.

The welts on her arm were more pronounced now. But, as of yet, he didn't see anything else. It didn't matter, though. This woman's very presence on their doorstep made everything suspicious.

Their visitor stood with a forced calm just beyond the aluminum threshold that defined their space. The concreted balcony attached all the front doors, much like a motel—not the nicest place Helio Systems Tech had put them up, but it was clean and near the site.

Dr. Achebe's hand swatted absently at a bug, and she offered a small, disturbed noise followed by, "May I please come in?"

Joule offered one short nod and stepped back. She held out the ID, seemingly as satisfied as she was going to get with it. But the way she held it and moved backward simultaneously, it was almost as though she were baiting the doctor in through the doorway.

The twins didn't know her.

And the timing was odd.

Cage took a moment to assess that they were in their own home, and there were two of them, and hopefully the fact that they were black belts would work in their favor. But it wasn't enough. In his world, information was king. "I don't understand. Why are you here?"

Even though they had no real idea who this woman was, they wouldn't leave her outside where the bugs swarmed. Reaching around her, Cage pushed the front door shut. He glanced briefly beyond the woman, looking to see if he could spot any of the small swarm that had gotten a hit on his sister.

He didn't see them now.

His thoughts flashed to the several he had managed to scoop into the cup and tape down to the paper. They now sat, angry prisoners, on his dining room table.

Dr. Achebe's shoulders visibly relaxed with the sound of the door clicking behind her. "Let me start over," she said, her soft expression changing to a warmer one.

Cage felt his muscles tightening in response. When had he grown so suspicious of people? Maybe he wasn't overly suspicious—maybe it was simply because this woman from the CDC had shown up just as he was monitoring his sister. But he couldn't think about that, or he'd miss important information. The woman was talking.

"My name is Dr. Noemi Achebe. I am with the CDC entomology research department. We received information and paperwork that came from Helio Systems Tech that was a theoretical link between mosquitos and the outbreak of systemic anaphylactic reactions that have taken too many lives on the east coast."

At least she sounded like a researcher.

"The names attached the data were yours. So, I looked you up and decided to come here."

It still didn't fit. Not fully. Cage shook his head. "The CDC doesn't think it's the bugs. They think it's the food."

"But you still believe it's mosquito-borne. And you think something is being transmitted by a bug bite?"

"Yes." He felt awkward saying it, but it was the truth.

It was clear Joule didn't want to tell their side of things either —at least not until they understood what this woman was all about and if she was really with the CDC. But at least everything she'd cited was true. Helio Sys had sent data to the CDC in several small batches. And the Mazur name had been all over it.

Still, this all seemed very odd.

The three of them were still standing in the center of the open space, no one yet willing to concede and sit down, to be vulnerable.

The doctor looked them up and down before saying, "I see your sister has two fresh bites on her arm." She pointed with one only slightly raised finger.

"Actually three," Joule said, then pointed downward to her leg. "And another on my calf. I stepped out into a swarm of them this morning."

Something about the way she spoke hinted at caution, and Cage decided to follow suit. Though whether Joule was cautious because there was a stranger standing in the small entryway of their apartment, or because she was feeling some internal reaction, he didn't know.

"I've seen your data, and you're correct. The official stance of the CDC is still that this is a reaction to some irritant, or contaminant, in a food source."

"But it would have to be a large distributor for all the places these cases have come up," Cage said, his mouth running as she repeated data that he couldn't help but correct. He stepped slightly further back and wondered if it had been a mistake to draw the doctor into their small apartment.

Aside from Joule's bow and arrow and the handgun that they'd taken from the house years ago, they had no weapons. Certainly nothing of use for a fight in the small living room.

"Your data is solid," said the doctor, still standing softly, as though trying to make herself not appear threatening. "I'd like to pursue it."

Cage felt his spine snap to attention and watched as his sister did the same.

"If we are right, and it is transmitted through bug bites, your sister is at risk right now," Dr. Achebe said, again pointing at Joule's arm. She changed her focus to Joule. "How long since you were bitten?"

Joule looked up at the clock on the wall. "Maybe twenty minutes."

"Oh!" The surprise in the researcher's voice was clear, and it felt to Cage as if this were her first non-controlled reaction since he'd opened the door. "That's not long enough to be out of the woods then."

"I know that," Joule replied.

"That explains why you're looking at me like I'm a threat." Her whole demeanor changed. "There is a threat here, it's just not me."

Cage wasn't sure this new intruder got to declare that, but she suddenly seemed much more genuine.

"Have you taken antihistamines?"

Joule shook her head. "No. We have EpiPens."

"You should take antihistamines now, before you have a full reaction."

Joule rattled off that she avoided most antihistamines, as they tended to knock her out. But the doctor came back with several options.

"I think we have some of that." Cage looked at Joule as if to ask if that was okay.

The doctor looked Joule up and down. "Try taking two. It's double the over-the-counter dose, but it should be safe. And it can stop this before it happens."

"*It can?*" He was halfway to the kitchen, and he pulled up

short. Was that right? Could they have just dosed Kelsey and saved her damn life?

Suddenly, thoughts ricocheted through his skull and it took an effort to stay on track.

The doctor nodded quickly. "They can. It doesn't always work, but you shouldn't wait to have a full reaction. You might stop it beforehand."

The words tumbled out of his mouth. Cage—still a bit stunned—couldn't stop them. "How did we not know this?"

"I don't know why it's not more common knowledge." The doctor shrugged at him sadly. "But it's not. I have some on me, if you'd like…" She reached into a brown leather purse that was as tidy, clean, and generic as the rest of her outfit. Pulling out a bottle, she held it out. "I have everything in there, but I understand if you want to go check and take your own medications."

True. While he had extreme trust in taking medication the CDC recommended, taking it from someone who showed up on his doorstep wasn't quite the same.

Joule had easily moved past him, not having been stopped by rampant, wayward worries. She rummaged through the small medicine cabinet they took with them each time they moved and found one of the medications the doctor had recommended.

Coming back to where Cage and the doctor now stood in the middle of the room again, Joule held out her hand. The pills sat in her palm. She had a glass of water in the other hand. "If I take this now, we won't ever know if I had a reaction."

33

"**D**o you really want to be a data point?"

Joule was locked onto the doctor's gaze as Noemi Achebe asked her the pointed words.

It was a harder question to answer than she'd expected it to be. There were a lot of advantages to the data. And maybe she could control it... but after weighing her odds, she said, "No."

The doctor tipped her head at the two small, yellow pills in Joule's hand. "You could still be one anyway. The medication isn't a guarantee."

Wonderful. Joule tossed the meds to the back of her throat and swallowed some water as a chaser. Her brother offered a small nod.

He hadn't answered the question for her, but it was clear that she'd made the decision he wanted her to make. It was fair. If it had been him deciding, she would have wanted him to definitively *not* want to be a data point. Their data points didn't fare so well.

Medicine taken and first decision made, she rotated her arm, looking at the welts, wondering again if they would do anything else. She looked down at her legs and then she looked back up at the doctor. "Why don't we sit down?"

Joule couldn't handle any more of this "wild west," standing in the middle of the room, staring at each other, intellectual guns drawn stuff.

As the three settled uneasily around the table, Joule decided it was time to just own up. "I'd like to call the CDC and check up on you."

The doctor nodded. "Please do."

That sounded positive but, as Joule whipped out her phone, one dark skinned hand came out, the paler palm motioning her to stop. "I do work for the CDC, and you should call and check. They will, however, inform you that I'm on vacation."

Joule watched as the realization dawned on her brother's face, and she could only imagine she wore an identical expression. "So, this isn't official CDC business?"

"No. But it involves official CDC business."

"Explain," Joule demanded.

"Officially, the CDC has rejected your idea. But unofficially, there are a handful of us still working on the angle that it's not the food. And, specifically, that it is a strain of mosquito. There are even more options for what could be triggering it—chemicals in the air, a medication, even a different insect—but those are the front-runners."

Joule hadn't considered the possibility that both options might be wrong. What if it *was* something different? Poisoned medication, even? Her eyebrows must have climbed close to her hairline, because the doctor nodded.

"I have vacation time, and I was willing to come up. But we've been mostly shut down, and the expense of an employee or two for this was denied. Still, the whole team wanted to talk to the two of you personally. You have anecdotal evidence that might be helpful."

That much was true, Joule thought. How many other people

had seen victims in multiple locations? And why the hell did this shit keep happening to her?

Though she periodically had that fatalistic thought, she knew it wasn't just her and her brother. There was so much shit going on: hundred-year floods every fourth year; strange blizzards, sometimes out of season; extreme storms; and even mudslides in places where periods of drought and rain had razed the landscape and the roots could no longer hold back the deluges.

The truth was, it wasn't just them. This was simply the latest thing that they'd run into.

Noemi was talking again. "The CDC isn't willing to fund the research, but they aren't fully rejecting the idea yet, either. It's just not their main avenue of pursuit. So, with me, you have access to at least some of the CDC resources."

"But you had to go on vacation to do this?" Cage's words were technically a statement but, the way his voice lifted up at the end, he was clearly asking.

"We wanted to get to you sooner rather than later. Wanted to know where you've been. And we suspected, given the data that your team handed in, with your names at the forefront, that we might find something like that—" She pointed to the upside-down, clear plastic cup and the three or four—Joule couldn't quite tell—mosquitoes buzzing angrily or climbing the walls. "I assume these are not the ones that bit your sister?"

"Unknown." Cage nodded as he said it. "But caught from the same swarm."

"What were you going to do with them?"

Cage looked at Joule and Joule looked back to him. She was the engineer here and not the biologist, but she answered anyway. "Identify the species first. See if we could find anything they were carrying. We have a basic, school-grade laboratory microscope here in the apartment."

"Of course you do." The words were offered with a smile

though the doctor was looking at the cup, respectfully not touching what wasn't hers. "May I?"

Another quick glance to her brother and Joule nodded. They agreed in unison.

The doctor picked it up, the tape holding the cardboard in place. Though Joule felt her muscles tense, none of the little fuckers escaped.

"They definitely look like *Aedes*." The doctor set the cup contraption carefully back onto the table. "They don't look like *Aegypti*."

Joule watched the woman. She still hadn't dialed the CDC, though she held her phone in her hand. Her brother must have had a similar thought, because he voiced what she was thinking.

"So, what exactly is it that you want to do with your vacation time?"

The doctor folded her hands. "I still do encourage you to call the CDC. Verify that I am who I say I am. I'm an MD-PhD, with the PhD in pharmacology. Check whatever you want with them, because they'll be asking for personal information so my lab can do a background check and you can see the results of your work."

That made Joule want to question everything. She did not want to hand over that kind of info to a stranger. But she remembered seeing the lovely little scramble of letters following the doctor's name on her CDC badge. The woman rattled it off as if she had a lot of practice explaining it. She sounded legitimate, though Joule wasn't sure she felt solid about it yet.

She was still explaining. "Then I'd like to see the locations where you've had people bitten. I have other sites to visit here, not just the ones you were at. There are other suspected cases that weren't fully reported. Also, because I'm not official, I'm hoping you can help me gain access to the private property where you work. We want to collect samples and send them back to the CDC for further testing."

She paused and then motioned to Joule. "You need to make your call, because then I'm going to tell you something else. And I think it's very important that I'm verified before you hear it."

The doctor folded her hands gently on the table in front of her.

Joule did what her mother had taught her and looked up the main number for the CDC herself. She knew better than to simply call a number she was given where some Yes-man on the other end could corroborate anything, whether or not it was true.

She wound her way through being placed on hold through several departments as she asked the same question repeatedly. Eventually they wanted more information, and Dr. Achebe supplied her with answers. So, Joule said, "Pharmacology department... epidemiological pharmacy research... Warren-Achebe lab."

At last, she was told, "Yes. Dr. Noemi Achebe is one of our lead team researchers. She is on vacation right now. May I take a message?"

Joule looked across the table, then answered as Noemi prompted. "Actually, I'd like to be put through to Dr. Warren please. Tell her it's Joule Mazur." Within a few minutes, she'd talked to the woman Dr. Achebe directed her to, and she was telling Dr. Helenie Warren, "Joule Lovelace Mazur."

She handed over her social security and driver's license numbers. Then Cage got on the line. "Faraday Carson Mazur."

"Faraday? Cage is a nickname? I like that!" There was a small chuckle in Dr. Helenie Warren's voice, but Joule didn't feel it.

"Okay," the CDC researcher said at last. "We'll get you verified."

Joule hung up. "I just gave a lot of personal data to a stranger. What was this thing that you're going to tell us?"

34

"What?" Cage asked, his head inclined to the side, his eyes staring at the woman. He would have looked at his sister, but he didn't have the spare energy or focus for it.

"We're working on a cure," the doctor repeated.

"And the CDC is funding this?" he pressed. "Even though they don't believe the mosquitoes are causing the deaths?"

She nodded, but her tone hedged a little. "Either way, it is a reaction. And it's taking lives. So, there's a little more push behind it."

"Just . . . what? Make it so there was never a reaction?" Joule asked. His sister was leaning forward, all her attention on the doctor, too.

But Dr. Achebe stayed cool. "We hope it will be a cure. But that's possibly a strong word. Even a highly effective treatment would be good."

"Define highly effective."

She didn't hesitate. "Better than seventy-five percent improvement over no treatment."

Cage did the math. If half the people died from it and they

could save seventy five percent of that half... It dropped the death rate to well under fifteen percent. He could get behind that. But Joule had more questions.

"What does it entail?"

"We are looking at an injection. It's very preliminary right now." The doctor reached into her purse and pulled out a folded stack of documents. She handed over the pages, one by one. The first was a print of a chemical formula, labeled as a possible allergen in the mosquito saliva. Another was a second chemical, labeled the same. The third was a listing of methods from a clinical trial. And the last a small print rundown of side effects produced.

"You inject people who are reacting?" He wondered where they would find them.

"No. We've only been able to inject non-reacting people, simply to be sure that it doesn't have any harmful side effects in and of itself. We'd like to attempt it on a person who is reacting—"

"But it's highly experimental," Joule filled in as she nodded along.

"True. But if you're about to die, then you want to try it."

"Kelsey," Cage murmured, but he hadn't meant to.

Dr. Achebe nodded. "Your friend who died."

He nodded again. "She had a heart condition. She died because she had a heart condition."

The doctor shook her head and corrected him. "She died because she had a reaction *and* a heart condition. Either of the two alone should have been survivable."

Her statement hit him like a push to the chest, metaphorically knocking him off balance. He'd not thought of it that way, but Noemi Achebe was right. Kelsey had the heart condition all along and she'd survived just fine every day until then. David had survived his bite, and they'd gotten Kelsey the epinephrine injection in time. She'd come back.

Cage felt his lips press together but he couldn't fight the sense of loss.

"I would have liked to have a medication to try on her." The doctor's voice was soft, though if it was only concern or concern plus a need to win the twins over, Cage didn't know. "If our idea works, it wouldn't have stressed her heart."

"She would have survived but for a lot of *ifs*," Joule said.

The doctor didn't seem offended by his sister's accusation or her forthright tone. They weren't quite fighting words. But they weren't comforting, either.

"You're right. It's a lot of *ifs*. Which is exactly why I'm here. I'd like to knock as many of those ifs out as we can."

Before Cage could jump in, Noemi turned her focus solely to Joule. "How are you doing?"

His sister stopped and looked at her legs, flipped her arms over, and checked her skin.

"No rash." She then obviously swallowed as if to test. "Throat feels okay. Actually, it feels a little better."

"Do you think you were starting to have a reaction?" He couldn't keep the panic out of his tone. It bothered him how much just the idea twisted, even though Joule was saying she was fine. His family was at fifty percent, too. He and Joule were the only ones left and he'd be damned if it all came down to him.

"Hard to tell." His sister lifted her hands in a legitimate, cartoon-style shrug.

Now they would never know. But he wouldn't have to deal with jabbing an EpiPen into his sister's leg. For that alone, he was more than grateful.

The conversation lulled for a moment and Cage sat quietly, his thoughts turning to Kelsey. If the doctor had arrived a week earlier, his friend might still be alive. He wondered if Joule was thinking the same thing.

The doctor, however, had not met their fellow Helio

Systems Tech employee. She offered only a moment of silence before asking pointedly, "Are you two due at work today?"

Cage shook his head. "I called in and took the day off because of..." he pointed at his sister's arm. "We wanted to wait. Be sure we were ready. We work in separate divisions, so we just wanted to have a real close monitor."

"Even better," the doctor announced with a smile of her wide, white teeth. "If you're up for it, I'd love to get started. We'll keep monitoring your sister for—" she lifted her wrist and looked at a shiny, analog watch. "—another ten or twenty minutes longer, to be sure. But it does look like you're out of the woods."

Cage watched his sister visibly exhale, her shoulders dropping. He and Joule knew all of these things. He'd had the same thoughts, but there was something about hearing it from a third party that made it all sound much more official.

"First, I'd like to test these guys." The doctor gave them no time to breathe. She pointed to the cup on the table. "If I can go out to my car, I can get several supplies. I fully intended to be doing field work while I'm out here. I do have several sites to check."

"Do you have other people to interview?" Joule asked.

For the first time, Cage wondered if Dr. Achebe had come up here to assemble a team.

The doctor only laughed. "No. Other people who get bitten and survive don't collect the data and then email the CDC with it."

That was fair. He and his sister were rather odd ducks in that respect. When he nodded, suggesting that Dr. Achebe do exactly as she'd said and head out to her car, she stood up. But Joule jumped up first.

"Do you need bug spray? We know there are some out there." She held her arm up as evidence.

The doctor laughed softly. "I'm already doused in it."

Of course she was. If she was here, then she believed that the mosquitoes were a legitimate threat. And if she believed that, then she would definitely protect herself against them.

Cage just hadn't smelled it on her. Maybe because he and his sister were their own clouds of anti-bug fumes.

The doctor grabbed her purse and left to head down to the car, closing the front door behind her to keep other bugs from getting in. But as soon as it clicked shut, Joule turned to face Cage, a puzzled expression on her face.

He looked around the room. Dr. Noemi Achebe had taken everything with her that she'd brought in. She'd put the mosquito cup back exactly where she'd picked it up from. There was no evidence that the doctor had even been here.

But he could go into the kitchen and look out over the little window carved over the sink and watch her go to her car.

"Did that really just happen?" Joule pressed.

He understood the odd feeling. The morning had taken a complete turn.

"The person at the CDC who confirmed her said she was on leave for *two weeks*. Does that mean *we're* now on leave for two weeks?" She stayed seated, leaning over the table, questioning him as though he would have the answers.

He had almost said *maybe*.

But even as he thought the word, he felt his fingernails raking the skin on the back of his hand. He saw Joule following his motion before he looked down and saw the mark for himself.

She looked up at him. "You've been bitten."

35

Joule glanced sideways at her brother, trying to surreptitiously inspect him.

He seemed to be doing well, but looks weren't enough. Knowing what could be lurking right around the corner, and that he was susceptible to reactions to bites, she jumped up. In the kitchen, she pulled down the same bottle she'd just put away a while ago and grabbed two more of the antihistamines.

As she'd smacked them into his hand, he'd only shrugged and started to protest. "I'm not—"

But she'd interrupted him with, "You don't want to be a data point, *do you*?"

Her own antihistamines were now at an hour. She felt fine. She had no rash. No constriction to her breathing, nothing. Though she wasn't sure if the welt of Cage's bite had taken a long time to appear or if they simply hadn't noticed, her brother looked really good. Either the medication was working, or he didn't need it.

Dr. Achebe, however, wasn't helping as much as Joule had expected.

Though Joule had cleared the small table and offered the space, the woman had taken over the whole thing, grumbling. "It's very small. Is there more room?"

She'd stood up straight and looked around the apartment.

There was no "more." The coffee table was wicker and barely worthy of holding a drink, let alone lab equipment. The doctor had barely refrained from rolling her eyes.

That was first time Joule had actually liked the woman. It *was* a small table. Previous to that, she'd simply seemed a little overly pleasant—as if her sole goal was to be so nice that Joule and Cage could not refuse. Her grumbling at least made her human.

But when the complaining went on, it began to grate. Still, there was nothing Joule could do about it. They had no more table space to give. The apartment was what it was.

The researcher had pulled a compound microscope from the back of her car. Though Cage had already gotten theirs out when she'd gone to the car, it looked like a child's toy next to the one she brought. Joule quickly moved it down to set it on one of the chairs.

Then the doctor announced, "We need these mosquitoes dead."

"Shaking them will break them," Cage commented, but offered no other solutions.

"We can drown them," Joule said.

"We can. But a dry kill will give us better evidence."

Joule and Cage had looked sideways at each other over the term "a dry kill." It made sense, but Joule had no idea how to do that. And it sounded a little serial killer-y. Though, Joule supposed, she was about to become a mosquito serial killer.

A few minutes later, with a few chemicals procured from her purse in a way that didn't at *all look sinister,* Joule thought, Dr. Achebe had punctured the cup with a needle and syringe and injected a few drops of liquid into the set up before tipping it so the cardboard was up.

As the plastic cup steamed inside, Joule was grateful this wasn't her table. "Is it going to eat through the cup?"

"Oh no." Dr. Achebe sounded calm, as though vaporizing liquids were an everyday occurrence. She casually taped up the injection hole in the cup. "It would have gone through the cardboard, though."

With a shrug of resigned acceptance—they were in it now, weren't they?—Joule and Cage leaned over and watched. Whatever was in the little droplets had the mosquitoes crawling awkwardly and looking as if their bodies didn't quite work. One by one, they dropped like proverbial flies.

"Is it safe for us to touch it?" Joule asked as the last one fell.

"No." The doctor quickly handed out blue, non-latex gloves.

This was not how Joule had expected to spend her day. She thought she would go to work. Get back to checking pillar strength and testing the ground for stress. Maybe determining the angle of the solar panels that they'd be installing or whether the roofline would need to rotate. She'd not expected to spend her day sacrificing specimens.

The doctor must have slipped a number of things she needed into her purse when she'd gone to the car, because next she produced small petri dishes, forceps, and more. It was a bizarre Mary Poppins-type scenario. *Unless she carried them all the time?*

Joule thought it but didn't want to ask. She watched as Noemi Achebe opened the top of the cup and deftly transferred one bug into a small dish and placed it on the stage of the scope.

"Look," she said. "It's *Karnatakan.*"

Joule and Cage leaned over to look. This scope didn't have a singular ocular piece, but a small screen that let them both look simultaneously.

The mosquito, in death, didn't look so menacing. Its legs were curled. Limp proboscis sitting unused.

Within a few minutes, Joule was in on the game. Wielding the forceps for herself, she placed the analyzed dead mosquito on a page inside a little drawn square, labeled and numbered. While Dr. Achebe took pictures, Joule moved the fresh specimens into petri dishes, handing them off to Cage, who declared that one was *Anopheles* and the other three were *Aedes*, specifically *Karnatakan*.

"Are the swarms more likely a singular kind of mosquito?" Joule asked.

The doctor didn't look up, but she nodded. "They have very short lifespans. So, they most likely travel together in clusters with others from when they first took flight. A swarm is dependent on the eggs laid in a particular location. That means it's most likely a singular type, maybe two." Finally, she looked up at the corner of the room, as if thinking. "Maybe as much as three varieties, depending on the water source. Also, when the eggs in a particular location hatched."

Joule followed along. "So, you could walk into one area, maybe out in a field, and be relatively safe. But then you walk a hundred feet over and step into a whole host of disease-carrying bugs."

"That's what we think." Dr. Achebe was looking down at the paper. All four of the mosquitoes were now laid in their inked squares. Joule had printed the genus and species beside each and now that she knew, she could see a slight difference with her naked eye.

"What's next?" Cage asked.

Joule thought they might grind them up, check their DNA. Do some of the blood tests that Cage sometimes did.

But the doctor shook her head. One by one, she loaded them into separate small petri dishes. She labelled and taped each one closed. "These are going back to the CDC."

She added a sheet with the location and the date and time that they were caught, getting the latter from Cage. With the last thing written, she began gathering up her supplies.

She capped the syringe and dropped in into her purse as though it were a pen. She put the petris into a labeled clear bag, but that went into her purse too. She collapsed the microscope setup and clicked the latches shut, picking it up like a small briefcase.

Joule again thought that Dr. Noemi Achebe had become the weirdest Mary Poppins she'd ever met.

"Thank you so much. You've both been so helpful."

Joule felt her neck jerk back a little bit. *Was that it?* It had originally sounded like they would be collaborating.

The doctor went on. "I have two more sample sites to visit today. I didn't expect you to be home until this evening. It looks like I got lucky and found you at the right time, though."

Had she?

Noemi Achebe held out a business card. "My number is on here. You can call if anything comes up. But if I don't hear from you, I'll get back in touch with you later tonight."

That at least was *something,* Joule thought. But within moments, the woman had thanked them again and then she and her middle-management outfit and almost-too-warm smile were out the door.

Joule looked around the apartment. Aside from the dismantled cardboard and plastic cup contraption, it was almost as though she'd never been here.

With a *did that just happen?* look on her face for the second time today, Joule looked to her brother.

Cage, of course, said, "I need lunch."

Just as Joule was saying, "You know who we need to call."

36

"No, nothing like that," Cage said as Joule made a frantic motion to him. He tapped the phone to put it on speaker and laid it on the table.

His sister was not a fan of speaking on the phone. She made him dial and do all the preliminaries. But now that the conversation was going, she wanted to be part of it, too. "Hi, Dr. Brett. We're both fine."

"That's good to hear. You had me worried."

"We had us worried, too!" she said.

With a motion to his sister to wait a moment, Cage chatted about the job and the weather. They got the same from Dr. Brett, until he rolled around to something bigger. "Laura is sick."

Cage felt the concern pull at his features. "Oh, do you need to go?"

Maybe she needed her husband to deliver soup or Tylenol.

"Not like that. It's more long-term."

"Oh." The word fell out of his mouth without permission as the idea sank in. "How are you holding up?"

The tense feeling spread throughout his body as Cage

thought about the veterinarian. They'd just been there visiting. Laura hadn't been around. Had Dr. Brett known then? Cage didn't ask.

"It's rough, but I'm doing okay." There was a slight pause. Even Joule, who tended to plow ahead, understood to step back and let the doctor fill in the space.

"It feels wrong to be doing okay when Laura needs more. Her sister's coming tomorrow to sit with her through chemo."

"It's cancer?" Joule asked, the obvious conclusion for chemo.

"Multiple sclerosis," Dr. Christian replied.

"I didn't know they did chemo for that."

Cage almost reached out and smacked at his sister for saying that. But the good news was, Dr. Brett already knew Joule. He knew she would be as interested in the treatment as she was sympathetic for his wife. She showed her love for people by learning everything she could about them and what they needed.

The doctor quickly filled them in. "The treatment is kind of new. They've been doing it for a handful of people. It's for more advanced cases, though."

"So, you've known for a while?" This time Joule looked up at Cage right after she asked it. He could see from her expression that she'd come to the same conclusion that he had earlier: that maybe this had been going on when they'd visited.

"Not really. She was initially diagnosed with migraines, and over the course of about the past eight to ten years, they diagnosed her with one or another additional thing. They kept changing the diagnoses and then stacking them. It was only within the past few months that one of the doctors put it all together and realized what was actually happening."

"I'm so sorry," Cage said. "That must be stunning."

Their own problems seemed small now—bug bites, really. Small in the larger scheme of things.

"It's almost a relief because, previously, she just kept racking up new diagnoses. We never knew when the next one would come along. She always had things that her diagnosis didn't explain. This, at least seems to be working." Dr. Brett sounded like he meant what he was saying, and that made Cage feel a little bit better. "The downside is Michelle."

"What's Michelle?" Cage couldn't help but ask. At least it sounded funny to him. Maybe a little levity was needed.

It worked, as Brett chuckled. "Her sister."

"Not a fan, huh?" Joule asked, and Cage felt some of the poison of his helpless sympathy begin to ebb.

"It's what Laura wants. And Michelle is really good. She's an RN. She knows what she's doing, and she takes care of everything. But I can't do anything. I'm just in the way."

Interesting, Cage thought, though it was not the right time to jump into that conversation. Reaching out, he grabbed at his sister's wrist, squeezing as her mouth opened to do exactly what he'd already thought and discarded.

"So, what's going on with you guys?" Dr. Brett asked, turning the conversation away from MS and chemo and missed diagnoses.

A small wave of shame passed over Cage. Aside from when they'd stopped by to see him when they were home, they didn't call unless they needed something. They often contacted him when there was some struggle, and now they'd done it again.

"Actually..." Cage paused, and he could almost hear the veterinarian smile on the other end of the line.

"It's okay, tell me. Michelle's coming tomorrow. I need something to cheer me up."

"Oh, this is not going to cheer you up." Joule added.

"You never know. I like weird things."

They filled him in on what had happened, eliciting such responses as "full systemic anaphylaxis?" and "*Aedes Aegypti*, right?"

The conversation moved rapidly, the targets changing as Dr. Brett easily kept up.

"The CDC thinks it's the food, though," the veterinarian said.

So, he'd already heard something about it. The twins could hear that he'd moved around the house while talking to them. In the background, they heard key clicks as he was looking things up as they went.

On the one hand, it was tempting to tell him they'd already looked at all of it. On the other hand, who knew? Cage stayed quiet. Worst case scenario, Dr. Brett would repeat their work. But if he knew another term, or simply checked it a different way, he might find something helpful.

"Now you're... *what?* collecting samples?"

"We don't even know if we're going into work tomorrow." Joule tipped her head at him, and Cage felt the width of her thoughts.

"I'm not sure we want to," he added as his sister nodded along. If Helio Systems Tech had pulled them off of the bugs, and Dr. Achebe was here, then maybe it was time to step away. *They could stay safe, not get sent out into the fields to collect lizards amid the swarms of mosquitoes*, Cage thought.

"You know," the doctor said, his tone changing, "I'm about useless around here."

Cage felt the offer before it was spoken out loud.

"Do you want another pair of hands?"

Cage hadn't considered it. They'd called the veterinarian to get his take on things, thinking he might have a good idea. They had expected him to maybe give them the life advice their parents no longer dispensed. Cage hadn't expected to lure him to Charleston with their possibly poisonous bugs.

"But what about Laura?" Joule asked.

"She has Michelle."

"We'd love to have you!" Cage blurted out before he thought better of it.

Within a few minutes, it was decided. They made preliminary plans and hung up with the promise of seeing each other tomorrow or the next day.

They called Dr. Achebe to let her know what they'd decided, but the call went to voicemail. Joule—whom Cage had insisted make the call this time—only left her name and said, "Please call us back when you can."

The twins spent their time grabbing dinner and trying to figure out where to put Dr. Brett in the tiny apartment or where else he might stay. They figured out what to say to Dr. Murasawa the next morning—how to tell her they wouldn't be back for a while. Then they waited impatiently for Dr. Achebe to get back in touch.

Two more times, they called but got thrown immediately to voicemail. Still the clock rolled onward. They played a stupid card game three times through, nearly getting into a fight about the rules. But at nine, as Joule gave in and turned on the TV to watch her favorite bad emergency show, she asked Cage the question on both their minds.

"Why haven't we heard from Dr. Achebe?"

37

C age looked up at his sister's frustrated expression, but she only huffed at her lunch and said, "It's weird."

She held the phone in her hand, and he realized she must have called again.

"Is it, though?" he asked. "At least Dr. Brett's getting here this evening."

"The whole thing is weird." Joule almost entirely ignored the upside, though he knew that she, too, was excited about their friend's visit.

They'd called off work for another day, claiming illness. Neither of them was quite ready to pull the trigger and leave the job, but they weren't willing to go back, either.

With both their parents gone, Doctor Brett was about the closest they got to having a parental figure. Their grandparents were stuck in grandparent mode, sending birthday presents and enjoying annual visits, but they didn't parent. They also didn't ever talk about the fact that their own child, the twins' father, had simply disappeared.

Cage wondered if they should tell their grandparents that they'd gotten the death certificate for their dad. They were still in the window where they could claim they were getting around to it, but pretty soon, enough time would pass that it would become obvious they hadn't.

There wasn't space for his thoughts in the tiny room. Then Joule stood up and began pacing, squeezing her phone as if her fist might be strong enough to break it.

"No, it's *weird*," she insisted.

"Dr. Achebe was weird," Cage countered again. "She shows up out of nowhere, with miraculous equipment—"

"And stole our specimens as though they were hers in the first place!" Joule interrupted, her anger clear, though she'd been nice enough at the time.

"So honestly, it's not impressive that she invited us on a date and then stood us up." He shrugged at her. There wasn't much they could do.

"It's not that," his sister insisted. "It's the phone."

Cage wasn't sure if she was making a mystery out of a molehill or what. But she got his attention.

"Her outgoing voicemail changed. I mean, I agree with you, she's not obligated to talk to us again. But I called her once this morning and I got the same message as yesterday. I managed not to call her again until right now."

Cage looked up at the old schoolroom clock that someone had hung in the living room, probably thinking it was "decor." It was 2:30.

He admired his sister's restraint. Joule wasn't known for her patience. "I thought it was going straight to voicemail anyway."

"It was. First it rang through, and I left a message. Then later it said the mailbox was full. Now it doesn't ring at all, just goes straight to the message—"

"So her phone is off?"

Joule shook her head, then changed her mind. "Probably. But the issue is, the *message* is different. Here."

She dialed the number one more time, and Cage thought

that it would be funny if Dr. Achebe answered and asked them to please stop calling her. But if that was a problem, she shouldn't have given them her number. Joule put her phone on speaker and very quickly it transferred over to the message.

"You have reached Doctor Noemi Achebe. I'm working on a very important project and I've made strides!" There was a slight pause, then she repeated the last word with more stress: *"Strides."*

Cage felt his facial features twist. *That was odd.* But Joule motioned for him to keep listening.

"I think I found the next breakthrough. And I'm so excited to tell you about it. So call me or... Track. Me. Down... whenever you get this message—"

It cut off as though she'd run out of time and didn't have a chance to re-record it. The words were strange, too, with her pointed emphasis on *Track me down.*

"What did it say before?" Cage asked.

"Hi, this is Dr. Noemi Achebe. Please leave your name and number and a brief message and I'll call you back." Joule's voice was almost mechanical sounding in her impression of the scientist. "It sounded clinical."

"She changed it when?" Cage asked. Joule was right, and he didn't like any of this.

"Sometime between nine this morning and now."

"Did you leave a message?"

"I can't. The voicemail is still full. It cuts you off and hangs up on you." Joule paused for a moment, her hands on the back of one of the dining chairs as though to brace herself. "Should we go *track her down*?"

"No." Cage's answer was quick and sharp. "That can't be for us."

"She said she found something!"

"Again, probably not for us." Creepy CDC Mary Poppins—which they'd taken to calling her—had packed her toys and left. "She didn't even call us when she was supposed to, so why would she leave a cryptic message for us?"

"How do we find her, anyway?"

Cage didn't like where his sister was going with this. "The fact that we don't even understand the message, I think indicates that we shouldn't be doing it."

But Joule had different ideas. She was tapping at her phone and then holding it to her ear. Only then did he realize she'd dialed someone. Whoever it was, she'd made the decision without his input, and he was left to sit on the sidelines and wait and see what she said.

What she said was "Pharmacology," stumping him. After a moment's wait, she said, "*Research* pharmacology."

He realized her exceptional memory was letting her walk the same path and get to whomever she'd talked to the first time she called to confirm Dr. Achebe's employment. He shot her a look that asked, *What are you doing?*

Joule made it clear, putting the phone on speaker and setting it in between them so he could follow along.

The voice came on the line, female and competent and clear. "This is Dr. Helenie Warren. You've reached research entomology and pharmacology. How can I help you?"

Joule almost grinned. Whatever this was, it was what she'd wanted.

"Hello. This is Joule Mazur again—"

"Oh, hello!"

The sudden recognition was not what either of the twins had been expecting. Joules' mouth was still moving, as if she was just continuing the sentence she'd planned out. The voice changed. "We got your clearances started. Did Noemi reach back out to you?"

"Well, that's what we're calling about," Joule said, "and just so you know, you're on speaker with both me and my brother Cage."

"Cage? Oh yes! I'm sorry I couldn't talk yesterday. So, what did Noemi tell you?"

His sister offered a brief rundown, but that was when the conversation changed.

"She didn't tell us she had samples." The confusion in Dr. Warren's voice was clear.

"She had four. One *Anopheles* and three *Aedes Karnatakan*. She took them with her when she left here," Cage explained, but now he was getting confused, too. Dr. Achebe had said the samples were going to the CDC, but Dr. Warren was at the CDC …

"When was that?" Dr. Warren's voice told him they were all confused, and the person who could untangle this mystery wasn't reachable.

"Yesterday…. Just after noon," Joule said.

The pause in the conversation told Cage that Joule was right. Something was very wrong with Dr. Noemi Achebe.

38

E verything in Joule stilled at Helenie Warren's words.
Joule had suspected something was off, but she
hadn't quite expected this. She'd figured calling the
CDC would clear everything up. But this was only making it
worse.

Joule had to ask, "She hasn't checked in with you since
yesterday?"

"No, and we thought it was strange. But honestly, we're
swamped. The number of deaths has our particular lab
pushing the clock day and night." Dr. Warren sounded almost
as if she hadn't realized it was already the next day.

"Her voicemail changed today. Why?" Joule threw the next
wrench into the fray. The break of yet another stretch of silence
told her more than she'd wanted to know. "I can hang up so you
can call her."

"No, please just hold on. I'm on the work line. Let me grab
my cell and call her there."

The twins sat almost silently, looking at each other,
attempting to communicate with only their expressions. *Aside*

from the fact that it was all a mess, they were doing a piss poor job,
Joule thought.

Maybe, just maybe, Dr. Achebe would answer for her
friend... or her colleague, and it would all be a worry for nothing. So, the twins waited while Helenie Warren listened to Dr.
Achebe's voice message. It became clear though, just from the
small noises on the other end of the line, that Helenie Warren
thought the same thing they did.

"That is weird."

"It's not just weird," Joule said, figuring if she was in for a
penny, she was in for a pound. "It sounds *directed*. Maybe to
you, or someone else there at the lab. It sounds like a missive to
track her down."

"It does sound that way..." The words trailed off and Joule
appreciated that she could almost hear the woman thinking.
"But honestly, I don't know who it would specifically be
directed at. We worked together and I like her but, I mean,
we're not....um..."

"*Outside of work* friends?" Cage asked.

"Exactly. So, I have a really hard time imagining that was
left for *me*. Still."

"Should we get in touch with her other friends?" At least
Cage was on board now. Joule had been the only one who'd
thought the whole thing was bizarre and that it was their
problem.

"I don't know that she had any. I mean, I don't know who
they are. However—hold on." She must have put her hand over
the receiver of some old-fashioned phone system. "Pablo?
Chuck?"

Whatever she was covering, it didn't quite work. So, while
the twins couldn't distinguish the individual words, it was clear
the doctor was issuing instructions to the two men.

Joule didn't like this. She was only halfway part of the
conversation. Then again, maybe Cage was right and that was

all that she needed to be. This wasn't her boss, and she didn't work for the CDC. They'd called in and alerted the staff to the problem. Maybe they were done here. They would pick up Dr. Brett at the airport this evening and go on their own way.

"Can we text you at this number?" the doctor asked, the words rapid and sharp, as though they were important.

"Yes. And my brother..." She rattled off his number, too.

"Perfect. We'll message both of you.'

"I don't understand." *Was Dr. Warren hanging up?* But it seemed she wasn't. Both Joule's and her brother's phone pinged simultaneously with a message just a moment later. She looked down at the unknown number.

"That was you?"

"It was Chuck. Hold on. Here's my number." The researcher rattled it off almost faster than Cage could pick up his own phone and punch the numbers in.

"Can you repeat that? Just to be sure?" Joule asked. With the current concerns about Dr. Achebe, who apparently had not answered for her coworker, Joule wanted direct ways to get in touch with everyone at the CDC that she could muster.

"It's Helenie—H-E-L-E-N-I-E—Warren." And she spit out the number again, with Cage nodding indicating he had actually gotten all of it the first time.

"Okay, so there's a link. I'll be honest, I'm a little suspicious of strange links sent by unknown numbers."

That at least elicited a small chuckle. "Yes. That was Chuck."

"It's a map," Cage told her. He' d already clicked it.

"What?"

Joule didn't touch her phone, not wanting to inadvertently disconnect the call with a person who seemed far more helpful than Dr. Achebe herself. So she looked over as Cage pushed his into the space between them. A map with a purple line strung its way through Charleston.

"Hold on," Joule said, her brain catching on something disturbing. Reaching down, she expanded the view on her brother's phone. She thought she'd recognized at least one of the locations. And when she put her finger on it, she looked pointedly to her brother—who said out loud what she'd been keeping quiet.

"The map line goes *directly by our apartment*."

"Yes. That's where Noemi has been in the past forty-eight. Noemi and Chuck set up trackers. And that's her phone."

"Eleven thirty-seven a.m. Eastern time!" a voice came from the background.

Joule became even more confused. Why was someone rattling off the time? The *wrong* time? It was well past two. "What?"

"That's when her phone shut off. It looks like it ran out of battery."

Shitmonkeys, Joule thought. "This morning?"

"Yes."

Just a few hours ago. Joule didn't like the creeping sensation of dread forming in her chest. "Can you send someone to find her?"

Who knew where she was now? They only knew that the last ping from Noemi Achebe's phone looked like it was out in the middle of nowhere.

"We can," Dr. Warren assured them. However, as Joule let out her breath, Helenie Warren added, "But we're in Atlanta. We're hours away."

Was that a hint to ask them if they could do it? Dr. Warren didn't come right out with it, and Joule wasn't quite ready to offer.

"It's very bizarre," Cage said, holding his hand up as if to stop her. Her own brain was still untangling everything they'd been handed. "Should we all just keep trying to get in touch with her?"

He wasn't offering, either.

"Definitely. Hopefully, she'll get her phone recharged soon."

If the researcher had hoped they would offer, she wasn't going to push it further. The conversation paused and once again, Joule thought she wasn't quite ready to do anything more. Not after the way Dr. Achebe had come to their home then disappeared with their samples.

When nothing more was added into the empty space, Dr. Warren added, "We'll get right on this. The earliest I think somebody can make it there is tomorrow morning, but we'll keep you posted. Thank you for letting us know. Like I said, we're snowed here. We had no idea no one could get a hold of her."

"We're happy to help," Cage said. And after a few more moments, they signed off.

Joule stared at Cage.

"At least we have a direct number now for Dr. Warren," he said. "And Chuck, too." Cage shrugged as if to say, "at least it's something."

But what even *was* that something? She didn't know.

Then Cage started thinking out loud. "They have a record of the entire path of where she went. And even knew that her battery had died."

Joule thought it was odd, but not quite worthy of the way her brother was reacting. "So? A lot of parenting tracking apps have that kind of thing. It's relatively easy to do."

"It's not the tech that's bugging me," Cage said. "It's the fact that they were monitoring an adult—an MD PhD from the CDC."

Joule almost laughed that she fully understood that gobbledygook string of letters he'd rattled off. But he was right, and she didn't like where that led either.

Cage pushed further. "You and I are our only family members left, and I'm not tracking *you* to that extent."

That was true. "I wouldn't agree to it."

"Exactly."

She caught on then.

Cage stood up, his hands pressing down on the flimsy dining table. He stared at her until she asked the right question.

"So, what was Dr. Achebe doing that she thought someone needed to keep tabs on her like that?"

39

"It's probably not a location of where she *is*, it's just where she *was*," Cage argued. "It's just where her phone died."

He thought they'd agreed to let the CDC handle this, but Joule was pushing hard. It was really his own fault. She'd pretty much let it go until he brought up the idea that the doctor was allowing her colleagues to track her every move.

"It's a place to start, and we know exactly where to go." Joule wasn't going to let go. But that shouldn't surprise him. He didn't like it, but he had to push back just as hard.

"It's in the middle of nowhere." Then he added, "There will likely be bugs."

Joule had seen the map. The area where Dr. Achebe's tracker line ended was rural, with several small spots of water nearby. In the Carolina lowlands, the water often formed standing puddles with perfectly still surfaces—wonderful for breeding mosquitoes. So much so that while he and Joule had only intended to be here for the summer, and the duration of the job, they'd figured that they would encounter the mosquitoes for the duration of their stay.

He'd since heard one of the locals say that the biting bugs

were a year-round issue here. He was not eager to go out even closer to their breeding grounds during the worst months.

Joule just stared at him. "She came to our house. She took our samples. Her phone battery died at 11:30."

"Yes, we already knew that." *He was going to lose this fight, wasn't he?*

He and his sister were both smart, but Joule was wily.

"Her calls started going directly to voicemail yesterday afternoon."

So? He tried to explain that in a rational way. "Maybe she'd already switched her settings or something by then. Or she hung up on you when she saw you calling."

Joule frowned at him, but she was considering this. Maybe he'd scored enough of a point that they could get out of this. But he knew his sister, and the answer was, probably not.

"Call me," she demanded.

"What?"

"Call me." Though this second time her tone was a little more cheery, Cage could still hear the demand behind it.

With another deep sigh and the feeling that he was about to lose this argument for good, he picked up his phone and dialed her. It rang on his end, once, then twice... even though Joule was intently watching the screen and hung up on him immediately as she saw her screen light up.

"Her phone didn't even ring for me, yet mine rang for you." She said this as though it should mean something.

"It didn't ring while it was connecting for me yesterday or again this morning. Then it didn't. Which means something had been off on Dr. Noemi Achebe's phone yesterday afternoon. And probably not just a silent ringer." Joule stood still, having made her case.

He countered with the only thing he had. "The CDC will be here tomorrow."

"Yes. And whatever they find, it'll be theirs. We won't even know what that was."

Cage didn't want to know. Well, he *did*, but he not enough to pay the price to find out.

"Does she even know she was being tracked?" Joule asked suddenly.

Cage didn't have answers for that one, either.

His sister wasn't done. Her brain was racing and so was her mouth. "Who carries all of that in their purse?"

He guessed he could admit it was weird. "I mean, I wouldn't do it."

"You rarely carry a purse," Joule pointed out, almost as if she was arguing his side.

He protested again. After the bites of yesterday morning—though some were admittedly his own fault—he didn't feel like leaving the house. "We can't go do this. Dr. Brett gets in tonight."

"You're right. We have limited time." But she wasn't conceding. "We should get ready now, so we can make sure we're back in time. Keep the trip short."

Cage found himself a short while later, heading out the door, doused in bug spray, trailing his sister. Joule hadn't quite blackmailed him, but she had mentioned the possibility of going on her own if he didn't want to come. It was close enough.

So, he found himself driving, with Joule navigating, or "naggrivating" as she'd named it when they were little. She'd called it that since their parents often snipped at each other on road trips and disagreed about which route to take.

Joule followed Dr. Achebe's tracker data on her phone as she led them straight out of town, and then commented, "Here. We'll pick up the doctor's trail here."

Cage made turns where Joule directed, and they followed exactly where Noemi Achebe had gone.

"Is there a shorter path?" They were winding their way over

God knew where. But Cage couldn't see the map. He was just taking the turns as he was told.

"I don't think so. The roads out here don't all line up."

Cage had noticed. They weren't in the city anymore. The houses had grown farther and farther apart. Some were newer and huge, some older and small, and some in between. They passed one small, dilapidated house that was doubling as a junkyard for old washing machines. Someone either had a penchant for rusty machinery or somehow had believed they could fix them all. A far too dingy, but hopeful, sign in the front yard read, "washing machines for sale."

"Oh shit," his sister said, sounding frustrated. "I don't think there's a road up here. I think she started going on foot. Because it's in between these two farms."

"Oh, no." Cage shook his head. "Just no."

"What? You didn't think we'd be able to drive to exactly where she went, did you?"

He hadn't thought about it at all. He thought they would come out here, find nothing, then leave. It's not like a grown woman would just drop dead with her cell phone in her hand in the middle of nowhere. But no, he had not really considered that they would need to trespass on someone's private property.

He turned his head and looked at the house beside him. Something said these people would likely be the kind who would protect their tall grasses and occasional cows with guns. He hadn't told Joule, but he'd brought his. It wasn't as if she could conceal her bow and arrow. But he'd packed his own bag with extra sunscreen, extra bug spray, a little bottle of antihistamines, and cold waters. All of those, his sister knew about.

"Here," she said. "Turn off here."

But he hadn't told her about the gun. He didn't like the feeling that having it gave him, and he liked the feeling even less when she pointed to the side of the road.

"Look, Cage. That's her car."

40

J oule felt her heart rate kick up. She'd thought all along that Cage, in his skepticism, would ultimately be right. She'd just wanted to know what happened. She just wanted to check the box and go home—she wouldn't sleep without it. She needed to know that Dr. Achebe hadn't lain injured in a field without help overnight. Joule had needed this, despite the fact that she was not the woman's biggest fan.

Now, seeing the car, she felt her pulse thrum and her chest squeeze. It was clear she wasn't going to check this box easily.

"How do you know it's her car?" her brother asked.

"Remember, I looked out the window. I saw her rummaging in the trunk."

"It's a pretty common-looking model." He sounded skeptical. Joule disagreed, but she loved him for it.

The brown Toyota Corolla practically screamed *researcher car,* Joule thought. Still, she agreed with him. "It's true. It's an older model. But it looks just like what she drove to our apartment, and it's exactly here."

It was parked literally ten feet before the tracking line

turned and headed across the open field to their right. Cage drove past the car.

"What are you doing? We have to turn around."

"I wasn't ready to park." He did slow down and scan the area.

Joule looked back and forth. It was a rural road, two lanes, homes with yards or fields with fences lined either side of the road. Dr. Achebe had taken one of the few places that a car could park safely on the side.

"I don't want to park directly behind her." Cage talked through his decision. Joule appreciated it. "I mean, it's possible she came out and went camping. She was just collecting her research samples and her battery went dead."

That was when Joule raised her eyebrows at her brother. He was spinning quite the story, though she had to grant that it was possible. A researcher checking samples might very well stay out overnight. Her thoughts took a different turn. "Are there different mosquitoes out in the evening than in the day?"

He shrugged. "Like I know?"

"I'm asking David." She quickly tapped on the phone. Her brother still looked at her as if she were absolutely bonkers, then he dropped it.

"I don't want to park directly behind her," Cage repeated. "If she's here and if she's fine and she leaves or comes back while we're back there looking for her, I don't want her to come out and find our car bumper-to-bumper with hers."

"Well, in that case, we just might pass her on the way back," Joule offered.

"That would be lovely," her brother argued, but he obviously didn't think that was the most likely scenario, because he used a nearby gravel driveway and did a quick three-point turn. He passed Dr. Achebe's car and stopped about twenty to thirty feet away.

Though Joule thought he could get closer, she'd argued about enough already. She was unbuckling her seatbelt and putting her backpack on when his hand shot out to grab her arm. "We need a plan."

She didn't quite agree. They would just walk in and look around. That was the plan. But her brother shook his head. "No, I didn't want to come out here. I agreed to come out here with you. I don't like this."

She had to stop then and really take stock. "Do you have a bad feeling about it?"

He sighed and let his head fall back against the headrest. "I've had one since she showed up yesterday morning. The phone call today didn't make it any better."

"We'll be careful," she promised, but his words sobered her.

"We have to be. And something else: Yesterday, I got bit going out and collecting those mosquitoes."

"I know." *What was his point?*

"I was covered in bug spray, Joule, when it happened. And I still got bit! That was on *our front doorstep* in the middle of our concrete parking lot, with a few patches of green behind it."

She got it then. Their front door should have been relatively low-risk. He'd been slathered in two kinds of bug repellent, yet one of insects had still gotten through. It occurred to her then... "You also managed to scoop up four of them."

This time it was he who looked at her like she was a fool.

"You didn't repel enough to keep them beyond arm's reach," she pointed out. "You got close enough to scoop a small handful."

"Shit."

Revelations were not her thing. She was not a fan.

Then he told her about the gun. If his words and his expression hadn't made it clear to her before just how much he didn't like this, that would have done it.

But she was his twin. She was his only remaining family. At least it all made sense to her. Now she felt bad about goading him into coming out. She'd wanted it and she'd manipulated him to make it happen.

"Cage, I'm sorry. We can turn around and go home if you want. We've seen her car. I can even call the CDC right now."

He started to think for a moment, but Joule knew the right thing to do. He didn't want to be here so much that he'd thought he might need the gun.

If she was smart, she would follow his lead. He started to reach for the door handle, but she shook her head, still scrolling through her phone and pulling out the number.

The voice answered immediately. "This is Dr. Helenie Warren."

"Hello. It's Joule Mazur again." She rattled off where they were.

Dr. Warren's voice perked up when she heard that it was Joule. "I didn't expect to hear from you again so soon."

"We followed the map."

"What?" Dr. Warren sounded confused.

"You sent us the map the tracker provided. Or Chuck did." She paused as she heard Dr. Warren catch up. Then she added. "We followed it. We're out in the middle of nowhere, well, in between two farms. It looks like she trespassed."

"I doubt she would have done that," Dr. Warren said. "I'm sure she would have gotten permission from the homeowner."

"Did you find out where this is?" Joule asked. There was a pause and Joule turned to look at her brother. She held the phone between them on speaker, though she hadn't mentioned that part to Dr. Warren.

"She told us she was collecting samples from sites where there'd been incidents," the researcher filled in.

"Was there an incident out here?" Joule's eyes flicked across the open field to the line of trees separating the two farms and as far back as she could see, where they merged into a stand of woods.

"No, not that I know of," Dr. Warren conceded.

"So, you have no idea why she was cut here?"

There was a pause from the other end of the line, and Joule had her answer.

41

"This worries me. I'm going to call your local police."
Helenie Warren's voice matched the words.

"I think there might not be police services out here," Joule said, looking around as though she might see an officer. "Probably a sheriff.... They might not even have 9-1-1 service."

"It sounds like she's still out there then. A dead battery, maybe a broken ankle?...Hold on a minute." Helenie covered her mouthpiece with her hand again, and again only succeeded in slightly muffling the sounds.

Joule held the phone over the center console between the seats as she and Cage waited an interminable amount of time. Someone in the background—maybe Chuck, maybe Pablo—was getting hooked through to the sheriff's office.

Sure enough, when the researcher came back on, she didn't sound happy. "It's going to be an hour or more before the sheriff can get a deputy out there."

"Why?" The woman was likely in danger. It was terrifying that no one would come faster than that.

"She's a grown adult. There's no official missing person's

report. There's no evidence of foul play or anything... or is there?"

This time it was Joule who said, "Hold on!"

Cage was already jumping out of the car, and she followed him down the street. Joule knew her breath was huffing over the phone line, but she didn't care. They inspected the brown Toyota as best they could, looking in all the windows and trying the door latches, but nothing opened.

"No, no sign of struggle at her car," Joule reported. But as she said it, Cage rolled his eyes at her.

When she quietly shook her head that she didn't understand, he wiggled his fingers and then waved his open palms toward the car, indicating they had just left their fingerprints over all over what might be a crime scene.

"She probably went in and twisted her ankle. She's probably just sitting out there waiting for help with a dead phone." Dr. Warren's scenario sounded innocuous enough.

Then Joule looked over the top of the car at her brother, who was shaking his head. They would never leave a person in distress, and she couldn't imagine being stuck out there all day like that. She knew Cage wouldn't do it either, no matter how much he hated the situation.

"What are the time frames on this? When did she arrive out here?" Joule asked, only to be told to hold on again.

This time, they waited on the side of the road. Motioning to her brother to follow, Joule wandered further down until she was standing at the point where the purple line on her phone took a sharp right into the field.

A small gap exposed broken barbed wire and told her this was where Dr. Achebe had gone through.

"It looks like she parked around 7 a.m." Dr. Warren came back on the line. "But her phone reached that last position much later."

And died at 11:37. A quick glance to her brother told Joule he was coming to the same conclusions, and none of them good.

"We'll go look for her," Joule told Dr. Warren.

The researcher didn't even give lip service to trying to stop them. She just asked, "How is your phone battery?"

That was a very important question, one that she hadn't thought to ask. "Eighty-three percent."

"Ninety-two percent on mine," her brother added, "and I have a back-up battery."

"And there's two of you." Dr. Warren let out a sigh of relief that was audible over the phone. "Chuck has a flight up there tonight. We are sending him, but I can't thank you enough for doing this. Please keep me posted."

Joule was opening her mouth to reply when Helenie Warren filled in, "And yes, the sheriff still has someone coming out. Is there any way to leave markers to follow if the deputy gets there before an hour?"

"I have colored tape with me." Joule had packed everything she thought they might need. The map showed they'd be out in the middle of nowhere.

"Seriously?"

"We did some... hunting... when we were in high school.... In the woods."

"Well then, you may be better equipped than the sheriff." Another pause, then, "Noemi said she'd found you guys yesterday around noon. It was the last time she checked in. She said we would like you."

That, at least, made Joule smile. Her father had always told her that somewhere in the world were people who would appreciate her particular brand of crazy. It felt good to find another one.

Hanging up with the CDC researcher, she slid sideways through the break in the fence. Her brother slipped carefully through behind her, and they started to follow the purple line on foot.

Thirty or forty feet later, he asked, "You know what this means, right?"

She didn't.

"Dr. Achebe didn't get permission. You don't go knock on the front door, and then break through the fence."

Shit, Joule thought, looking at the map again. The doctor's phone had not been carried to the front door of the farmhouse. The building was far enough back that the tracker would have shown that. They were officially trespassing.

Stopping, Joule turned around and scanned the area. The twins had a brief discussion of the pros and cons of knocking on the door. The farmer might insist on following them, or tell them no. He could grab a shotgun and tail them.

"I don't see cars in the driveway," she commented, as though that might mean no one was home.

"There are four barns and a garage," Cage pointed out, as if to say *why would they leave their cars out?* "The grass is relatively tall. And it's now the middle of the day." He looked up at a bright sun and peeled his jacket, tying it around his waist, indicating just how hot and muggy it was.

Cage did not get warm easily.

"We're covered in bug spray. We're here. It's possible she's hurt and just needs a hand getting out." Joule didn't know if she was arguing the points to her brother or to herself.

"And I've got my gun," he added, as if that were anywhere near the same argument. She accepted it.

Ten minutes later, they'd crunched their way across the grass, tracing the tree line, which Joule hoped kept them hidden from anyone who's land they were illegally traipsing on.

They entered the stand of trees and she saw that the woods went far back. Maybe it was even the edge of a state or national park. Ten minutes after that, she checked the phone map again, noting that she was getting less and less signal as they moved.

"We're not even a third of the way," Joule commented, not liking the result.

Cage checked the time. "It should get dark before Dr. Brett gets in." Neither of them wanted to be out here after the sun set. "We're going to have to pick up the pace."

Joule had pulled her roll of thin, pink marking tape from her bag and left her third streamer tied to a low branch. The sunlight only cut through the leaf cover infrequently and the temperature must have dropped. Hopefully, so had the amount of bugs.

They walked farther in silence and Joule pulled out a pack of crackers, offering one to Cage, which he took, and a second which he refused. The warmer blooded of the two, she'd always assumed she needed more energy. She ate the rest of them down with the bottle of water as she went.

The going was a little harder than they expected. Their phones periodically lost signal and Joule eventually screen-shotted the map so they could follow along when they lost service. She made Cage text Dr. Warren when their signal popped up again briefly, letting the CDC team know where they were and that they hadn't found Dr. Achebe yet.

"We're not going to get to go home before we go to the airport," Cage said, and she could practically see him calculating the time. But she didn't argue. He was right.

Five minutes later, she put another piece of pink tape on a passing tree and told him, "We're very close."

His hand went out across the front of her, as if that could hold her back. But it did effectively stop her. "Do you smell something?"

Joule did. And it wasn't good.

42

"Is that—" Joule was asking as Cage held his hand out to stop her.

Whether he thought there was danger and she needed to stay quiet, or if he just didn't want her to say the words, he didn't quite know. Slowly, he reached into the bag he carried and pulled out the gun.

For a moment, he squeezed his eyes shut, not liking any of this, but then he did what he had to. He racked the slide and chambered a bullet. He'd just alerted anyone nearby that he was carrying and loaded. He'd either just made them run away, or he changed what could have been a friendly exchange into a gunfight.

Cage had no idea right now which one he'd done.

Joule took another bold step forward, her heel catching a twig that cracked loud now in the silence their own quiet had carved out. Luckily, birds still chirped, and he took that as a welcome sign. It was worse when the wildlife all disappeared.

Looking to his sister for a moment, Cage started moving forward softly. But there were no call-outs from anyone in the brush and no noises that made him think someone was just beyond where they could see. So, he figured he'd give it a shot. He yelled, "Dr. Achebe! Dr. Achebe!"

No answer came, only a few chirps from birds and a rustle a short distance away that let him know he'd scared something smaller than himself. It was close enough that he felt he should have been able to see whatever it was, but he couldn't.

Was it better or worse that no one answered? He didn't know.

Joule held her phone up, her finger tapping at the purple line to let him know they'd reached the end of it.

"Dr. Achebe's phone should be right here," he whispered, though Cage suspected they'd find much more than that. The smell got stronger as they got closer. Though it wasn't overwhelming, he stepped forward through the trees. This time, as he turned a corner in the trail, he saw something lying sideways across the trail.

A small bird had landed on it and began to peck. His stomach rolled again.

Joule seemed to feel nothing of this sort though, even though she'd just seen the same thing. Instead of stopping, she picked up her pace. There was nothing he could do but follow.

In a few moments, they stood over Noemi Achebe's body, her shiny dark skin now dull and waxy. Her brown eyes were whitened and blank. Her jaw hung slack, neat rows of teeth showing. Her button-down shirt had been traded for a long-sleeved but lightweight, white T-shirt. Her flats had been traded for sneakers, but for being dead, she looked much the same. Her head was rolled to the side, her hand lying limp, palm up, as though she had been laid out this way.

Cage turned away. He was the biologist. He could probably much better explain what was going on here than his sister could. However, she was the one who was able to look at it with a clinical eye. "We're past the last signal point of the phone."

He didn't respond. Old memories surfaced in an unexpected rush. He had seen his own mother after she'd died a gruesome death. That had elicited a wholly different reaction. This was outdoors; he was in the woods. He told himself it was a different situation and that he was fine. The bird that sat on the body pecking at it had flown off as they approached. Small spots of red and pink and white showed at various points on the corpse where rodents or birds had ventured to have a go at it.

He looked first for obvious signs of allergy but found none.

"I don't see any welts," his sister commented, obviously thinking along the same track as he did.

It made sense to think she'd died of an allergic reaction, didn't it?

"Her lips aren't blue," Joule added.

"Actually, on people with darker skin, lips turning blue isn't the hallmark. We need to check her gums."

Joule looked up at him, her own lips pulled tightly, eyes staring sharply. It was clear she was not willing to check the gums of a dead woman. Neither was he. So he added, "No, I don't see any welts either."

Even as he looked at the dark skin of the researcher, he realized he needed to look at his own. Had he been bitten while he was out here? He'd been so tense, he didn't know if he would feel it.

They were back in the cover of trees. Were there standing puddles back here? He didn't know, but he heard the buzz and hum. The woods were full of insects. Quickly, he inspected his arms and the exposed skin on his legs. Lastly, he ran his hand along his neck where he couldn't see.

"You're clear," Joule said without being asked. Then she turned her head away from him, exposing the back of her own neck to him. Her hair was pulled up into a ponytail. Maybe it would have been better if she had left it down. *Too late now.*

"You're good," he said.

In unison, they turned back to the body.

The path was narrow and with Dr. Achebe's body crossing it, they couldn't go any further. They would have to step over her, and Cage wasn't willing to do that. He didn't believe in zombies, but he got a lot closer to it when there was a body in front of him.

As he watched, Joule swung her backpack off her shoulder and plucked out the spray bottle before liberally covering herself in bug repellent one more time. Without a word, she handed the small container to him, and he figured it was a good idea. But only as she disappeared into the trees did he realize that she'd had a further purpose.

Staying back from the body, she picked her way through the dense underbrush off the trail. A few times the trees and scrub were thick enough that she almost disappeared from view. Just the corner of her backpack or a rainbow charm she had on it let him know she was still there, moving slowly along.

"I'm not getting close," she told him. "Not stepping into a crime scene!"

Was it a crime scene? He didn't know.

As she merged back onto the path on the other side of the body, Cage held his phone up. There was very little signal here. The bar had blinked off and on as they were traipsing in here, just enough for Joule to have reported in once in a while. It was enough to get them to this spot, but not enough to send anything out now. He wrote a text and hit send but didn't try to attach a picture. After watching the phone attempt to do its job for a few seconds, he gave up. It would send when it sent.

Still, he reached out and snapped a few pictures—of the body, of the area. They'd have to report this—

"Cage?" Joule's voice was full of worry.

"Take a picture," he told her, not meaning to sound so crass, but he wasn't in any position to correct himself or be more polite. He was standing over the dead body of a woman he'd met only yesterday. "We have to call this in."

Joule held her own phone out at arm's length, as though she didn't want to get too close. She was staying several feet back, and constantly looking down at her feet as though there were some invisible line she wouldn't cross. He could hear her sucking in a breath. Whatever she'd seen on the other side, it disturbed her.

"Look for her purse and her phone," he told his sister, wondering what was bothering her now. She hadn't seemed affected at all when they'd first spotted the dead body.

"Cage, wait!...Cage!"

He saw the purse just then. The brown leather blended in with the woods, but the shiny hardware had glinted and caught his eye. His sister's voice tugged at him again.

"Come back here!"

He stood and turned around, having a straight shot through the trees to see the worried look on his sister's face.

"We didn't see it from that side."

Of course, they hadn't. *Was she being stupid?*

She wasn't.

"Cage, from back here, I can see that her head is blown open. She was shot."

43

Cage's brain scrambled as he tried to untangle what his sister had just said.

The body looked *laid out*. Was that because it had actually *been* laid here?

Joule was working her way back to his side of the trail, holding her phone up, trying to get a signal. He hated that the move reminded him of Florida and everyone trying to get signal to save Jeff's then Clara's lives.

But his sister wasn't being melancholic, she was being practical. "We need to call 9-1-1."

Cage shook his head. "There's no way to get a call out here and the sheriff is already on his way."

"In an hour or more…" His sister looked at him pointedly. "Do we just leave and let the deputies find this?"

Cage fought the urge to grab the gun in both hands, take a sturdy stance, and turn a slow circle, ready to shoot at anything. But they'd been out here poking around for a while now, and no one but the bird had said anything. He tried to think reasonably. "Her phone died at 11:37. Hours ago."

It seemed whoever had killed Dr. Achebe was long gone,

but it didn't stop the hammering of his pulse or the roiling in his stomach.

"It's a crime scene," Joule said. "We shouldn't touch anything. We need to head back out and find a signal."

She was right. The sheriff's office thought they were checking out a possible missing adult and a dead phone. Not a homicide.

Cage debated. "What's our best option here? If we leave her and we don't touch the scene, what happens if someone comes back?"

That would ruin everything, and all they would have to give the sheriff was pictures.

Joule tipped her head, thinking. "One of us stays and one of us goes until we get signal."

A visceral twist almost took him down. His body shouted "No!" They couldn't split up, but he tried to speak it reasonably. "We only have one gun. We have to stay together."

Joule nodded emphatically. Maybe she'd just been tossing ideas around, not actually suggesting they do that. They'd learned before, the hard way, that splitting up was dangerous. He was absolutely unwilling to do it now.

He'd fought her about coming out here and he'd fought her in the past on other topics. He was glad he didn't have to fight his sister on this one.

"I guess we take a shit ton of pictures, and we walk away." Joule put her hands on her hips and surveyed the scene as though it were a dirty kitchen and not the body of someone they somewhat knew. "As soon as we get signal, we call the sheriff and see what they say to do."

Though he was nodding along, Cage added, "I found her purse. Do we take it with us?"

Joule frowned again, one hand still on her hip. She faced him, her back to the body that was already starting to smell. The weather was so warm, Dr. Achebe was probably fully heading into decomposition. "If we take it, we tamper with evidence…"

Before he could even answer, she offered her own counter-point. "If we don't take it and someone comes back, all the evidence is missing."

He hated this. He wanted to get out of here now. He also wanted to do the right thing. Dr. Noemi Achebe needed some level of justice. Of that much, he was certain. But he wanted his sister's opinion, too. They always worked better together. "Come look at her purse with me. Then we'll decide."

Though he didn't want to stay any longer than necessary—and he didn't want to explain it to an officer later—together, they stepped off the path again. Leading her over to where the purse was tipped sideways, he watched as Joule took more than a dozen pictures before turning to scan through the trees. She stepped away.

Cage was walking in short circle around it, not quite sure what she was doing until she came back with a stick. Pushing the tip of the stick into the open zipper at the top of the purse, she pried at it, tipping it upright and letting them peer inside.

"Here." She held out another sturdy piece of wood to him and said, "Help me."

She held the bag precariously upright and open as Cage used the second stick to poke around. The bag was simply an open cavern, not the complex accordion of pockets and zippers his mother had favored. Two pockets were sewn into one inside lining, but they didn't close, and he was able to easily look inside without tampering with the evidence too much… he thought.

Joule frowned and looked up at him. If she was upset by the smell, or the fact that they were standing so close to a dead body, she didn't show it. She was concerned about something else. "No cell phone."

"Look at this..." he said, using the stick carefully on a small, gray plastic container. "An EpiPen."

He flipped it over and almost jolted backward. "It's used!"

"Why would she be carrying a used EpiPen?"

He shook his head as if to say he didn't know, but maybe he did. He tugged at the thought, talking it out. "I would think she would carry a full one. So, she probably used it. If she came out here, she got bitten..."

"If she used it, then that means she had a reaction." Joule finished the thought, her face rolling through one emotion after another, her expressive features conveying everything he felt. He wondered if he looked the same.

"So, she got bitten and had a reaction—" He stopped himself there. He was missing something.

Joule looked down into the bag again, taking his stick from him and pushing things around while still holding it open with the other stick. "There. A small vial of antihistamines."

"She would have taken those first," he agreed. "So, they must not have worked."

"Then she used the EpiPen, and it didn't work, either."

It was getting stranger and stranger, Cage thought. His arm began to itch. He reached down to scratch, grateful to see no changes in his skin. It was just psychological, or else the welts hadn't risen yet, but there was nothing visible there. He pulled his other hand back, telling himself he didn't itch and there was no need to scratch.

The story still didn't add up. "She didn't die from the reaction. She was shot in the head. So, it *did* work."

Looking down into the purse again, he watched as Joule continued to stir the contents. "Oh my God. There are two full syringes in here."

He wanted to say, who carried syringes, but the answer was clear: Noemi Achebe did.

"Is one of them from whatever she used on the mosquitoes yesterday morning?"

"It doesn't look like it. There's a third one. ... It's empty."

Taking the stick back from her, he continued to poke around, exposing one of the full syringes. "It looks like a pale yellow liquid... hold on."

Grabbing his phone with his free hand, he used the flashlight to aim down into the dark recesses of the bag. "It's actually almost clear. The same in both. And the used one."

"Well," Joule said, looking around, "I guess it's appropriate to keep the used one, right? It's not like there are biohazard sharps containers out here."

So maybe it wasn't as odd as he'd thought, but it was still weird as hell. "Does she have any marks on her?"

His sister shrugged up at him. "How would we know? She's in long sleeves and long pants."

She'd tried to protect herself against the bugs, and Cage now wished he and Joule had dressed to stay covered rather than stay cool.

Joule was still working the scene, though. "We have to bring the purse with us. We can't have somebody come back and get this... or worse."

"So where is her phone?" he asked, by way of agreeing with her.

"It lost battery back there..." She turned and pointed. "But that doesn't mean that's where it is."

Cage agreed, it had run out of battery on the trail, so it was probably still with her. "Her pants pocket?" He reached out to take the second stick from his sister. Using both of them for strength, he looped them through the purse strap and lifted it, holding it awkwardly away from him.

Shit, he thought. He needed two hands for his. "Take the gun."

But Joule refused, reaching out and taking the purse-carrying contraption instead. With the gun in his hand making him feel a little better, they picked their way out of the dense foliage. Together, they stepped over and through small brush back to the path where the body lay.

Joule set the purse down and used one of the sticks to poke at the doctor's pockets. She shook her head, seeming to find nothing. "Unless it's tucked in her shoe..." Joule used the stick to check as best she could. "Nope. No phone—"

Her head snapped up just as he heard it. Something pushed through the nearby underbrush.

Cold fear gripped him, ice crystals forming in every limb.

Had someone been here the whole time, waiting and watching quietly?

Had they pissed this person off by moving the purse?

A short quick nod of his sister's head told him that whatever it was, she agreed with him. They needed to get out of here and fast.

44

"No." Joule huffed her answer to: "Did you touch the body?"

She was pretty sure this was the forty-fifth time she'd been asked that. She'd heard that police would ask the same question repeatedly to be sure that people gave the same answers. Since she only ever said "No," she was confident she was remaining consistent.

Twenty feet down the road, Cage's expression looked much the same as she felt: Exhausted and irritated. His patience was far superior to hers, so she felt justified knowing that his was wearing thin, too.

"We have a guest arriving at our home," she told her inter-rogator and pulled her phone from her pocket. Looking quickly at the face of it, she tried to calculate how much longer this would take.

The officer offered her an irritated, chiding look. She wasn't supposed to play with her phone, but she needed to know the time. "He's arriving in town in another thirty-five minutes. We have to pick him up at the airport."

When the officer didn't respond, and only continued to look

irritated, she realized that goading the officer wasn't her best bet. So Joule pointed out, "You know where we live. You're more than welcome to come and ask us all the questions you want. But it's getting dark, and our guest doesn't have anywhere else to stay. Follow us if you want. Come meet him."

Though the sheriff's deputy continued to frown at her, her hope kicked up as the other deputy walked up close. Her brother was trailing behind. Maybe they were about to get out of here.

There were now cars parked all down the side of the road, mostly county sheriff cars. The farmer who owned the land where they had trespassed—and Dr. Achebe had trespassed before them—was now out talking to the deputies himself. His wife stood behind him and both wore scowls.

Joule understood. They hadn't even known they'd been trespassed and now their property held a murder scene. She wanted to wave at him and tell him she was sorry, but she wasn't going to apologize for anything in front of the deputies. The officer might take that as an admission of guilt.

With her brother now five feet away, Joule looked up at Cage. An officer had parked himself between them, though that wouldn't stop the twins from communicating. The two officers conferred quietly for a moment, then one turned to both of the twins. "We're going to let you go for now. But don't leave town."

She wanted to laugh at that last command.

She understood. They had been the ones to find the body and Cage did have a weapon on him—one he'd had to surrender. But she'd watched as the tech at the back of a nearby van had swabbed it and declared it hadn't been fired at any time in recent history.

The officers kept the gun "as evidence" anyway. That had pissed her brother off to no end. Joule wanted to remind him that she still had her bow and arrow. She knew she could take down a large animal with it, or even a human if she had to. But none of it was the kind of thing to say in front of officers who seemed bent on coming after them for murder.

What a shitty day.

They'd handed over the doctor's purse to the crime techs, and then their phones. They'd both agreed to let the techs copy their phones looking for evidence. The phones had only just been returned; Joule hoped it was because there was no evidence against the twins. Besides, their own phones and cell tower triangulation had put them on the other side of town during any window when Dr. Achebe might have been murdered.

She and her brother wouldn't go down for this. She just had to not be a bitch until they got out of sight of the officers.

The officers had still treated them as if they were killers.

The two stood in the road, watching the car as Cage and Joule drove away. She sat on the passenger side, looking in the sideview mirror. The officers stayed still, arms crossed, as though sending a signal.

"That was exhausting," Joule sighed. "I wonder if they found her phone."

"I wonder if they're tracking ours," her brother immediately replied.

Joule hadn't thought of that, although it was entirely possible. There was absolutely no reason that the techs wouldn't install a tracking app when they'd pulled all the data.

"We are their only suspects as of yet."

She hadn't thought of that either and she didn't like it.

"Okay, well, I'm still calling Dr. Warren. I hope these jackasses are listening in." She dialed quickly.

"Joule!" Helenie answered, her breath gulping. "Are you okay? The sheriff's department called me."

"Yes. We're fine—"

"—though we were questioned relentlessly," Cage threw in. "But they just now let us go."

"Oh, good." The relief in Dr. Warren's voice was palpable. Joule didn't add that they were still on the shortlist of suspects. She didn't think they'd be there for long, so that was at least helpful.

"We didn't find her phone." Joule paused wondering how much the officers had told Dr. Warren. "And Dr. Achebe was shot."

"She was shot?" Helenie blurted, obviously surprised. So, the sheriff's office had not told her that part.

"Yes, we didn't recognize it at first. She was shot in the head." Joule added the last part to clarify that it hadn't been something random. Dr. Achebe hadn't accidentally shot herself, and the likelihood that it was a stray bullet from a hunter went down with the precision of the hole in her temple.

There was silence on the other end of the line for a moment as neither of them quite knew what to say.

Then Helenie picked up the thread, offering what she could. "About her phone...."

The tone in Dr. Warren's voice told Joule there was somehow even more to this than they already suspected.

"We misread the tracker. The battery didn't go dead. It was shut off."

45

"Are you good back there?" Joule asked Dr. Brett.

The whole day felt surreal and so did having Dr. Brett Christian sitting in the back seat of her car while Cage drove. Joule turned around and looked into the backseat to have her conversation. Dr. Brett was the adult here. Even though she and her brother were truly adults now, it felt somehow wrong or *off* for him to refuse the front seat.

"I'm fine. Give me a second." He seemed to be messaging his wife and commenting to Joule while he did it. "She and Michelle decided to have two days of girl time, since I left them alone before she starts her chemo."

"Were you being kicked out of the house?" Joule asked.

"I'm not kicked out per se. But it's wise to spend at least a week traveling."

Joule loved the idea that they had Dr. Brett helping them for a full week. It was better than she'd hoped. She looked to Cage then, as their friend finished his message home letting his wife know he'd arrived safely.

"We have to talk to Dr. Murasawa," Joule told her brother, who nodded along. They had not said the words out loud, but they agreed they wouldn't be going back to work—not for the foreseeable future, anyway. At least not until someone solved whatever this was.

"Okay." Dr. Brett pocketed his phone and leaned forward. "Tell me what happened today."

The twins had sent a slew of texts letting him know they were being interviewed by the sheriff's deputies, that there was a dead body, and more. The poor man had been on the plane and had likely been inundated with all of it when he landed.

Joule suspected he hadn't untangled any of it yet.

"So, you found a body today? A real dead body?"

She nodded, rocking to one side as Cage took a turn she didn't see coming because she was still facing backwards. "It was the researcher who visited us yesterday. Her phone messages were weird. When we tracked down her coworkers, they said they traced her phone and it had gone silent hours before. Since we were here, and they're in Atlanta—"

"Her coworkers are in Atlanta?" Dr. Brett jumped in. He'd seemed to be following this crazy-ass story until that part.

"She's from the CDC." Joule filled in the missing pieces until Dr. Brett was relatively caught up and Cage had pulled into the drive-through at a local burger joint.

Her mother wouldn't be proud of her diet. Joule knew they needed to start cooking more. Having Dr. Brett here seemed a good excuse to eat better, but right now, everyone was close to starving and there was too much to do to even whip up mac and cheese. They pulled away from the restaurant with the bag of food at Joule's feet and the smell of hot food filling the car. Her stomach rumbled even louder than it had before.

They'd barely made it to the airport to pick up Dr. Brett after his luggage had finally been offloaded. They were both still in the clothing they'd traipsed the woods in. Until the food had entered the car, she could still smell faint traces of the bug spray they now wore everywhere.

"So, what does it mean that they said the battery didn't die?" Dr. Brett dove back into the story as Cage hung a right turn out of the lot and took a deep breath.

He'd let Joule tell most of the story before, but he chimed in now. "They thought the phone had died because the last report on the tracking program showed only a two-percent charge. The record showed it had been losing juice all morning. So, it made sense that the battery had died."

"But it didn't," Dr. Brett filled in and then added, "And you said you didn't find her phone?"

"No. Someone shut it off ... maybe her?" Joule surmised. "Her purse was there and there were still medications in it."

"That makes sense, though. Who would take medications?" Dr. Brett asked, "unless they were narcotics?"

"Not narcotics," Joule answered confidently before she reconsidered. "Or at least, I don't think they were." She looked to her brother as he shook his head in agreement. "But who would shoot a CDC researcher out looking for mosquitoes?"

"You're certain it was a murder?"

"It was one clean shot to the temple." Joule thought back and spoke while she tried to double-check the pictures in her mind. "She was lying on the ground with her head turned to the side. The entry wound was near her temple, aimed downward. Her hair was thick so we didn't see that there was a wound at first. Not until I walked around behind the body and saw the back of her head—"

"You didn't notice the blood on the ground? Head wounds bleed a lot." Brett was leaning forward, looking at her with concern. He was bringing up things she didn't know. Things the twins hadn't considered.

Joule felt her own neck jerk back. "No. I didn't see any."

She looked to Cage for confirmation, and he immediately shook his head.

"Was the back of her head blown open?" Dr. Brett asked.

Such an odd conversation to be having over a bag of hamburgers and fries.

Joule sipped at her orange soda for something normal to anchor her thoughts. The drink would be gone before she even got to the burgers and she would force herself to have a glass of water. "No, not really. It wasn't all blown away, but it was open. Definitely an exit wound."

She said it with confidence before dialing back a little bit. "Not that I really know what an exit wound looks like."

"Well, it's going to be much bigger than the bullet," Brett filled her in. "It looks like a wet, red sponge has been blown apart. And you can usually tell that it was blown *out* of the skull and not *into it.*"

"That would be it." She was finding it interesting that they had a friend who could and would have these conversations with them casually. They arrived back at the apartment faster than she'd expected, Cage finding a parking spot in front of their unit and then helping Dr. Brett with his suitcases through an unspoken agreement.

Joule carried the food. Jostling the bag made the smell waft up and her stomach protest again that it hadn't been fed yet. They didn't discuss the body, the bug bites, or Dr. Achebe's work as they passed a small family coming down the steps.

Eventually, they were all inside the unit, Dr. Brett looking around and Joule feeling as though she wanted to explain.

"It's a company rental."

He nodded. "It looks comfortable enough."

That triggered another series of thoughts. Joule set the paper sack on the table and turned to her brother. "If we don't go back to work, how long do we have a company rental for?"

"I don't even know." He blinked at the suggestion. It seemed he hadn't thought about that until now either.

If they were renting the place themselves, they might have until the end of the month to run their lease out. But Helio

Systems Tech held the lease and could kick them out tomorrow.

"Shit." Joule did something she could do and began pulling the food out, unwrapping each burger to figure out which was whose. She was not eating that monstrosity with egg and pickle that Dr. Brett had ordered.

Cage disappeared into the back with the suitcase and then reappeared, somehow also having managed to go to the fridge and pull out the ketchup.

But Dr. Brett had already picked up his burger and started eating when he dove back into the topic. "So, she was shot in the head once?"

The twins nodded.

"The exit wound didn't fully blow out the back of her head?"

This time they shook their heads and Joule wondered where he was going.

Dr. Brett sat in his chair and picked up his soda as though he were analyzing a TV show, rather than the dead body of a woman they'd just met. "So, it either wasn't a large caliber bullet, or it wasn't at very close range. And she wasn't killed where you found her."

46

"What?" Cage was still processing everything he had heard. The burgers had all been eaten, the sodas sipped down to the dregs a long time ago, and his lemonade had basically turned to slightly sweetened, warm water. Each time he took a sip, he regretted it.

"You're sure she wasn't killed there?"

"She couldn't have been. With an exit wound like that there would have been obvious signs. That kind of open hole leaves brain matter and blood spray in the area. Also, head wounds bleed a lot," he repeated.

"What if she were shot standing up and she fell over?" Joule said.

Even as his sister spoke the words, Cage figured that made more sense. But Dr. Brett was shaking his head.

"She would have fallen down very quickly. She would have still been bleeding when she hit the ground. It would have soaked into the ground. You should have seen it—"

"Because head wounds bleed a lot," Cage filled in. The twins looked to each other then they looked back at Dr. Brett almost as though the move had been planned. "Why kill a CDC researcher?"

"That I don't know. And why move the body?" He stopped and thought for a moment, wadding up the waxed paper from his burger. "I don't know that either. I mean, this isn't my area of expertise. Now, give me a Zombie Apocalypse. For on-the-ground treatment, veterinarians are in the zone. We can fashion medical supplies and tools in almost any size and out of almost anything. But I'm not really sure about dead human bodies. I don't work with humans that much."

Joule grinned, but Dr. Brett was talking about Dr. Achebe again, and Cage watched as her grin faded.

"You found the purse..." He added, almost like question. "Was there anything near it?"

Cage was catching on. "It would make sense that she dropped the purse when she was shot."

"That's what I'm thinking... Then the body would have been dragged into the trailway so people could find it."

"If they didn't want it found, they would just leave it off the trail. All of that makes perfect sense," Joule added, "Until we have the issue that the phone was actually turned off."

"Did you hear anything about time of death?" Dr. Brett looked between the two of them.

Cage needed to fidget with something. Moving a rejected pickle off his wrapper, he set it aside then folded the paper neatly corner to corner, thinking while his hands moved. "So, they took her phone and turned it off. Further back on the trail. Probably before she died."

"But I don't think they shot her there." Joule was looking into the middle distance, probably seeing the scene in her head.

Cage shook his head, once again neatly folding the wrapper end to end. "We passed the spot where the phone disappeared—or at least where the signal did. If they'd shot her there, we should have seen blood spatter or something on the ground."

Dr. Brett nodded along, confirming his thoughts, then added his own two cents. "If they'd shot her there, why move her further down the trail? She would have already been on the trail. Right?"

"Yes," Joule said, tapping her own phone and holding up the map for him to see. "This is the path through the woods that the phone made. It stopped dead in the middle of our walking path... but a little ways before where we found her body, and her purse was in a different place."

Joule made the map bigger and then tapped her finger on a spot just off the trail. "Probably right around here."

"But we didn't see anything near the purse," Cage added.

Joule thought for a moment and shook her head before reporting to Dr. Brett. "No. I didn't see blood spatter there, either. Not anything, though we weren't looking for it." She turned back to Cage. "Don't you think we would have noticed if there were brains on the tree, or blood on the purse?"

"On the purse? Definitely."

Joule added, "I didn't see anything on the trees, but I honestly don't know if we would have seen it. We were so focused on the purse. I can tell you there was no blood puddle on the ground near it."

"Was there any evidence of a struggle at the point where the phone disappeared?" Dr. Brett took a sip of his coke without paying attention and obviously didn't like what slurped up. He set the cup further away.

Cage looked down at the table. "I don't know. We weren't looking for anything like that. We thought we were going to find her with a twisted ankle." Or he'd hoped they would. They'd gone into the woods calling out for her. "We thought maybe her phone had died and we wouldn't find *anything,* that she would have walked out the other side."

"At some point, it had been suggested that she might even camp out to collect samples," Joule piped up and Cage wondered if they were lying to themselves.

Had he had an inkling all along that Dr. Achebe was already dead? For the life of him, he couldn't tell now. Cage tried putting it all together. "Someone or something turned her phone off back on the trail. They took it. They didn't take anything from her purse. And somehow her purse made it to the side of the trail."

"Maybe they scared her when they got her phone, and she ran," Joule said. "Maybe she dropped the purse, and someone shot her."

"Did someone maybe take the phone after she died and bring it back to that point and turn it off?" Dr. Brett asked.

"No, that point is as far as the phone went." Joule once again flipped her own phone around to show the map. "The line would have tracked over here to the purse or up the trail to here if that had happened."

"That's a good tracking program then. If it's showing that much distinction."

Or was it? Cage wondered. The service in the area had been sketchy. That line might be their only saving grace, though.

"So, Dr. Achebe was executed, and her phone was more valuable than whatever the medication was in her purse," the veterinarian said, trying to put the whole mystery together. "Was there anything else in her purse that was interesting?"

Cage and Joule looked to each other.

47

"I'm about to lose my fucking mind." Joule heaved in a breath and looked at Cage and Dr. Brett as if they might have the answers for her.

She'd eaten part of her toaster waffle in a relatively calm manner, she thought. Cage and the vet had dug into bowls of cereal, the size of which she couldn't comprehend. But now, both looked up at her with startled expressions.

"It's been three days. Helenie Warren hasn't called. The police haven't told us we're off the suspect list. We don't know if we're going to lose our apartment. That could happen at any moment." She waved her hand around as though tossing disgruntled fairy dust everywhere.

"At least we don't have that much to move," Cage commented.

The apartments always came fully furnished. The twins had worked jobs with Helio Systems Tech for a few years and had quickly learned to bring only the essentials.

Joule shook her head at her brother. That wasn't the problem. She was a pro at these moves. She was not a pro with looming changes. She handled the sudden, the unexpected, and the emergent just fine. It was the expected that always seemed to drive her crazy. Especially when it didn't turn up as expected.

"We have lots of samples, and we're getting good data," Dr. Brett pointed out. Though that maybe bothered her as much as anything.

Clear plastic cups now littered the apartment, taped upside down to stiff papers, holding in the buzzing and irritated "samples."

At first, they'd used small pieces of cardboard. When they ran out of those, they'd turned to stiff ad slicks from their junk mail. The small room wasn't big enough for all of it.

Chuck from the CDC had shown up the day after they'd found Dr. Achebe's body, as promised, despite the fact that the twins had already located the missing doctor. He'd insinuated himself into the sheriff's investigation, using the CDC as a pry bar. It also helped that he alibied out of her murder quite cleanly. He'd talked the deputies into letting him into Dr. Achebe's hotel room and then into giving him the CDC microscope that she'd carried and its cute little silver briefcase. The expensive equipment was, after all, clearly marked as CDC property.

The sheriff's deputies and the Charleston Police, who had jurisdiction over her hotel room, had taken a while to agree. Then Chuck had surprised the twins by leaving them all of her supplies, so they could continue the work.

"With Dr. Achebe not doing 'vacation' stuff while she was on vacation time, we are under extra scrutiny now. But, if you want, you're now set up to do everything you need," he'd told them as he unloaded the trunk of his rental car into their already crowded apartment.

"Can we send you samples?" Joule had asked, as though she were the biologist here.

"Of course."

So whatever scrutiny the team was under, it didn't preclude them from running specimens from a set of twenty-somethings in their Charleston-adjacent apartment. Or from handing over CDC lab equipment to them.

The apartment was now swimming in small petri dishes, syringes, mosquito samples, and more. They even had a thermally insulated bag in the fridge that held vials of who knew what? The trio hadn't had time to go through it all, though Chuck had assured them they were standard, lab-grade chemicals.

"It's not a lab," Joule protested when neither of the men spoke. "It's supposed to be home."

But was it? Once the words had come out of her mouth, she realized it *wasn't* a home, and it wasn't supposed to be. It was a temporary waystation at best. Aside from going out once for groceries and a handful of times to try to collect mosquitoes—some attempts successful, some not, but all of them terrifying—they'd been holed up in this apartment.

The entire time she ranted, both Cage and the vet leaned back in their chairs contemplating what she said. Dr. Brett scratched at the back of his hand and then the underside of his wrist. Joule had thought *she* was suggestible, but he was even more easily influenced than she was. The mere talk of itching made him start scratching and left her on constant alert, trying to surreptitiously see if he had any more bites or welts appearing.

"I want to go home," she whispered. The sound was far too plaintive even to her own ears.

She meant home to Rowena Heights. Home to the house she'd grown up in. She was glad they hadn't leased it, though Kayla and Ivy had definitely started putting out feelers for renters. It still might be something they did in the future. The more she thought about it, the more it settled, satisfied, in her chest.

She wanted to get away from the bugs, back to something she knew. Once they got the air conditioning turned on and she'd made her bed, it would at least feel more like her home of old. There, she had neighbors she knew. Dr. Brett lived nearby —he wouldn't have to go home at the end of the week.

Cage's voice interrupted her wishful thinking. "We can't leave town. Remember?"

Joule felt her head drop back with an exasperated sigh. "The sheriffs need to get over this. There's absolutely no evidence against us."

"Is there any evidence *for* you?" Dr. Brett asked.

"No one's telling us!" Which was another point Joule had taken issue with. If she was going to be a prime suspect, someone should be telling her what was going on. No one agreed with her on that—certainly not anyone in the sheriff's department.

She flipped her old phone over, face down on the table next to the new phone. She and Cage had gone out and each added a second phone for general use. They were now supporting four lines for the two of them. If they had been living entirely off of their own salaries, it would have been a major budgetary crunch.

It had taken the three of them less than an hour to find the tracker on Joule's phone. Once they'd found that, it was easy enough to locate the same hidden app on Cage's.

"What do we do?" Joule asked. She hadn't touched the second half of an already small toaster waffle. The men's spoons were scraping the bottoms of their bowls. Dr. Brett had tipped his back to drink the milk. As he set the bowl down, both he and Cage opened their mouths as if they had an answer for her.

Even as they did it, the phone rang—her old one.

She'd given everyone the new number, but the twins had decided to keep the old ones activated. They took the new ones with them when they went out; the old ones didn't leave the apartment much. But the twins left them running and even still used them a little. There was no point in tipping off the sheriff's techs that they'd gotten new ones. Still, she was more than happy to use the old phone for basic information. They could scan that all they wanted. She wasn't guilty.

Joule saw the number flash and she picked up the phone. "Dr. Warren?"

Helenie offered no polite hellos or small talk. "We got the autopsy report. And it's beyond interesting."

Joule was about to ask, *What happens now? Can we see it?* But Dr. Warren was ahead of her. "I'm emailing it to you. You should read through and call me back."

"Okay." Joule ended the call, clicking the buttons to download the report onto her phone. As she did, she realized it would be better if it was on her computer, where the three of them could read it together—and it wasn't logging on the traced phone. Stepping away from her half-eaten waffle, she clicked her way through folders and browsers, pulling up the same email she'd just opened on her phone.

She was about to swing the screen around so the three of them could read it together, when Cage's old phone rang.

She looked up to the worried expression on her brother's face.

"Yes.... What? ...Okay." Cage's tone was sharp, his worry bleeding through the whole room, despite the fact that she heard nothing useful from his side of the conversation.

He put the phone down, already lifting from his seat. "That was Dr. Murasawa. She needs us ASAP."

48

Cage fought the steering wheel as the car tried to veer first one way and then another. As it bumped through the grass he was taking at far too high a speed, they all felt each pit and rut he couldn't see.

His heart was pounding. He'd started sweating, the worry dripping down his spine. It would have curled his shoulders in if he hadn't been so tense just trying to keep the car on track.

They'd all shoved their feet into their shoes and bolted out the door—Joule swinging down to grab her ever-present backpack, Cage loading his pockets. They'd made it all the way to the car before realizing they had no bug spray on them. Both had been bitten at the front of the apartment complex already.

Still, they'd slammed the car doors and Cage had peeled out before the three of them were even buckled. Dr. Brett was asking where they were going—but he hadn't balked, just run. Joule sprayed them down in the car and they'd all coughed their way through the next two miles, opening the windows to let the microdroplets of bug spray escape rather than going into their lungs. But Cage could still taste it in the air. His internal organs were the one place he was relatively confident he didn't need to be protected.

The car lurched down then back up. It bounced and tried to jerk quickly to the right. Yanking the steering wheel to the left to correct for that, Cage spotted the group off in the distance.

It had to be another bite. Another reaction. But even as he thought that, he wondered, *Why call them?*

Didn't all the team leaders have EpiPens on them now? What was happening that he and his sister—both officially on leave—had been called in with emergent tones?

They'd been at their apartment. They weren't even already on the jet lab campus. Surely everyone else and their brother was closer than them. But Dr. Murasawa had only demanded that they come in, and neither of the twins nor the vet had even questioned the order.

Joule, seat-belted in but leaning forward, one hand wrapped around the back of her chair, twisted sideways and smacked on the dash. "Stop!" she yelled at him. "Stop!"

As Cage tried to roll the car to a slower speed, the bumps managed to hit harder. Quickly he gave up, smashing into the brake and lurching the car to a full stop. Joule was already opening the door.

"We're faster on foot." She was probably right.

Their car was older. Neither of the twins had wanted to replace it because it worked just fine. But it was absolutely an old sedan, not made for four-wheeling. He was out the door just behind her and running, arms pumping, feet pounding the ground. His ankle twisted as he stepped on a rock he hadn't seen, but Cage kept going. Too much adrenaline to know if it hurt.

Adrenaline, he thought. Was that the problem? Still, why call them? But he didn't slow down. He heard the thumping of Dr. Brett's feet as he, too, pounded his way through the soft ground and too-high grass behind the twins.

Dr. Murasawa saw the car coming and ran toward them. Why was she out with the group in the field? She usually worked indoors. Now, she waved her arms over her head as though the three of them weren't already booking it across the field as best they could.

She turned away from the trauma at her feet and came toward them, fast. She ran well, her movements confident and not what he'd expected.

As she joined the group, Cage managed to huff his question out, having slightly overtaken his sister for the lead. "A bite?"

Before his boss could answer, he was on top of the small group. He didn't look at faces. He didn't need to. He saw Melinda lying on the ground, her face pale, welts covering her skin under a thin layer of sweat.

"You were right," Dr. Murasawa said. "You were right. It's the bites."

Melinda, who'd always been a fan of the official CDC announcement that it must be the food, took two labored breaths and looked up at the arriving trio. "I haven't had anything to eat since dinner last night and I got bitten. It can't be the food."

Joule dropped to her knees next to the woman, her EpiPen already out but still capped. They'd both seen this enough to know not to jump to stabbing someone. Cage had already grabbed his as well, the plastic growing warm in his fist.

As he stepped closer and hovered over his team leader, he realized that towering over her was the worst thing he could do. He, too, dropped down next to her, watching as the others scooted out of the way for him and his sister, as though they knew anything more than anyone else.

"When did you get bitten? Where?" Joule was asking, looking over the woman as if to find the original pink mark in the sea of rash that had bloomed.

"Right lower leg." The words wheezed out of Melinda's

lungs, soft and wet as she pointed one finger. The action made it seem as if Melinda was already exhausted.

"You gave her an EpiPen?" Cage asked as he looked around at the others, still breathing heavily.

Some of his coworkers were on their knees, crowded in close. Others stood back a few feet, waiting and watching. It was clear no one quite understood how to help. He wasn't sure he did, either. His only advantage was experience, but his survival rate was no better than anyone else's.

Breathing heavily, even though she'd only run a portion of the distance they had, Dr. Murasawa tilted her head and said, "No."

"Why not?" Cage asked, startled. He'd thought that this was a case of the pen not working. Dr. Acheoe had said sometimes the pen itself didn't work, and sometimes the pen worked but the medication didn't, for whatever reason.

"She never struggled to breathe."

"She's struggling now!".

It was Melinda, still lying, laid out on the ground, who shook her head. "Not my throat."

She opened her mouth and though she struggled to breath, they could see her airway was open.

"What?" Cage didn't mean to ask out loud. The word had been there, pushing itself out into the crowd, not letting him just think it quietly.

"She was bitten." Dr. Murasawa stepped back, her hand going to her forehead. Nervous energy rolled off her in waves. "Almost immediately, the welts started showing up everywhere. So, we laid her down. We tipped her head back. We were ready to help her breathe..."

His boss stopped and sucked in a breath. Cage noticed and did the same. He needed the air himself. He didn't understand. Beside him, his sister looked just as confused as he was.

Dr. Murasawa continued, though she wasn't any more

certain of what was happening than any of them. "The welts spread everywhere. But... ah... her throat never closed."

Cage turned and looked at Melinda.

"It maybe felt..." She paused, breathing heavily. "A little scratchy..."

"And now?" Joule asked.

Melinda shook her head slowly, one side to the other, as though that effort itself were what was exhausting her. "No."

Then she said something that startled them both. She looked to Joule first, and then to Cage and said one word:

"Fever."

49

J oule put her hand out, first placing her palm to Melinda's forehead. She snatched her hand back, realizing that was stupid. Not how her mother or father had ever done it.

Flipping her wrist over, Joule placed the back of her hand against Melinda's skin.

It didn't matter which side she used, though. Melinda was burning up.

Her hand came away wet. Though she'd seen it when they'd run up, she hadn't quite placed that the woman was sweating profusely. Looking up at the others, she asked, "Breathing?"

As soon as it was out, she figured it was the stupidest thing to say, and the dumbest way to ask it.

Still, Melinda understood. She took another slow, heavy breath and said, "Difficult."

Cage looked around, almost frantic. "Does anyone have a stethoscope?"

"I do."

Joule didn't recognize the young woman, and she was pretty

good with faces, which meant this person had come to the project after she and Cage had left. "Did anyone call 9-1-1?"

The new tech held up a soft-sided, insulated white bag with a red plus logo on the side. "We already did."

On the one hand, Joule was surprised someone had a whole kit. On the other hand, she wasn't. There was a reason she and her brother had joined Helio Systems Tech in the first place. It was part of the same reason that they had stayed for as long as they had. Their coworkers were smart and prepared.

The woman stepped forward, opening the not-fully-zipped bag as she did. Her movements indicated they'd been in it already, and she was just standing by, ready to use it again. One hand clutching the handle, the other pulled out the stethoscope and handed the limp piece over to Joule, who immediately handed it to Cage.

She wouldn't even know what she was listening for. But her brother possibly did.

Several of the team members frowned as he put the bell of the stethoscope on the upper right side of Melinda's chest.

"Her lung sounds awful. I'm no doctor, but I know they aren't supposed to sound like that."

"Like what?" Joule asked.

Even as she asked, Cage was shaking his head. She could tell he'd screwed something up. It was the look he made when he was irritated at himself. Before she could decipher it, he turned around and handed the stethoscope over his shoulder.

Dr. Brett was on the ground in a heartbeat, taking Cage's spot. "I've got you," he told Melinda as he next asked her to roll slightly up.

It was an effort, but she did it. The vet leaned over, his eyes focused on the back of her white t-shirt as he placed the stethoscope on her ribs at her back. He listened, intently focused for a moment before asking, "Can you take a deep breath?"

To her credit, Melinda tried.

"Rales." He pronounced the one word clearly, though no one seemed to understand except Melinda.

"Of course." She almost pulled one side of her mouth up, not even coming close to a real grin. Melinda was generally upbeat, Joule knew. Cage had worked with her since they'd started in Alabama, and he liked his team leader a lot.

"It's a crackling sound in the lungs," Dr. Brett explained. "Almost like saran wrap or plastic. It means there's fluid."

"It's barely been half an hour since she was bitten." Dr. Murasawa jumped back in, her tone and her expression not bothering to hide how worried she was. "Well, half an hour when we called, over forty-five minutes now."

"It can happen fast sometimes." He motioned to Melinda, leaving his hand in place behind her shoulder blade, as though he were gently laying her back on the ground. Then he moved the stethoscope, placing it on her sternum and listening again.

After moving the bell slightly and pausing, he frowned again. He stopped, lifting his hand, he motioned to the group with a harsh expression to be quiet.

Joule felt herself freeze.

He'd heard something he didn't like. She knew the man well enough to know what his happy face and his worried face looked like.

He honestly wasn't that concerned about his wife getting chemotherapy. He knew what to expect. He knew her prognosis was very good. He knew she was in the best hands. He probably completely understood how the drugs worked at the molecular level.

He knew it wouldn't be easy, but he clearly had faith in his wife. He had faith in her nurse of a sister, and he had faith in the treatment itself. Here, he had faith in nothing.

As the group responded, their sounds abruptly cut off, like an old stereo with the button smacked. He leaned over again, his head down low, almost as though he were using an old horn version of a stethoscope rather than the rubber tubing kind that had been in the kit.

Was it not a good enough stethoscope? Maybe it was a cheap field version. But the man leaned back, sitting on his heels, and pronouncing, "Her rhythm is irregular and weak."

He pushed the woman's long, thin sleeve away to get at her wrist and Joule noticed for the first time what the group was wearing. Even if they hadn't fully believed it was bites and not something in the food, they'd covered up. Every single one of them wore lightweight, light colored clothing that came down to their ankles and hands.

Dr. Brett placed two fingers on the pale inside of Melinda's wrist. After waiting a moment with an expression that said it wasn't going well, he turned it over and tried again.

"Shit," he said. "I'm not that good at this."

"You're not a doctor?" the young woman with the medicine bag asked the veterinarian.

This time she sat down and shoved him out of the way. She'd hung back but now she was in motion. Her sleek black hair swinging as she moved, her dark eyes focused. "My dad's a nurse—ICU—I can find a pulse."

Sitting on her own knees and nudging Dr. Brett out of the way, she grabbed Melinda's wrist. Even as she did it, Melinda's head lolled to the side, as though the small effort of keeping her face aimed toward the sky was too much.

"It's thready and weak," the new tech pronounced.

Joule didn't know quite what that meant, but she had stepped back, watching the action rather than trying to get into it. She knew that wasn't a good thing, though. If the pulse was bad, then Melinda's heart wasn't working fully. This time, when she breathed, the team leader opened her mouth wider as though the very act itself were more effort than she could sustain.

Dr. Murasawa grabbed Joule by her elbow, not the kindest

of gestures, as she hauled Joule to her feet. But Joule wasn't going to complain. They were all doing the best they could, and the focus was Melinda.

"Help me look. Help me listen," Dr. Murasawa demanded.

Her boss was standing tall and scanning the area.

"They told us it would take a while but it's taking too long. It's too long!" Dr. Murasawa was getting frustrated, her worry bleeding through every word.

"What is?" Joule asked.

"The ambulance. We only called you after they hung up."

"They *hung up*?" Shouldn't they still be on the phone? Joule thought they had to stay on the line until the ambulance arrived. "I don't understand."

"The operator had to take a different call. They're understaffed and overwhelmed." The doctor sounded like she was more trying to explain it to herself than reciting actual facts to Joule. "I don't know."

What was even happening that the dispatch operators were so busy? "They can't send an ambulance to a woman dying in a field?"

There was no answer. Behind her, the group fell strangely silent for a moment.

Joule's lungs clenched. They'd all heard her, and she shouldn't have said that. Was Melinda even dying? She'd meant it as a scathing rebuke to an ambulance service that wasn't even here, not a pronouncement about Melinda's chances. Joule wasn't even qualified to guess any of it.

The noise of the people behind her had stopped. Joule had to force herself not to cry. She felt like shit for saying it. But she had a job and she had to be useful. Her eyes couldn't cloud as she scanned the horizon and the streets in the distance for the approaching ambulance.

She listened for sirens in the distance, but the only sound was the audible effort of Melinda's labored breath.

50

C age held onto Melinda's wrist. At first, he just wanted to double-check, to feel the weak and thready pulse the other woman had said she felt. He needed to have something tangible to judge by.

While he'd been checking, Melinda's hand had gone limp in his. Looking up, he caught the other woman's deep brown gaze. Her Asian features were cut with worry as he asked, "Did she pass out?"

"I'm not sure," she answered softly, though he'd meant it more as a rhetorical question.

It was clear to him that Melinda had passed out.

But Dr. Brett was scooting back in close, situating himself next to the young woman as he placed the stethoscope on Melinda's chest once more. "I don't think she passed out. Her heart stopped."

Cage let go of her hand—not because he intended to but as a knee-jerk reaction. In the slow motion of surprise and confusion, he watched as the limp arm hit the ground. He saw it then: The ashen color that had crept through her skin.

He'd thought before that she was turning bluish, and he'd

assumed it was because she wasn't breathing well. But her lips hadn't turned the blue-gray color of cold, so maybe he hadn't interpreted it correctly.

With a quick motion, Dr. Brett grabbed at the Y of the stethoscope and expertly removed it one-handedly from his ears. He pushed it toward the young woman working next to him. "What's your name?"

"Ji Lee." But she wasn't looking at any of them. She was looking down at Melinda, her fingers moving to the side of Melinda's throat, now exposed by her limp head.

Though her expression appeared frantic, Ji Lee's movements were calm and efficient. She shook her head to Dr. Brett. But, like him, she expertly placed the earpieces into her ears with one quick flick of her fingers.

Yeah, Cage thought, *he shouldn't have been the first one listening*. Ji Lee had simply hung back until she'd been asked to step forward and he should have asked sooner. He and Joule had just come blazing in because they'd been called. Like everyone else, they'd assumed they had the most experience. Hell, Dr. Murasawa had assumed it, too, calling them on a day they weren't even on site. So maybe he wasn't just an arrogant piece of shit here.

They had not asked Ji Lee to take care of Melinda before. It was clear now that whatever was going on had progressed to something different from anaphylactic shock. It was well out of any jurisdiction he and his sister held.

"She needs a breath," Dr. Brett told Ji Lee.

Ji Lee quickly and emphatically shook her head, *no*. "We don't breathe with CPR anymore."

"I know, but we need to be sure that her throat is open. So, we need to breathe into her mouth so that we can see her chest rise. That way, we'll know if our chest compressions are moving air in and out of the lungs, or merely pumping her heart." Then he sat back, his head popping up as he scanned the area and the edge of their group. *"Where is the ambulance?"*

Joule and Dr. Murasawa were standing sentry, but the two of them shook their heads. It wasn't here and they didn't see it in the distance.

"I thought I heard sirens." Cage jumped into the fray. *Hadn't he?*

Joule turned around, looking bewildered. "It went right by us. There was an ambulance out here—on the main road—" she pointed, "—and it wasn't for us."

He turned back, watching as Ji Lee leaned in and pinched Melinda's nose and tilted her head back to open her airway. Though Cage waited for his team leader to shake them off, irritated, and tell them to get back to work, it didn't happen. Melinda didn't protest in the slightest. That might have driven home the severity of the situation more than the original pronouncement did.

His new job was doing nothing but being out of the way and holding the medical bag Ji Lee had thrust at him when they changed places. Cage watched now as Dr. Brett pushed on Melinda's chest. Ji Lee lowered her head down, aiming her ear toward his manager's open mouth. "I think so, but it's hard to tell. We should start compressions."

Dr. Brett looked up to him, and adrenaline spiked in his own system again. "Check the bag!"

As the vet described what he was looking for, Cage had already unzipped it and was trying not to paw through the contents like a madman. He located the face mask and handed it over even as he noted the filter in the middle and the mouthpiece on the other end.

Apparently, grabbing Melinda's nose and tipping her head back had just been a check, not the CPR of old he'd expected. Ji Lee yanked it from his hand and had it fitted expertly over

Melinda's mouth and nose, breathing into it before he could even quite figure out what was going on.

"Yes!" Dr Brett sounded excited. That had to be good. "Her lungs expanded. So, her oxygen is poor due to lung function and not a swollen and closed trachea."

"Do we need to breathe for her anyway, even though it's not part of standard CPR?" Ji Lee's head popped up, her gaze momentarily off of Melinda's face.

"I was thinking the same thing." Dr. Brett was still moving, all of this conversation happening in staccato movements and rapid decisions.

Even as he said the words, he was moving into a classic position to perform chest compressions. His fingers laced together, palms down, he moved them along Melinda's sternum.

His boss still hadn't reacted, Cage thought, and he wasn't okay with it. *Wake up! Tell us to back off!* But she didn't.

"Tell me I'm in the right spot?" Dr. Brett looked to Ji Lee, who shook her head at him for a moment as if asking why we was even asking. He reminded them all. "Veterinarian."

She nodded and waited while he did the compressions. Cage felt his eyes open wide as he heard the soft lyrics coming from his friend and mentor.

"Rising up... back on the street..."

Was the man singing Eye of the Tiger?

Even Ji Lee had turned her head to look at him oddly. But Dr. Brett was not deterred.

Ji Lee must have been counting, because she motioned for him to stop as he hit the chorus. Leaning over, she offered two long breaths into Melinda's lungs.

They all watched as the woman's chest rose and fell with each attempt but didn't make any motions of its own. If Cage was one for praying, he would have done it then. Hell, he might start right now.

Dr. Brett laced his fingers and relocked his shoulders and elbows. Ji Lee motioned for him to wait, her fingers moving to Melinda's throat, checking for a pulse.

She shook her head no and Dr. Brett began singing again.

Cage looked up and around, joining his sister and Dr. Murasawa in watching for an ambulance that didn't seem to be coming. It was the only thing useful he could do as he heard the second chorus to the old eighties hit Dr. Brett used to keep time.

51

Cage leaned over Melinda now, his own elbows locked as he took his turn pushing at the woman's chest. Surely, they'd cracked a rib or two by now. But it wouldn't matter if they couldn't manage to save her life.

Dr. Brett had worn out, the ambulance still hadn't arrived, and Cage had no idea how much time had passed, only that it was too much. Like all of them huddling over their friend and coworker, he was running on sheer hope.

Melinda's skin was clammy to the touch. She'd been sweating with the fever, but that seemed to have stopped a while ago... or had it? And how long ago? He didn't know.

Cage was in a fever dream of his own. The rushed, adrenaline-fueled haze was hard enough when it was someone he didn't know. It was too much when it had been Jeff or Clara. It was worse, far worse, with Kelsey and David. Somehow, it was even harder to take now with Melinda.

With Kelsey and David, he'd jabbed a needle haphazardly into their leg and sat back and waited. He hadn't been responsible for saving Kelsey after her heart attack. But now? This was on him, and he pushed a harsh rhythm on the torso of a woman he admired, as if she could come back to life fueled by his own sheer spite.

"Slower," Dr. Brett said, his hand reaching out and gently touching Cage's elbow.

He tried to decrease his rhythm, but his brain was running too fast, time too slow. Though Dr. Brett motioned him again, and Cage tried, he shook his head, though he didn't stop.

The vet was exhausted. Even lifting his arm to tap Cage on the elbow had seemed a rough effort. He dropped back on his heels and was taking his own slow, deep, labored breaths. Was he just tired? Or was he sick, too?

"Sing."

Cage couldn't risk looking up. "*What song?* I don't know that one."

He'd easily recognized "Eye of the Tiger" but he couldn't sing it.

"I Will Survive," Dr. Brett told him, but again Cage shook his head.

"Another One Bites the Dust," offered Ji Lee.

Though Cage knew that one, he couldn't bring himself do it. He couldn't hover over one of his favorite managers and do CPR on her singing those words.

"Girls Just Want to Have Fun," Dr. Brett threw out, as apparently every CPR song was from the eighties.

His own father was a fan of eighties pop. While Joule had always thought of it as just something their father liked, Cage had built his own musical collection around it. He knew this one.

He took a breath. "I come home in the morning light..."

It was, he found, easier to do it with a rhythm, to dance his way through CPR, despite the fact that he was frantic and his own heart was pumping like a madman. Between the adrenaline of the situation and the effort of the rhythm, he needed some Cyndi Lauper to pace himself.

"Harder," Dr. Brett told him.

"It feels wrong, but do it harder," Ji Lee had chimed in right behind him.

At last, his thirty compressions were up and Ji Lee leaned over and breathed again. She hadn't traded out her position, but it wasn't nearly as high impact an aerobic workout as what Dr. Brett had done until Cage relieved him.

"Ambulance?" the veterinarian had shouted again, the question carrying across the group.

Ji Lee was done, and Cage leaned over, lacing his hands together again as Ji Lee checked his positioning. He began singing again.

Though he tried to block everything out, he couldn't. He had no filters in the midst of the emergency. Dr. Murasawa's voice came through to him.

"They're not even answering 9-1-1 right now."

"Are we out of jurisdiction?" he heard his sister ask, but he kept his rhythm, his whole upper body moving with the work.

They'd moved a lot as kids. At one point, the twins had lived in a home that was technically beyond the city lines. They had 9-1-1 for emergencies, but had been surprised that dispatch sent the sheriff and not the police as they didn't have any city services. His mother had commented that they were lucky that at least they had 9-1-1. Some places didn't even have that.

"No. We're just beyond city limits, but they answered the first time," Dr. Murasawa said.

He leaned back, another thirty compressions done, to see her brows pulling together and her mouth turning down. Her jaw clenched as though it were the phone's fault and not anything else. "They are supposed to be on their— Hello?"

Her attention had shifted, her entire body stiffening as she said the word. Then she jerked the phone away, another frown marring her features as Cage leaned over, once again training his attention on his own exhausting work.

Whatever it had been, it hadn't been an actual person.

"Hush!" his sister yelled out to the crowd, but he kept singing under his breath.

From the corner of his eyes, he saw her hands go out, palm down, as if she could stop the earth, or at least the people around her.

Everyone else quieted. He even lowered the volume of his singing. He had to preserve his energy anyway, but he couldn't stop. Cage let Ji Lee count the number of compressions he was doing. Under his breath he finished off a chorus, "Oh, girls just want to have fu-un."

"I hear something," Joule said. She motioned Dr. Murasawa to step away from her so the woman could keep her phone to her ear.

Beside her, David had stepped up, ears alert. They looked like a small band of desert animals listening for predators.

David began nodding excitedly. "I hear it too."

Ji Lee had tapped him, and Cage leaned back, breathing heavily. How had Dr. Brett kept this up for so long?

No one asked if it was worth it. Volunteers waited for when he grew tired, too, but they would have to pull him off. He was angry as hell that he had to fight to save another friend's life.

They would keep going until the ambulance arrived. There were enough of them here. They would rotate through. If Melinda died, it wouldn't be because they hadn't tried.

Ji Lee leaned over, too, continuing with her two long, deep breaths again. He watched with only the mildest satisfaction as Melinda's chest rose and fell. His managers preternatural stillness spoke to him more than anything else. It chilled him deep in the marrow of his bones. He didn't think they would be saving her.

It was perfunctory now. No one willing to quit. Because she was the boss? Because they liked her? Or simply because she was one of them? He didn't know, but every face bore the same determination he felt.

They weren't going to lose another one.

He was leaning over to start again. But Ji Lee motioned him to stop. He'd moved too early as he saw her fingers move to Melinda's throat, once again feeling for a pulse. He should have known that Ji Lee would check on every round, but he hadn't quite caught on.

A slow shake of her head to the left then to the right, told him Melinda still didn't have a pulse of her own.

He leaned in, elbows locked, shoulders square, body positioned over what he was now certain was his friend's body. He pushed again as Joule and David yelled, "Yes!" and took off running.

52

J oule took another step back as the paramedics finally showed up. They wore the same uniforms as the other team had the day Kelsey died. She didn't like that.

Would there be different companies operating in the Charleston area? Would they be equally well-trained? Were these guys the best? She had no answers to her questions as the pair from the back of the truck hit the ground running.

Though it seemed to take forever for them to check all of Melinda's vitals and come to the exact same conclusions anyone here could have told them, Joule understood they were working very quickly. It was just her patience that was slow. Within seconds, they pulled out the defibrillator and charged the paddles.

Everyone else moved back.

Dr. Brett, Cage, and Ji Lee were all sitting, exhausted, on the ground nearby and they, too, pulled back a little. The grass wasn't wet from morning dew—the day was too hot for that— but it was still damp from the moisture of the air. Their clothing had to be sticky, one of Joule's least favorite feelings. But she knew none of them would notice until later.

She wondered if she had towels in the car for them to sit on so they didn't get the seat wet or grassy. A stupid thought, it gave her brain a needed break. It didn't last long as she watched them jolt Melinda's body and Joule prayed for the manager to come back to life.

"Charging," they called again. "Stay back." Though it was more a command to each other, as no one else had stepped into their field of care.

The first time hadn't worked. They'd checked for a pulse, looked at their little machine and shaken their heads at each other. They charged it again. They'd never said *anaphylaxis* as the group had told them when they'd arrived. Melinda's throat had never closed, despite the rash that covered her body.

Even the blotches had faded now. Joule saw where the woman's shirt had been pulled up to reveal skin for the paddles. The irony, Joule thought, that the rash—once the hallmark of sudden terror and maybe death—now seemed to be the least of it. The EpiPen would have saved her from that.

Only then did she realize she still clenched it tight in her fist. How had she not cracked the plastic with her tense grip? She didn't know, just a miracle of the physics of cylinder type shapes or the modern marvel of durable plastics. She considered then, for the first time, putting it back into her bag. But she wasn't willing to let it go. She clung tighter, as though it were a talisman, or a last hope, or a magic potion.

This time the dark haired one declared, "I've got a pulse!"

Joule felt the tension release from her shoulders. Her chest opened up and she gulped in air. She heard Dr. Murasawa do the same. But she didn't take in enough air, didn't feel enough relief to fully relax.

The EMTs began moving around, quickly running an IV, patching Melinda with various stickers attached to wires and reading the monitors. Joule would have thought she was pretty decent at understanding what was happening but, right now, none of this field setup was making sense to her.

She looked to her brother. Leaning back on his hands in the grass, he let his long legs stick out in front of him. He wasn't in the way, and his pose was almost indicative of having played flag football at a summer picnic and being tired. He nodded to her, as if to say *we did it.*

As the EMTs worked on their friend and Joule forced herself to breathe evenly, the driver showed up. He was rolling the gurney from of the back of the ambulance and walking it out toward them. They must have worked fast if he was only just now showing up, but it had felt so long. He dropped the movable bed down low, ready to transfer her over, the backboard waiting on it.

It seemed they were getting ready to move her into the waiting vehicle. Joule considered that the best possible case and she let herself take another sigh of relief. When she did it, the voices started again. "No. We're losing her!"

The beeping of the little machine wasn't quite as loud as it would be in a hospital room, but it had changed rhythm, taking too long between certain beeps. Joule stood to the side, exhausted from her own tension, her hand coming up to cover her mouth in an unconscious gesture, her fingers digging into her cheek. She didn't mean to, as if anything she did would affect Melinda on the ground, ten feet away.

All she could do was stay out of the way.

It felt wrong to breathe the open air when someone near her couldn't. By the same token, Joule knew the best thing she could do for Melinda was not distract anyone's attention or cause any more trouble. So, she counted her own breaths, taking over for her autonomic nervous system. She looked frantically to her brother and Dr. Brett, making sure that they were doing okay—as if she had any authority to check them out. At least they didn't seem to be sporting any sprained wrists or broken bones. They were both breathing heavily. Still wrung out from what they'd done, but seemingly okay.

Over Melinda's body, the flurry of activity continued. They shocked her again and again.

Joule felt someone's fingers reach across the palm of her hand and squeeze her hand so tight it hurt. She squeezed back. She didn't need to look to see that doctor Murasawa was standing next to her, her terror as deep as Joule's own or maybe worse. The clench of their hands together grounded Joule as best it could in the surreal situation.

The two EMTs worked frantically but professionally. It was clear this wasn't someone they knew and the work was clinical. The entire team formed a loose circle around them until, simultaneously, the professionals sat back, one of them looking at a wristwatch. Fully digital, it required him to tap it twice before it displayed any numbers.

"The patient is deceased."

She'd known it, Joule thought. She'd heard their tones change even though they'd kept working. Every Helio Systems employee had probably understood as the EMTs moved from life-saving measures to throwing Hail Mary passes.

Passes that hadn't worked.

Melinda, who'd been pale when the twins arrived, didn't even look human anymore. She looked like someone had left a bad polymer doll of their friend lying out in the field. It wore Melinda's clothing and had her face, but it didn't feel like her.

Joule's stomach turned solid, her breathing stopped, her jaw went rigid as she tried to deal rationally with what she was seeing. Logically, she knew that Melinda was really gone. Her brain refused to accept it.

With an economy of motion, the EMTs flipped the machines off. One of them leaned back and held his hand up, and the driver readily supplied the backboard. When they put Melinda onto it, they moved with a new economy. Their motions told everyone that they were no longer gently handling a human patient but removing a body.

Cage and Dr. Brett had taken to their feet with the announcement, scrambling upward and moving away, almost as though her death was their personal failure. It had been anything but. Both men scrambled over to Joule, and she would have moved to meet them halfway, but she was unable to move or function. Dr. Brett's hand landed on her shoulder, as if she needed him to anchor her to the ground while the world swirled around her.

Dr. Murasawa somehow managed to squeeze her hand even harder.

She wouldn't pass out. She clenched her jaw and told herself not to, though it had happened twice before. Even though they had declared Melinda dead, Joule would not steal attention from her coworker and her brother's friend.

Cage's hand twisted into the fabric of the back of her shirt as if he needed to hold onto her to stay upright. Her eyes squeezed, tears coming out despite the fact that Joule didn't want them to.

This wasn't right.

"It wasn't anaphylactic shock?" Dr. Brett asked.

Even as Ji Lee shook her head, the dark-haired EMT said, "No."

The second added, "It looks like a reaction to an infection, but we can't diagnose." Then he heard the radio and the driver answering back. Whatever was said, he understood, even if Joule didn't.

"We have to get going. We have another run," he announced. "Today has been crazy. Whatever this is, it's the third one we've had this shift."

53

"No." Joule pushed back more forcefully when Cage again suggested food.

She wasn't hungry, though the thought of eating didn't turn her stomach. It didn't turn anything.

Dr. Brett looked between the two of them. "We should eat." He added, "Numerically, we should," when neither of the twins responded. Joule got the feeling that Cage was suggesting food for the same reason the vet was.

Dr. Brett gave up on that tactic and Joule thought he didn't feel like eating either. She shifted gears as he asked, "That was your third case?"

Joule didn't understand.

"The third one you've seen die," he clarified.

This time she nodded. They'd also seen Dr. Achebe's body. It was too much, the number of people they'd watched die in the last two months.

They were still on temporary leave from work, and right then it crystalized that she didn't want to go back. Even being on leave, she'd been called in for the worst part. She hadn't gotten to help set any beams or test any forces. Joule hadn't been able to talk with people she knew, make plans and have discussions to determine where the solar panels should go. She'd merely been asked to show up for a death—the one reason she had taken a leave.

Plopping down onto the couch, she let her head slowly lean back so she didn't wonk it on whatever piece of wood was directly under the cheap construction. The furniture looked nice and relatively new but, beneath the surface, it was low-quality with crappy padding.

She reminded herself that David had lived. Jeff had lived. She and her brother had both been bitten and lived. That was likely thanks to Dr. Achebe and her antihistamine trick.

Had anyone given Melinda antihistamines? Joule didn't know. Now wasn't the time to ask, maybe never. Melinda had been declared dead *right in front of them*. Questioning what the others had done would only make it seem as though someone had screwed up.

Joule didn't think it was possible to screw up in a situation like this. There was only the bad you survived and the bad that you didn't.

The three of them had each sat down, separating themselves to different quadrants of the small room. Cage sat at the table and Dr. Brett had taken the armchair as far from Joule as possible, as though they couldn't even stand to be in someone else's human space.

No one spoke for a while, each needing the silence. Joule felt the jumble of emotions tumbling through her, unfettered. Melinda hadn't been her friend. While she had liked the woman and enjoyed her company the few times they'd had dinner as part of the group or had sat at a lunch table together, Melinda had not been her direct superior.

Good bosses were hard to find. When they'd started, they'd had Dr. Radnor. He'd died in Alabama and had been replaced with Dr. Murasawa, who'd stayed on.

Melinda had been there all along. Joule knew Cage had thoroughly enjoyed working for her and with her. She wondered how much worse this might be for him right now. She couldn't even open her mouth to ask him. He shouldn't have to answer, anyway.

All of it added up and she didn't want to go back. She knew that a good job that paid well was worth everything. While she had the occasional coworker she didn't like, it seemed they didn't last very long with the company—as though no one liked them or they just didn't fit. Helio Systems Tech had specific designs on the way they wanted to run things. Joule and Cage had fit in very well.

Would this be a deal-breaker? Would they really just walk away from three years on a job that kept them together and gave them satisfying work?

Then again, should she really question whether the death of several of her coworkers was a deal-breaker? It seemed like it absolutely should be, though none of it was the company's fault.

Eventually, she peeled herself off the couch, headed over to the table, and pulled her laptop out of the bag. That set her thoughts twirling off on another tangent.

Something deep and needful twisted and ached at the thought of going *home*.

Instead of doing anything about it, she opened the laptop, checked her email, and then opened the one she'd come for.

She looked up at her two companions, still sitting in their own silence, inaction their only action. They were all refugees from a tragedy—one that might have been preventable, or maybe not. One that hammered home the problem that they might not be able to save anyone. Would this drive them further into their own silence or maybe bring them closer? She asked the question to find out.

"We have the autopsy report on Dr. Achebe. Do you want to see it?"

She let the words hang in the glaring silence. For a moment, she waited for her own voice to echo back, but it didn't. No one said anything.

Slowly, Dr. Brett and Cage migrated over to sit on either side of her, even picking up the chairs and moving them closer. Maybe this was good. Not that reading an autopsy report was *good* in any measure, but if it snapped them out of the melancholy another death brought, Joule was willing to use it.

The three of them leaned in, Joule scrolling the screen only when they'd all finished each page. No one spoke until they hit the end of the paperwork.

Sitting back, she said, "There was a needle mark in her thigh."

"The EpiPen." The first words her brother had spoken in hours. He made sense.

"What about the one in her arm?" Joule asked.

54

"You do it." Joule had pushed the phone across the table toward him. He didn't need her phone, though. He had his own.

"Fine." He simply hadn't called Helenie Warren himself before. Joule had always done it.

"Cage!" the researcher responded with his nickname. While she didn't sound *pleased* to hear from him—and under the circumstances who could blame her?—she also sounded like he was an old friend. He took that as a positive.

"Hi, Dr. Warren—"

"Helenie, please. This is all way too messed up for titles."

That at least made him smile. His whole day was way too messed up for titles. Way too messed up for food and everything else.

"Is Joule there?" she asked.

He nodded before realizing how stupid that was and added, "Yes."

"Hi ... Helenie." He heard his sister stumble slightly over the first name. "Dr. Brett Christian is here, too."

There was a pause. "Is he the one you talked about? The veterinarian?"

"Yes," Cage added.

"Welcome, Dr. Christian. We're glad to have you."

He quickly joined the conversation, doing as she had and brushing away the title. "We're in too deep for titles, like you said. I'm just Brett."

Though as he said it, his head turned from side to side, and he made a pointed stare to each of the twins, making it clear they should just call him "Brett" from now on, too.

Interesting, Cage thought. They'd grown up a lot since they'd first met him. They'd been high school kids back then and the title had been appropriate. It was an odd moment, though, to realize that while Dr. Brett had referred to himself around them as just "Brett," on only a few occasions had Cage felt comfortable using just the man's first name. Maybe it was official now.

"We read the autopsy report," he told Helenie.

"What did you think?" An interesting tone shaded her voice, and Cage found it reassuring to be consulted by a CDC researcher.

There was silence for a moment, as if they didn't think anything, but Cage was actually convinced they all thought too much. Helenie filled the gap with her own thoughts.

"I'm a biopharmaceutical researcher. Cage, I'm sure you have much more human physiology experience, in the broad sense, than I do. And, Brett, you've got such a wide scope of physiological knowledge that I'm hoping together we can put it all into one piece."

Joule, the only non-biologist in the group, grinned and sat back as though she'd been dismissed, though Cage doubted that was actually the case.

He dove in. "She had a needle mark on her thigh, which we're assuming was from self-administering the EpiPen." He'd seen the screen for that in the report. Maybe, given what had happened or with a nudge from someone at the CDC, they'd known to specifically check adrenaline and found it to be high.

"Yes, that's what we thought, too," Helenie added. "The bullet hole is my main concern."

There was a deeply wounded chuckle underneath the wording, as though she were trying to cover her own damage. She had worked with Dr. Noemi Achebe for who knew how long, Cage thought. He and his sister had merely met the woman the day before. The timing was concerning, but he hadn't lost a friend in the woods at the beginning of the week—only on the field behind the jet lab this morning.

"The autopsy said the gunpowder residue indicated it was at relatively close range. That's what scared me." This time Helenie's tone was softer. "She faced her killer, and the person got close enough for her to probably see them. I'd been telling myself that it was a hunter out in the woods. That it was an accident."

"A hunter who'd missed with stunningly good aim?" Cage questioned her. He'd not believed that for a second, though one of the sheriff's deputies had suggested it and he'd understood it was a freak possibility.

"It's what I told myself." It was clear she'd since given up on that angle. "I decided I didn't want to dive into the murder angle unless I was forced to."

"We've been forced to now," Joule finally piped in. Of course, she wasn't letting anyone slide. Typical Joule.

"So who would have been after her? And what would they want?" Brett asked.

"I wish I knew," Helenie lamented. Her tone indicated that she wasn't certain this person wouldn't come after her, too.

It was a thought that hadn't occurred to Cage before now. If one CDC researcher was in danger, were *all* CDC researchers in danger? But the conversation kept moving and he didn't get to dwell on it.

"They took her phone," Joule added. It wasn't part of the autopsy report, but the twins had told Helenie that before...

"I've been telling myself that the last point it pinged from was just the last place she had it on. Maybe she turned it off herself."

That was possible, Cage thought, but it didn't solve the problem of her phone not being on her or in her purse.

"Why is the phone valuable?" He pressed what he understood was Joule's point.

"Chuck was tracking her, so he and Pablo knew where she went. But honestly, I don't know why she was killed in the first place. So, it's very hard to determine why the phone itself would be valuable. Maybe she turned it off *because* the battery was low, and she was saving the last bit for when she needed it."

"Maybe..." Joule breathed the word out as she stared at nothing. She was thinking about something, hopefully about to put some valuable pieces together. The researcher couldn't see that, and when Joule didn't pop in with anything brilliant, Cage asked what he thought was a big question. "What about the needle mark in her arm?"

"Had she used the empty syringe in her purse?" Joule asked, now focused back on the conversation. He had no idea if she'd come up with anything.

Cage looked to his sister. Had they told the researchers about the empty syringe before? He couldn't remember. They'd left the scene, picked up Dr. Brett at the airport, and spilled the whole story to him. They'd crashed that night, and then they'd talked to Dr. Warren a few times over the week. They'd all been waiting for this report.

"There were several syringes in her purse. Two with a very pale, yellow, clear liquid in them and one that was used and recapped." He filled in the details now.

"That's weird." Helenie seemed distracted by the information. "I'm not sure what that would be."

Joule added, "We figured she was being environmentally sound by recapping and pocketing it. Littering used needles would be bad."

Cage could almost hear the CDC researcher's eyebrows lift as she put more odd pieces together. "But they didn't take *that*?"

"Well, if they took anything, they left that behind." Cage realized for the first time that he didn't know how many syringes the woman had started with.

"The phone was turned off..." Helenie had veered the conversation back to the phone. She, too, was trying to puzzle it out. "So, whoever took it from her turned it off...."

Her words trailed away, but Dr. Brett picked them up. "If they knew she had a tracking program, that would be the immediate first thing to do."

"As soon as they turn it back on, it will track again," Joule pointed out.

"Oh!" Helenie and her team apparently hadn't thought of that yet. "We have the program here. We can track it now. Pablo! Chuck!" she called back over her shoulder.

It was only Friday. He'd been losing track of time, but they must all still be in the office. Cage thought *everyone was there*. "Have you not tracked the phone again?"

There was a scramble, and a silence drew out as they checked.

"Nothing." Cage heard the word in the distance before Helenie repeated it directly to them.

"So," Joule added, "whoever has it, hasn't turned it on yet... Wait, that doesn't make any sense. Why steal it and not turn it on?"

"But we should be able to get a warrant and get most everything from it, right?" Helenie asked.

The three of them looked at each other. It seemed none of them knew.

Joule added back into the non-answer. "Or they removed the tracking device somehow. Was it a device?"

"No. It was a program..." Helenie replied. Then she called back over her shoulder again. "It was just an app, right?... Yes. Chuck and Pablo have it too."

More than just Noemi, Cage thought but didn't ask. Joule was still speaking. "Then they didn't turn it on. If it was an app, it would have activated as soon as they turned the phone on. There shouldn't be any avoiding that."

"So, why take the phone and not turn it on?" Cage posed to the group.

"Maybe to remove it from circulation?" Joule suggested, but then she had a thought.

The three all looked to each other for a moment, and he thought it at the same time that his sister said the words.

"If she faced her killer, then Dr. Achebe might have known she was in danger. I wouldn't imagine a shot that close would be a complete surprise."

There was another moment of silence as they all contemplated the concerning issue his sister had laid at their feet.

But Joule wasn't done. "If she knew the phone was valuable, maybe she turned it off herself and tossed it away."

55

"We can cross here." Joule motioned as she tucked one finger carefully under the barbed wire and lifted. The middle strand was missing between these posts, and she wanted to believe they could climb through without catching or cutting themselves.

What were they even doing? she'd asked herself for the whole drive here.

They were breaking onto private property... *again*. This time, if they were caught, they'd surely be arrested.

That wasn't stopping any of them though. The light of day was fading, and she hoped that would work in their favor. It would definitely work against them locating a dead phone easily, but her highest priority now was not getting hauled in for questioning on a murder she was already a suspect in.

The fact that it wasn't stopping Dr. Brett—just *Brett*, she corrected herself mentally—was the only reason she was continuing on. She'd decided he was the adult in the group, so when he'd given this outing the green light, she'd had no more excuses.

Now, he reached out, hooking his finger through the bottom

strand of wire, and held it down. He motioned Cage through the bigger hole they had made. On the other side, Cage reached back and took the piece from Dr. Brett, holding the tension. He and Joule held it while the vet hunkered down and played a careful game of winding his body parts carefully through the odd opening with not quite enough light to see.

Joule looked over her shoulder, careful not to drop the wire. There was a farmhouse in the distance, but no one was outside. Another was down the street, though that house was a distant dot and would require someone with free time and a pair of binoculars aimed exactly the right direction to see them. She held out hope that no one was watching, though they were essentially in the open and only about fifteen feet from the roadside. They'd dressed in relatively dark colors and had their personal phones turned off.

"Joule!" Cage snapped and she turned back to the task at hand and climbed through.

She wondered if alarms would go off when she set her feet on land she didn't own, but nothing happened—nothing she could hear, anyway. The farmer owned cows, but they didn't seem to be in the area where Dr. Achebe had walked, and they didn't seem to be here, either. Still, she tried to watch where she stepped as she moved quickly toward the trees.

Behind her, the two men released the barbed wire and it snapped back into place as she looked at the new phone they'd bought. Hoping to mark a GPS spot, she checked the map, but already the signal was too poor.

Frustrated, she stopped, still out in the open, still exposed should a driver come by. The two guys marched right past her, but she wasn't having it. In a move she'd perfected with years of carrying a backpack rather than a purse, she swung it forward and unzipped it with one hand. Reaching in with a "Were you really going to walk away?" look on her face, she coughed to get their attention and held up her roll of pink marking tape.

It was notably smaller than it had been when she'd come to Charleston. The job in South Carolina was one of the last places she'd expected to use marking tape for a trail. But here she was.

Ignoring her expression, but following her unspoken instructions, Brett backtracked a few feet and reached out to take the tape from her. "We can't mark the fence, it's too obvious."

He turned around, tape roll in hand, scanning the area. "Which way do we think we're going?"

"That way." Cage pivoted his phone, holding up the screen and reading the stationary map because the signal certainly wasn't aligning them with GPS. "It should be over there that we found the doctor's body."

The property was too open for her taste, and Joule was now itching to get out of sight.

When the three agreed, they traipsed with the tape remaining in Brett's hand, unused. Once they headed into the cover of trees, relief slowly infused itself through her system. She wasn't out of the woods yet. Literally, she was just *into* them, but it already felt safer.

They paused as the eldest among them turned and ripped a piece of pink tape and tied it where they could easily find it on a tree. It was bright enough to spot in the dark, as surely it would be full dark by the time they returned. They would need it to signal them that this was the right place to leave the woods, to orient them back toward the break in the fence and the way to get back to their car, but it wouldn't flag anyone driving by on the road.

They'd parked away from the break in the fence, away from the point they'd seen where they thought they could get through. They were also on the other side of the farm from where they'd come in when they were first tracking Noemi Achebe. Confident that if they parked the same car in the same spot they had when they'd found the dead body earlier in the week, the sheriff's department might catch on.

"We should have rented a car," Joule said now, even though it was far too late.

"I don't think it matters. It's been five days," her brother added.

"We're confident no one will be out here?" she asked the veterinarian, as though his adulthood made his answers more solid.

"Absolutely not. I don't normally break into other people's properties to illegally mess with crime scenes."

She raised an eyebrow at him, as if he were insinuating that she and her twin brother often did. This, at least, was new for them, too. With everything else they'd done, maybe it was surprising that tampering with a crime scene was something they'd never checked off their list before. She tipped her head and headed further into the woods, ready to get this over with.

It took a few wrong turns and crossed paths, trying to match where they were to where they wanted to be simply off maps on the phone, but when they arrived at the point they thought was correct, they stopped.

There were no markers or anything indicating this had been a crime scene. Should there be something here, five days later? Joule had no idea. The trail looked as though people had come through, but ... what she was looking for, she didn't know.

"Is this really it?" Joule stood in the middle of the trail, turning a circle before she realized she wasn't confident that she wasn't standing in the spot where they found the body. Surely, standing in the exact spot was bad juju. She shone her phone light on the littered trail and stepped aside.

They'd decided it was dark enough and they were far enough in to use the flashlights to make their way through. No one should spot them. It still wasn't enough to make her confident that *this* wasn't the spot.

Cage shook his head. "I have no idea. We came from the other direction last time."

So, they walked past the point they thought was right, then turned around and tried to trace their steps from the other day. Dr. Brett trailed behind them. He hadn't been here at all before.

When that didn't work, she stopped again. Cage sighed in a way that told her he had nothing to contribute either.

Turning to Dr. Brett, Joule confessed. "They're all trees. I don't know enough to distinguish one tree from another. It's not even the same time of day. I have no idea if we're in the right space."

"We need to go further back," Cage told them. "If we're in the right place, we should be able to pick it up from the other side."

Without any better ideas, they backtracked again. This time, they went farther than before. They had to have crossed the spot where her body was, though Joule had no idea exactly where that might be.

"I was hoping there would still be crime scene markers or something that would make it obvious." This was harder than she'd expected. The sheriff's deputies and whoever else might have been investigating had removed all their little yellow tents with numbers that had marked the evidence. The body was long gone. "Would there be any blood spots on the trail?"

"It'll be there where she was killed," Brett answered, though he didn't look at her and did his best to keep his eyes on the trail. "We may have to brush the leaves out of the way, but the blood stain will still be there. It will look like a darker spot of soil."

"But we didn't even see blood on the trail when we found her and that was just a few hours after she died." Joule wasn't ready to try finding the bloodstain yet.

"Which just makes it harder."

She kept her eyes on her brother and on the surrounding

area. If anything, the farmer should be patrolling his land much more thoroughly now that he'd dealt with an influx of investigators and a dead body, which he'd clearly been upset about at the time.

"Got it!" Cage announced.

"This isn't it," Joule protested. She knew that much. They were not even near the right spot now. "This is definitely too far back."

But her brother seemed to understand, so he held up his phone up. His own GPS had picked up their trail. That was probably the "Got it!" he'd meant. It was now overlaid on the map of Noemi Achebe's last trip.

Peering close to the small screen, Joule saw that they were well past where they wanted to be, but holding a signal was at least a little easier than hooking into one in the first place. They managed to let their own tracker dot follow the path for a while. This time when they arrived back at the site, the signal was still gone, but they were more confident.

Joule paused and turned a full circle again, pointing into the trees. "Alright, that means her purse was over here…"

Without further comment, they each wandered into the brush and did as thorough a search of the surrounding area as they could. They spiraled out from the point where they suspected the purse had been, but it yielded nothing.

When they gave up, the three regrouped on the trail where the dot was last marked.

"This was where she turned it off." Cage held up the phone again. "If she tossed it, maybe she tossed it from here. Maybe it was the first move she made, trying to keep her data safe."

Cage swept an arm wide. "Maybe if a person was behind her on the trail, she threw it the other direction to keep them from finding it."

They began searching the leaves and debris in new directions. Forty minutes later, they found the phone.

"It was under some leaves, but the metal casing glinted from my flashlight!" Dr. Brett had pulled gloves from his pocket before picking it up, carefully pinching it to not destroy evidence. "Should I turn it on?"

"No!" The twins practically yelled it in unison.

Joule added, "There's a tracking app on it. You'll alert anyone who's watching it."

Cage seemed to have already figured out that part, but now he looked to his sister. "If we can't turn it on, what do we do with it?"

56

C age unlocked the apartment door and stepped inside with Joule and Brett following closely behind. The three of them had returned from the farm without a word spoken, until the door was closed behind them. The night had settled in around them while they'd exited the woods pulling down their markers as they went, hoping they hadn't missed any. The moonlight guided them back to their exit spot in the barbed wire.

Joule now looked to them, though it was clear to Cage that neither he nor Dr. Brett had any answers. "If we turn it on, anyone tracking it pinpoints us here."

"That's just the CDC tracking it though, right?" Cage asked, but even as he'd spoken the words, he'd wondered...

"Don't risk it," Dr. Brett warned.

He'd almost just hit the button when he found the phone. What had changed his perspective? Cage almost asked "Why don't you think so?"

Brett looked back and forth between them. "The doctor who carried this phone, she was out in the woods, right?"

The twins nodded in unison.

"On private land. Right?"

They nodded again.

"Literally in the middle of nowhere."

Cage put it together then. "And she'd been killed. Someone had tracked her to that exact point."

Joule was agreeing now. "They killed her with one single bullet at close range. Someone besides the CDC was tracking the phone."

"Or it *was* the CDC," Cage offered quietly and with a shrug. Though who at the CDC would kill Dr. Achebe? Chuck? Pablo? *Helenie?* He didn't want to believe that. They spent a tense hour debating what to do next.

Then they packed.

Everything. Their favorite tumblers that they brought to every job site. The waffle iron they carried to each new location. All their clothes and toiletries. They emptied the drawers and checked behind the couch. They logged out of any programming on the TV and made Dr. Brett do a full idiot check.

They were leaving. They had a potentially deadly piece of equipment in their hands. They could not be found at their last known address. No one at Helio Systems Tech understood they shouldn't tell anyone where to find them. Though Cage didn't think anyone at work would give out their address, he couldn't be here if they did. And the sheriff's department was tracking the old phones.

The twins spent time hand-inputting their contact lists into the new phones. They couldn't have anyone just link into the old ones and latch onto the new ones. That would defeat the whole purpose. They were interrupted regularly by Brett calling out and asking if something belonged with the apartment or if Joule had meant to leave her shampoo behind.

"It's almost empty!" she called out, as Cage watched her gaze never lift from the contacts list she was checking and double checking. A switched number might mean the person was lost to them forever. He double- and triple-checked his own. Data entry was not his strong suit.

At two in the morning, they carried everything down the stairs, hoping the dark would cover them. One bag held samples, various mosquitos they had caught and tested during the three days they'd spent researching with Dr. Brett. They shoved in the supplies Chuck had left with them from Dr. Achebe's car.

Finally, everything was stowed in the trunk and backseat. They'd eaten nothing but fast food for the past twenty-four hours. Cage's stomach was starting to protest, and it wasn't going to get any better in the middle of the night. They drove through the one fast food place that was open then headed to the airport.

They rented a new car and left theirs in long-term parking.

It was the height of paranoia, Cage thought. However, when Brett said it was maybe a good idea, he'd put more stock in it. Only after they transferred everything over did they hit the road. Four hours later, they were getting close.

"Here." Joule pointed up ahead, indicating a turn-off.

He remembered the city and the freeways were always busy, or at least they had been every time Cage could remember coming through. They'd get there soon enough.

Brett appeared to have fallen asleep, his head on a pillow propped against the window. He was wedged in with the gear and suitcases creeping well past the midpoint of the back seat. He'd not complained at all, and had even offered again to take the back, though Joule had almost fought him for it.

It felt odd to be fleeing with the car full, rather than heading out on a grand adventure. They'd not ever done this before—quit their jobs in the middle of the night and cleared out the unit they were in.

Cage had been ready to call Dr. Warren and tell her that

they were on their way as soon as they'd made the decision. But Joule had pushed him to wait.

"It's her cell and it's still early."

He agreed with her. He didn't add that, if it was someone at the CDC who'd killed Dr. Achebe, then no one knowing they were coming until the last minute might work in their favor.

No one suggested calling the sheriff's department and letting them know the twins were, in fact, leaving town. No one from any law department had contacted them after the roadside interviews. They made what they felt was a reasonable assumption that the *don't leave town* order couldn't possibly still hold if it hadn't been reiterated.

Cage wasn't sure how well that would work if someone in law enforcement actually did come after them. But if the department was watching, they would catch on really quick when the phones didn't move. The twins had left them—the only personal items left behind—turned on and placed squarely on the kitchen counter.

If anyone asked, he'd answer. He had no problem telling law enforcement where he was, he just had issues with being tracked in general. He had objections in the specific when one of the researchers who was being traced had likely been killed because of that tracker.

"I'm going to call Dr. Murasawa." Joule held up her phone, speaking relatively quietly so as not to wake Brett in the backseat. The "too early" argument didn't work there.

He listened to the one side of the conversation as Joule left a message in her kindest, gentlest words saying that they were abandoning the apartment. She said they were traveling, and the apartment would be open if Helio Sys wanted to put anyone else in it.

Thinking about that made the feeling settle a little deeper into Cage—maybe they were doing the right thing. Finding Dr. Achebe's phone had lit a fire under all of them.

Joule hung up, her expression pensive but her thoughts already turning to the next thing to take care of. "We probably have an hour to eat something for breakfast and then get to the CDC before we meet up with Dr. Warren."

"It's Saturday and she just lost a colleague. I suspect she'll come in whenever we ask. She might already be in," Brett commented from the back seat, more awake than Cage had expected. None of them had truly slept.

"Maybe she'll meet us somewhere else, not on the CDC campus," Joule suggested.

Cage shook his head. Seeing Dr. Brett offer the same reaction from the backseat, he tried to keep his eyes on the road and wait for signals from his sister about where he should turn off. He let the vet explain.

"From what I've heard, I don't think our killer is Helenie. But we don't tell any of them where we're staying, and we don't meet them alone."

"Somewhere that a killer could put a bullet in the three of us and disappear with the phone," Joule filled in, backtracking her earlier idea. "The CDC might be best. It should at least have security cameras."

It was a shitty game, Cage thought, and he didn't know how to fight it. The Night Hunters had been biological, and they acted like biological creatures. So had the sharks. The tornadoes had been a weather problem. In the end, they were just physics—maybe physics they couldn't quite predict, but they had still been physics. He wasn't quite sure how to face down *people*.

"We keep ourselves safe at all costs," Dr. Brett added from the backseat, now leaning forward. Only then did Cage even put together the added idea that Brett had a sick wife to go home to. They'd been getting updates, but his wife hadn't been part of Cage's sphere and he regretted forgetting about her. Still, Brett seemed in for a pound on this adventure and he was still giving out advice. "Which means we feed ourselves something decent. My stomach's about to turn upside down."

So it wasn't just him, Cage thought. They stopped at a restaurant serving a solid, sit-down breakfast. They ordered omelets and sides of fruit. Joule got a salad on the side of hers, surprising him. Then, as they climbed back into the car, Dr. Achebe's phone still safely tucked into Joule's backpack, they faced the final step in fleeing their life in Charleston.

Cage didn't start the car yet as Joule pulled out her phone and called Dr. Helenie Warren. They all leaned in, waiting for the researcher to answer as the line rang.

57

"Thank you. We appreciate it," Cage said into the phone. Joule leaned in next to him as he held it over the center console. Dr. Brett hung forward from the back seat.

Cage figured they were officially homeless right now, but that was okay. No one could ransack a hotel room they didn't have.

"No," Helenie added. "Don't thank me. I want you in the lab. It's where we'll all be safest."

Her words drove home the concern she had for their well-being, too. It was easier to brush it aside when he could tell himself he was just being paranoid. But he couldn't hold onto the worry; Dr. Warren was still talking.

"I need Dr. Brett Christian's full name and social security number to get him in as a guest. You two are already cleared from earlier."

"Are you ready?" Brett leaned forward and rattled off spellings and the rest of his information.

Cage guessed Brett would trust these researchers if he and Joule already had.

Helenie got what she needed from him. "All right. It's going to be an hour or two before I can get you through this security check. We're a little thin of staff on the weekends, but there's always someone here."

They got directions to the lab building and where to park before they hung up.

"We have two hours to kill in Atlanta," Joule told them.

"Let's go find the CDC." Brett was still leaning forward over the seat. Though the offices were just slightly north of Charleston, it didn't feel any cooler here. "Turn the car back on, please. I'm about to die here. I was not built for a Southern summer. I've never been to the CDC before. Once we know where we are going, we can spiral out and look for a nearby hotel."

Cage turned the key, and the air conditioning flooded the car again, thankfully reducing the heat.

"Ah!" Brett let out a relieved sigh that almost made Cage laugh. His next words shut that thought down. "I'll put the hotel room in my name in case anyone's looking for either of you."

"Shit." Cage looked to his sister. "What if they *are* looking for us? What if the CDC background check brings up that we're wanted in a murder trial?"

Joule shook her head. "It's not a murder *trial,* it's just a murder. And we're not wanted, we're just *persons of interest.*" She made air quotes as she spoke, brushing him off. "I doubt that the County Sheriff's Department has managed to put some national BOLO out on us. Also, Helenie said we cleared."

That calmed him down considerably. They had been warned not to leave town, and they had, in fact, left town. They'd even left the state. But there wouldn't be any warrants on them. Nothing like that unless the investigation had progressed further and turned up something on the twins that made them actual suspects. He hated not knowing.

It took longer than planned to reach the CDC building.

Apparently, exactly as Brett had suspected, it took a little while to find the right entrance and locate the building Helenie wanted them to park at. It was smart to have come here first.

Cage paused, driving slowly around the campus but entering nothing he wasn't allowed. It was kind of wild to be here. He looked up at the big buildings covered in glass, the blue signs splashed with the CDC logo that he'd only seen in pictures and on TV.

"That bird looks a little too close to the post office logo," Joule said. "Someone should have checked the trademark."

He'd almost laughed.

Brett sat in the backseat, looking out the window almost like a kid.

"How come you've never been here before?" Cage asked over his shoulder.

"When would I need to? I did vet school in Knoxville and, aside from a few things I've gotten notice of and all the standard things I've vaccinated people's pets for, I haven't dealt with any infectious diseases before. Certainly not any emerging ones."

"Yeah, well, neither have we," Cage added. It suddenly hit him, that was exactly what they were doing. This was an emerging disease. Maybe not just an allergic reaction to a tainted or oddly processed food.

He took a turn, not knowing where he was going. He drove them aimlessly around the campus as the trio looked at everything. He wondered if their car making odd little turns and going to too many buildings like tourists was triggering anyone watching surveillance. But his thoughts were cut short by the phone ringing.

He turned away from the campus, intending to leave. He let his sister pick up the line and say, "It's Dr. Murasawa."

He found himself in a somber conversation as he tried to watch road signs in a strange city. Their boss had returned the call. Joule had to tell her that yes, the decision was serious, the apartment was empty, and they were already out of state and couldn't come back.

"We're sorry to lose you from this job, though I do understand why you left. We want you to know that we will offer you another position in the future on another site, if you want it."

"I appreciate that. Please do keep us in mind." Joule used her best professional voice, but Cage felt some hope bloom in his chest. He hadn't known if they'd shot themselves in the foot by leaving this way. But finding out what was on Dr. Achebe's phone was a necessity. The rest wasn't.

Cage didn't like letting his bosses down. He didn't like the feeling that still snuck in at the edges of his lungs, even though Dr. Murasawa wasn't upset with them. He'd never cheated on a test except for that one time in third grade, and he still felt bad about it. His parents had raised him that knowledge was king. Loyalty was tantamount. And family was everything. He considered—and was confident Joule did, too—Helio Systems Tech people were his work family. His failure and sudden exit felt like he'd let them down.

"We should go look at the hotel first, before we take the room," Dr. Brett said, not quite catching the twins' emotional turn. "Sometimes they're not what they look like in the pictures."

With a nod, Cage pulled himself together and they followed the vet's directions.

"It looks fine to me," Joule said as they pulled up in front of the four story building. "More importantly, it looks perfectly average."

Brett filled in his thinking on choosing it. "It's a chain, which is good. And it has indoor room entry. That will make it harder for anyone to get to us."

"Good point," Joule said. "Lord knows Dr. Achebe just walked up and knocked on our door with no one knowing."

This did feel more secure, Cage agreed. He was already parking in the lot just in front of the lobby. They were all unclicking their seatbelts, but Brett had other ideas.

"I'm heading in. You guys stay out here." He was gone before there was a chance to protest.

Cage added, "It's like we're his kids."

Joule didn't counter his comment. Maybe it was good to still be someone's kid.

Sure enough, Dr. Brett returned, having checked them in under his name. He leaned in the car window and told them, "You're not on the paperwork at all."

Together, they scoped the room out and sat down for a while.

They brought in only the suitcases with clothes—nothing they couldn't afford to lose. Nothing they didn't need the CDC to see. Without any time to relax, it was already time to leave.

"We'll run late if we wait any longer," Joule had said, heading back into her room and stuffing her phone back down in her backpack. She stood at the door as she expertly slipped one strap over her shoulder.

Cage checked the room he was sharing with Brett. The vet had gotten them a suite and he and Cage took the twin beds in one room, leaving Joule the other room to herself. The advantage of being the lone one of her gender, as if any of that mattered. He patted down his cargo pants to be sure he had everything before they climbed into the car and retraced their path back to the CDC.

They retraced the directions Helenie Warren had given them.

"What do we need to bring with us?" Joule asked, but she was already popping the trunk. The answer wouldn't be "nothing."

They pulled the CDC equipment Chuck had loaned them, as well as the samples of mosquitos and the data log notebook

Cage had insisted they keep. They were hauling supplies in. Probably not the usual visitors.

On the other side of the security panel, Helenie—red headed younger than expected—smiled at them and waited for them to get checked through. It took a while to process everything. Joule's backpack was x-rayed, and Cage had to empty all of his pockets. The guard had looked at them oddly as they'd scanned equipment already clearly engraved with the CDC logo.

"They're with me," Helenie assured the guard, who was just doing his job. "We lent them the equipment."

It probably didn't help that they'd packed their samples in the small suitcase they carried. They really looked like they were coming to stay. The guard dutifully scanned the suitcase, too. Surely the petri dishes full of individual mosquitoes laid out and fixed could not be news to him.

Eventually, they were wanded down and allowed to pass through. On the other side, Helenie greeted them with visitor badges that bore their names and some stripes and coding that Cage was sure told everyone but them what they could and couldn't touch. Each tag had a photo, likely pulled from their driver's license pictures, Cage thought.

Cage and Joule grinned at each other and tipped their tags like fools. Their tags both said "Consultant." Dr. Brett was relegated to "Guest."

The sheriff hadn't put out enough of a warning to stop the CDC from letting them into the labs. As Cage grinned at the thought, Dr. Warren was turning around.

"Follow me." Then she was walking them back to the lab.

"We have to restart that phone. But you're not going to believe what we found."

58

"Hi, I'm Mike." The tall, dark-haired man met them in the hallway outside a lab marked "Achebe-Warren." He reached a gloved hand out to shake.

Joule held her own hand out before realizing it was probably a bad idea with his glove on. Yanking her own back just as he did, she grinned as he apologized.

"Sorry. I'm just in the lab so much." Peeling the blue glove, he then reached out again barehanded. "Nice to meet you."

"Joule Mazur," she added, pointing to her "Consultant" tag with a grin.

"She and her brother, Cage," Helenie added, "are the ones I was telling you about. They were some of the first to link what we're seeing to the mosquitoes." Then she turned to the trio and explained. "Mike is from the lab next door to mine. He's in the Abellard-Brookwood lab."

Mike shook hands with Cage and then with Brett, each of them getting introduced. "Our labs work on different projects," he explained, "but oftentimes we realize they overlap."

He walked down the hall to his own door. Or he treated it as such, even though Joule saw the plaque read "Abellard-Brookwood." "Jordan and Jillian— Abellard and Brookwood—went to India last year, testing an outbreak of what appeared to be Sleeping Sickness."

So far, Joule followed along. She felt she was able to follow the sentences as well as her brother, but figured that would change relatively soon.

"Sleeping Sickness itself is considered sudden-onset, but this variety—or new disease—is even more rapid onset. Victims are falling severely ill in under an hour."

Dr. Warren was hanging back. It seemed she and Mike had already figured this out. Joule paid attention to Mike, since he was the one dispensing information, and it was on her to keep up.

"In fact," Dr. Warren added, "Mike and I started discussing this yesterday after you went looking for the phone. We only just realized the connection."

At least, Joule thought, no one had been holding out on them.

"How does that even work? The one-hour onset?" Cage asked and Joule felt the conversation beginning to slip away. "How would viral replication even reach that kind of a load in that small amount of time after infection? Were you sure it was one hour?"

"Not at first," Mike added. "For exactly the reasons you mention, we were confident we were missing something." Then the scientist got a look Joule had seen so many times at work. *This was where it got interesting.* "So, were the mosquitoes able to transmit such a high inoculating dose?"

Yep. Joule had thought she followed along, but she was now scrambling. Cage was not. Brett was not.

"It's not that high, but it is a high dose in the initial injection through the interaction we call a 'bite.' However, it turns out it's not the viral load that's hurting the patients. It's the specific points at which the virus is attacking the cell. It's triggering cells to signal *en masse* almost immediately upon infection."

"I'm sorry." Joule looked between them. "I'm an engineer, not a biologist."

"Gotcha." Mike turned to look at the other two as though asking if they needed further help, too.

Joule answered for them. "Oh, no, I'm confident they understood you."

With a smile and a nod, the scientist continued. "Most viruses enter a cell, and it takes anywhere from three to five days for them to replicate enough to make a person sick enough to feel symptoms. The virus uses the body to replicate itself. This high-level replication creates enough virus in the host for the person to become a vector themselves."

He paused. Joule waved her hand. This explanation was working, but she did ask her question. "A vector can transmit it to someone else?"

"Exactly. The high viral load allows the person to breathe, sneeze, or bleed out enough to infect someone else. Here, damage is happening well before that, within the first hour. The virus isn't even getting to replicate. It's simply changing the cell signals."

"Enough to make people sick immediately?" Cage asked and Mike nodded in reply.

Helenie jumped in, helping Joule out. "When you're sick, you don't actually feel the virus or the bacteria in your system. What you feel—the fever, the aches, the heaviness in your lungs—that's mostly your body's reaction in an attempt to fight the infection. With this new disease, the virus is signaling the body to do all of those things well before it's even replicated enough to need the body to fight it."

"Okay," Joule thought she'd caught up. But it didn't matter, the race was on and everyone else was ahead of her.

"Then what's the point?" Brett asked. "Even generically

speaking, that's a horrible way to evolve. If it kills its host immediately and doesn't replicate, then it doesn't get to jump to the next host and the virus dies with the patient."

"We were thinking the same thing," Mike added. "But we found that ultimately, it didn't matter. Humans aren't the reservoir for this disease, the mosquitoes are. As long as it's replicating enough somewhere else, then the virus doesn't die out. Also, enough people survive that it doesn't matter if it kills a handful along the way."

"Is fifty percent enough?" Joule asked, appalled. That was what the survival rate they'd seen was.

"It is." Mike's answer was solid and unflinching. "Not for us, but to viruses, it's a perfectly acceptable percentage."

She didn't like that answer.

There was a pause as the scientists seemed to give her a moment to absorb the random cruelty of nature.

Helenie hopped in, as though her information would soothe the cut Joule had just suffered. "Brookwood and Abellard should be getting in this afternoon. They're just returning from yet another research trip to India. They've been doing blood draws on a variety of people to see if some of them are repositories for the virus, that they survived initial infection, maybe even completely asymptomatic."

"Taking a bite on those people would give the mosquitoes enough virus to transmit to the next person?" Joule asked. It sucked being the only engineer in the room.

"Right now, that's the working theory," Mike answered her. "I'm here, running samples and sitting on my assays."

Cage and Brett laughed at something Joule didn't quite catch, but the conversation moved too fast.

"The other researchers went to India..." Joule was putting some of the pieces together. So was her brother.

"That's the region the *Aedes Karnatakan* mosquito is named for."

Joule asked her next question, just trying to organize all the scrambled pieces she had. "So, when the mosquito came here, it brought the virus with it?"

"That's what we think." Then Mike added, "It may not matter. It's nice to know the history of the disease. Sometimes knowing the origin helps us fight it, sometimes not. Right now, Brookwood and Abellard are checking to be sure it's the same thing. Then, if we have a solution for there, we have one for here, too."

Joule was nodding along, grateful that everyone was willing to speak in English plain enough for her.

"Do you want to come see the labs?" Mike asked then.

Joule was more than willing to give her brain a rest for a moment and readily agreed.

Helenie nodded, seeming anxious to get them in. "We'll charge the phone and once it's got a little juice, we'll get it turned on and see what's on it."

Joule handed over the phone and Helenie stepped aside with it, finding a charger and plugging it in. Joule found she felt calmer that the woman hadn't left their sight. It would have been easy to swap out the phone or move it away. Had she realized her guests might suspect everyone? Either way, the phone sat in plain sight and Helenie moved back to join the little tour.

Mike started in his own lab. The place was large. Two scientists in white coats stood at the counters, pipetting something into micro test tubes.

"You're working on the weekends?" Cage asked.

"Some of these tests take five or more days to run." Mike shrugged at them as if to say, *What are you going to do?* One of the scientists look up and nodded at him confirming that it was, in fact, a multi-day test.

She added, "If we don't start on Monday, we work through the weekend."

Joule could only nod along, once again thinking that she

might be the slow kid in this parade, but she wasn't having to pipette reagents on the weekends.

"Over here, next door, this is my lab.... Well, it was mine and Dr. Achebe's." Helenie waved at her door, though her eyes cast down. "We didn't do the same experiments, but we overlapped a lot. Not like Brookwood and Abellard."

Joule looked up, wondering what that meant. Mike filled in. "They're married. Consistently investigating as a team, which is not the case for most labs around here."

Joule chuckled at that. It was clear that doctors Warren and Achebe worked together and equally clear that they weren't in each other's pockets. There were obvious missing pieces that Helenie didn't have about the researcher who'd come to their door and had been murdered the very next day.

Still, Dr. Warren was clearly friend enough to add, "I've been dealing with some of the funeral preparations. Dr. Achebe's family is Igbo. Her parents were refugees, and she was their only child."

Joule frowned, and Cage tapped the back of her hand with the back of his and turned to explain. But Helenie filled in a little more. "Refugees from the last wave, apparently. They had Noemi relatively late."

This time, her brother filled in where she was still confused. "From Nigeria. There was a huge wave of refugees after the local civil war, I think. In the sixties and even seventies."

That helped, Joule thought. Helenie was still going on. They'd all lost someone to these bites or the fight to save people from them. She and her brother weren't the only ones.

"The funeral is in two parts," Helenie added. "The first is the burial, and the family is taking care of that. The second part is a celebration of life. They've asked us to be very involved, but we don't know when it will be."

Joule nodded along. Would it interfere with the investigation? Would she attend Kelsey's funeral or Melinda's? Had

Kelsey's family already held it? She didn't know. There were too many different parts of life intersecting, and she was trying to ignore it. She didn't have to plan Dr. Achebe's funeral or her celebration. She probably wasn't invited to either.

Cage asked more questions, seemingly very interested in the culture. While Helenie answered what she could, disclaiming that she was no expert, she didn't know more than they did. Joule wandered the new lab they'd been let into. No one was working here this weekend, and Helenie seemed to have the place to herself.

"What is this?" Joule asked, pointing to but not touching a tray that looked like a DNA sample. Colored bands crawled their way up.

"It's a DNA gel. It's reading a specific sequence of a specific portion of the mosquito DNA. We believe it's an identifier for the new disease."

"Huh," Joule said and was ready to move on.

Her brother looked at her oddly asking, "What is it?"

He wanted to know, *Why this tray?* They were out all over the lab. Photos were taped up of other gels they had run. The lab hoods held trays of more of them. She shrugged at him. "They had the exact same one in the other lab."

"They do run gels as well," Helenie answered, and Mike tipped his head, agreeing with her.

"Yes, but different sequences."

"No," Joule said, frowning. *How well did she trust her memory?* But that kind of thing—quickly memorizing a geometric design—she was really good at.

"This DNA sequence—" she said, pointing at the tray again, still being careful not to get close or even hover her fingers over it, lest she shed some of her own cells into what might be a very touchy project, "—is the exact same one as in your lab."

"It's not," Mike smiled as he countered her.

"It is." The more they told her no the more confident she became.

With a frown and a snap of a new pair of gloves he reached out to pick up the sample. He waited only a moment for an unspoken nod from Helenie. Disappearing around the corner, he was clearly planning to come back and prove Joule wrong. But when he reappeared in the doorway, he looked concerned.

"She's right. We have the same sequence."

59

J oule stood back as everyone bustled around her, looking at the gel samples she'd pointed to.

"That's why we come in on Saturdays!" Mike offered the proclamation while carefully tilting the sample he'd brought over from his lab as a gesture. "These were just developed from samples sent back from India. That kind of match is exactly what we are looking for!"

At least no one was upset with her. In fact, they all seemed downright gleeful.

Everyone else gathered around the plates with Cage and Brett trying to see but also not pushing their way in. There were small exclamations of "They do match!" and "Yes!" as she listened.

"Glad I could help?" It was the only thing she could think of to say.

"You definitely sped the process up a bit. We would have had to compare all of them, and hopefully soon. But it might not have happened until Monday or Tuesday when the full staff is in." Mike was still grinning, gloves on his rapidly moving hands, and Joule was beginning to think he lived in them.

"But it does mean—" Helenie said as she leaned back against the lab table, "—that what you guys are seeing in India is the same thing we're seeing here. What is that sequence from?"

"It's a genetic marker that we found in the saliva of some of the *Aedes Karnatakan*. We think it's what people are reacting to."

"The initial anaphylactic shock?" Joule jumped back in at the part she understood. "So, they don't all carry it?"

"No," Mike answered quickly, and then backpedaled a bit, "at least not the ones from India. What about here?" he asked Helenie.

She immediately shook her head. "We don't know yet. It wasn't anything we were looking for. We can check the samples that we have, though."

Cage motioned to the small suitcase they'd propped in the corner when they arrived. "We brought a ton from Charleston."

Brett added in, "We spent three days traveling the area and collecting samples. We gathered a lot of *Anopheles* and a good amount of *Aedes Aegypti*, but there's enough *Karanatakan* in there to run some solid numbers."

"Is everyone allergic to it?" Joule asked, still trying to figure out why some people were falling ill and some weren't.

"We don't know that either," Helenie sighed this time. "It's still very early in the game. This is the way diseases unfold. We have to see the disease first and then, once we have enough people with something strange, we work to identify the source of it. After we identify the source, we then have to work to find out what specifically in the genetic coding of the virus or the bug or the insect or the mouse—if there's a vector—is causing it or helping it. It's absolutely a learning process and at no point do we think we know everything. We just do the best we can with what we know so far. Right now, the upside is that no matter what it is, it's causing an anaphylactic reaction in a lot of people."

Joule's head jerked back at the harsh comment. Even if she tried, she'd be unable to hide her reaction that she didn't think it was an *upside* at all. She'd watched people die from this thing.

"I meant that we can at least treat that with epinephrine. EpiPens are relatively easy to get."

"They were getting bought out in Florida and in the Charleston area. Actually," Joule added a little sheepishly because who was she to be telling the CDC what she'd researched? "I called random pharmacies all over the south. Everywhere that people had these reactions, the pharmacies were all running short on EpiPens. Other places I spot-checked weren't."

"Other places?" Helenie asked.

"Colorado, Montana, California."

"That's pretty good sampling," the researcher praised her.

Joule, who'd passed her basic chemistry classes and understood scientific method relatively well, shouldn't have felt as flattered as she did. But she did.

"That matches exactly what we've seen here. Again, part of the problem with identifying this is that only a small group of us were working on it. Most of the other labs are trying to find a foodborne allergen or contagion."

Joule still didn't understand why they would think that. Her brother didn't either, and the researcher must have read it on their faces. Joule had learned to keep her mouth shut, but she'd never had an "inside face."

"Unfortunately, all of it makes sense. Here." Helenie led them over to her computer and invited them to watch as she pulled up a screen. "This is why we had to get you guys cleared. If you look at this map..."

When she didn't fill in the end, Cage did. "That's the infected area map, right?"

"Actually, while it would be easy to think that, it's a map of one southern vegetable distributor's district. The vegetables come in from South America, and this company distributes them to the outlined region."

"Oh." Joule hadn't meant to say anything, but the map really did look like exactly where they'd found cases.

"Wait, it gets better." The sarcasm in the researcher's voice was unmistakable as she clicked another button. Another map pulled up, overlaying the first. The red shaded area was now also green. And the green covered a very, very similar swath.

This time, Joule knew better than to assume. "What's that?"

"A meat distributor. Oh, there are *two more*." Helenie flipped buttons, again overlaying the map with two other colors.

"They are all food distributors, that so perfectly match this map?" Joule was stunned. Her home was being fed by entirely different sources than she was getting here.

"Look, I'm not saying it isn't foodborne; I'm not saying they're wrong. I'm just saying the *Aedes Karnatakan* distribution overlap is identical to each of these. So you can see why the bulk of research is going into checking foodborne contamination."

"That's a lot of testing to do." Joule felt better about being ignored now. Though really, they hadn't been ignored at all. They were standing in a CDC lab they'd been invited into because of the research they'd sent.

"Exactly. It's a metric ton of testing. We're just the holdout lab who thought it was a virus with an insect vector."

Joule gestured behind her to where Mike was lining up the gels they'd run, looking for matches. "It looks like you're right."

"It's looking more like it now. But it could have gone any direction. That's why Dr. Achebe wanted to go find you guys. We had limited resources."

"And we were producing data and sending it to you," Cage added with a grin.

"It's always handy when it happens that way," Helenie said, smiling.

It made more sense now. Why Dr. Achebe wanted all of their information and to clear them. Joule felt better having met Dr. Helenie Warren in person and seeing some of the information. Still, there were too many questions.

Joule dove into the reason they came booking down here through the early morning on a Saturday. "We were called into our job for another case. We watched another coworker die."

But she didn't get any further.

"Why are your coworkers falling like flies?" It was Mike this time. He'd left Chuck and Pablo with the samples and joined the group again.

"Well, we explained to Dr. Achebe that we're building on the city outskirts. We're constantly taking samples and testing out in open field."

Helenie nodded. "So, you're encroaching on the mosquitoes' territory."

"Right." Cage nodded along, seemingly sad for the mosquitos getting nudged out of quality solar space.

"This coworker ..." Joule continued, though she felt wrong not calling Melinda by her name and using her merely as data at this point. But that's all she was to these people, and it was what she needed to be. Better that Joule did it this way then that Cage had to. "She had a rash, but not full anaphylaxis. I think I'm saying that right. Her throat didn't close up."

Cage took over the story. "They never used the EpiPen, but she had a sudden onset fever, and she couldn't breathe."

"She drowned in her lung fluids," Helenie added thoughtfully as though she knew what she was talking about. As if that's exactly what this disease did, and it sounded like it was.

"The thing was, maybe what really put us on the road—" Joule began. Her brother watched as her and Brett's eyes narrowed. They knew where she was going with this. "—the

EMTs were late. They might have saved her if they'd gotten there earlier, but they took almost forty-five minutes to arrive. Cage and Brett and I were only ten minutes away, and when our boss called us in, we made it there well before the ambulance."

"Cage and I did CPR for almost twenty minutes waiting for the EMTs," Brett added softly. It wasn't a brag when the patient didn't make it. Joule watched as the researchers' faces all reacted to the new information.

"Another ambulance drove right by us on the street. It was going somewhere else while we waited. When..." she couldn't say *Melinda was dead*, "they were done. they packed up quickly and said it was their third case of the day. It was eleven a.m. And this was the *third* case they'd seen already."

Helenie looked back and forth between them, obviously as concerned as they were by that number. "We'll be getting that data in the next handful of days..." she mused, and then asked, "Is *Aedes Karnatakan* taking over the percentages?"

"I don't know what it looks like now," Joule said, even as Brett added, "I think so. They seem to be outbreeding every other species."

Helenie didn't have the same attachment to Melinda and her story that Cage and Joule did. She turned her attention to Brett, who explained. "Cage and Joule have graphs of distributions they found early on at their worksite. Unfortunately, the data is not an apples to apples comparison. But what we sampled out and around shows *Karnatakan* breeding at a much higher percentage."

"What about at the worksite?"

"We didn't get to go back," Cage filled in softly. "We were off, and our boss told us we weren't allowed on site because we weren't covered."

Helenie nodded. "So not a consistent comparison over time."

Joule shook her head. Then she asked the question she'd wanted to for a long time. "What about the cure?"

"What cure?" Helenie asked as Chuck turned and tipped his head at her, frowning, as did Mike.

At the other end of the lab, Pablo knocked a beaker onto the floor, shattering the glass and splattering a clear liquid all down his pants and shoes as he yelped, "Shit!"

60

C age's head swiveled to the back of the lab, as did all of theirs.

Pablo looked up, then down. "I have to clean this up."

The man couldn't have looked more guilty if he tried.

"Was it acid? Base?" Mike asked, even as Helenie seemed to be stepping forward to help with the cleanup.

"Just DI water, but there's glass everywhere," Pablo explained, still not quite making eye contact with any of them and only then slowly shifting his feet out of the splash radius.

Had he knocked the beaker off himself to distract from Joule's question?

It wouldn't work. Pablo apparently hadn't met Joule. *At least there wasn't more to clean up*, Cage thought. He'd seen worse.

"I'll get the broom." Pablo jumped up to take himself out of the equation.

Yup. Even Joule was looking sideways like *Do you believe this guy?*

"No," Helenie told him as she motioned to Chuck. "You get the broom."

Chuck seemed to protest for a moment, but the lab manager's pointed glare shut him up before he said anything. Then she turned her gaze back to the other lab assistant. "Pablo, what did you do?"

Pablo shook his head.

"You know about this *cure*," she accused again.

He tipped his head one way then another. Shrugged one shoulder. Looked away. "Not really."

That sounded like *something* though. Cage also stared at the man, not because he had any power but because he was such a crappy liar. Lack of game recognized lack of game.

Under all their combined glares, Pablo broke. "I can't!"

With those words, Cage felt his chest constrict and his anger sharpen to a laser focus. "People are dying, Pablo!" Cage bellowed. "Your coworker died! Two of my friends died and another one almost did. So if you know anything..."

Cage was leaning forward, shifting his weight onto the balls of his feet. He hadn't even realized he was doing it until Joule put her hand out, open, on his shoulder. She didn't grab him or actually hold him back, but she softly motioned him to back down.

Both he and his sister were second-degree black belts. While neither of them was the kind to fight much—neither had wanted to go to state championships or anything like that —the old training occasionally came in handy. He was ready.

His father had always told him he liked that the twins were trained because, if either flipped their switch, whoever was on the other side of the ring—or the lab, in this case—knew that they were going up against someone who could take them down.

It was even funnier when Joule did it. Though she was tall, she was incredibly lightweight. Still, no one wanted to mess with her when she got that glare in her eyes and rolled into a stance that told others that she knew what she was doing. Cage wondered if maybe that kind of demonic glow had finally hit him.

"I— I—" Pablo choked out in response, but couldn't finish.

"You better fucking tell everyone right now," Joule demanded. Stepping forward, she pointed her finger at the ground, but she didn't move into a fighting stance. It was almost as if Cage was her chained dog, and Pablo would definitely want to deal with her.

The lab assistant didn't look like much of a fighter himself... at least not any better than he was a liar. Cage watched the man's attention shift to Joule, as though he couldn't tell his bosses or any of the other lab workers, but he could tell her. "We don't know if it's a cure, but we think it might be."

"*What?*" Helenie asked, stunned.

Cage reached out and grabbed the scientist's hand. He squeezed it, silently asking her to step down. If Joule was getting answers, they needed to let her.

Under Joule's directed stare, Pablo kept talking. "Dr. Achebe found a sequence that she thought might work. Oh God, this is so illegal!"

He dipped his head back and looked at the ceiling, while they all waited on pins and needles, hoping he would say something useful. *If it was incredibly illegal,* Cage thought, *Pablo was only getting himself in trouble.* But if he didn't tell them, other people might die.

This time, Pablo looked at them as though he were standing before a firing squad. He spoke with righteousness in his tone and words. "No one here was working on it! When she sent her findings out, the higher-ups told us it didn't work. That we were wrong. They had almost the entire CDC—except for this one lab!—studying food contamination."

He was clearly mad that he and his boss had been ignored. *But the CDC had kept this lab working on this direction,* Cage thought. Pablo was still ranting.

"They said it was maybe something that the cows were being fed that was making it through into the meat." He waved his hands angrily, as though this explanation helped.

Helenie's mouth hung open, as did Mike's, the two of them leaning further forward with every piece of information. Cage could tell they wanted to demand answers. But he'd been here before, and demanding didn't work very well. So, he waited and reached out one hand on each side, tapping them. He could only hope that Pablo didn't see the move as Joule strode forward. She was going for blood.

"You have to tell us or more people will die." She reiterated her brother's words, and Cage would have laughed. Joule was a numbers girl. She liked data. She believed in telling the truth and wasn't one for cajoling people. For whatever reason, she'd adopted Cage's stance on this one. She was right.

Pablo nodded. "Noemi has a friend at a biopharma company."

Helenie and Mike both shrugged at him as if to say, *Who cares?* Chuck, who'd been standing close, sweeping up the last of the glass still near Pablo's feet, looked at him as if to say, *Don't we all?*

It was just the industry, Cage figured. He had scientist friends in other industries, too. Joule had architect friends and friends who were project managers for construction companies. But Helenie then caught on to something more.

"She took the data to them."

Maybe it was easier that somebody else had said it. Pablo closed his eyes and nodded.

"And they developed a cure." Something about the way Helenie said it made Cage think she was more hopeful than angry.

He shouldn't have done it—he shouldn't have taken the attention off Pablo's confession, but he turned and looked at her, his expression asking *Why?*

She shrugged. "A cure is a cure. The way they obtained it may be *horrifyingly illegal*—" She added emphasis to the last two words, tipping her head and aiming her glare back at Pablo, who seemed to shrink under the non-verbal reprimand. "But a cure is a cure. People are dying."

When the rest of them seemed to accept that, Helenie asked more calmly, "Who's the company?"

Pablo shook his head no.

"Just tell me who they are so we can get in touch. I won't out you. I won't out Dr. Achebe."

Cage thought that was too late, though. Pablo shook his head again. So, Cage spoke the words that Pablo couldn't, because Pablo's expression wasn't about being stubborn at all. It was an entirely different emotion that Cage was reading. "It's not about who the company is, is it?"

Pablo didn't answer, but Cage could see he was right. This time he did step forward, leaning onto the balls of his feet, anger shooting right through the core of him. Whatever Pablo and Noemi had done, it was worse than he knew.

Pablo again closed his eyes and shook his head as he choked out the words, "I can't."

Cage strode across the room, almost as though he were going to throttle the lab assistant. He stopped when he realized Pablo offered no resistance. The man would take whatever anyone dished out, because he knew now just how deeply he had fucked up.

Cage turned around to face everyone. For whatever reason, though he didn't mean to do it, it seemed he was shielding Pablo.

But he said the words Pablo couldn't. "They tracked Noemi and they killed her. They're coming after Pablo next."

Behind him, he heard a soft sob as Pablo almost managed to silently agree.

The looks on everyone else's faces fell. Whatever the cure

was, it wasn't coming their way. It wouldn't be anything they could get their hands on. Just to make matters worse, Joule's voice piped up.

"Whoever else is having their phone tracked, you need to turn it off right now. Everyone in this lab now knows at least part of what they killed Noemi for."

61

"We have to power her phone on," Joule said. After their realization about the trouble Pablo had brought to the lab, she'd moved to stand next to her brother.

Though she'd done it unconsciously, she'd formed a line of solidarity. *Odd*, she thought, *or maybe not*. She knew everyone in the lab was on the same side—except Pablo—and the outside world might be coming after all of them. But it had always been her and her brother against the world.

Behind her, Chuck finished the last of a quick mopping of the floor. Pablo leaned against the countertop, though surely that wasn't in compliance with lab safety. He sobbed quietly, but she didn't feel that sorry for him. Had he even taken the gloves off his hands? Joule found she honestly didn't care. Let him contaminate himself. Then again, he already had.

"It should be charged enough to turn it on," Helenie said, and Mike looked at her oddly.

Helenie explained to the other lab worker what had been going down with her people. "Noemi seemed to have turned her phone off and maybe thrown it. Probably just moments before she was killed. These guys—" she motioned with one finger, pointing to Cage, then Brett, then Joule, which felt almost like a physical touch, "—figured it out. Then they went out and found it."

"The killers didn't take anything that we know of. They just killed her. They might have needed her phone, but they didn't seem to want anything more than for her to be dead."

Joule heard Pablo sob slightly as she said it, but again, she found she didn't have much sympathy for him. She added, "Maybe they were just silencing the knowledge."

When no one else added anything—and how could they? She and her brother had found the body and the phone—Joule turned to Pablo again. "That knowledge has now contaminated all of us."

Helenie nodded. As a pall settled over the lab, they all wondered who had killed Noemi and why. Though they still didn't have the details, they'd figured out some parts of it.

"How safe is this lab?" Brett asked.

"I mean, you saw what it took to get in here," Helenie said, as though that were enough.

"Yes, but we were coming in with good intentions. Someone with bad intentions? What would it take them to get in here?"

That made her change her stance. "Scientific credentials."

She laughed, her arms lifting up in a shrug to match the bitter sound.

"Could they get guns in here?" Brett pressed her. Despite her sudden understanding that they weren't safe, he wasn't going to leave it at that.

"*Guns?*" Helenie repeated, almost as though she didn't understand the words. Then she answered, "I think they'd struggle to get guns in here."

Mike joined in. "However, if you know what you're doing, everything in here can be a weapon."

This time it was Brett who closed his eyes and whispered, "Shit."

Joule and Cage scanned the lab. She and her brother had both had several upper-level chem labs in college. Joule more than Cage, and Brett probably had even more. She was certain everyone standing in this lab right now knew which beakers to pick up and throw into faces. Or what they might drop into a drink or onto a sandwich to poison someone.

She bet several of them could quickly make bombs from what was out on the countertops. A chem lab exploding wouldn't even warrant further investigation, especially when the CDC was focusing so much attention on connecting this disease to foodborne contaminants.

Who would suspect that it had been on purpose? That something in this lab was worth destroying?

Without speaking, Mike moved quickly and locked the doors. "No one comes in."

Helenie nodded. She and Mike were the ranking officers here.

But Mike pulled his phone from his pocket and checked something. "Brookwood and Abellard are due back any time now. I'll let them in when they get here."

"You trust them that much?" Helenie asked, her gaze wary.

"Don't you?"

"My trust is running a lot thinner today." She paused for a moment. "But yes, I do trust both of them. They've been here longer than me."

Joule's eyes bounced back and forth, following the conversation, until they decided who else they could let in. Whoever Brookwood and Abellard were, they'd waltz right in. Joule hoped the trust was well-founded.

"If we don't let anyone else into this lab, we should be relatively secure."

"Great." Cage let the word slide out on a dollop of strong sarcasm. He'd been hanging out with her for too long.

Joule figured everything would be fine until they had to eat or pee, but she didn't comment yet. There were more important things right now. "Before we power the phone on, we need to know what we're doing with it."

Chuck stepped in close. They all hovered around the phone as if it were a bomb they had to defuse. The analogy wasn't horribly wrong.

"I'm going to uninstall the tracking app. What else do we need to do?"

"Well," Cage added, "turning it on is going to locate this phone to here. Whoever killed her probably hacked into her tracking GPS and followed her. That's why they managed to kill her in a remote spot and not be seen. If they still want her phone, they'll be watching that same tracking app and waiting."

"It's going to be a homing beacon the second we put it on. So, we can turn it on and uninstall the tracker..." Joule added, "but that makes *this* the last known site of the phone."

Her brother understood. "They'll know we have it and that we brought it back here."

"They'll know *someone* did," Brett gently corrected him, but Cage was quick with a reply.

"Who else would it be? The deputies didn't collect her phone. They said that, and everything else, loudly enough for all the neighbors to hear."

Brett hadn't been there, but Joule remembered.

Cage looked to each of them. "They can come right to us here. So, the question is, how much of the tracker data do we need? And how much do we get if we uninstall the app? Does it take all the data with it?"

That was what Joule had been worried about. If they uninstalled it, would they lose something important?

"I don't know." Helenie shook her head.

"I think so," Chuck chimed in, and then he looked sheepish. "I found Noemi and Pablo loading the tracker app, and I did, too, so I could track her. Seemed like a good idea, since she was striking out on her own. I didn't realize there was more going on."

Joule turned to question Chuck specifically then. "You forwarded us her tracking info, so we still have everything from after she left our apartment. But we probably need tracking from days before that. Did anyone download that and save it somewhere else?"

No one said anything.

She figured they were tracking each other, but it didn't become important until Noemi stopped answering her phone.

"We need to get that data before we uninstall anything."

Helenie and Chuck looked to each other, then turned in unison to Pablo.

"I don't know!" he protested, maybe a little too hard. Then he took a deep breath and told them what he could. "She had a handful of days off that she used before, too."

Helenie nodded as she absorbed what Pablo was telling her. Then she turned to explain to the others. "Noemi was the kind of worker that *always* worked. Her job, and her prestige from being a scientist, were everything to her. Even I knew how much it meant to her family and to her community that she worked at the CDC. She never used her time off until... about a month ago?" She turned to Pablo as if he might clarify.

Joule was realizing now that Chuck mostly worked for Helenie, and Pablo was Noemi's assistant. This, though, was something he was more than willing to share.

"She started taking one or two days off at a time, and yes, it was about a month ago."

Helenie turned back to the group as though she were confessing something. "Maybe that's why we thought this two-week break wasn't such a big deal. Noemi had also mentioned that she was going to go find you guys and look at your data. We were all behind that."

"And she *did* come see us," Joule filled in, understanding better why the lab workers weren't suspicious of her and Pablo before now.

"We need to know where she went on those other trips. Hopefully, it will tell us something about which company she met with," Cage filled in as they all turned to the lab assistant.

Pablo looked back at them as though offended that they thought that. "I truly don't know! She just told me what she was doing and I helped her organize the data." He looked down at the floor then. "She offered me a cut."

"A *cut*?" Helenie asked as the rest of them figured it out. There was money in play. A cure would be valuable, and even more so if it could be delivered quickly after someone was bitten.

"She's my boss." He whispered it as part explanation, part apology.

This reaction—disease, whatever it really was—went down fast. Joule tried to calculate how much a company could charge if everyone had to carry the antidote on them. Almost like the EpiPens.

Holy shit.

Those were expensive, and the company that cornered the market had been driving the price up for years. Her heart lurched at the thought of what kind of money they were playing with.

"What did Noemi get herself into?" Helenie whispered.

They'd probably all been thinking the same thing.

Pablo tried again to defend his actions. "The CDC wasn't doing the work. Honestly, she did think we'd get rich off it. She told me we could both retire. But we did it because it was going to get something made that would actually save people! We—" he made a circling motion with his finger, indicating everyone in the lab, "—believed it was an insect vector. We knew we could be wrong, but we were taking that risk and so was the company. The CDC certainly wasn't designing anything! They weren't even putting resources into studying this! We only still had this lab going because we fought for it!"

His righteousness bled through the room.

For a moment, Joule bought into it. Then her anger quickly returned. "All of that makes sense. I understand why you did it. I hope you still agree with those choices when they're gunning for all of us."

The room fell silent for a moment.

"The proper protocol is to send this up to the director." Mike looked around the room. *Definitely a rule-follower*, Joule thought.

Pablo stiffened. Could that mean jail time for him?

But Joule's thoughts didn't matter. All the CDC people were looking at each other in a way that communicated something over her head.

Then Helenie asked, "Who else did she tell?"

"I don't know." Unfortunately, Pablo's answer seemed genuine.

It was Mike who declared, "Then we can't report it. Not until we know who we can trust."

With that harsh directive, they simultaneously came to a horrifying realization. Even Joule. There were no safe official channels. They were on their own.

Helenie made the first decisive move, heading to her desk with Noemi's phone in her hand. Everyone followed her as she asked, "Are we ready to turn it on?"

62

C age stood behind the group gathered at the lab door. He stared at the back of his sister's head. Brett stood next to Cage as if the two of them didn't know what they were doing—or maybe he just didn't want to be at the front.

The other two CDC doctors—the Brookwood and Abellard everyone talked about—had called in, but Mike had told them not to come to the lab. Now they were all leaving in small groups, phones off, no tracking. Just in case activating Dr. Achebe's phone had brought someone here.

Cage held his breath as Chuck and Helenie turned around. She told them, "It's only fair that we're the first ones out. We know what's normal, so we can spot what's not. We worked with Noemi, so if anything blows back, it should be onto us."

Cage actually thought it should blow back onto Pablo, but he didn't say it. Helenie was re-issuing instructions. They'd be out of contact for a while.

"Once we hit the train station, we'll message. Then we'll get rental cars and find a place to stay. We'll wait for you to update us after that."

Cage nodded, but Joule turned around and tapped Brett and the two slowly moved away. It took a moment to see that she was leading him to the lab's other door. They peered through the small window. *It should probably be watched, too*, he thought.

The escape setup was both simple and elaborate. Simple in that they were all to avoid anything that could be tracked. It was elaborate in all the strange methods and double-checks that one principle made necessary.

"Ready?" Helenie didn't wait for them to answer, just undid the lock and stepped into the hallway. She slung her purse over her shoulder like any normal day and she headed away, not looking back.

Chuck followed, his messenger bag stuffed with information and samples. He wasn't quite as nonchalant as Helenie, but following his senior lab manager down the hall helped him blend in. She started a conversation with him that sounded perfectly trite. Cage only caught a smidgen of it before Mike closed and locked the door behind them.

Joule pushed her face to the other window before quickly stepping back. "The hallway seems empty."

"How long do you think we have before they check in?"

"It shouldn't be that long before they hit the station." Mike motioned them all to get away from the doors. It would look suspicious if anyone walked by and peeked in. He pulled the burner phone from his pocket and set it on the table as they all waited for it to buzz.

It was Cage's new phone they watched. Joule had handed hers over to Helenie. They'd all memorized both new numbers, and the lab members had turned off all their phones a while ago.

Cage thought about pulling out his copies of the data they'd downloaded from Noemi. No one had the time to go through it yet. Their first goal was to get everyone out quickly.

They stood, watching the phone and making small talk. Mike recommended a restaurant in town, then rescinded it. "I go there a lot. If someone knows that, they'll look there. After all this dies down, though, I recommend it."

After all this dies down was hopeful. Cage wasn't sure what he believed.

Even as he questioned everything, the phone beeped and the message came in. Helenie and Chuck had arrived and seen nothing unusual.

Turning to his sister and Brett, Cage offered a tense grin. "Our turn."

Their threesome was leaving together. They worked well together, but they didn't have anyone who worked at the CDC to lead them out. The walk back here had been a little bit convoluted, but Joule was confident she remembered the right path back to the security desk. Mike had reiterated it for them. He was staying behind with Pablo. They'd be the third and last wave.

They needed to split up so that anyone coming for them couldn't take them all out together. While sneaking down the hall felt like a game, it could prove a deadly one.

"Ready?" Cage looked to his sister. Her backpack was full of information they'd printed before erasing it from the computers. Dr. Brett hadn't carried a bag, just his wallet and keys. Helenie had handed Cage a spare messenger bag she had from a conference she'd attended.

They looked quickly up and down the hallway.

"Wait!" Joule stepped back from the door, trying not to raise any suspicion. A man was walking by.

The three of them tried to look busy at the counters as the feet tapped their way down the hall. Once the man was past, she asked Mike, "Did you recognize him?"

"I think he's one of the other scientists, with a lab down the hall, but I can't be sure."

Cage looked out the window again, making sure the man was out of sight. The chances that he was dangerous, and specifically dangerous to *them,* were relatively low. But not as low as he'd thought they were yesterday.

With a glance back to Joule and Brett, Cage said, "Go."

He offered only a nod to Mike as he followed the other two out into the hall.

Joule was in front. Cage didn't like that. If they encountered anything, she would take the brunt of it. But one of them had to lead, and Joule remembered the way out. They were less likely to encounter problems if they looked like they knew what they were doing, like they belonged, and his sister was good at that, too.

She plowed her way to the T at the end of the unit and took a hard left, almost spinning as she went. The other two tried to step into line behind her. Cage was grateful when her next right turn dumped them at Security. The outside doors were just steps away and he tried not to sweat bullets.

This time, they just walked past the detectors and all the gates. It seemed no one really cared what they were leaving with. He offered a small nod to the guard, hoping that seemed normal, and pushed the outside door open.

He was free.

Or was he?

Had he been holding his breath the whole time? He couldn't tell. Still, it felt markedly better to be in the fresh air.

Joule seemed to be trying not to run as they headed toward the parking lot, but their pace was definitely clipped. It was Saturday. Maybe someone would assume they were just eager to get home.

As they approached the car, Brett fished the car key from his pocket. Joule's hand came out to stop him, her eyes scanning the parking lot.

If they clicked the button from yards away, they notified

anyone who might be following them of which car was theirs. Cage didn't know anyone here, so everyone was a potential threat.

In the next lot over, one lone man was climbing into his car. Everything was easy to spot because there were only five cars in the open space. At the last minute, Brett clicked the button, setting the car off, honking and blinking at a volume that made Cage almost jump. Anyone following them knew where to aim.

Climbing in quickly, they each slammed a door shut. Joule had crawled into the back this time, though there was more space without their luggage.

Brett started the car—he'd only had Cage drive on the leg down because he'd been so tired. Neither of the twins was authorized to drive this car. But putting their names on the rental agreement was expensive and possibly made them searchable for anyone looking.

It was entirely possible, Cage thought, that *no one* was looking for them. That whoever it was that had killed Noemi Achebe had finished the job with her. At worst, they were looking for Pablo. At best, they didn't even know he existed. Maybe the killer thought Dr. Achebe had done all the work herself.

It was equally possible that someone was watching everything closely. If the killer had hung out near the crime scene, they couldn't have missed Cage and Joule being interviewed by the sheriff. They might have seen Brett at the twins' apartment.

But Cage and Joule had their next task to get to.

There was no one to message and nothing they could do. They were completely without contact, having handed their phones over to Helenie and Mike. So, they pulled out of the parking lot, took a right-hand turn, and hopped onto a busy Atlanta freeway.

They needed a store, and Cage tried to operate the car's GPS to find one.

Ten minutes later, Brett said, "Shit. I think we're being followed."

63

"Turn here!" Cage tried to point and grab for the dash to steady himself at the same time.

Brett made the sharp turn at the last minute. "Where are we headed?"

"I don't know. We can figure that out once we shake them. Is it still following us?" Cage waited a beat and then another.

Brett's eyes flicked to the side view and rearview mirrors before he said, "Yes."

"Which car?" Joule asked as she slouched down in the seat, not wanting to openly turn around and stare out the back window.

She peeked up and over the headrest as Brett told them, "White sedan, three cars back."

That was how it had made the turn, even though they'd taken it at the last minute with no signal. Their stalker was lingering far enough back that even their sudden moves wouldn't fool it.

They pulled up at a light, and somehow even Cage's ribs felt tense. Needing something to do, he began tapping furiously on the dashboard GPS. They didn't have any cell phones to call for help, and no one was tracking them except this white sedan. They had no way to even take pictures to show anyone. But maybe he could find a way out.

He located them on the map and scanned the side roads for somewhere to go. If they could get far enough ahead, that might help. He pointed to the screen. "Go fast, get ahead. Maybe keep driving around here. See if we can make a light that they get caught in."

"Got it," Brett said and swung a right onto a smaller street.

This area was mostly like a grid. *Not helpful*, Cage thought. "Take a left here!"

The roads began curving, the area looking much more residential, and he wondered if they could lose themselves down a side street or duck into an alley and let their follower pass them. Could they simply pull up into someone's driveway and act like they lived there?

"Turn here," Cage said, again pointing to the light. Unfortunately, making a left meant waiting for traffic to clear.

"It's still back there," Joule informed them from the backseat. She was rotated into a bad position. If they were hit or had an accident, her seatbelt would hurt more than help, but her information was valuable.

"Please turn back around." Cage tried not to beg. He wasn't just worried about some impending accident. He'd noticed the person in the car next them looking at his sister oddly.

"This sucks monkey balls. We don't even have any phones!" she declared. "Is the dash connected to a call program?"

"No, we turned that off, remember?'

"Hopefully, we can reconnect it if we get stuck in a ditch somewhere." She seemed satisfied with that but, Cage thought, they would all have to be. It was their only option.

What would happen when they didn't check in?

Cage noted the time. Mike and Pablo should have left the lab by now. They'd been the last ones out so they could lock up.

"Here!" Cage pointed quickly again, and they took a quick succession of right and left turns that threw them against their seatbelts and into the doors. "There's a parking lot! Turn in!"

Cage pointed frantically to the right, trying not to make a grand gesture that could be seen from other cars.

Brett barely made the turn, tires squealing as he ducked in quickly. Another car screeched to a halt and the vet peeled past them, too, offering a tight smile and a small thank-you wave as consolation.

"Here," Cage pointed to a space, "Park!"

"If we park, we'll be stuck if they come up behind us," Joule protested.

"It's probably also the best place to hide." The parking lot was busy.

Brett took the chance and twisted the wheel, bringing them to a stop between a huge truck and an SUV. They were hidden but couldn't see well. It was a gamble, and Cage counted slowly to ten, trying to silently wait out fate.

They sat for a few moments, no one saying anything.

Cage knew he was only hearing his own pulse in his ears, but to him it sounded like he could hear all three of their heartbeats.

"There!" Joule shouted, then repeated it again softer. "There!"

In the rearview, he spotted her slowly sliding down in the seat, and he and Brett did the same. Cage still didn't see what she'd pointed at. He just had to trust her, but his heart pounded.

"He just drove across the end of the aisle." Joule had no sooner said that than Brett was cranking the car on and backing out.

"Not too fast." Cage motioned with his hand, as though he controlled the gas with witchcraft and gestures. "We don't want to draw attention."

It was clear that Brett was desperately trying to do "normal" when they'd all left normal back on the freeway. At the end of the aisle, they swung a hard right and then another and headed back out to the main street, hopefully leaving the white car touring the parking lot searching for them.

Three blocks later, Cage sighed in relief. "I think he's gone."

"I haven't seen him," Joule said, once she'd turned around and peeked over the backseat. "Now what?"

"We still need the phones." Cage hadn't been able to stop thinking about it.

Twenty minutes later, they'd wound their way through sections of town, taking a path that no sane person would. Cage pointed out a gas station and then cucked in and bought a single burner phone with cash.

Climbing back into the car, he handed it to his sister to set it up and text the other two phones what had happened. "Next up, big store."

They needed four more phones. He used the dash GPS and found one. This time when they arrived, all three of them went inside. They weren't willing to split up for that long. They'd already split the main group into three, after Helenie's warning that they shouldn't all be able to be found together.

Cage knew that by "found" she meant "exterminated."

They bought two more phones with cash and exited quickly, Joule tucking them into her bag to set up. As the car doors clicked shut behind them, Joule said something she'd been holding onto for a while. "Mike replied while we were in there. He and Pablo are getting off the train."

They'd taken Mike's car and hidden it, abandoning it before walking to a bus stop. They were on their way now to a car rental on the other side of town from Helenie and Chuck. There would be records of the rentals, but it would add another layer that somebody would have to go through to find them. Looking for the cars they owned would yield nothing.

In the back seat, Joule worked diligently, setting up the two new phones and sending messages on the one she already had running. This time, they stopped at another gas station in another section of town and Dr. Brett ran in. He pocketed two more disposable phones.

They'd acquired them from three different locations, so hopefully it would be harder for someone to track them. The phones would track back to different sources and different batch numbers, should anyone try.

Sitting in the driver's seat again, Brett asked, "Where do we go now?"

"I think we go to our hotel." Joule didn't look up from her work, so Cage became the eyes of the car. He'd not seen the white sedan again, though he wasn't breathing easy.

"Is it safe?"

"All our things are there. I think we have to go check the place out and then we can decide if it's safe."

Cage was tense enough on the ride to have broken out in a cold, clammy sweat. It took too long. They'd wound their way to the other side of town with no thought of getting back. The sun was starting to ride low, and he didn't want to arrive after dark. Though he was ready to jump at anything, nothing jumped out at them.

On the way back, Joule fielded updates on what would become Brett's phone. "Helenie has a rental car. They are on their way to Chuck's." "Pablo got a rental." "Pablo and Mike are at Mike's place, all clear."

The white car wasn't there waiting for them. No one watched the lobby. Even the hotel clerk seemed to not care about the people coming into his building. They headed up to the room and entered carefully. Anyone watching the hall footage later would know they were being paranoid. Hopefully, it wouldn't come to that, but being followed from the CDC had him concerned about their chances.

Inside the suite, they each looked over their own things before meeting back in the middle.

"I don't think anything has been touched," Joule said and when the two men agreed, she sent out a message to the group.

They sat on the couch and stared at the wall for a while, trying to calm down.

Cage double- and triple-checked the locks on the door, developing a deep appreciation for people who lived with this anxiety all the time.

But someone *was* really chasing them. Someone willing to *kill* them.

He turned around. "Now what?"

"That was wild. I don't think I've ever driven like that before." Brett paused for a moment and Cage couldn't decide if the vet had found the chase invigorating or terrifying or both. But then he looked calmer. "We should probably look over the things we got off Noemi's phone."

Cage welcomed the distraction.

Joule said, "I think we just have to wait for messages."

She handed Brett a phone, declaring it his. The other four would get traded to Helenie, Mike, Chuck, and Pablo when they returned the two Cage and Joule had loaned them to get off the CDC campus. They'd already loaded their contacts and more onto those.

Only now did Cage stop to think that he'd handed the others everything they needed if they *weren't* on his side. Or even if they were willing to sell him and his sister out when the chips were down. But it was too late to get it back now. He could only hope he'd trusted the right people.

The phone sitting in front of Brett went off and all three of them jumped, though no one commented on that.

"What does it say?" Joule asked, but the look on Brett's face wasn't good.

"Pablo's place has been ransacked."

64

They'd been so close, Joule thought, *to making a clean getaway.*

All they each had to do was check their homes to be sure that nothing was disturbed, that there were no obvious signs anyone was coming after them, and then they'd meet up.

Mike's place had cleared. Helenie's place had been cleared. Even their place remained untouched.

But not Pablo. Was it wrong if she consoled herself that Pablo was the one closest to Noemi? That maybe all this was partly his fault? But it didn't matter.

The phone would eventually become Brett's, but right now it belonged to their pod. Still squeezing it after getting the shitty message, Joule decided to do something. So, she hit the button and called Mike. "Is everyone okay?"

"Yes."

"Is anyone still there? Still searching or watching for Pablo?"

"Not that we can tell."

"Did they take anything?"

"Not that we can tell," he repeated.

She was being as bad as the sheriff's deputies that had interrogated her and her brother, but she couldn't stop. They all needed these answers.

"Hold on," Mike told her, clearly distracted. "Helenie is calling."

A moment later when he came back on, Joule continued her interrogation, trying to be softer. He wasn't a suspect, as far as she knew. "Are you safe?"

"As safe as I think we can be." There was a shrug to his voice, but he didn't sound terrified. "We need to meet up."

When she agreed, he added, "Brookwood and Abellard are home. They'll want to join us."

Joule had no idea what that really meant. Were they nearby? Would their meetup be relatively local?

"They'll be able to help. They've been working on this for a while," Mike added, seeming to take her silence for dissention.

Maybe it was. "Do we want to bring them into this? Clearly this isn't safe."

An almost chuckle came through from the other end of the line. "They've been through worse."

Was that enough of an excuse? Joule had been through worse, too. Or had she? Maybe human killers were worse than disasters.

From the couch, her brother's voice carried across the room. "Have you seen this data? These pictures?"

Joule hadn't. She'd scanned the downloads from Noemi's phone like the rest of them, but nothing had popped out. Not in the short time she'd had with it.

Mike's voice pulled her back to the call. "Of course, we need Helenie and Chuck, too. However, if we do that, it puts all of us together and makes us a target."

It was true, but weren't they already targets? Wasn't that the problem? They needed to think about it another way. "Being separated makes it harder to take all of us out in one fell swoop."

Then again, maybe not. They had discussed the possibility of a bomb before. They might not be in a lab, but would it be that much more difficult somewhere else?

"Where are we meeting?" Joule asked, finally accepting that this was the way it needed to be. They needed to put their heads together, and being in four separate places wasn't helping.

Brett snapped to attention at her question. She shrugged and shook her head, as if to say, *I don't really know.* But obviously she'd accepted the meetup for them all. "You're not there with the other two researchers, are you?"

"No, we're just leaving Pablo's. We'll have to let them know where." She could almost hear the shuffling in the background, maybe the door clicking shut. "You need to pull out a map and pick a place."

"We don't know the area."

"That's the point." She heard them getting into the car now. "Everyone else lives here. Everyone else will pick based on what they know and if they've been watched..."

"Then whoever's following us will have a better chance of finding us." Turning to Brett and Cage, she handed the assignment off to them.

"Library?" Brett asked.

That sounded good. "Hold on."

Within a few moments she was rattling off an address for a public library that they hoped was central to everyone. "Maybe we can get a private room."

"Interesting," Mike said, indicating that she'd most likely fulfilled his prophecy of them picking some place that none of the rest of the group would.

"I'll call Helenie and Chuck, you call the other doctors and make sure they turn their phones off."

Shit, she thought, *they hadn't bought burners for two more people.* They'd have to live with it.

Decision made, she placed her calls and went through a nearly identical discussion, ending with Helenie and Chuck agreeing. As she talked, she watched Cage and Brett get everything in order to leave.

"It's getting dark," Brett said as he moved to stand at the side of the window. He slid slowly to where he could see outside into the parking lot behind the hotel.

It was all very cloak-and-dagger, making Joule wonder where a veterinarian got skills like that. Or was he just doing things he'd seen on TV and in movies?

"Guys, you need to see this," Cage said. But Brett's hand came out, palm open, waving him down. The abruptness of the gesture sent a chill through Joule's spine.

"There's a white sedan that pulled into the parking lot. And no one's getting out."

65

"Joule is."

Cage's words startled her. He'd answered quickly when Brett asked, "Who's our best evasive driver?"

"Am I?" she asked, but he immediately tipped his head.

"I saw you in driving class in high school."

She had gotten a lot of bad marks there. It was the one class she hadn't gotten an A in. She firmly believed she should have been getting more of the kind of instruction they gave to police officers and FBI agents.

It didn't seem to take much more than Cage's words, and Brett tossed her the keys. She protested. "I'm not authorized to drive the car."

"We're not authorized for a lot of this," Brett said, waving his hand around the room, indicating maybe their whole existence right now. "I'm not going to die with a bullet in my brain."

The unspoken words, *I have a wife to get home to* hung in the air.

Once again, Joule had forgotten about Laura. She'd been so busy, so worried about the situation at hand, that it hadn't occurred to her. She didn't have anyone to leave at home these days, even her kitten Toto had gone to live with her grandparents. Now she worried about Doctor Brett's wife. Her chemotherapy ended later this week, and he would need to return home. Would he be safe?

She curled her fingers around the keys, holding them tight, as though they were a good luck charm.

"The car's still there," Brett reported, slowly moving to look out the window again. "I think someone's sitting inside."

"We're parked on the other side," Cage said. "Do you think we can get past them, or will they follow us anyway?"

"Is our car tracked?" Joule was wondering how they'd found them so fast.

Her brother tipped his head and raised his eyebrows. "It's a rental car. They're always tracked now."

Shit. "So, anybody who can find the rental can follow us."

The other two nodded at her as if to say yes, it was obvious.

"But who would figure out about the rental?"

Brett shrugged. "Once they figure out I'm with you two, it might not be that much of a stretch."

He didn't seem to be mad that they'd brought this to his door, but Joule was now doubly committed to getting him out safely. He slowly stepped away from the window and turned to scan the room as if calculating how big it was, but that didn't make any sense to Joule.

"What are you looking at?"

"I'm trying to figure out if they can see us moving. Maybe shadows on the ceiling." He was still looking at walls and the ceilings. "Obviously we don't turn off the lights, but will opening the door signal them?"

Joule glanced up and around now. 'I don't think they can see us moving around. But if they know we're leaving, they'll follow us."

"I'm hoping that we can get out without them knowing." He

took a deep breath and looked at them, his expression asking if they were ready.

Cage was gathering up the pages he had spread out. They'd distributed only paper printouts, having tried to destroy all the digital copies in the lab. Now Joule was thinking they needed to get pictures on these phones, to preserve the information.

There wasn't time for that idea now. She followed Brett, who was slowly sliding to the other side of the room, his eyes checking to see if he was casting shadows on the ceiling or something that might signal they were leaving.

Also, she thought, they might be able to release Noemi's information to the press and ruin whatever someone might kill for. If it wasn't a secret, there was no need to kill to keep it. She could only hope that might be an option.

Motioning with his hand, Brett directed them to skirt the outside of the room before he unlocked the door, checked the hallway, and slowly slid sideways through the smallest crack of the door.

So far, she was safe. Joining them in the hallway, Joule slung her backpack over one shoulder, car keys still clutched tightly, as the three of them slunk furtively along.

They hit the steps just as the elevator dinged. Cage spun around and pushed at the stairwell door, waving the others through and trying to shut them in faster than the hydraulic closure wanted to let them. As the opening far-too-slowly reached a slim crack, he peeked into the hallway.

What if whoever was in the hallway had noticed them? That would be suspicious.

Why was he still standing there? *Someone was on their hallway. That wasn't suspicious.*

But it was.

Her brother's back visibly straightened as he turned and whispered, "They're going into our room with a keycard."

So slowly that it resonated deep inside her ribcage, she whispered to her brother. "Shut that door."

They could only pray whoever it was didn't hear them. The steps were metal, the stairwell concrete. Even their breathing seemed to echo. Surely, the sounds would alert everyone where they were.

The three rushed down the steps as quickly and softly as they could, two completely impossible tasks. They burst out the side door, sucking in fresh air.

Should they peek into the back lot and see if someone was still waiting in the white car? *Hell,* she thought now, *maybe there were two of them.* When no one suggested it, Joule decided to follow the other two and crept around the corner. Brett took the lead and whatever he saw or didn't see, he deemed it clear enough and, with an open hand, motioned them forward.

Joule ran hell for leather toward the car, sliding into the driver's seat without bothering to take off her backpack. It felt solid behind her and right now that was okay. As tall as she was, she was still the shortest of the three. This way, she didn't have to slide the seat forward.

Without her seatbelt on, she cranked the engine and threw the car in reverse. The rental was pulling out even before Cage had his door clicked shut. At the road entrance, she turned entirely the wrong way, but this direction didn't leave the car in view of anyone sitting in the back lot. Taking the first freeway ramp, she drove ten miles before she finally let out her breath.

"Is anyone behind us?" she asked into the open air, still watching traffic.

"Not the white car," her brother answered.

"I don't see anyone else either," Brett told her, so Joule took the next turn toward the library.

"That guy was not only going to our door, but he also had a card key," Cage reiterated into the space of the sedan.

Joule thought about her suitcase and everything she'd left

behind. It might all be gone. Or searched through. At least the most important things were in the car.

Eventually, they would need to go back and check to see if anything had been disturbed. There were no obvious signs anyone was coming after them now, so she tried to slow her rapid heartbeat and found she couldn't.

Even as she thought about the logistics of where she might escape, and which streets she might duck down if they found they were followed, Cage spoke up from the back seat.

"Did you guys see anything on the data from Noemi's phone?"

Joule had seen plenty, but nothing useful. She kept her eyes on the road, trying to drive like *normal*. The last thing she needed was to get pulled over, although maybe that was second to last. The last thing she needed was to get followed by whoever had killed Noemi.

"It's really interesting," Cage was saying. "The good news is —at least I hope it is—I think I found something."

66

"I don't think anyone knows about you yet," Cage said after Brookwood and Abellard introduced themselves and said they didn't think they'd been followed.

Jillian Brookwood had dark hair pulled back in a ponytail, and she moved like a bundle of energy. Jordan Abellard was taller, more thoughtful, and moved in tandem with her—which looked to Cage like no easy job.

"They will now," Joule said. "You might be followed on the way out of here."

"Were you followed on the way in?" Dr. Jillian Brookwood's sharp gaze turned to his sister.

"I don't think so." Cage looked around the room. They'd been the second set to arrive, after Helenie and Chuck. Thank goodness, because if they'd walked to find just the two new doctors, he wouldn't have known they were his people. "However, someone did seem to be entering our hotel room as we left."

"Did you go back and check?" Pablo asked.

The three of them shook their head simultaneously.

"We were on our way here," Brett said, as if to brush off having their room broken into.

"How would you know if they took anything?" Chuck countered.

Cage had learned that letting go of things was much easier than letting go of people.

"They maybe got our clothes, some toiletries, a few hotel shampoos." Everyone nodded along at Joule's clear rebuttal that they hadn't left anything worth taking.

Dr. Brookwood was already leaned over the table where everyone had laid out their printouts. She tried to remove duplicates before lining things up in some level of order. There were maps from where Noemi's phone tracker had found her, the dates printed across the top of each. There was a copy of every picture from her phone—including several smiling shots of her parents, clouds, and a heron she'd found in the creek.

Though Jillian Brookwood was already busy studying the data, the rest decided that no one had actually been followed here, though it was clear that several of them had already been targeted. With introductions done and the requisite *Is everyone okay?* finished, nine heads now leaned over the table. Quietly, each of them examined every scrap of evidence Dr. Noemi Achebe had left behind.

In turn, they each started tapping on their phones, looking up what they were missing. At one point, Helenie turned to use one of the computers at the edge of the library room. But even as she reached for it, the whole room gasped.

"Yeah, I just realized ..." She yanked her fingers back. "Maybe *not* searching on a system that has public access is a better option."

The whole point of being here was to not be somewhere they could be found. No one knew yet what they were searching for. But whoever had killed Dr. Achebe did.

"Here." Joule pointed to a spot on one of the maps. Almost

simultaneously, Jillian Brookwood did the same on another map, three positions down in the row. The two women looked to each other, Jillian's ponytail swinging. Joule's curls bouncing.

Cage followed both their fingers. Though the paths were different, they had pointed to the same spot on the map.

"BioStride OneGen Pharmaceuticals," they both announced.

The entire room turned to listen, and Dr. Brookwood gave the floor to Joule. *A nice move*, Cage thought, as Jillian was obviously the senior researcher here. The twins were nobodies from a solar systems company stationed out of Texas.

"BioStride OneGen," Joule told the room without hesitation, "is a small research pharmaceutical company. They're up and coming. They got started developing a system of reading multiple genetic markers to speed up the genetic matching process. Most places that run genetic testing are now using a process that involves a patent held by BioStride."

She paused, then added, "However, they've had no major successes since then."

"And have been desperately looking to score one," Jillian added.

Helenie looked up. "This has to be it. Noemi's message said she was making *strides*."

The other faces around the table turned, looking to each other. They didn't have to say it. However, aside from the name and general info, they stalled out.

Cage began scanning through Noemi's trove of mosquito pictures. Brett stood beside him, helping him sort. Their skills had improved. Once he'd looked at a thousand of these little suckers, identification was faster. Sure enough, he began moving them around.

"How are you sorting?" Jordan Abelard asked, because it obviously wasn't by date.

"*Anopheles*," Cage said, pointing to the largest grouping of the most innocuous genus. Then, "*Aedes*." This group was split into three. He named each set in turn. "*Aegypti*, a small quantity of *Albopticus*, and *Karnatakan*."

"The *Karnatakan* cluster is way too big for this section of the US," Jordan told him. "Where were these taken from?"

"Atlanta, Georgia coastline, Savannah, Charleston." Cage rattled off the locations as he handled the eight-by-eleven photos that made the mosquitoes look alarmingly big.

Together, the three of them began scanning for more pictures. They shuffled past pictures of Dr. Achebe visiting her parents on multiple occasions. Then her days off showed trips to what was likely BioStride and then some location in the Florida Panhandle. Some of the mosquitoes she'd collected from Jekyll Island had been from earlier days off.

Joule had moved over to stand by him. "If you look at the dates on this, she was collecting mosquitoes very early on."

Cage filled in for the rest of the group. "We saw one of the first cases, we think."

"In Florida, Gulf side?" Jillian asked and Cage and Joule both nodded.

Cage kept going. "It looks like Dr. Achebe's work started just a week or so after that."

"Does it?" Jordan asked, looking up as the room went quiet. "Or is that simply the point you downloaded the data from? Was she working on it before that?"

67

The group worked for several hours until their stomachs began openly rumbling. The library was about to close, and Joule wondered what was going to happen next.

"We're only open for fifteen more minutes." A library worker had come through and knocked, then stuck her head into the room to warn them.

The group nodded to her as though everything was fine.

"Well, that was smart," Joule muttered and when everyone looked at her, she added, "She saw all our faces. *Shit!*"

She wondered if maybe she shouldn't have sworn in a roomful of scientists when she was the youngest one here. Actually, she wasn't. She was two minutes older than her brother, but that probably didn't count.

They had gathered enough information to be relatively certain BioStride Pharmaceuticals was the culprit. They had Noemi's path relatively well-mapped, because she'd been letting her friends at the CDC track her.

Just as the thought that it was odd entered her head, Jillian asked, "Why did you put the trackers on the phones?"

Chuck explained. "Our lab is entomology-based, so we were the obvious ones to collect mosquitoes and other samples. Noemi came back with a bite one time, and she and Pablo decided to track each other. I horned in, thinking it was a good idea. Not realizing I'd stepped into illegal data-selling." He glared at his fellow lab worker. "She'd be out on her own a lot. If she was affected, or hurt, we wouldn't have known where to start looking for her."

"You should have known where she was collecting samples," Jillian said with a frown.

"Yes. But it was a large area. And if she thought another location might have standing water, she absolutely would have moved out of the designated area to sample it. So, we decided to be overly cautious."

"I have a question," Cage said, and everyone turned to look at him, the library clock ticking down. They would have to gather everything up and get out relatively quickly.

"These plants—" he said, pointing to one picture "—keep showing up. According to the data with the pictures, they're not all the same plant. It's the same *kind of* plant showing up in different locations."

Joule moved in concert with everyone else as they scooted in closer to see.

"I think these are the same two, even though this one has little flowers," he added.

Jillian quickly confirmed it. "They are... Do you think they're related to her *cure*?"

"These other plants," Cage continued, holding up individual pictures. "They only show up once. They're well-framed and pretty. I think these were her taking pictures she liked, maybe a reference for something in the future, but not what she was after. This plant, however, shows up—" he lifted the picture and read the tracking data "—at Jekyll Island, then

Tallahassee,—" he picked up another picture, then another "—outside Charleston, Hilton Head…"

"You think she was using something from that plant to develop whatever this cure was?" Joule asked. *Was she the only one who didn't have enough biology to follow along?* The murmurs and shrugs that answered told her she wasn't lagging too far behind. No one else had quite figured it out, either.

It was Jillian who straightened her back. "We have to leave."

"The library is going to close any minute," Helenie concurred as she checked her burner phone. "And the librarian *did* see all of our faces. We should not have her come back here again."

"We need to leave in small clusters. Same groups we came with," Joule said. "It would be suspicious if this many of us left the library together this late at night. But small groups shouldn't raise flags."

Everyone nodded as Joule waited, thinking surely someone had a better idea. The thought of going back to their hotel made her stomach tighten down and twist itself into knots. She needed to see what they had done, but she also knew that going back could put the three of them in the crosshairs again.

Jordan Abellard looked at Helenie and something passed between them. Joule figured, they'd worked the labs next to each other for who knew how long? They'd probably shared data and all kinds of things. Maybe they'd even evaded capture and murder together before. What did she know?

Helenie took over. "We leave in small groups. And we all need to get to Charleston."

That made Joule's head snap to the side. "We're going back?"

If nothing else, there were so many mosquitoes there. She'd felt relatively safe inside the city limits of Atlanta. It was built up enough that she hadn't seen many insects. She didn't think her brother or Brett had had a single bite in the time they'd been here.

Why would they go back?

Jordan jumped in. "We need to get the plant. We need to find it and test it to see if we can figure out her formula."

Joule wasn't sure how they would do that. "Bring it back *here*?"

Maybe they hadn't meant *everyone* needed to go to Charleston. In the next few minutes, she found out that's exactly what they meant.

"Pablo and Mike," Helenie said, handing out assignments. "I want you two to head south of Atlanta, maybe an hour, then turn on Noemi's phone and download everything you can... Not onto your phones. We don't want any digital connection."

That might link their phones to any signal trace they couldn't cover and then make either of them into beacons.

"We'll buy a tablet or something."

Helenie agreed, adding, "Once you do that, turn around and head up to Charleston. Take whatever route you want." She turned back to the others. On her phone, she pulled up a map, the program offering several routes. "Jordan and Jillian, you take this route. It's going to take you a little out of the way and should put you right in proximity to find one of the plants. Get samples."

She turned to Joule and Cage and Brett next. Joule bit her lip, ready for instructions.

"You head directly to Charleston." Helenie held up her phone, pointing to the main route for them. "Find us a place—actually *places*—where we can stay."

Then she addressed the group as a whole. "Chuck and I will take the longer route and talk to the sheriff's department."

That had all eyes whirling to her.

"We need to get the contents of Noemi's purse," she explained.

No one argued the need, but... Joule asked, "How will you do that?"

Were they going to break into the evidence locker or something? She was pretty sure it wasn't as easy as people made it look on TV.

Helenie grinned. "I'm going to use the power of the CDC and explain that the government agency needs its materials back. I don't think we'll get the whole purse, but we should be able to get the pertinent pieces."

Not a bad idea. The sheriff's department hadn't struck Joule as being very high-tech.

Helenie was already telling Pablo and Mike, "Grab what's yours off the table and go now."

There were only a handful of minutes left before the library closed.

As they were leaving, Pablo turned around. "Everybody check in every hour."

They all nodded.

Joule and Brett and Cage were the second group to be jettisoned out. The groups were barely separated at all, but maybe it would be enough to not arouse suspicions.

They drove through the nearest fast food joint, not being picky but needing to quell the rumbling in their stomachs. Dr. Brett was at the wheel again. After all, he was the only one licensed to drive the car. He headed east at a sedate pace, taking them back to the wet fields and lowlands that held far more mosquitoes than Joule was willing to deal with.

She had a bad feeling about this.

68

"I don't like this." She didn't protest loudly, but Joule protested.

"Me either," added Helenie.

Not the response Joule had expected. She knew how her brother was reacting—his shoulders were tense, his movements stiff. He felt the same way she did.

Helenie had provided them with nets, much like pool skimmers, so they could reach out and gather samples. Joule smelled like a bug spray factory and an essential oils multi-level-marketing scheme all at the same time. They all did.

Pulling back a once again-empty net, Helenie sighed. Brett, Chuck, and Cage all turned to look at the two women.

"Any luck?" Helenie asked, but they all shook their heads no.

The group had divided into two factions. Pablo had headed out with the Brookwood-Abellard lab group, which included Mike. The hope was that Pablo—perhaps the most vulnerable of them—was safer placed with the three least vulnerable of them. Each group had a map and a list of places to collect samples from, but collecting was turning out to be difficult.

"We're far too repulsive," Chuck told them.

Joule felt her brows rise. That wasn't something she was usually called.

"We have mosquito repellent all over us," he clarified. He wasn't wrong, but...

"With good reason," Cage retorted just as Joule was opening her mouth to say the same thing.

"Sure, but we can't get samples if we're actively repelling those same samples."

She and her brother had thought about this before. "What's more important? Collecting samples or not getting bitten?"

She expected a rousing chorus of "not getting bitten!" but the group stayed silent.

Helenie shrugged both with her shoulders and her expression. Then she addressed everyone. "I'm asking this openly, but what happens if we *don't* get the samples?"

Fuckballs. Joule hated the answer. If they didn't get the samples, they couldn't test them against the liquid in the syringes that Helenie and Chuck had collected from Noemi's purse. They'd managed to convince the sheriff's department that the syringes were government property and the department had had them for evidence long enough.

Pablo had confessed that he knew Noemi left with four syringes in her purse. One was missing. The conversation had turned grim, and that last puzzle piece help snap the rest together. They figured Noemi had realized she was being followed and turned off and thrown her phone. That was either to stop her killer from getting the plant information or to stop the CDC from getting information about Noemi's extracurricular activities.

Then her murderer had killed her in one place, moved her body one direction, and dumped her purse in another... after taking one of the syringes. The misdirection had worked, too. Police never would have found the purse. And had Pablo not mentioned what she was carrying, they would never have known one was missing.

This morning, they'd set about determining that the two remaining syringes held the same substance; each group now carried one. The plan was to collect samples, look for reactions, and run serum tests. There was every possibility that the syringes Noemi carried weren't even her "cure," but they had to find out. The news last night had reported three more deaths in the Charleston area from the mysterious new disease.

Joule knew a better way to study it would be to test against already-infected people. Unfortunately, the window of time was so short that no one knew how to get to them, and they couldn't just inject people with a syringe of unknown compounds. They might know something soon, though.

Mike had collected a portion of the liquid from their syringe and shipped it back to the CDC for a thorough analysis. It would be tested with NMR, mass spectroscopy, and IR in hopes for reverse-engineering the formula.

Whatever it was, they still had to see if it worked. In turn, that meant they had to catch these mosquitoes. So, the answer to Helenie's question was that the risk was necessary.

Fuckballs.

All eyes turned to Chuck as he pulled a fancy bottle of lotion from his bag.

"What? You think I haven't spent the past four years collecting mosquitoes? I know what attracts them." He put some of the lotion into his hand then rubbed it along the edge of the net. "Normally, I just squeeze some of this into a spot to attract them, but I'll try getting the net, too."

He walked about five feet out and squirted a dollop into the grass. Joule thought it was crazy, but figured he knew best. Lord knew, she'd had no need to catch live mosquitoes before now and she hoped she never would again.

She asked Chuck, "How did you do this before this plague?"

"I just didn't worry about getting bitten." Then he shuddered.

Joule thought that probably wasn't an option now. Luckily, the scented lotion seemed to work. They quickly realized the mosquitoes were attracted to Chuck's hand, too, and they jumped to wipe him down with disinfectant wipe and re-sprayed him with repellent so that only the end of the net was attractive.

Three hours later, they had collected samples from five different points.

"Not my usual haul," Chuck lamented, and Joule had to wonder, *how many mosquitoes did he normally catch?*

This was already a disturbing amount.

"We have enough to keep us busy testing tonight," Helenie declared.

Though it hadn't been specifically designated, she was their leader. So, Joule asked her, "Where to?"

"Our place," she told the team as she began to pack up her gear. "Separate routes. Like usual."

Joule had booked them four separate, two-room suites under four separate names—the ones least likely to be checked on, she hoped. Each suite afforded the team an open space where all of them could gather. Today, they'd be working in their two separate teams and compare results at the end, so as not to influence each other.

They piled into their cars now, splitting themselves, the samples, and the equipment. Helenie didn't say it, but Joule suspected that she was constantly splitting materials and samples in case one of them was intercepted, things were stolen, or people or parts were somehow removed from the game. Joule didn't like to think about what that *somehow* might be.

Brett drove them through yet another fast food place, and Joule had never so desperately wanted a home-cooked meal.

She hadn't said it yet, but she was hoping she and Cage could go visit their grandparents when this was over. Her grandfather cooked like nobody's business. Her system would need to rewire itself for healthy food.

She fantasized about sitting at the table with her grandma and grandpa, a table set with homecooked food. But the now-empty mosquito nets were propped next to her, crumpled wax paper wrappers were shoved back into the food bag, and her Coke was sipped down to its last dregs. Her fantasy was interrupted by the words from the front seat.

"Don't scratch," Cage commanded.

"What?" she leaned forward, her reverie dissipating like smoke.

"He's got a bite," her brother told her, the words tense and unwanted.

Brett held his right arm out for inspection as he continued to drive, his eyes on the road.

Joule looked at his forearm and the small welt that had risen there. "How do you feel?"

"Scratchy," he replied. Though if he was being snarky, or trying to calm her, she didn't know.

She watched as he pulled the arm back, scratching again, seemingly unconsciously. This time, she leaned over the seat to look, and she watched as a second, and then a third, welt rose on his arm. Then he began coughing.

69

Cage watched from the passenger seat as Brett's breath slowly became more labored. He'd already handed the man antihistamines and the last of his lemonade to take them with. But it didn't seem to help at all.

"How many did he take?" Joule asked from the backseat. She didn't wait for his answer. "Give him two more. He needs it now, before his throat closes and he can't swallow anything."

Cage hadn't thought that far ahead. His panicked brain was scrambling to hold on to the thoughts that whizzed by. He pulled the little bottle from the dash where he'd slapped it after passing his friend the first dose.

They sat on the side of the road, traffic whizzing by and making the car rock each time a semi passed. It was bizarre to him—though appropriate—that his world would be literally rocking right now.

Dr. Brett looked at him and nodded as he took the pills. This time, he swallowed the medicine with considerably more difficulty. Cage could see his throat working.

Joule stayed hovering between the two bucket seats and the

twins watched as Brett tipped his head back trying to breathe easier, but the headrest made that difficult.

"His seat," Joule said, "push it backward."

Brett heard her and grabbed the lever. He was still mostly functioning, and he had to be cognizant of what was happening. With the seat reclined, tipping his head back was easier and it seemed to buy him a little more air. That, in turn, brought Cage a fraction of relaxation.

He could only hope it worked.

Cage gripped the EpiPen tightly in his fist, and only then it occurred to him that maybe now was the time to use it. He held it up in front of his friend's face. "I'm ready."

He heard Joule's voice from the back seat then. She was leaning away but her tone stayed frantic. She was calling 9-1-1. "What mile marker are we at?"

Cage looked forward and back but couldn't see one. She rattled off an exit that she thought they had just passed. "We're in a small blue sedan, a rental, on the right-hand side of the road."

She tried to offer landmarks, though Cage was afraid they were the same landmarks that would occur between any two exits here.

"An ambulance will be here in ten to fifteen minutes," she told him but left the phone line open.

The twins stayed calm and quiet, at least on the outside. On the inside, Cage's blood rushed through his system, pounding in his brain and scrambling his thoughts. Even his fingers pulsed with it. He fought to keep his breathing slow, feeling guilty for being able to do it.

Though the twins didn't speak, to Cage it was clear: They were both trying to lower their pulse rates in an effort to keep Brett from panicking. The more he panicked, the faster whatever was harming him spread through his system.

It might already be too late, Cage thought. He watched the dash clock and yearned for an old analog watch where he could watch the second-hand sweep. All he could do now was stare at the unchanging screen. *Why didn't the minute change over? Why didn't the ambulance get closer?*

The seven ticked over to a rectangular eight and he heard the sound of Brett dragging in breath now.

"No... not... yet." The words were whispered individually, as though putting two syllables together would be too much effort.

Cage pulled the cap off the EpiPen, but Brett's hand lifted up, telling him to stay.

Shit. He didn't want to go against his friend's orders, and his friend was far more educated in this than he was, but Brett was also getting worse. That's when Cage saw it.

Through the ashy tone of Brett's skin, the sweat had begun to bead on his forehead. His eyes looked puffy as they squeezed shut. Was he in pain?

Just like Melinda.

There was no question now. Cage leveled a hard stare at Joule and mouthed the words "check yourself." He needed to know if he was caring for one sick person or two.

Quickly, Joule examined her arms, lifting the edges of her sleeves and her pant legs. Why hadn't Brett worn long sleeves? He'd said it was too hot. *Was it too hot for this?*

The anger flared, though consciously, Cage knew he was more scared than angry. Still, it was hard to fight it down.

"You need this?" He held the medication up for Brett to see. But his friend shook his head.

"Sick. I know."

"But your throat is closing."

"Too much." Somehow, Brett had forced out the two words, and Cage understood that he meant the adrenaline to his system might kill him, too, since he was sick.

The raspy, wheezy effort of breathing said there weren't many options left.

"How far out is the ambulance?" He shouldn't have yelled at his sister, but Joule relayed the question to the dispatch operator and answered, "Five minutes."

Another raspy intake from Brett left Cage holding the pen ready.

This time, his friend couldn't speak.

"Tell me no," Cage demanded. "Tell me yes or tell me no."

Brett's eyes were rolling back into his head. His chest heaving with the effort of breathing, sweat rolling down his temples. As the veterinarian's color turned gray, Cage plunged the needle into his friend's leg.

70

"Who are you to the patient?" The nurse or intake admin or whoever it was blocked the path as the twins ran into the ER, attempting to follow the workers hauling the gurney.

Brett was still alive. Cage balked for a moment. He wanted to follow, but they'd been stopped. He blurted out, "We're his kids."

Did it matter if they weren't really? Brett was the closest thing they had to a father right now.

"Your names?" the woman asked, still not budging as she tapped on her tablet.

"Cage and Joule—" He paused. "Christian."

That would be the name on Brett's driver's license.

"We'll need you to help fill out his paperwork."

Cage nodded. It's what Brett's child would do, right?

"His full name?"

Cage froze. He didn't know, but Joule rattled it off. Cage wasn't surprised she remembered it. When the intake nurse asked for his home address, Joule rattle that off, too. She had a phenomenal memory. Usually, she taunted him with it. Now, he was beyond grateful.

"Zip code?"

But she didn't know.

"They moved recently," Cage told the admin. It was a good excuse, and had the benefit of truth, Cage thought.

"Health insurance?"

For the rest of the questions, they simply shrugged off that they were adult children and hadn't kept up with their parents' paperwork.

"He carries it in his wallet, though," Cage said with confidence, like a child who would know. He thought of his own father's driver's license. He'd carried it in his wallet since they'd found it, years ago, when his father went missing.

Being of no more help, the twins were directed to hard, orange plastic chairs and told that they needed to wait.

Even sitting felt wrong. He was so tense. They had managed to keep Brett alive, though their friend might have been right. The adrenaline may have hurt him as much as it helped.

Joule reached out, sliding her hand into Cage's and squeezing far too hard. It was an anchor he sorely needed. They'd just eaten, so there wasn't even the pretext of fetching snacks from the vending machine to keep himself busy.

"Laura?" Joule asked him, and it took a moment for Cage to place the name.

Shit. He hadn't even thought of calling Brett's wife.

Brett had stayed in touch with her the whole time he'd been here, but thirty minutes ago, he'd seemed fine. How long had they been sitting here? Did he need to call her now? He did.

He nodded to Joule and stepped outside to make the call. It was maybe one of the most painful he'd made in his life.

"She's on her way." It was all they said as he sat back down and watched the analog clock on the wall tick. He regretted wishing for one earlier. Now he watched the sweep of the thin, red second hand, letting it tell him it had only been minutes and he couldn't expect anything.

Twenty minutes later, he and Joule had said nothing more. They just sat silently as the ER waiting room bustled and shifted around them. He thought of nothing until he heard, "Cage and Joule Christian?"

A young man in purple scrubs and tablet in his hand scanned the waiting room to see who reacted.

Thank God he'd given their first names correctly or he wouldn't have recognized the summons. Now his legs straightened of their own accord, his back stiff as his hope soared. They were getting called back.

"Come with me." This time, instead of being blocked they were escorted through the swinging doors. They passed closed curtains. Some of them were quiet, some of them beeped, and behind others he could hear and see shadows of activity as ER staff tried to save whoever was in the bed.

Though the young man had introduced himself, Cage had paid zero attention. He now motioned to the last curtain. "He's in here. One of our nurses is monitoring him. We'll do everything that we can, but we're not confident there's much left that we can do."

"What?" Joule asked, her tone accusatory. But the man in the purple scrubs didn't take it personally.

"We've given him every medication that's available. Most anything else we could administer will cause more harm than good. Now, it's a waiting game."

Only then did Cage hear the beeping beyond the curtain. He didn't wait. He simply grabbed the open edge and ducked through. His hand still connected to his sister's, he pulled her along.

Brett lay unmoving in the white sheets. His eyes closed, his skin almost the same color as the linens except for a pale rash. Everything looked wrong. An IV hung above him and dripped into his exposed arms. The machines behind him beeped and blinked.

Cage watched as the rhythm slowly degraded.

Dropping his sister's hand, he reached out and grabbed one of the hands that lay still on the sheet. It didn't clutch back as his brain flashed to a thought: *Wherever Brett was, it wasn't here.*

Joule rushed to the other side of the bed, grabbing Brett's other hand and willing him to get better.

Cage didn't know if he was even breathing. He'd lost his mother in a violent clash that he'd heard, and he'd known what to expect. He'd lost his father by the man simply slipping away and disappearing. Cage and Joule had almost gotten to decide on their own whether and when their father was truly gone.

He didn't even register the change in the beeping and buzzing of the machinery as the staff rushed in and shoved him and his sister out of the way. Standing back, his limbs stiff and cold, he watched the staff push medications into the IV, then stand back and watch.

They pushed something else and waited again. Chattering amongst themselves. Words he didn't understand.

His throat constricted, but it didn't matter because he wasn't breathing anyway.

Cage watched as Brett slowly slipped away.

71

"Where have you been?" Helenie looked up, her eyes scanning the twins, as she opened the door of the suite.

The looks on their faces must have said everything, or at least enough.

"Where is Brett?" Helenie demanded now, more concerned than anything.

Joule only shook her head. How was she still upright? She was numb.

Was she dead? And she just didn't know it yet?

"He got bitten." Her brother spoke the words. Somehow, they were both far too simple and far too complex.

"Where is he?" Helenie didn't process the answer or didn't want to. But Joule could see the trepidation on Helenie's face.

In the room behind her, Chuck was kneeling down, doing lab work on the standard hotel room coffee table. He looked up. "What?"

Joule shook her head again, tears pressing at the back of her eyes, all her muscles clenching against getting the words out. "He didn't make it."

What a stupid phrase.

She wanted to yell, *He's dead!*

The stupid bugs had killed the one thing she'd found after her parents had gone.

Seeming to get her bearings, Helenie ushered them into the suite and closed and locked and bolted the door behind them. Only then did Joule remember that they were in danger from far more than just whatever this disease might be.

She hated it. And she hated the whole world right now.

"What happened?" Helenie pressed, though she did it as softly as possible.

Joule could only listen as her brother managed to recite the facts of the afternoon.

Chuck's eyes flitted back and forth. They'd all been covered in bug repellent, but they'd also attracted the mosquitoes so they could catch them. Had it cost them one of their team members?

Was it just a fluke? Joule wondered. *Or was nature that cruel?*

She wasn't ready to deal with what had been thrown at her. Not in the slightest.

Walking into the room, she ignored Cage and Helenie discussing details. She sat on her knees next to Chuck feeling like a child at the low table, but she didn't care. She was angry and she needed something to take it out on. She needed tests and she needed an answer. Blinking back her tears and her rage, she asked, "What can I do?"

"Here." He handed her a rack of micro test tubes and talked her through the tests they were running.

Chuck handed her a pipette and watched carefully, but she wasn't concerned. She knew enough lab technique to be useful here. She didn't mind being checked though she was more than angry enough to be a furious perfectionist.

Behind her, Helenie asked her brother about the cure.

Fuckmonkeys, she thought, sitting back. Helenie and Chuck had it with them.

"We don't even know what's in those syringes yet," Helenie offered by way of consolation.

Joule told herself the same thing. Because if they did have a cure and the twins simply hadn't used it, how would she ever forgive herself? Had they lost Brett because of the flip of a coin?

The teams traded who was carrying Dr. Achebe's syringes simply so that anyone following them couldn't know who to attack. Helenie and Chuck had been the designated carriers on this trip.

And Brett had died.

Joule swallowed that thought, as bitter as it was, and threw herself into the work because she couldn't do anything else. She followed Chuck through the tests and learned from both Chuck and Helenie what they were looking at.

At three a.m., she pointed out a handful of petri dishes. "These reacted."

They separated those from the unreacted ones and ran another test that would take five hours. While she waited, Joule tried to reconstruct Noemi's travels before the tracker. She used social media and phone records and tried not to think of all she'd lost today.

At four a.m., they got an update from Mike. He sent documents to a fake email that they opened on the tablet that he and Pablo had picked up when reloading data from Noemi's phone. At least she could read the analysis, Joule thought, as the whole team scanned through the massive download.

Ultimately, the liquid was a combination of four molecules. One was water, and another was a common delivery solvent. Two remained unknown.

At six a.m., she managed to fall asleep on the couch for two hours. At eight, when she woke, Helenie and Chuck stood over her.

"How are you doing?" Helenie asked, as sympathetic as she could be to the young woman on her couch.

Joule only shrugged. For a moment, she'd wondered why they asked, until the day before flooded back at her and drained her. She'd been ready to say, "I'm fine," but the idea of "fine" slipped out of her mind. She was most definitely *not* fine.

She was angry. She was in despair. She was empty.

"As good as I can be," she replied.

"We're splitting differently today," Helenie announced. "You come with me. Cage is going with Chuck."

"Why?"

"We got a call from the sheriff's department. Someone came in late last night and tried to access Noemi's purse."

Joule felt her eyes widen.

"They said they were with the CDC."

Joule could hardly believe that. *They'd managed to snag the samples by hours. They'd been lucky. Wait...*

"*Was* it someone from the CDC?"

Helenie shook her head solemnly.

They were being followed. Maybe hunted.

"So, we're going in four groups today," Helenie reiterated, wanting Joule to get moving.

Joule wanted to protest, but neither of the twins was in any shape to drive or even be in charge of anything. Helenie would be lucky if Joule wasn't flat-out useless.

There was still the unspoken idea that they shouldn't be all together. It hung in the air and taunted her. They'd been split up, and it still hadn't saved them.

In the chair beside her, Cage somehow stayed asleep. Joule envied him the escape.

"He and Chuck will leave when he wakes up. We wanted to let you guys sleep as much as you could." Helenie offered a sad smile.

"As much as they could" didn't seem to be very much. Cage

had still been awake when Joule had finally passed out last night. But she wasn't willing to just leave him there.

Gently, Joule rocked her brother until he opened his eyes long enough to understand she was leaving. She had a fatalistic sense now that every goodbye might be the last. She should care more. She should be more afraid for losing her brother.

But she didn't have anything left in her.

She was in the car with Helenie before she even thought to ask, "Where are we going?"

72

C age had woken groggy but then been jolted by the memories of yesterday. They hit him hard and fast, and he looked around the room for Joule... who was missing.

Once he remembered where she was, he calmed down. Chuck was anxious to get going, so Cage found himself in the passenger seat, heading down the freeway before he called her. "Where are you going now?"

The team had all been sharing locations, but not via text or anything recorded. So he hadn't expected a message.

"We left the first site and we're out in a field, south of Charleston." She rattled off better information about their location.

With that information soothing what it could, Cage leaned back in the passenger seat. He'd given the keys to Chuck. Despite the fact that Cage knew the area better, it was clear he was in no shape to drive. He'd ceased to care that the only person registered to drive the car was not even with them.

Someone else had come for the syringes in Noemi's purse. Cage figured that going four different directions made them less likely to get pursued, but more likely that someone would get bitten.

And he cared. He truly did. He knew logically that he did, but there was no room to *feel* any of it. He decided to keep tabs on his sister the best he could. Everyone else was an adult who could make their own decisions.

"Where are you headed?" Joule asked in return. The twins might not be good for decision-making today, but they could keep the teams updated on their location. "We're on the road where—"

A harsh sound from his sister cut through his speech. "Joule?"

She hissed at him again and went deadly silent.

He wanted to ask what was wrong but was left sitting and waiting. Every joint locked and his hands trembled as he waited.

"What?" he heard her ask but stayed silent. For some reason, he was confident the question wasn't for him.

A moment later, he heard a stranger's voice demanding, "Turn off the phone."

His eyes flew wide and he motioned frantically for Chuck to pull off the freeway.

His panicked gestures at least got Chuck's attention and Cage held tight as Chuck cut across lanes and pulled down an exit ramp.

Cage listened as his sister said, "Okay."

Shit, he thought and waited for the line to go dead.

Instead, the noise changed and he heard the crackle of background noise. Had she hit the speakerphone instead of the off button?

He had maybe a few moments before she realized her mistake or before whoever it was discovered the phone was still on.

"Show me," the voice demanded.

Cage didn't know what was happening, but he didn't hear a reprimand. He waited, breath held as Chuck motioned to him, asking where to go.

They both realized they had to be silent. Anything they said could alert whoever was with Joule. Cage didn't know what was going on, but his sister hissing at him to shut up made him wait.

Was there a mute button? He checked frantically but couldn't find anything he was willing to hit while Joule waited on the other end. Reaching into the cup holder, he pulled out a receipt and grabbed a pen, motioning again for Chuck to stay quiet. He scribbled directions to where Joule had said they were and held on again as Chuck peeled out.

If Joule was in danger, so was Helenie—and Helenie was Chuck's boss. He'd already lost one lab member, and he was gunning to get there in time today. At least they weren't far away.

Cage couldn't hear most of what was said, but it didn't sound friendly.

His heartbeat hammered in his ears as he held the phone up. When Joule finally did speak it was loud and clear. Maybe she said it for him. But her words chilled him to the bone, and he felt the car accelerate.

"Don't you dare turn that gun on me."

73

J oule narrated as best she could for her phone to catch, but her brother and Chuck were too far away.

Jordan, Jillian, Mike, and Pablo had also split into different groups. *Were any of them close enough to help?*

Did any of them have any idea what was happening?

Beside Joule , Helenie had frozen in place. She'd been checking something in the grass, her back to the man. Joule had turned to face him, to show that the phone she'd been holding to her ear when he first commanded her was now turned off.

It wasn't.

Thank whatever Gods were watching over her that she'd been facing the other way. She could only hope she'd pulled it off. Her hands had been shaking with the adrenaline rush of the immediate threat. She'd heard him step up behind her and the chill that ran up her spine told her she wasn't likely to get out of this.

Somehow, the fear of dying was the only emotion that had broken the hard shell around her. This morning, she hadn't cared if she lived. Suddenly, she did.

Glad her brother wasn't here because he was both her best hope and because she didn't want both of them to be here, Joule had hit the speaker button instead of hanging up. Then she'd immediately turned her screen black.

When he demanded to see that the phone was off, she'd shown him the blank screen and could only hope it was still broadcasting.

But what if it wasn't?

Her brother was almost definitely on the way. He would have called back if she'd hung up on him. But the phone didn't ring. How long would he wait? Did that mean she was successful, and he was listening in, even now?

There were too many questions. Too many things she couldn't count on.

Whether or not she'd successfully put her phone on broadcast didn't matter. This fucker had picked the wrong day to pull a gun on her. Brett was gone. Her brother wasn't here. And as much as she would do everything to protect Helenie, Joule didn't have it in her to do anything that *wasn't* stupid.

The only reason she hadn't already rushed this asshole was because he was too far away.

For all that she was angry, and for all that her anger made her feel superhuman, she still knew she was not faster than a bullet.

She also knew the gun was not an idle threat. She suspected this man had executed Noemi.

Beside her, Helenie now stood up slowly, her hands coming up as she did. Whatever she'd been holding had been left in the grass.

How smart was Helenie? *Smart,* Joule knew. But how good was the woman in an emergency? That was entirely unknown.

"What do you want?" the researcher asked, her tone timid.

Helenie being strong was possibly their only hope of surviving. That faded with Helenie's unhelpful response.

"Where is it?" the man demanded, and Joule tried to memorize his face—the wide nose and eyes that should have been beadier. His hair and his shirt were dark. He was broad but maybe a little soft. She calculated all of it.

The fact that he was letting them see him did not bode well. Her stomach clenched, but she ignored it. The only way out of here was through him.

Joule was getting out or she was going to die trying.

"Where is what?" Helenie took a small step forward, faltering as though standing was problematic on the uneven ground.

The gun swung from Joule to Helenie now and Joule watched as her partner flinched and pulled back. Just the threat was too much for her.

"The formula!" He apparently did nothing but demands.

"Noemi had it. We don't have it." Helenie cowered under the threat and Joule stayed still.

She had one hand still up, holding the phone with the screen that she couldn't see now. Turning it slowly, she hoped he didn't notice. She tried not to show her sigh of relief when she moved it just far enough to see the screen was still off.

Hopefully, no one else could call her.

"Yes, you do," he demanded. He wanted the formula.

"No!" Helenie sounded like she was going to cry. "We don't have it. Our coworkers do!"

Fucking Monkey Balls, Joule thought. Helenie had just thrown them under the bus.

Or had she? How many partners did this guy have? If it was just him, maybe the better move was to divide his attention.

"It's true," Joule volunteered and watched the gun swing back to her. She felt the change in her body as it reacted to the threat. It was bad enough having the gun nearby. Staring down the barrel ratcheted the tension in every muscle, took over her breathing, and set her heart on high alert. But she tried to stay focused on her goal.

Get.

Out.

Alive.

In the periphery of her vision, she caught a subtle shift in Helenie's stance.

"I can get it for you. *We* can get it for you." Helenie changed her words, her head motioning to Joule. Only then did Joule realize that Helenie was afraid her words would mean he could drop Joule and take Helenie as ransom.

Joule was glad the woman was at least trying.

Helenie asked another question before Joule could do anything.

"Why does BioStride want it, anyway?"

He looked between the two of them for a moment but didn't answer.

"You're with BioStride!" Joule jumped into the conversation again, hoping to pull his attention back and forth.

"I was. Not anymore." He seemed to think his comment was almost comical, but that made no sense.

Joule still tried to follow along, though she didn't think Helenie was in any shape to lead. She saw the researcher's expression change again.

"Then what could you possibly want with this? A single person can't handle this kind of distribution."

What kind of surreal world was she in with a gun aimed at her, too far away to fight back? Her brother possibly listening through the phone but too far away to do anything helpful... Two other teams of people might save them but probably didn't even know what was going down right now.... And Dr. Helenie Warren was discussing *distribution routes!*

He took a moment and then he answered, "I can handle it."

Helenie prodded him again. "You need me. You need her,

too."

Again, she tipped her head toward Joule, making motions to keep them both alive.

What on Earth could he need Joule for? Maybe Helenie was handling this better than Joule had given her credit for. As his attention turned back to Joule, she saw Helenie's expression harden for a split second before she remembered to wince and cower.

Yes!

"We don't have the formula," Helenie offered with what Joule now realized were fake tears in her voice. "We split it up so that you can't take any one of us."

His eyes flickered back and forth, and Joule tried to school her expression to say, *Of course we did, we're smarter than you.*

"But she and I together, we can put all the information back. We tested it. We got the molecular makeup. We can get that."

He nodded for a moment as if deciding what to do. Would he kidnap them and demand science that Joule couldn't pull off? Her heart pounded and her brain raced.

Never let them take you to a secondary location, she thought.

But Helenie was keeping him occupied. "How will you manufacture it? How does the formula help you?"

Joule figured he could just sell it, but she didn't dismiss that Helenie was buying them time. It just probably wouldn't be enough time.

He grinned, clearly thinking he was smart. "I've already sold it to a company in India."

Sonofanighthunter, Joule thought, and his next words confirmed her suspicion.

"I don't need the formula. I already have it. Noemi gave it to me. I just need to make sure that *you* don't have it."

As he aimed his weapon at Helenie, Joule rushed him, and she felt the world tremble as the gun went off.

74

J oule had her hands up, ready to push the gun out of the way. If he cooperated, she could use a technique that could pull the gun from his hands and put it in hers.

But it didn't matter.

He'd aimed at Helenie, who had also rushed him when she saw Joule move.

The meek voice and cowering had been only an act. Joule saw the determination on her partner's face, and then the surprise as the bullet hit her.

Helenie stumbled backwards and for a fraction of a second, Joule's brain flashed: *Another one gone.*

She was the only one left and she had to save herself. Helenie took two more steps before she fell onto her butt in the grass, blood staining the front of her long-sleeved t-shirt, the pale color marking what would surely be her death.

Whatever switch Joule had, it flipped.

She growled an unearthly sound, her anger and her loss stripping her of every concern about the outcome. She charged at the man from the side before he could swing the gun back to her.

Trying to knock it from his hand, she struggled, but all she could do was get on the other side of it, where he couldn't aim it at her.

It fired again, the retort loud. The ringing in her ears told her she'd been way too close. Joule didn't stop to check if she'd been shot.

As much as her head buzzed and vibrated, his had to be the same, so she tried to take advantage of it. Grabbing for his arm, she attempted to pull him across in front of her, putting the gun further out of her own harm's way.

In the distance, she spotted Helenie on the ground, face up in the grass, hands on her chest, unable to stop the red that bubbled up from underneath. But Joule couldn't pay attention.

She fought for everything. She fought with everything.

She had the killer's beefy arms in her grasp, but he was too big to be controlled by her slim fingers. His weight and willingness to do real damage gave him an advantage over her knowledge and intelligence. Somehow, her anger fueled her forward.

A sound rang through her head, but she couldn't quite make it out.

He growled at her as he turned, one meaty fist coming up to punch. She took it on the jaw.

Though she'd smartly sidestepped and avoided the full force of it, his fist still clipped her. It would have stung if she could have felt anything.

Joule spun back to face him again. She wasn't done, but as she came back around, she found the muzzle of the gun directly in her face.

Her brain buzzed with something again, but the ringing still stopping whatever it was from getting through.

He seemed to hear it too and, for a moment, his gaze flicked away.

Taking advantage of what little gap he gave her, Joule

lowered herself, aimed at his midsection, and bolted forward with everything she had.

She only managed to make him stumble backward.

His arms flew up, perhaps in surprise, the gun still firmly gripped in his hand.

Even as she pushed at the immovable mass that he was, something grabbed at her.

Helenie?

Joule felt herself suddenly yanked backwards.

Helenie was still on the ground.

He had an accomplice.

Joule was whirling to fight whoever had grabbed her, but she caught the gunman's face. He looked stunned, just as surprised as she was that she'd been pulled from their fight.

Her head was still ringing, and she could only watch as she was now pulled back into range for him to turn the gun on her. He didn't pause for long, maybe a split second. As he got his bearings, he lifted the gun, aiming directly toward her.

Who was behind her? Who was holding her here?

She felt a thought race through her brain. How stupid this was! He would shoot and, at this range, it would go directly through her into the person behind her. He didn't seem to care though, friend or foe. They were both as good as gone.

The gunman aimed and she saw his finger start to squeeze the trigger.

But in slow motion, as she resigned herself to the same fate as Helenie, she saw a familiar face rise up behind him.

A thick branch was clutched like a baseball bat. The heavy swing aimed directly for the assailant's skull as the gun went off one more time.

75

"Joule!" Cage yelled. "*Joule!*"

He called again and again as he ran across the field.

He wasn't close enough and he could only run as his sister fought.

As he and Chuck had scrambled from the car, he'd seen the gun. He wanted his own gun, but it was still in the custody of the stupid fucking sheriff's department. He wouldn't have been able to distinguish hitting the killer or his sister from this distance anyway. So maybe it was better that he didn't have it.

He saw Jordan Abellard grab his sister, pulling her backward from the fight.

Abellard had put himself in the bullet's path. The stranger's sudden appearance had startled the attacker.

Then Jillian had popped up behind the man holding the gun and clubbed him, dropping him like a rock.

Even as Cage finally got close, he watched Jordan kick the gun from the man's now-limp hand. Cage barely registered that as he ran to his sister, dropping onto the ground where she'd fallen. She was hunched over, and he couldn't see anything.

He should have said something nice, but all he could do was grab her by her shoulders and shake her until he could see.

No major cuts or gashes, but she had bruises and scratches everywhere. No bloom of blood from a bullet shot. He grabbed her and rattled her again, unable to do better. "Are you hurt?"

She shook her head at him, no.

Jesus, he'd heard three shots and she'd been close. *So close.*

Instead of believing her, he turned her one way and then another, looking her over again. Joule shook her head at him again as if to say *no*, she was fine. Not that any of them was fine.

He hugged her fiercely, the only thing he really had left. And for a moment, she let him.

Beside him, Chuck was leaning over Helenie. He'd peeled his shirt and was wadding it up, pressing it to her wound, trying to stop the flow of blood.

"My phone," Joule yelled at him and wiggled free of his hold. Cage made a motion to her to lower her volume. But she didn't. "My phone!"

"Yes," he said. "That's how we found you."

"Nine! One! One!" she yelled, correcting his assumption.

Jesus, he thought shaking his own head. "Yes."

Helenie needed an ambulance. They needed the police for whoever this asshole was. It seemed he was still alive.

Jordan had peeled his shirt, too, though he and Jillian seemed to be looking around for something. It only now occurred to Cage that they were trying to find something to tie the man up with. They had nets and petri dishes, but not zip ties or cables.

He watched as Jordan also pulled his belt and used it to tie the man's hands, tightening it as much as possible. Catching the shirt when he tossed it, Jillian anchored the man's ankles together. He would come back around and he would struggle when he did. Jillian tightened the knots as best she could. Their attacker shouldn't be able to get anywhere.

At last, Jordan looked up at them. "Is she okay?"

Cage shook his head. He didn't know. He only knew that Joule was motioning him to do something, and it took a moment to figure out that this time, she wanted him to help find her phone.

Together they searched the ground but didn't see it.

"Call me!" She was still talking too loud, startling everyone each time she spoke.

Again, he motioned for her to lower her volume, fumbling in his pockets where he had dropped his own phone when he began running. Quickly, they located her phone as it rang. She couldn't hear it, but she'd caught the flash of light on the screen.

Flipping it over, she dialed 9-1-1. Like a fool, he realized then that he could have called from his phone, but Joule was the first to call. There was too much going on. For a moment she stared at it, and then seemed to realize she couldn't hear anything and thrust the device at her brother.

She would hear again, he thought. It was just the retort from the bullets that had temporarily deafened her. Should she have her hearing back by now? But the voice on the other end said, "Nine one one, what's your emergency?"

He found himself going blank.

He had far too many emergencies.

Joule seemed to recognize that he wasn't speaking, and she pointed to Helenie. With a direction to aim, he began describing their situation.

"I need police. I need an ambulance. I have a gunshot victim." He did his best to direct the emergency services people to the middle of a field in the middle of nowhere.

The operator kept him on the phone, but they seemed to have Helenie's bleeding under control. He wound up telling the operator they were collecting mosquito samples and had been attacked.

Eventually, when he was assured that everyone was on their way, he looked up.

His sister smiled at him, proudly. "I heard some of that!"

Breathing one sigh of relief at that, he continued to relay information back and forth about Helenie. She was mildly alert, the bleeding heavy, but the team was following the instructions the operator gave them, applying pressure and waiting.

They'd looked for an exit wound and applied pressure there, too.

Jillian must have whacked the attacker hard because he'd not yet come around. She leaned over and placed her fingers on his throat—obviously repulsed by doing so—and announced, "He's still alive."

It sounded as if she was disappointed in that fact.

Joule was now speaking in a far more normal tone. She stood up, looked around, and took it on herself to survey everyone. Somehow, she managed it with a wider eye than his own.

She passed Jordan and Jillian and managed not to kick the man who'd held a gun into her face more than once. *That took willpower,* Cage thought. She moved over toward Helenie. As Joule paused, Cage worried about the researcher. Was she bleeding too much?

That wasn't it.

"Chuck," Joule said, grabbing his attention. She pointed to his back. "You've been bitten."

76

"I'm fine." Chuck waved her off.

Joule wasn't having it. "You need antihistamines."

She reached for her backpack only to find that it wasn't there.

Spinning wildly and unable to control herself, she spotted the bag in the grass, several feet away. Had she thrown it? Had it been thrown? It didn't matter.

She bolted for the bag, grabbing it and digging through. When she came back to Chuck, she had pills in hand. She didn't have water, but that didn't matter. He swallowed them and she watched until he shrugged at her and turned back to take care of Helenie.

Cage was hovering over their leader on the other side now. Joule pulled out the spray. Without permission or warning, she doused Chuck until he complained. "You're getting it on Helenie!"

"Well, she needs it, too," Joule countered.

Hell. They were in the middle of a mosquito collection point. They suspected that infected *Aedes Karnatakan* were breeding here. That was exactly why they'd come.

Now they were stuck waiting for police officers and an ambulance.

She turned back to Jillian. "How did you find us?"

"Helenie called and left her phone line open."

The same as she'd done, Joule thought. To think that she'd been concerned Helenie would fold under the pressure.

Cage's head popped up and he stared into the distance. Did she hear a siren? Or was that just leftover ringing in her own skull?

She watched Chuck closely for a moment, unable to distinguish sounds enough to do anything. Then she began spraying each of the others, though at least she tried to get consent first.

Jillian accepted, as did Jordan. Like Chuck, bare-chested Jordan had far too much exposed skin. There was nothing she could do about it except try to keep him protected. They weren't carrying jackets in this heat. They weren't even carrying extra shirts.

Joule looked at the gunman, thinking to aim her spray his direction. Then she held back out of spite, because *fuck him.* Also, he was covered relatively well. *Let him lie in the grass. Let the ants and the bugs eat him.*

Chuck and Cage were hovering over Helenie, doing the best they could. Cage stayed on the phone with the operator. Jordan and Jillian stood over their attacker. And Joule looked around until she spotted the gun in the grass, a short distance away.

She walked over and was leaning down to pick up the thing that had threatened her, when she heard a voice. Even as Jillian commented, Joule stopped herself and nodded. "It was a stupid thought. I can't touch it. It's evidence."

Jillian agreed. "You certainly don't want to put your fingerprints on it."

As Jillian smiled, glad that Joule agreed, the expression faded from her face.

Following her line of sight, Joule turned to look at Jordan.

He held his bare arms out, looking down at them.

They all watched in horror as a rash climbed along his skin.

She hadn't seen a bite on him. She wanted to protest that this couldn't happen. Did that matter? *Something* had gotten him, and he was reacting.

She scrambled in her bag again, thrusting histamines at him. This time she doled out four.

Fuck doing it in reasonable doses.

He swallowed them dry, just as Chuck had. For a moment, she swung her attention back to Chuck. Was he reacting, too?

For now, his pale skin was clear except for two welts that bloomed on his lower back. They were the same ones she'd seen before. She called out to him, "How are you doing?"

He simply waved her away as he continued to hover over his boss. "I'm fine!"

Joule turned back to Jillian as she hovered near Jordan.

Joule watched as—right in front of her, in rapid time—his skin turned an ashy tone, and he began to sweat.

His breathing started sounding labored.

"Is it your throat?" She moved in close, as if she could diagnose anything. She'd seen this before and she needed that damned ambulance *now*.

He shook his head, no.

Fuck. She thought, *fucking fuck*.

If it was his throat, then they had the EpiPen and the EpiPen worked. She'd seen people survive it, and she knew what to do for that. So far, no one had survived the sickness.

She looked to Jillian, but Jillian was staring into Jordan's eyes. Some kind of communication passed between them, and Jillian looked up at Joule. "Get the syringe."

"What?"

Jillian tried again. "Pablo has our copy and he's too far away."

Joule started to catch on. Pablo and Mike were probably *en route*.

Jillian didn't wait for Joule to play catch up. "Who has your copy?"

"Chuck did."

She was ready to run and get it, but Jillian started to yell. "Help me!"

Joule rushed to Jordan's side. He was starting to waver. He protested, "I'm fine."

Though he seemed to find his footing, he clearly wasn't fine. His skin tone was wrong, and he was sweating profusely.

"Lower him down!" Jillian almost yelled the instruction. Though whether it was for Joule or just to let Jordan know what was going on, it was enough.

She helped him into a sitting position and watched as he started to slump over. Jillian grabbed his shoulders and told him "High Fowler!" Whatever that meant, he made the effort to straighten up.

"Get the syringe!" Jillian told her again.

This time Joule scrambled.

"Chuck!" She was hollering before she even got close. How were they so far away?

"Not now!" Chuck didn't even look up, but Cage did.

"We need the syringe!"

"The EpiPen?"

"Syringe!" Did she yell it? Joule could still hear her ears ringing. "Do you have it? Jordan needs it!"

That got Chuck's attention and he turned from Helenie for just a moment. Joule could see the woman was starting to fade.

Where was the fucking ambulance?

"We don't know that it works," Chuck protested, but Joule held her hand out for it anyway.

Jordan was dying right in front of their eyes. No one was

here to help, and if they didn't do something, he would be gone, too.

She waited for Chuck to dig around in his own pockets, her hand still out as she looked into the distance, finally spotting flashes of blue and red.

Not the ambulance. The police were welcome but they were not the people that she needed.

For a moment, it flashed in her mind that she and Cage were wanted in association with another murder. *Would they be hauled away?*

She had to get the syringe to Jordan first.

Looking down, Joule saw Helenie's eyes were struggling to focus, and her color was pale where Jordan's was gray. Chuck began snapping in Helenie's face, trying to keep her conscious.

But he held the medication out behind him, and Joule grabbed it from his hand.

"It's not even a full dose," Cage reminded her. They'd sent part of it back to the CDC for testing. But it was all they had.

She ran back, hoping she wasn't too late. Could Jordan have gone that far downhill that quickly?

She heard the sirens but it didn't stop her. The earth pounded at her feet. The grass twisted beneath her, and her ankle turned. She kept going.

"Here!" She shoved the syringe out to Jordan, knowing what he intended to do.

He still struggled to sit upright, but as he grasped the medication he gathered some strength, even pushing Jillian out of the way as she tried to take over.

"If this doesn't work, you can't be responsible."

The stunned look on Jillian's face told Joule the woman hadn't considered this possibility.

But the ground around her was about to be littered with bodies, Joule thought.

Should he even do it?

It wasn't Joule's decision, and it was all they had.

"Put your hands in the air!" The words were yelled out with the kind of authority police officers must be taught in training.

Jillian caught her gaze and motioned for Joule to do it, though she didn't yet move from Jordan's side.

"Everyone, hands up in the air!" the voice repeated.

"We can't!" She heard Cage yell back. "We have a gunshot victim on the ground."

"Everyone hands up!"

Did they not hear? Could they not see?

Joule squeezed her eyes shut, trying to comply and hoping that if *she* did, the others could get away with staying where they were.

She heard Jordan's voice, though it was strained, as he told her and Jillian, "Noemi was an amazing researcher. I'm going to trust her."

"Hands up!" the voice yelled again.

This time, Jillian slowly began to stand and raise her hands. As if the two of them complying would be enough.

They both watched as Jordan grabbed the cap of the needle in his teeth, yanked it free, and plunged it into his own arm.

His eyes rolled back and he slumped onto the ground.

77

C age sat on the grass with his hands cuffed behind him watching as the ambulance hauled Helenie away.

There had been a big jumble of confusion as the EMTs tried to decide who needed attention first.

Joule sat beside him, and Jillian huffed on the other side of her. Chuck had been pulled aside to be questioned first.

Joule twitched, and it only occurred to him then that they were sitting in a bug infested area. *Shit.*

"Hey!" he called out to one of the officers ignoring him.

"Stay put and stay quiet!" The officer pointed a flashlight at him. It was off, but why did she even have it out anyway? Cage didn't know.

"You need to know this!" Cage yelled. Beside him, Joule and Jillian offered a small nod.

"What?" She walked over, clearly irritated with being interrupted at whatever she'd been doing.

Jillian spoke up. Probably better, because she had the credentials. "I'm a scientist with the CDC."

"So?"

Wow. Cage's feet weren't tied and it was tempting to lash out and take this asshat officer's feet out from under her.

Jillian was struggling to keep her temper under check, too. The obviousness of her struggle somehow made him feel better. "We are CDC researchers, and we were out here collecting mosquito samples when we were attacked."

"So?" The officer still didn't give two shits. "We'll get your side of it in a minute. Just wait."

Cage was done. "You're standing in—and keeping us in—a field full of mosquitoes carrying the disease that's killing everyone."

Joule picked up his thread. "You've now been warned. If you don't move us to the parking lot or somewhere less mosquito-infested, we'll be suing you for endangering our lives."

"No one's in danger here," the officer smirked.

Cage nodded his head toward Jordan, who was still out cold, but according to the EMT left behind to wait for the next ambulance for Jordan, his vitals were okay. It was the only reason the three of them hadn't thrown themselves at the officer in the first place. "Tell that to the man who is about to die from a mosquito bite."

It was a bit much, but Cage was done with this bullshit.

Jillian was, too. "No. *We* won't sue you. *The CDC* will."

For the first time, the officer's eyes flicked with uncertainty, and Cage pushed hard on that button.

"When you get bitten, which you likely *will* with that fair skin and—I'm assuming—lack of mosquito repellent? Everyone who can help you will be cuffed and stuck on the ground. Since we've already warned you, our sympathy level will be damned low."

Whatever god controlled the mosquitoes smiled on them for a moment. Or maybe it was psychological. Cage didn't care. The officer smacked at her forearm.

He felt Joule's shoulder move against him as she tried to hide a laugh.

On the other side of his sister, Jillian's eyes still trained on her husband. She wasn't finding the humor here. He shouldn't be, either. He and his sister were just too fucked up to do anything else.

"Our phones will show everything we report is true," Joule said, but Jillian had another agenda and she spoke through ground teeth.

"That's my husband on the ground. I'm a medical doctor. I outrank the EMT caring for him."

She was? Cage tried not to let his surprise show on his face. They needed to stick together.

The other officer came over, Chuck in tow, his hands still cuffed like a criminal. Cage's anger had bounced right back, and his arm twitched as though he could break away from the cuffs. He'd never been cuffed before or arrested. If these guys found out about Noemi's death, he wouldn't be getting out of them soon.

"His badge says CDC." The other officer held up Chuck's ID.

"That's what these guys are saying." The officer waved the flashlight end to indicate the three of them.

"That's because *we're from the CDC*. That's my husband. I'm an MD." Jillian ground out the words. Maybe it was not the best move to play, "I'm smarter than you are," but Cage was pretty certain she was the smartest one in their crowd, and that was saying a lot.

"You got a badge?" the more reasonable officer asked.

Jillian rocked to one side. "Hip pocket."

The redheaded officer pulled it out and huffed. "There's a lot of letters after her name, but two of them are M and D."

"Then let her go help her husband!" The male officer had clearly had enough of this bullshit, too.

Within minutes, they were all freed and all crowding around Jordan, though only Jillian and the EMT were working. Sirens blared in the distance, getting closer and closer. Then more EMTs were tumbling out of the vehicle, pulling the gurney behind them. They'd been updated by their partner on the ground.

Before Cage could breathe, the ambulance had swallowed them all back up, including Jordan and Jillian. Only he and Joule and Chuck were left with the officers.

Should he tell them that he thought ballistics would match this gun to the death of Noemi Achebe, or should he just keep his mouth shut?

78

"He doesn't seem any the worse for wear," Jillian said, and Joule felt the air rush out of her. "They've done every test in the book and a few extras that I demanded."

"Let me find Cage and tell him." Joule wandered through her grandparents' house, Toto following along like when he was little. The carpet was salmon-colored, the couch plaid, the designs much busier than her own parents had liked. Her father had grown up here and in the pictures of him as a young man, he always struck her as looking a lot like Cage.

It was good to see her father again. Even just in photos and a little now in her own reflection.

Finally, she found her brother downstairs, pounding out a tune and proving he was no musician. Their great-grandmother had played for the small church and had inherited two small pipe organs when the church closed. Now, Cage was doing them a disservice.

Joule relayed the message to him and watched him breathe an obvious sigh of relief. "Helenie, too? She's good?"

He called out as Joule switched the phone over to speaker.

One day, she'd have a phone conversation that was just her and one other person, but today was not that day.

"She's good, too!" Jordan's voice called out from the background.

Cage didn't seem surprised, but Joule had thought it was just Jillian calling in. "You're at the hospital?"

"I'm waiting on papers to get checked out!" Jordan sounded upbeat. Better even than the last time she'd talked to them, a few days ago.

"So, you still think it worked?" She'd asked this before.

"We have Mike on it, and the powers that be just put two more labs on it." There had been a huge dust-up in the CDC, what with one researcher selling their work out from under them. "Also, Noemi had a needle mark on her arm. We're pretty sure she used it on herself."

They all took a moment to absorb that. *Noemi hadn't died of the illness.* The empty syringe had been her dose...

Finally Cage leaned over the phone, thankfully no longer making horrible noises with a musical instrument. "When does Helenie get out?"

Joule knew that what he meant, but didn't say, was: Would Helenie be out in time for Noemi's funeral and her celebration?

"Two days. We're bringing her home with us. She needs care and we can't locate her dad."

Joule's heart froze. She'd been there, too. "Her dad?"

Jillian sighed. "He's a physicist and he got kicked out of his professorship for suggesting he could achieve time travel. Now he's in the wind somewhere when his daughter needs him." The shrug in her voice suggested her respect for the man was low.

Joule hoped she never earned that. Helenie was warm. Noemi had been a steamroller, but Jillian? Joule hoped she always kept that woman's respect. It didn't hurt that she had a little of it now.

They talked more about Noemi's findings, trying to decide whether her motives had been altruistic or purely selfish—that part had been hard to put back together. Jillian said they were working to not let her get posthumously charged. Her record didn't warrant it, and her family and the CDC didn't need to deal with it, either.

Then more voices entered the fray, and Jillian said the doctors were checking Jordan out. Hanging up, Joule turned back to Cage, but within minutes their grandmother was calling them to dinner. Joule was getting the home-cooked meals she had craved, but only for one more day. Then they had to go.

JOULE STOOD out in the open field. She wore black, despite the heat. She and her brother were in long sleeves and pants, though everyone looked at them oddly.

While there was news that hospitals had a new treatment and getting bitten wouldn't kill anyone anymore, she and her brother hadn't quite converted to feeling safe.

Everyone thought they were weird—everyone except Laura. Michelle was at her side, and they hung back as visitors formed a ring around the spot.

It would figure Brett would want to be buried as a tree.

It was stupid, Joule thought, but she couldn't stop the tears that came.

Did Laura know what she and her brother had lost? Would Joule ever know what they'd taken from Laura?

The guilt weighed on her, but it had lingered and waited. Held back by excuses, she'd been able to ignore it, until now as she watched the bundle of seeds and dirt and Brett's ashes get lowered into the hole. A stake was planted in the ground nearby with his name and his favorite quote printed on paper in a plastic sleeve nailed to the post. Laura had assured the crowd that it would soon be replaced with a crafted metal marker.

Joule waited through the prayer and the few words that Laura spoke to the crowd. It was difficult not to look at her brother or see the tears silently running down his cheeks.

Though it was selfish, she felt as though they were alone again. She hadn't been smart enough to figure out that they weren't alone until Brett was gone. So she hung back, her grief a cloud around her.

One by one, the people left. Only Michelle stayed with her sister.

At last, Laura approached them—Joule and her brother were the last of the mourners, staying to watch the dirt fill in as though that would end the chapter.

"He loved you, you know."

Joule couldn't hold back any longer. It was hard to speak through the tears. "We loved him, too."

She was nodding, as though that might make her broken words more intelligible.

There was no reproach in Laura's tone. Joule would have turned to her brother, but she couldn't bear it.

"He died doing what he loved."

"He should have been with you," Cage said, but Joule felt it in her heart. He should have been.

He would be alive if...

"No, he shouldn't. I had him for a long time. He thought of you two like the kids we didn't have. It meant everything to him that you called him when you needed someone." She paused. "It was a freak accident, and you did everything you could."

Joule couldn't think of anything to say. How could she thank this woman for the forgiveness Joule didn't think she deserved?

Laura looked away, then repeated, "It was a freak accident. I'm beginning to think everything is. I found him through a freak accident, too." She shrugged, seeming to accept that she'd lost her husband though he was far, far too young to be gone.

Maybe Joule could eventually accept it, too.

Laura hugged each of the twins and Joule didn't know if that made it better or worse.

Joule would go back to her house. She would go back to her empty dining room and her bedroom with only the bed and dresser.

They wouldn't rent. They had to stop for a while. Regroup. Get over losing their third parent.

Joule didn't know if she ever would.

THREE WEEKS LATER, Joule sat in front of the TV watching a show with Cage, Kayla, and Ivy. They'd made crockpot chili with Ivy's recipe, and she'd talked them into watching an art heist film then proceeded to point out all the inaccuracies in the film.

It was the first time Joule had felt at home in her skin. The first day she'd forgotten to check for bites. The first time she'd had a good memory of Brett that hadn't swamped her with fear and anger and grief.

She had friends.

She was safe.

Her phone rang.

She stepped out of the room and answered it away from Ivy's next critique. "Deveron? What's going on?"

"It's Sarah. She's missing."

ABOUT THE AUTHOR

A.J.'s world is strange place where patterns jump out and catch the eye, little is missed, and most of it can be recalled with a deep breath. In this world, the smell of Florida takes three weeks to fully leave the senses and the air in Dallas is so thick that the planes "sink" to the runways rather than actually landing.

For A.J., reality is always a little bit off from the norm and something usually lurks right under the surface. As a story-teller, A.J. loves irony, the unexpected, and a puzzle where all the pieces fit and make sense. Originally a scientist and a teacher, the writer says research is always a key player in the stories. AJ's motto is "It could happen. It wouldn't. But it could."

A.J. has lived in Florida and Los Angeles among a handful of other places. Recent whims have brought the dark writer to Tennessee, where home is a deceptively normal-looking neighborhood just outside Nashville.

For more information:
www.ReadAJS.com
AJ@ReadAJS.com

www.ingramcontent.com/pod-product-compliance
Lightning Source LLC
Chambersburg PA
CBHW020253030726
47499CB00001B/179